R0700230790
10/2022
O9-BTL-736
West Palm Beach, FL 33406-4198

ALSO BY GLENN DIXON

Pilgrim in the Palace of Words

Tripping the World Fantastic

Juliet's Answer

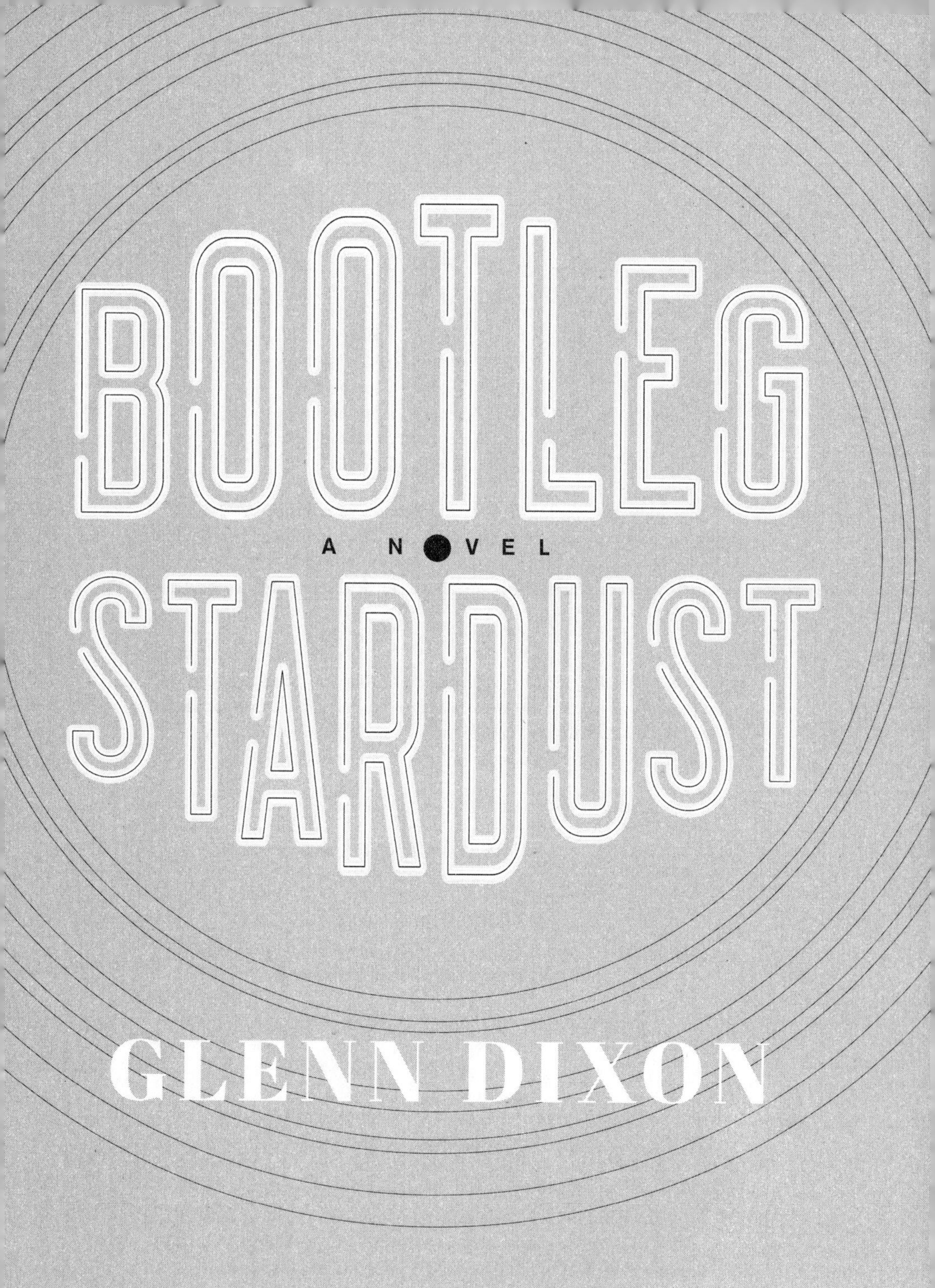

BOOTLEG STARDUST

A NOVEL

GLENN DIXON

PUBLISHED BY SIMON & SCHUSTER
New York London Toronto Sydney New Delhi

Simon & Schuster Canada
A Division of Simon & Schuster, Inc.
166 King Street East, Suite 300
Toronto, Ontario M5A 1J3

This book is a work of fiction. Any references to historical events, real people, or real places are used fictitiously. Other names, characters, places, and events are products of the author's imagination, and any resemblance to actual events or places or persons, living or dead, is entirely coincidental.

This Simon & Schuster Canada edition April 2021

SIMON & SCHUSTER CANADA and colophon are trademarks of Simon & Schuster, Inc.

For information about special discounts for bulk purchases, please contact Simon & Schuster Special Sales at 1-800-268-3216 or CustomerService@simonandschuster.ca.

Manufactured in the United States of America

1 3 5 7 9 10 8 6 4 2

Library and Archives Canada Cataloguing in Publication
Title: Bootleg stardust / Glenn Dixon.
Names: Dixon, Glenn.
Description: Simon & Schuster Canada edition.
Identifiers: Canadiana (print) 20200307401 | Canadiana (ebook) 20200307452 | ISBN 9781982144654 (softcover) | ISBN 9781982144685 (ebook)
Classification: LCC PS8607.I92 B66 2021 | DDC C813/.6—dc23

ISBN 978-1-9821-4465-4
ISBN 978-1-9821-4468-5 (ebook)

For Desiree,
my personal muse

Ordinary riches can be stolen. . . . Real riches cannot. In the treasury-house of your soul, there are infinitely precious things, that may not be taken from you.

—Oscar Wilde

Contents

BOOTLEG STARDUST

The Blues Don't Live Here No More

Our keyboard player quit but we turned up for the gig anyway. It didn't matter. At most, the Salty Dog pub had about five people in it, and that included the bartender, who felt sorry for us and brought us a pitcher of Molson beer. He said he liked the way we played "Space Oddity." Not many bands covered David Bowie, he said, so it was pretty good to even try.

That was the last song in our opening set. It wasn't a disaster but there wasn't much to get excited about, either. I was sitting with Rudy and Katrina at a beer-sticky table near the stage. Rudy was our bass player. Katrina played drums. Together, we were all that was left of the band called Breakwater.

Rudy tipped his head toward a window near the front door. "It's still snowing," he said, as if that weren't obvious. We'd loaded in through a spring snowstorm—Calgary still gets tons of snow in April—and I'd only worn my jean jacket, the one with the corduroy collar. It was warm enough, but my Adidas runners weren't so great. My socks got wet and they squelched a little when I walked.

"That's why no one's here," Rudy went on. He was grinning that big dumb grin of his, trying to be helpful, but Katrina cut him off.

"I thought 1974 was supposed to be our big year," she said. "Levi, are we even getting paid?"

"I don't know," I said. "I'm just happy to be playing."

"Right." She crossed her arms and wouldn't look at me again.

The Salty Dog wasn't great, that's for sure. It smelled a bit and they had fishing nets hung up on the walls, just tied ropes really, hung with plastic starfish and conch shells. At the back, a pool table sat under a big fake Tiffany lamp.

"Maybe we should just start the second set," I said. Rudy and Katrina both nodded grimly, and we plodded back up onto the stage.

As soon as I strapped on my guitar, though, I forgot our troubles. I had a Fender Stratocaster with a sunburst finish and a rosewood fretboard. That's a pretty nice guitar in case you didn't know, and just to hold its weight in my hands was to dream, to imagine I was a rock star, onstage in front of thousands. And at the Salty Dog—even with no one there—at least I got to try out my moves. We started into our first original and I did a Pete Townshend windmill and that felt pretty good. I bobbed my head and whipped my hair around, then stopped when I saw Rudy staring over at me. I was growing my hair, but it kind of fluffed out more than it hung down. Still, I was trying, and that's what's important.

Just the other week, Rudy said I had droopy eyelids like Paul McCartney. He said I could probably pose for *Tiger Beat* magazine and that all the girls would go nuts over me. I told him to fuck off. Rudy, just so you know, had straw-colored hair that was as stiff and straight as a scarecrow's. He was a little paunchy too and kind of short.

We were pretty good, though, all things considered. Katrina wanted to do more Motown, but we drew the line at that. Me and Rudy wanted to do stuff like Pink Floyd and Bowie, and most of all we wanted to write more of our own songs and become famous.

A couple of songs into our second set, some construction workers came in, still in their orange overalls, their hard hats tucked under their arms. They headed straight for the green felt of the pool table like it was the promised land. They dropped their hard hats, chalked up their cues, and started racking up the balls. We were playing one of our own songs, "Hello Juliet," when one of the pool players stopped to check us out. He listened for a moment before yelling out for us to play "Smoke on the Water."

I stopped. "We don't really do that one," I said into the mic, and it might have come across as a little too brash.

He grimaced and strode across the empty dance floor toward us. He was a big guy, and he had the pool cue balanced over his shoulder like a fishing pole or something. "Buddy," he said, but he was eyeing Rudy. "C'mon. I'll give you five bucks to play 'Smoke on the Water.' "

I don't know why he was going after Rudy. I was the one on the microphone. The stage was small and maybe six inches higher than the dance floor. Rudy was short, like I said, so he stood about eye level with this guy.

Katrina leaned out from behind her drum kit, peering between the cymbals. "Rudy," she said, "I'll give you ten bucks *not* to play it."

Rudy took a step backward. This guy was big, and Rudy wasn't exactly John Wayne. "We don't know any Deep Purple," he blubbered.

The big guy scowled and reached for Rudy's guitar cable. It was a long one, looping around all over the stage. He just reached down and yanked on it, hand over hand. Rudy had the end of it tucked under his guitar strap so it wouldn't pop out and the guy just hauled Rudy over. Rudy fell sideways, and the guy kept pulling on the cord, reeling Rudy in across the stage like he was a fish. Poor Rudy floundered a bit, then rolled onto his back and started playing the riff from "Smoke on the Water." He wasn't the best bass player in the world, but still, I give him credit for that.

"Too late, buddy," said the big guy.

I stepped forward. I mean, jeez, I didn't want to, but I kind of had to. I lifted up my foot and kicked at the guy, like some sort of bad karate move, and my soggy running shoe caught him right in the middle of his forehead. His eyes bore a confused expression for a moment and I could see the imprint of my tread on his forehead before he toppled backward. Rudy scrambled back onto his feet. Katrina stood up from her drum stool, gaping at us, holding up her drumsticks like she didn't know if she should start the next song or not. And far away, in the back by the pool table, this guy's buddies all turned to gawk at us, their big cow heads swiveling around to take in what had just happened.

"Run," I said.

And we did. I took my guitar and Rudy had his bass. Katrina had her sticks but we left the rest of the gear and peeled out of there, out the back door, out into the cold, our breaths huffing out in cloudy blasts. We ran for our van and I struggled to get the keys out of my pants even as I was running. Just as we got to the van, the front door of the pub flew open and this guy's buddies were all trying to squeeze through it at the same time like the Three Stooges or something. I hopped into the driver's seat while Rudy and Katrina piled in through the sliding door on the other side. I thumped the van into gear and we tore out of there, fishtailing a bit in the slush. The snow was coming down hard now and it seemed like the end of things. Probably because it was.

♫

We practiced in Katrina's dad's garage. Her dad had to move his station wagon out on Wednesday nights so we could fit all our stuff in. He had tools hung up on nails above his workbench and they rattled when we played. Along the other wall were a couple of bicycles and a pile of empty paint cans and a snow shovel.

One time he came in to check on Katrina, and he stayed to listen for a while. We were playing our Bowie stuff again, *Ziggy Stardust and the Spiders from Mars*, and he nodded his head and said I sang it really well. So, I liked him. He seemed pretty decent.

On the Wednesday after our gig, Rudy was a bit late because he had to come straight from his job at Kmart. Katrina wasn't saying much. I could tell she was still mad about the Salty Dog. Someone had punched holes in her snare drum when we'd left it behind, and she'd put pieces of duct tape to cover the damage. It sounded a bit flabby, if you want to know the truth.

We only made it through a few songs before Katrina quit playing. She sat on her drum stool and sighed heavily, wanting us to notice.

"Jeez," said Rudy, slipping off his bass. "That sounded pretty good."

Katrina sighed again, heaving herself up like a balloon, then deflating.

"Everything cool?" I asked.

"I don't know," she said. "I think—"

"Aw, shit, don't say it."

Rudy was looking from me to her in that hurt way of his, trying to understand what was happening.

"I'm sorry," she said. "I just don't think I want to be in this band anymore."

"C'mon," I said. "We need you."

"No you don't. All the songs are yours. You're the singer, you're the guitar player—"

"No, no, I need a drummer."

"Yeah, but you don't need me." She looked down. "Besides, I got accepted to the U of C for the fall."

Rudy considered the hanging chisels and screwdrivers. He thought for a moment. "Can we still practice in your dad's garage?"

"Don't be a dink," she said. "What if I want to start another band?"

♫

A couple of days after Katrina quit, I was listening to Cat Stevens on my record player. I lived in Rudy's basement, or I guess I should say, Evelyn's basement. Evelyn was Rudy's mom. The place wasn't much but at least it was mine. It had orange shag carpet laid down right over the cement, so it was still cold in April. I tried to spruce up the walls with posters, like Pink Floyd's *Dark Side of the Moon* and a couple of sci-fi movie posters like *Planet of the Apes*—the first one and still, obviously, the best. On the other side of the room, I had my records lined up on shelves made from bricks and boards. The albums weren't in any alphabetical order, that's for sure, but I knew where everything was.

I loved album covers. There were some really good ones, like Yes and Uriah Heep—with dragons and wizards and zeppelins crashing. That was pretty cool art if you ask me. It made you think.

I was listening to that song about fathers and sons when Rudy called down from the top of the stairs.

"What?" I said, plucking the needle from the record. The turntable whirled to a stop and I lifted the vinyl carefully, the tips of my fingers touching just the rim. I blew on it and slid it into its paper sleeve, then slipped that down into the cardboard of the album cover.

"Stroganoff," Rudy called down. "We're having beef stroganoff."

I went over to put the Cat Stevens album back in its place.

Rudy came down a few steps, eyeing me from under the roof beams. "Levi? You coming up?"

"Yeah, in a minute."

Rudy trundled down the rest of the stairs. "Mom says to wash your hands." He swept his gaze around the basement. I had a school desk we'd found on the side of the road when I first moved in two years ago, and lying on top of that were the manila envelopes.

"You got the demo tapes ready to go?" he asked.

"Just about."

We'd been putting the tapes together for weeks. We'd recorded six songs—three originals and three covers—on a reel-to-reel belonging to Katrina's dad, and I'd been copying a bunch of cassette tapes from it to send out to record companies. I switched up the songs, though, so each tape was slightly different.

Mixed with our originals were very specific cover songs. We did "The Weight" by The Band, who were signed to Capitol Records. And "Space Oddity" by David Bowie, who was with RCA Records. And last, we'd recorded "The Blues Don't Live Here No More" by Downtown Exit. Everyone said we sounded like them. They were on Labyrinth Records.

For each record company, I put our cover of their band's song as the first track on the tape. Which was either the dumbest idea I'd ever had or a pretty good one.

Rudy was waiting. "What are we going to do about the band?"

"Well, I was thinking, if we get signed, we could maybe get the drummer from the Barrel Dogs to join us."

"Levi, c'mon. We're not going to get signed."

"No," I said. "I think it's a possibility. It could happen."

"I'm not that good. It's just you, Levi. You're the band. It's exactly what Katrina said."

"Screw her."

Rudy's gaze went to my Raquel Welch poster, the one from *One Million Years B.C.* where she was this sexy cavewoman. Under it, my Stratocaster sat on its stand, its lacquered top shining. My old acoustic, a Martin D-28, was leaning against the sofa. I didn't have a stand for that one. It was a bit bashed up. The fretboard was worn down and one of the tuning pegs had been replaced with a mismatched part, but it still sounded good.

"I don't know, Levi." Rudy came over and plunked down on the sofa. "I don't know if I want to be in the band anymore either."

"Shit, Rudy. You're the bass player."

"Mom's been leaving these brochures around. You know, to sign up for college classes and stuff."

"What kind of classes?"

"To be an electrician or, I don't know, maybe I could get a job in a recording studio."

"That's cool."

Rudy considered me. "I can't work at Kmart forever."

"I know."

"She got some brochures for you too."

"Shit."

"She thinks you should do some remedial stuff. Get your high school diploma once and for all."

"Oh, man," I said, and shook my head. "I'm not going back to school. I'm done with all that."

"I know," said Rudy. "You're going to be a famous musician."

I couldn't tell if he was making fun of me or not.

"Jeez," I said. "It's not that easy."

"No, it is," he said. "For you. You're good. You know that, right? You're really good."

"Thanks, man."

Upstairs, we heard the door to the basement creak open, and we both froze. This one time Evelyn had caught us smoking up. She'd wrinkled her nose at the smell and we could tell she was angry, but she didn't really say that much. Just "Don't do it again." So, mostly, we didn't.

"Boys," she called down. "You get up here this instant."

"Yeah, Ma. We're coming."

Rudy and I locked eyes for a moment before he got up off the sofa and plodded over to the steps. He sort of lumbered when he walked, maybe a few extra pounds on him. I followed him up the stairs.

At the top, the kitchen was one way and the living room was down the hall the other way. I could see the upright piano down there, with a book of Beethoven sonatas set up on its music stand. On the wall above the piano was that painting by Renoir, the one with all the people sitting around a table, the men wearing boating hats, the women in long dresses and ribbons. I remember I used to look at the painting when I was practicing. I used to pretend I was playing for them, and Evelyn noticed. After that, she taught me a bit about art too. She knew a lot of stuff.

Evelyn stood there in the kitchen waiting for us. She was wearing a floral-print dress and her lips were compressed indignantly. She looked a little bit like Queen Elizabeth, if you want to know the truth. Queen Elizabeth, except without the money.

"Well," she began, "I'm more than a little ticked off at you two." Behind her, on the table, dinner was laid out, but she wasn't letting us by just yet.

"Aw, Mom," said Rudy. "I told him dinner was ready."

"It's more than that. Have you seen the electricity bill this month?"

"That's not my fault," I said, though I knew I'd been playing records all day.

Evelyn glared at me. "I don't mean just you. And I don't mean just the electricity bill." She paused. "There have to be some changes around here. It's time you two took some initiative."

"Ma," said Rudy. "I told him already, about the brochures."

Evelyn gestured for us to go and sit at the table, then she patted down her dress. She had a whole speech prepared. I could tell.

"We're going to send out those demo tapes," I tried, pulling my chair out to sit. "It shouldn't take too long before—"

"Levi, you're twenty years old, for heaven's sake."

"I'm almost twenty-one."

"That's even worse. You can't live in my basement forever."

"I know." She was eyeing my socks. One of them had a hole so that my big toe stuck right through it. I sat down pretty quick so I could tuck my foot under the table. Rudy sat opposite me.

"I want to see some action around here. Either you go back to school, or you get proper jobs. That's the deal. Both of you."

"That's not much of a deal," said Rudy.

"You need to start planning for your future." She slid gracefully into her seat. "Look at me. I worked hard and I made something of myself."

"You teach piano to little kids," Rudy said, and then slumped down like he knew right away that he shouldn't have said that.

She pinned him with a look. "Rudy Wheeler, you mind your manners. You have no idea what I've been through. And you," she said, pointing her fork at me. "I don't even know where to start with you."

♫

Evelyn started teaching me piano when I was still a kid. For a while I was pretty good. In fact, I was her star pupil, and that meant a lot to me because, up until then, my childhood had been pretty shitty. I'd been shuffled around different foster homes for a long time. How it works is, when you're a baby, you've got a shot at getting adopted. But by the time you're in elementary school, well, no one really wants you anymore and you just get moved around from one place to another.

When I was twelve, child services put me in this group foster home, and that was the worst one of all. I hated the group home so much I actually wanted to spend more time at school. They had a band room there, and after classes I'd fool around on the piano. The band teacher let me play it even though I wasn't in band, and sometimes, when he wasn't busy marking papers or stacking chairs, he'd show me a few things. He told me I should probably get some proper training, and soon after that he arranged for me to get piano lessons.

That's how I met Evelyn. She took me on, and I started to really learn about music. That's also how I got to know Rudy. He was in grade six, one year below me, and he was always hanging around when I came over for lessons. He'd sit on the couch and watch when I practiced. It was all a bit weird. He was just this young kid, with wide, kind of sad eyes. But he liked to listen to me play, so I didn't say anything. I just let him sit there.

Rudy didn't really get music and I'm sure Evelyn wondered about that. Evelyn was amazing on the piano. She'd gone to Juilliard, which, if you don't know, is about the most important music school in the world. It's in New York City, and there was a time when it looked like she was going to be a concert pianist. There were photographs on the walls from when she was young, playing a shiny black grand piano. She wore a sparkly evening dress and she seemed really sure of herself. But that was before she got married. There were photographs of her husband too, Rudy's dad, but he died a few years ago. It was cancer, one of the really bad ones.

When I was eighteen, I got out of the foster care system. I'd already stopped with the piano lessons and was learning the guitar. I'd found an old Martin acoustic at her place and, pretty quick, I got really good on it. Evelyn wasn't thrilled about it, but she let me keep the guitar. Then I persuaded Rudy to get a bass and that's basically how our band got started.

Evelyn wasn't too thrilled about that, either.

♫

About three weeks later, I was watching *Gilligan's Island* on my little black-and-white television when I heard the phone ring upstairs. There was a pause and I heard Evelyn's heels click across the linoleum. "Levi," she called. "It's for you."

"Who is it?"

"Levi. You come and get the phone. How am I supposed to know who it is?"

I trotted up the stairs. Rudy was reading *Lord of the Rings* in his favorite chair in the living room. He sat sideways, his legs slung over the big upholstered arm of the chair. He glanced at me when I came in but then went back to his reading.

The phone was on a little table by the piano. Evelyn had left the receiver lying on its side, the coil looping across the glass top.

I picked it up, fingering the cord. "Hello?"

"Levi Jaxon?" It was a female voice.

"Yes?"

"You posted a package to Labyrinth Records?"

I waved over at Rudy frantically, signaling for him to put his book down.

"Yes," I said. "That's me."

"Very well, then," the voice continued. "We are running some auditions for Downtown Exit and your demo tape has come up. We wondered if you might be interested in coming in."

"To Labyrinth Records?" I said.

Rudy got up from his chair, his eyes wide. "Holy crap," he said, but I waved for him to be quiet.

"You would have to come to London," the woman on the line said.

"London? Like London, England?"

"Yes, Downtown Exit is currently recording in London."

"Are you sure you have the right tape?"

"I don't have anything else written here. Only that they'd like to see you for an audition."

"With my whole band?" Crap. I didn't really have a band anymore, but I didn't want to tell her that.

"No," she said. "Just you."

"Okay."

There was another pause. "This must be confidential. I need to make that clear."

Confidential, I thought. *Why?*

"Next Thursday. Two o'clock in the afternoon. Shall I put you down?"

"That's in less than a week."

Rudy was nodding at me. Yes, he was saying, say yes.

"Okay," I said.

"Right," she went on. "You will need to be— Do you have a pen?"

I put my hand over the receiver. "Rudy, get a pen."

He rummaged through the drawer under the side table and fished one out.

When she said the name of Abbey Road Studios, I just about barfed. "Abbey Road," I hissed at Rudy and he wrote it down.

"Be prompt," she said. She repeated the date once more and then said she had other people to phone.

I hung up and turned to Rudy. "Holy shit," I said, then we jumped up and down for a while. Evelyn called from the kitchen for us to simmer down and Rudy went in to tell her the news.

Evelyn was standing at the stove stirring a pot of tomato soup when I came in. She was going at it with a big wooden spoon, clanking it against the sides of the pot. "They want you to go all the way to England?" she asked. Her hair was just beginning to gray and I saw real concern in her eyes when she looked up.

"Yeah," I said. "I can't believe it."

She raised the spoon at me. "You're to be very careful with these people. Do you understand?"

"It's Labyrinth Records, Ma," said Rudy. "That's, like, one of the really big record companies."

Evelyn kind of harrumphed a little and went back to her soup. "I don't care who they are. I'm just telling you to be careful."

"Ma!"

"It's okay," I said. "I can take care of myself."

I heard her grumble at that, but she didn't say anything more.

♫

We went down into the basement after, to listen to the Downtown Exit record. Rudy studied the cover. "Their guitar player, that's Pete Gunnerson."

"I know," I said. I knew every guy in the Exits.

Pete Gunnerson was not my favorite guitar player but he was good. He sang a bit too. He did the lead vocals on "The Blues Don't Live Here No More." In fact, that's why we recorded that one—because my voice sounded a lot like his.

He wasn't the main singer, though. That was Frankie Novak. All the girls went crazy over Frankie. He could have been a movie star—with his slicked-back hair and anvil chin—and the guy could sing. That was for sure. He had this deep growly baritone, something you just have to be born with. You can't learn stuff like that.

"Do you think they're replacing Pete Gunnerson?" Rudy asked. His voice was a little whistly. He was more excited than I was.

"Maybe," I said. "I heard he's off his head on acid half the time. Sometimes they have to stop a show because he's too high to play."

"Holy," said Rudy. "I can't believe they got our tape."

I'd already listened to the Downtown Exit album about a million times, but I took the album cover from Rudy to look at it again. The front cover was just a brick wall and a guitar, nothing else, and of course their name splashed across it in white. I always liked their name. I liked the letter *X* in it. I always thought *X* was the coolest letter in the alphabet.

This was their first album and they had a couple of big hits on it. They were still pretty new but they were going to be huge. Everyone knew that. Even though the guys were American, they'd been signed by Labyrinth, a British record company, and their album was out everywhere on Earth. In fact, Rudy and I had just seen them a couple of weeks ago on my little television. They were on *The Midnight Special*, just before Creedence Clearwater Revival. CCR did their version of "I Heard It Through the Grapevine," but I thought Downtown Exit were easily just as good.

Frankie had paced across the stage like a panther or something, playing it up for the television cameras. They did their first hit, "Painted Ladies," which was raw and oozing with testosterone. Every girl I knew had gone bonkers. That's all they talked about for days. But I'd been watching the other musicians in the Exits and I could tell they were really good. Chester Merriweather was their drummer. He was this huge black guy and he towered over his drums, making them look like a toy kit. He hit the skins so hard you could see the drums vibrating. Pete had this sort of pirate thing going on, with a bandanna wound around his forehead and one big hoop earring in his right ear. He was definitely cool. Frankie, Pete, and Chester all grew up together in

New Jersey. The other guys in the band—the bass player and keyboard player—were top-notch session players who'd been brought in later.

I put the album cover down. "There's something weird about all this."

"What are you talking about?" said Rudy. "This is what you dreamed of. This is your big chance."

"Yeah," I said, "but I don't know—why would they want me? I'm nobody important."

"But they must have liked the tape. They phoned you."

"Yeah, but—"

"Don't be stunned, Levi." He shifted his big brown eyes onto me. "This is what you've been dreaming about. Isn't it?"

"I guess so." I mean, yeah, I was a pretty good musician and for sure I wanted to make something of myself, but all this seemed a little too good to be true. "But they never said they'd pay for me to get there," I went on. "It's London, man. How am I supposed to . . . ?"

Rudy gaped at me. "Holy jeez, man. What do you mean?"

"I don't have enough money." I considered my socks. "I don't have nearly enough money for that."

♫

A couple of days later I came upstairs into the living room. Evelyn was sitting at the piano wearing her floral dress with an old sweater on top of it. The book of Beethoven sonatas was open, and she had it propped up, with some lined staff paper next to it. She was copying out the music, maybe making a simplified version for one of her students. She penciled in a few notes, then laid her long fingers down on the keys to check on a minor third or something.

Rudy was wearing his Dr Pepper shirt, the white one with the long red sleeves, and he was sitting sideways in his chair reading his stupid *Lord of the Rings*.

"I've got something to say," I said.

Rudy looked up and Evelyn put her pencil down on the music stand.

"I've sold my guitar."

Rudy struggled to sit up properly in the chair. "You what?"

"I sold my Stratocaster. To Katrina's dad. He gave me five hundred bucks for it."

"Well," said Evelyn. "That's news."

"It's worth way more than that," said Rudy.

"No, no, it's really not."

"Jeez, Levi, that's your guitar. That's your Strat."

"I still have the acoustic—" I swallowed. I had a big lump in my throat just thinking about it. That Stratocaster was supposed to be my ticket to the stars. It seemed crazy that I'd have to give it up to make all this happen. "So," I managed, "he gave me cash." I fished the money out of my pocket. Five crumpled hundred-dollar bills. I'd never had so much money in my life. I lurched forward and pressed a hundred-dollar bill into Evelyn's hand.

Her forehead creased like I'd handed her something unpleasant. "No," she said. "Levi, I can't take this."

"It's for the electricity bill," I said. "And Rudy—" I gave him a hundred dollars too. He didn't put his hand out, so I just laid the bill down on top of his book. "That's for you to go to school."

"Aw, Levi."

"And the rest is for my plane ticket. I'm going to go to England."

"Well, that's certainly your prerogative," Evelyn said.

"I'm going to do this thing," I said. "I have to try. If I don't—" I thought of her and Juilliard, and how she never became famous, and I think she knew what I was thinking.

"All right," she said. She tucked the bill down into her sweater pocket, and when she looked up again, her eyes were just the slightest bit liquid. "I'll just keep this for you, for when you come back."

"No," I said. "Evelyn, if I go out that door, I don't think I'm ever coming back."

Sometimes Magic

I stood in the rain staring up at the doors of Abbey Road Studios. My runners were soaked and there were dark, wet patches on the shoulders of my jean jacket. The famous crosswalk was behind me, rain spattered and empty, but holy crap, there it was. Abbey Road.

I was about to go up the stairs and knock on the door when it opened anyway, and a security guard stepped out. "Off the property," he barked.

"I'm here for the audition," I said, and I kind of hoisted up my guitar case to show him.

The man gave a dismissive shrug. "You can stand on the sidewalk, but you can't come onto the premises."

"The woman on the phone told me to come," I protested. "For Downtown Exit."

"Hold on." He dipped back inside, and for a long moment I stood there on the wet pavement, waiting. When the door opened again, the man eyed me. "You can come in, but you're not to touch anything."

He waved for me to come up the steps. And then, holy, I was walking in through the front doors of Abbey Road Studios. Sometimes, magic happens in your life, real magic, and I was trying to take it all in. On the other hand, it was a really old building, like nearly two hundred years old, and the floorboards creaked. It smelled a bit musty too, if you really want to know.

The security guy stayed at the door, but there was a sort of reception desk in the front hall where a woman sat watching me.

"I'm Levi Jaxon," I said. "I'm here for the Downtown Exit audition."

She studied me and then glanced down at her clipboard. "You're number seventeen?" she said, and I could tell by her voice it was the same woman who had phoned. Now, in person, she had sharp little teeth and a sort of bird-of-prey look about her.

"I guess so."

She stood up and came around the desk, signaling that I should follow her.

I picked up my guitar case and trailed her through another door and down a long hallway into the heart of the building.

There were pictures on the walls, one of Ringo Starr looking at the camera like he was surprised and another of all four Beatles out on the front steps, the same ones I had just come up. They were doing a sort of high kick, all of them in a row, though they didn't look too happy about it, like maybe the photographer had told them to try it, like maybe he said it would be fun.

I had to hurry to keep up with the woman as she clicked along ahead of me. She led me down a staircase into the basement where the big studios were, stopping at one room that looked about the size of a junior high gymnasium. Other than a grand piano pushed up against the wall, it was empty. Just a stool and a microphone set out there in the middle of the floor.

"In there," she said.

My footsteps echoed across the floor. The woman remained in the doorway but she gestured for me to sit on the stool and put on the headphones that were hanging over the mic stand.

I sat and opened my guitar case. I lifted out my guitar and settled into place and plunked the headphones over my ears, and immediately there was a whoosh of, I don't know, ambience, like everything all of a sudden was super clear. I could hear myself squeak a little on the stool as I shifted the guitar up onto my lap.

I looked over, but the woman in the doorway was gone, and I was about to put my guitar down again when a voice came through the headphones. "Number seventeen." It was a gruff male voice, kind of tired sounding, with maybe a bit of Irish in it.

I looked around but there was no one there. Just me.

"Up here," said the voice, "for Christ's sake."

High above me I saw the control room, where a man in a pinstripe suit stood behind the plate glass. He was barrel-chested and mostly bald, and I knew right away that it was Bobby Malone, the manager of Downtown Exit. They called him Surly Bob, but not to his face. He was tough as nails. Everyone knew that. I think he'd been a boxer or something and right now he didn't look too thrilled to see me.

"All right," he said. "Play something."

"What would you like me to—?"

"Any bloody old thing. Let's just get a level on you."

Behind Bobby Malone, Frankie Novak was sitting at the mixing board and he looked famous, all right. He had a sort of James Dean thing going on, greased-back hair and dark brooding eyes and a cigarette burning between his fingers. He held up a glass of something, whiskey, maybe. I could hear the tinkle of the ice in his glass through the console mic. I also saw an engineer, but there was no sign of Pete.

Bobby made a circling motion for me to get on with it and I started in on a pretty little arpeggio from "Hello Juliet." I was pretty nervous but it sounded okay in the headphones.

"Jesus," Bobby said. "What the hell is that?"

Frankie, behind him, had lost interest. He'd turned away and was chatting with the engineer.

"Just something I wrote," I said. "I can . . . I can do something else if you like."

"Just hurry it up," Bobby said. He crossed his arms and waited for me to get going.

I shifted on the stool and rang off the first chord of "The Blues Don't Live Here No More." Then I lit into it. I sang the lead vocal too. If they were looking to replace Pete, this was my big opportunity, and I wasn't about to screw it up. I'd spent the whole week before doing nothing but practicing Downtown Exit songs, dropping the needle down onto their record and learning all the parts, note by note, every little bit.

I got about halfway through the first verse when Bobby put up his hand to stop me. "Play the guitar solo."

Frankie had shuffled around to watch again. He ran a hand through his perfect hair, and I could see his steely eyes were fixed on me.

I bent into the opening notes of the solo and gave it all I could. This was on my acoustic guitar, mind you, so I was at a bit of a disadvantage but I did my best, copying the phrasing exactly as it was on the record, exactly as Pete Gunnerson had played it. I finished up in a flurry of extra notes that weren't on the record, just something fast that I thought might impress them.

Bobby bent down to the console microphone. "You know all the Downtown Exit songs?"

"Yeah," I said. "I'm—"

He cut me off with a grunt, then leaned down to Frankie in a sort of huddle.

"He does sound like Pete," Frankie whispered. He squinted at me through the wisps of cigarette smoke. "But he looks like a bit of a hick."

"I can hear you," I said.

Bobby picked up a clipboard and studied it for a moment. Then he looked down at me again. "Where'd you get that guitar?"

I looked down at my old Martin. Five of the tuning pegs were the original silver ones, but the sixth, the one on the D string, was a replacement part, kind of a creamy plastic. "This?" I said. "I learned to play on this one. I've had it for a long time."

"I'm not asking for your bloody life history. I'm asking where you got that guitar."

"My piano teacher gave it to me."

"Jesus," he said. "What'd you say your name was?"

"It's Levi," I said. "Levi Jaxon."

"Aw, Christ," Bobby muttered. He cupped a hand over the console mic so I couldn't hear him and said something to Frankie. Frankie nodded.

"All right," he said. "You'll be getting a callback."

"For real?"

Frankie, below him, said something I couldn't quite hear. Surly Bob grunted. "You know we're doing you a bloody great favor, son."

"Yes, sir."

"Christ on a kite," said Bobby. "You better be good."

♫

Afterward, I phoned Rudy from one of those red London phone booths. I didn't know who else to call. I had to tell someone. I pictured the phone ringing in the living room in Calgary, the old upright piano pressed up against the wall, the fading William Morris wallpaper, a bowl of dried flowers on the coffee table.

It was Evelyn who answered. "Hello?"

"Evelyn?" I said into the tinny distance.

"Who's this?"

"Evelyn, it's me, Levi. I think I got the job!"

"Well, that's news."

"The audition went well. I met the band's manager, Bobby Malone. I even met the lead singer, Frankie Novak."

"Did you, now?"

"They said they'd give me a callback."

There was a pause on the other end. I knew her well enough to know it meant something.

"What?" I said.

"Levi, I just want you to be realistic."

"I am. Jeez, Evelyn, I'm telling you this is my big chance. These guys are famous."

"You are not to believe anything they say, do you understand?"

"Evelyn, c'mon. Is Rudy there? Put him on the phone."

"I can't do that," she said.

"Why?"

"Because he's not here anymore."

"What? Why?"

"Don't be such a dim bulb, Levi. He's gone after you, to help. I don't know why you ever gave him all that money."

"What are you talking about? I don't need his help."

"You can tell that to Rudy. He begs to differ."

"Evelyn. I don't—"

"Levi Jaxon, you know as well as I do why he's gone after you. I don't want to hear any more about it."

I held the phone away from my ear for a moment. I really didn't want to argue with her. Evelyn could be pretty bossy sometimes, but she did have a good heart. She'd taught me a lot. She'd even showed me how to read music, which, for me, was a pretty big deal. And I knew what she was worried about. There was one little problem.

"Evelyn," I said. "C'mon. I'm going to be fine. I can manage."

"I'm happy for you, Levi. Really, I am. Just promise me something."

"What?"

"That you'll be careful. At least until Rudy shows up. Now, where are you staying?"

I didn't really want to tell her that. I'd found the cheapest place I could—a youth hostel by Covent Garden—and I was pretty sure she'd tell me it was dangerous and that I should move.

"Evelyn," I said. "I have to go."

I hung up and stepped out of the booth. The rain was coming down harder. Springtime in London is pretty wet, I guess. I ran for the Tube station with my guitar case thumping against my thigh. I could feel a big black bruise forming there. The hems of my jeans had torn away so the ropy loops kept catching under the heels of my runners. I didn't really care, though, and I didn't really care about Evelyn. The audition had gone better than I possibly could have imagined. They were going to call me back and that's all I needed to hear. I felt like I was finally on my way.

I got a bit lost in the Underground, unfortunately. I was usually okay with directions and signs and stuff, but here, everything seemed backward. I wandered for a while, back and forth through the tiled corridors, trying to find the brown line—the Bakerloo line—that would take me back to the youth hostel. It took forever but I was kind of buzzing anyway. Bobby Malone was not nearly as terrifying as I thought, and I'd actually talked to Frankie Novak. I'd actually talked to a rock star.

♫

I could hardly believe I was in London. It felt like the center of the rock and roll world, home to Led Zeppelin and Pink Floyd and David Bowie. Not that I was ever going to run into any of them, but holy crap, it was kind of magical just to think they'd been here. I'd already walked by the Marquee Club where the Stones got their start and that gave me a huge rush. The Stones were in Europe now, doing their whole *Exile on Main St.* thing. The latest rumor was that Keith Richards was doing some quack treatment to get himself off heroin in Switzerland.

I wanted to walk everywhere, to see everything—Big Ben and Buckingham Palace and the Tower of London—but I knew I couldn't stray too far. I'd given them the phone number for the youth hostel and told them they could reach me there, so I kind of had to stick around.

I didn't have much money anyway. Everything I owned was stuffed into a little black duffel bag, like something you'd take to the swimming pool to do laps. If I angled everything just right, I could get the duffel bag and my guitar into the locker in my dorm room.

All I knew was that the Exits were supposed to be recording their second album. I had no idea what the new songs were or what they wanted me to play, but, sure enough, after a couple of days, the phone rang in reception and the Swedish guy who ran the place came up to get me. It was the same woman on the line, the one with the tiny teeth, and all she said was that I was supposed to get myself up to the band's rehearsal space in Twickenham.

Well, I didn't know where Twickenham was, but she gave me a load of instructions and I called them out as she said them, and the Swedish guy was nice enough to write them down for me. When I hung up, he helped me look it up on a map. It turned out that the rehearsal hall was on the River Thames so far out from the center of London that I'd have to take the Tube to Waterloo Station and from there change to a British Rail line.

I left early the next day and it still took me almost two hours to get there, which just goes to show you how big London really is. And I only found the right spot because I could hear the band playing as I came out of the Twickenham train station. All I had to do was follow the music.

The rehearsal space was actually an old boat factory, kind of like a great big barn with a cement floor and pigeons cooing in the rafters. A carpet in the center of the room marked out where their stage would be. Their gear was already set up and a row of lights illuminated their little circle of equipment, but the rest of the place was in darkness.

Right away I saw that Pete Gunnerson was there, alive and well, and most certainly still a part of the band. They were running through their new stuff—Frankie, Pete, Chester, and the two session players, Miguel Rosario on the keys and David Barrons on the bass. They called him Skinny Dave for obvious reasons.

Bobby saw me first and came charging forward. Close up, he was kind of short and squat, but he looked like someone you didn't want to mess with, that was for sure. "Bloody hell," he said. "What do you think you're doing?"

"I'm here," I said.

"Christ on a kite," he said, pushing me into the shadows behind the PA system. "Who told you to bring your guitar?"

"I thought—"

"You pretend you're road crew, right? You watch and you learn and you shut your gob."

"Okay." I didn't know what he was so mad about all of sudden. I thought they'd asked for me to come.

"And lose that bloody guitar."

He stomped off, waving at the guy who was working the lights. I could see now why he had the nickname he did. I tucked my guitar case in with a bunch of other cases and crates and tried to blend in as best I could.

The band had stopped playing but the amplifiers were still humming with electricity. Frankie wandered off from the stage set but Pete remained, standing under a single purple spotlight, with his black Les

Paul hanging over his shoulder and one hand on the top of it. He had long, straight blond hair with a red bandanna wrapped around it and he was wearing a silk coat, like a tunic, with big brass buttons and black leather boots that came up almost to his knees. It was that pirate thing again, which was pretty cool if you ask me. He also looked perfectly sober. It was Frankie who had a bottle in his hand. He was pacing back and forth behind the makeshift stage, taking swigs though it was barely two o'clock in the afternoon.

I hovered around behind the PA system, trying to keep out of sight, but Chester Merriweather, the drummer, spotted me. He was a big guy. He squinted at me and frowned, then got up off his drum stool and headed toward me.

"Hi," I said.

"Boss," he began. "You gotta make yourself a little more inconspicuous."

"Pardon me?"

"You're the new guy, right?"

"I guess so."

"You can't be hanging around here. Pete's gonna see you."

"Yeah, but—"

Chester looked me up and down. "You don't know the first thing about what's going on, do you?"

"I guess I don't."

"Well, shee-it," he said. "It's probably not for me to say. But you got to wait your turn. It's coming. All right? We got some shows up north."

"North?"

"Birmingham, Hull, Leeds."

I wasn't sure where those places were, and my face must have shown it.

"Smaller venues," he said, "to get ready for the big European tour. So you"—he jabbed a finger at me—"you got to bide your time. And you got to listen. You got to learn the tracks. Pete will be needing you."

Pete glanced over just then. He must have been wondering who the hell I was and what I was doing there. I was starting to wonder that now too.

"Go," said Chester. "Make yourself scarce."

I slunk back farther behind the PA stack where they couldn't see me and from there I watched them get ready to go again. They ran through a couple of their older songs—the ones I'd already learned—and I could tell they were working them out a little differently. They extended some of the solos and crashed into the endings harder than they did on the record. I studied Pete, how he was moving, or how he sometimes played the A chord on the fifth fret instead of the second.

And then I noticed a young woman over on the other side of the band, kind of tucked in behind the stack of PA speakers. It was kind of dark so I could just see her silhouette moving around over there. She had a camera and she was taking photographs, floating slowly around the set. I watched her come around the back, behind the drums. She stepped forward a bit and the wash of lights caught her face, and I don't know, I guess I'd seen some pretty girls before but nothing quite like this.

Maybe it was how the lights were set, but it was as if she'd stepped out of a painting, like one of those young women in the Renoir print above Evelyn's piano. When she slid back into the shadows, I kind of lost track of her. I tried to refocus myself on the band, but the truth is, I wanted to see her again.

I kept waiting for her to step out into the lights again, but she never did.

♫

The band was headed up to Leeds for a show a few days later and Surly Bob phoned me to tell me I was supposed to come. I just said, "Yes, sir," and tried not to show how excited I was.

"But, here's the thing," he went on. "There's not enough room for you in the van so we're putting you on the train. Chester's offered to go with you—he doesn't like driving on the left side of the road anyway. He says it's unnatural."

By now, I knew my way around well enough to find the right train station at the right time, and when I climbed on board I stuffed my guitar case into the luggage rack at the end of the carriage. Then I slid into a seat next to Chester. He didn't say much, so I didn't either. But somewhere past Northampton, he swiveled around and met my eyes. "Boss," he said, "how you feel about getting stoned?"

He opened his jacket, and in his inside pocket was a spliff the size of a felt pen marker.

"Whoa," I said. Of course, I'd smoked up before with Rudy, but I'd never seen anything like the joint he was offering.

"Helps the miles go by," Chester said.

We went into the washroom like a couple of kids, banging against the walls with the shunt and shift of the train. When we opened the door again, I had a moment where it struck me that I was hanging out with the drummer from a famous rock band. Downtown Exit had already hit it big in America, and in England, "Painted Ladies" was hovering around number five on the BBC Radio 1 charts. And here I was with their drummer, lurching back down the aisle, giggling like a kid. We eased into our seats again and a lady with a little dog gave us the stink eye.

Our train rolled past Nottingham and we saw a sign that made Chester sit up. "Did you see that? It said Sherwood Forest."

"No kidding?"

"Shee-it," said Chester, drawling out the word. "It's like being in a fairy tale."

"Crazy," I said. I was really quite stoned.

A British Rail guy came down the aisle with a cart, and Chester spotted the sandwiches and cans of soda. "Hey, you got a bob on you?"

"I don't even know what a bob is."

"A bob is money," he said. The cart was rolling past and Chester inspected it. "You think they got Tab in this country?"

"You mean like the soft drink?"

"Yeah, Tab. I'm dying for a Tab."

We looked at each other and laughed. The lady with the dog got up and moved to the other end of the carriage. The truth is I'd spent the very last of my money on a paisley shirt in Soho. Something I thought I could wear onstage. Mostly I was still wearing my jean jacket and my Adidas running shoes, but I knew the time for those was over. When I told Chester about the shirt, though, he pursed his lips and considered me sorrowfully.

"Boss," he said, "you ain't exactly going onstage tonight. Didn't anyone tell you?"

"Tell me what?"

"Aw, shit," he said. "You really don't know?"

"Know what?"

"Well, listen, I know you got good intents and all, but you're gonna be sitting on the sidelines tonight."

"So, I can't wear my shirt?"

"Damn, no. You don't need no shirt. You can play bare-skinned if you want. It don't make no difference."

"It doesn't?"

He studied me for a moment, then broke into a great bellowing laugh. "You got a lot to learn, Boss," he said. "You got a whole lot to learn about this business of ours."

And he was right.

That night, in Leeds, Surly had the crew set me up on a metal folding chair behind the curtain to the left of the stage. There I sat tucked away with the speaker crates and a tumble of guitar cases. They'd given me a Les Paul, a real beauty of a guitar, heavy as hell but with a real smooth neck. They'd set up a microphone for me too, on a little stand in front of my chair.

I watched Frankie from behind the curtain. He pranced out into the spotlights and the crowd began to bounce. I just sat there while the band worked through their first couple of songs. Miguel wore a silk cloak like he was some kind of wizard. Skinny Dave hardly moved, typical for a bass player. Chester was whapping on his drums and Pete was sending out pure bursts of energy on his guitar, throwing moves as cool as any I'd ever seen.

And then it happened. He started tripping. You could tell. His eyes grew big—like he was seeing something that wasn't there. He started missing notes and Surly signaled for me to get ready. I straightened up in my seat and Surly motioned to the sound guy. They'd rigged up this system where they could switch the amp from Pete's guitar to mine. They turned off his mic too, and all of a sudden I was live.

Poor Pete. He seemed lost out there. He knew that his hands weren't doing the things that were coming out of his amplifier. But he kept twanging away on his useless guitar. A couple of times, he wasn't even close to his mic while I was singing his backups, sitting behind the curtain like the goddamn Wizard of Oz. Eventually, he almost completely stopped, his jaw agape, his eyes like dinner plates, but I just kept on playing.

When they did "Painted Ladies" for the encore, I played the hell out of it. Frankie was out at the front of the stage and he shot me an appreciative glance. He just kept doing that jungle cat thing, stalking across the stage. He didn't miss a beat and neither did I.

After, when the band was coming off the stage, Chester veered off toward me, a towel around his neck.

"Good thing I bought that fancy shirt," I said.

He put a meaty hand on my shoulder. "Don't you never mind," he said. "You did good."

Pete had lurched off the other side of the stage with Frankie, so he never saw me at all. I tell you, it was the weirdest thing I ever did. I had just performed for two thousand people and they'd all gone nuts, but not a single one of them knew it was me who was playing back there. Not a single person knew.

♫

We did a couple more gigs in Sheffield and then Birmingham. Sometimes Pete was fine and he'd play the whole show. Other times, they'd switch over to me pretty quick. Before the shows, I was supposed to pretend I was one of the roadies, but I could see that Pete was getting suspicious. He'd seen me sitting behind the stacks, and once he'd caught me with one of his guitars. I told him Surly Bob had asked me to change the strings on it and he bought that. The guy had loads of guitars: the black Les Paul, an older sunburst model, a blonde Stratocaster with a whammy bar, and a whole bunch of others. I lugged my old Martin along, but mostly it just sat in its battered case, unopened.

None of it was what I expected. I didn't stay in the same hotels as the band and I didn't really get to hang out with them at all. No one but Chester ever said thanks, and I guess, when it came to it, I wasn't anything more than a glorified roadie after all. I also hadn't been paid yet, just some pocket change here and there, barely enough to get myself fish and chips. Evelyn had been right, of course. I hadn't thought to get a return ticket to Canada and now I was pretty much out of money, so basically, I was hooped.

When we got back to London, I figured that was that and I packed up my things to go home. Then I took one last trip out to Twickenham to get the money they owed me. Surly hadn't called me. I just went.

The afternoon was bright and unusually warm. For England, it was a pretty nice day. Still, I was feeling a lot of dread. I could hear the bass guitar thumping and the crack of the snare drum as soon as I got off the train, and the whole band came in as I got closer.

The big loading dock doors at the back were open and I walked right in. The mock stage was set up again, but it was less cluttered this time, and the guys were standing close to each other. They were rehearsing a new song they'd tried a couple of times up north called "29 Streetlights." It was a song about growing up in a small town, so small that the whole thing only had twenty-nine streetlights. The lyrics were about memories, about something that happened under each of those streetlights—like a first kiss or whatever. It was pretty long. It was like they had a different verse for every one of those damn streetlights.

None of them saw me come in and I made a beeline for Surly. I didn't want to draw this out. I just wanted my money. He was standing by the soundboard, his arms crossed over his chest, listening, and he didn't notice me until I tapped him on the arm.

"Hey," I said. He grimaced a bit and gestured at his ears like it was too loud to hear much of anything. "Can I get my money?"

"What?"

"Maybe, can we step outside for a moment?"

He grunted but followed me out through the loading dock doors and down the cement steps into the parking lot. "Right," he said, pulling a pack of cigarettes from his chest pocket and making a show of lighting one up. "What are you after?"

"Well," I said, "I'd like to thank you for the opportunity to—"

He eyed me through the smoke. "Bollocks. What do you really want?"

"I guess I was wondering if I might get paid."

"You're not done yet."

"Well, I was thinking that maybe I should be getting back home."

Surly Bob took a slow drag on his cigarette, then he sighed. "Listen, I just booked us another show. At the Hammersmith."

"The Hammersmith?"

"The Hammersmith Odeon. You know what that is?"

"Yeah, of course," I said, though I wasn't sure I did.

"It's big."

"Okay."

He took another puff on his cigarette. " 'Painted Ladies' is number three this week. That's better than it did in the States."

I nodded.

"So I got us the Hammersmith. All that rubbish up north, that was just prelude."

I knew what a prelude was, but I had a sneaking suspicion it was for the Exits, not me. "Okay," I said, "but then you'll pay me?"

"Bugger," said Surly. He dug into his pants pocket and pulled out a wad of British pounds—twenty-pound notes, the purple ones. He counted off five of them and slapped them down into my hand. "There's a hundred quid."

I stared at the bills. I wasn't sure what to say. I wasn't sure how much I was supposed to be getting paid. I hadn't signed a contract or anything. I guess it didn't matter. I just needed enough to get me home.

"Now, why don't you come on back inside? The boys are working out the new song. You'll need to be learning it too."

"Okay," I said, but I didn't move.

"Jesus, Levi. I'm trying to help you out here." He started back up the steps, but at the top, he stopped. "So, you coming or not?"

"Yeah," I said, "I'm coming."

The band had finished playing when I slunk back in. Chester tipped his head at me and I waved a hello at him. Frankie was off to the side, but Pete was still out there in the spotlights, and that girl, the one with the camera, was out there with him. She leaned into him and gestured like she was explaining a camera angle or something. He said something back and she smiled and walked off the set. Surly was watching them too, and before he could get away from me, I grabbed at his arm.

"Christ," he said. "What is it now?"

"Who is that?" I asked.

Surly followed my gaze. "What . . . Ariadne?"

"Her name is Ariadne?"

Surly grinned. I hadn't seen him smile before. He didn't have the best teeth, that's for sure. "Ariadne Christos." He said the name like I should know who she was. "Christos?" he repeated when he saw the blank expression on my face. I really didn't know what he was talking about.

"Listen," he said. "She's got nothing to do with you. You play your damn guitar and let me handle the business side of things."

"Right."

"Now, bugger off. I'm busy here."

♫

The day of the Hammersmith show, I headed out early to get a feel for the place. It was this crazy old theater from the 1930s—very art deco—with plush red seats and a semicircular balcony, and to the side of the stage there was a massive pipe organ like something out of a horror movie.

Chester, Miguel, and Davey were already there when I arrived. Chester usually liked to tune his drums himself, his tom-toms especially, so they made this descending thump of notes. He'd found himself a can of Tab and he held it up when he saw me.

Miguel was out front. He usually played keyboards but today he was perched on a stool on the half-empty stage holding an accordion of all things. It was shiny blue with little white buttons on one side and a miniature keyboard on the other, and it made him look like he was from another century. Miguel had long stringy hair and a wiry mustache like Salvador Dalí. His English wasn't perfect, but he knew his music, that's for sure. He was hunched over the accordion, swaying a little, pumping at the bellows with his eyes closed. It was kind of cool. Some old folk song thing.

I was off at the other end of the stage trying to figure out where I would be set up tonight when Frankie came crashing in. He pushed in through a side door behind the stage, swearing, hardly making any sense, with Surly Bob trailing behind him, his face grim, one hand out, trying to calm Frankie down.

Miguel stopped playing.

"Fucking police," spat Frankie.

"There's been an accident," said Surly Bob.

Chester glanced up from behind his drums. Dave retreated into his shell.

"Everybody," said Surly. "Stop what you're doing and gather round."

Chester raised an eyebrow at me. He came out from behind his drum kit and we all made a circle around Surly and Frankie. I stood behind Chester, unsure whether this really concerned me or not.

"Something terrible has happened," Surly said. "Early this morning, Pete went and fell off the balcony at the hotel."

"What do you mean . . . fell?" said Chester. Miguel's brow was furrowed like he wasn't sure what he was hearing.

"I was just sitting there with him," said Frankie. He stared down at the floor and shook his head like he couldn't believe it.

"Boss," said Chester. "What exactly are you trying to say?"

"We were out on the balcony," muttered Frankie. He started rubbing at his wrists. "We were drinking."

"Well, that ain't no crime."

Frankie's lips went tight. "Pete was really drunk. And he'd just popped another tab of acid."

"Aw, shit," said Chester.

"I was angry. He's so fucked-up all the time, and we were already plenty drunk so there was no point in—"

I stood as still as I could. Everyone was focused on Frankie.

"So I told him," said Frankie. "I told him he had to lay off that stuff or he'd be out of the band." Frankie looked up at us then, his eyes wet with tears.

"Damn," Chester said. "You said that?"

"Pete started laughing at me. He put his hands behind him and sort of humped himself up so he was sitting on the railing. *You?* he said. *You're going to kick me out of the band?* He was laughing so hard he was sort of jiggling, and I'm thinking that ain't cool, and that's when he started to tip over."

"He fell?" said Chester.

"His eyes got all big. He looked right at me like he knew he'd just done something really stupid. And then he was gone."

"Is he all right?" I asked. Surly signaled for me to shut up.

"Jesus fucking Christ," snapped Frankie. "It's eight floors down. No, he's not okay."

Miguel said something in Spanish and crossed himself.

Chester's face had gone all wobbly. "Pete's dead?"

Frankie bent over like he was going to throw up. His shoulders started heaving but he wasn't making a sound.

"We just came from the police station," said Surly. "They took Frankie in for questioning." He put a hand on Frankie's shoulder, but Frankie jerked out from under it.

"Don't you fucking touch me," he said. He pushed past us and kicked at a chair, my chair in fact, and it clattered across the floor. We all watched it bounce and come to a stop, then Frankie stomped off in the other direction.

Surly Bob held up his hands. "All right, all right. This is not the worst thing that can happen."

"*Madre de Dios*," Miguel said. "What is the worst thing that can happen?"

Chester was shaking his head like he couldn't believe any of this. They'd grown up together, him and Frankie and Pete, and I couldn't imagine what he was feeling.

Frankie was pacing in the cavernous gloom behind the stage. I could see him light up a cigarette, the end glowing red.

"Right," said Surly. "We have to get on top of this."

"What are we going to do?" Miguel asked, stroking his mustache.

"We tell Labyrinth the new album is almost ready," said Surly.

"But we just barely begun that thing," Chester said.

"And then we have the European tour, so that helps." Surly was nodding to himself, thinking out loud. "That will keep us paid, until we can finish the album."

I didn't say a word. Chester eyed me and I knew what he was thinking. I knew what everybody was thinking. I was going to be in the band now. It was obvious. It wasn't how I'd expected it to happen, that's for sure, but now there wasn't a choice. It was going to be me.

Frankie was still pacing back and forth, kicking at things, and when he'd had enough, he stamped out his cigarette and barged back toward us. I tried to stay clear, but he came in at me and jabbed a finger in my face. "And you," he spat, "you can just fuck off."

Chester moved to get between us. He was a big man and he pushed up against Frankie. "He didn't do nothing."

Frankie glared up at him. "And you can just fuck off too."

Chester stared him down for a moment until Frankie brushed past him, past me, and out through the fire escape door behind us. Then Chester kind of deflated. He sighed pretty heavily and turned to me. "All right, Boss," he said. "Looks like you're up."

Hello Juliet

We played the Hammersmith that night. What else could we do? Surly had pasted an *X* on the stage floor with duct tape to mark where I should stand, and it was way back behind the other guys like I was some sort of bootleg Pete. All of us had to slink out to our places in the dark, except for Frankie. He was to come out last, and so we stood there in the shadows, waiting as the red dots of the amps blinked around us.

Behind me, a wall of speakers hissed with twenty-four thousand watts of electricity. I could see the dark mass of the crowd, three thousand of them, shuffling and buzzing. Little specks of orange flared up here and there from the burning ends of cigarettes and joints.

And then, all at once, a row of lights blasted on and Frankie bounded out onto the stage. Chester cracked his drumsticks above his head to count us in and *boom*—this surge, this cauldron of sound, crashed over me. We slammed into the first chord and the electric sizzle of my guitar hit me almost physically. For a few bars, it felt like a galloping horse I had to wrestle under control.

Out front, Frankie ripped his mic from its stand and his vocals soared over everything. He was a good performer, I'll give him that. No one would have known he'd been a broken mess just two hours before. Chester was grooving too, his massive head bobbling back and forth in time with the music. The bass drum thumped deep in my chest and the floorboards trembled and everything just fell into place. This was music for the gods. This was unstoppable.

I had to remember to breathe, especially before stepping to the mic for my backup vocals. But half a song in, I just went with it, trying to ride the crazy bucking wave of energy.

In the glare of spotlights, I couldn't quite see the crowd anymore, but I could hear them roaring. It was sweltering under those lights and I felt rivulets of sweat dribbling down my forehead. Still, we rocked through the first song, and when we came to the last chord, we hit it hard, staccato, and in the split second of silence before the audience exploded, it was as if we had stopped time for a moment.

The truth is we tore the place apart that night. I gave it my all and Downtown Exit never sounded so good. Everyone knew it. Even Frankie whirled around once and caught my eye, a flicker of confusion dancing on his face. I think he thought that it was Pete playing back there—until he saw me. But it didn't matter. Everything gelled that night. The crowd was on its feet for most of the show and we had to play three full encores. And even when we left the stage for good, we could hear them thundering behind us, stomping and clapping and yelling for more.

After the show, Frankie disappeared but the rest of us went up to Chester's hotel room. I drank a ton. We smoked pot too, loads of it, and everyone tried not to think about Pete. We tried to just focus on how well the show had gone. We stayed up until five in the morning, and then I crashed on Chester's pullout couch. Surly had all the guys staying at the Dorchester, a posh hotel near Hyde Park, and without anyone really saying so, I knew I'd be staying there now too.

♫

In the morning, when the light came shattering in through the window, I struggled up and made a cup of coffee in the coffee maker. It was a lot better than the Nescafé at the youth hostel. I wouldn't be missing that. Chester was still snoring on the bed, and I drank a second cup before leaving to clear out my locker at the hostel.

Surly had mostly managed to keep Pete's death out of the news but the hard-core fans knew about it. Some of them—mostly girls—were huddled outside the hotel, heads bowed in a little circle, holding candles and singing an out-of-tune version of "The Blues Don't Live Here No More."

I didn't feel like chatting, that's for sure, so I tucked my head down, said excuse me, and elbowed past. I really felt like shit, if you want to know the truth.

It took me forever to get back to the hostel, and when I finally pushed through the front doors, I saw a guy slumped in a chair by the reception desk. His backpack was between his feet and his head was lolling back like he was asleep. It took me a second to realize that it was Rudy.

He looked even worse than me. His hair was a bird's nest and he was snoring a bit. His Dr Pepper T-shirt was untucked and rumpled. I kind of recognized that before I even recognized him.

"Rudy," I said. "What the hell?"

Rudy snorted and woke up, clamping a hand on the fanny pack around his midsection. I imagine he had his passport in there, his plane ticket, and all his valuables, and I was pretty sure every pickpocket in London would know that too.

He blinked up at me. "Jeez, Levi, you're a bit hard to track down."

"What are you doing here?"

"I came to see the famous rock star."

"Rudy, I don't need your help."

"You could've told us where you were staying," he said. "You could've at least done that." He wobbled up onto his feet.

"Rudy," I said. "Please. Don't wreck this for me."

He pinched his lips. "I'm not going to wreck anything."

"Look. Everything's changed. Pete's dead."

"What?" He took a step back and kind of tripped a little on his backpack. He had a foam mattress rolled up and strapped to the bottom of it. He didn't fall, though. He was wearing clunky hiking boots and he managed to right himself with a little jig step.

"Oh, jeez, Rudy. You can't just—"

"Pete Gunnerson is dead?"

"All I know is that now I'm in the band, for real."

"All right," he said. "So, you're going to need—"

"No, that's what I'm telling you. I don't need your help here. I'm good."

His lower lip started to quiver a bit.

"Okay, okay. How about we get you sorted out. You look like shit." The Swedish guy must have been upstairs. There was no one at the desk. I turned to go and find him, but Rudy stopped me. He was pretty out of it with the jet lag and all, but he fixed me with one of his serious looks. He zipped open his fanny pack and said, "I brought you something."

"What?"

Rudy rifled around in the fanny pack. It was a pretty big one and it hung under his stomach like a little pillow. "Here." He passed me a thin blue strip of cloth. "You forgot this."

"Aw, shit, Rudy." I held it up. It was the first-place ribbon I'd won at the Kiwanis Music Festival. The ribbon was so worn it was almost translucent. On the back, a little piece of paper was stapled to the top. The writing was kind of scribbly, but I knew it off by heart. I'd kept it for years. *Levi Jaxon*, it said. *First place, fourteen and under, piano.*

"You played that Bach thing," said Rudy.

"The Prelude in C Major."

"Holy. You were really good."

I remembered that day clearly. And not just because I'd won my division when I was a full year younger than most of the other kids. It was more about Evelyn, the look on her face, like she was really proud of me. But something else too. Like she didn't want anyone else to see how proud she was.

But still, it was the first time I really did anything good. It was the first time anyone really noticed me at all. That ribbon marked the day my life began to change.

I don't know. You get this feeling when you're tossed around from foster home to foster home. It's like you're not good enough to keep.

Like you're not good enough to love. I know that sounds like a lot of psychological horseshit, but it's true. I just kept getting ditched by people. They shuffled me around and I got sent to about twelve different schools, so I never really had time to make friends.

I never learned much of anything else at school either. I only learned piano, and then the guitar. I could play those things like nobody's business. It just came to me. It was the one thing I was truly good at and this little ribbon was proof.

"Okay," I said to Rudy. "Let's get you a bed. You really don't look so hot."

♫

The Exits had a couple more days booked at Abbey Road, but now, of course, they were without Pete and everything was up in the air. From what Chester had told me, they had a couple songs in the bag, and a couple more that were half finished. You needed maybe ten or twelve songs for a full album, so they weren't even close, and time was ticking.

When I'd first gone in for my audition, there was nothing but a stool and a microphone and that big old grand piano pushed up against the wall. Now the studio was filled with gear. Chester was there, setting up his drums behind the sound baffles in a corner. Skinny Dave was in the other corner and Miguel was sitting at the grand piano, fiddling around on the high notes. There were cables everywhere, snaking along the floor.

Surly Bob came clanging down the stairs from the control booth. He was wearing his pinstripe suit but it was a bit rumpled and maybe a little too small for him. "Miguel," he said, "quit buggering about on that piano. We've got work to do."

Miguel nodded and stood up from the grand piano. His keyboard rig was set up near Chester. There was a Vox organ, a Roland electric piano, and a Moog synthesizer all stacked on top of each other. Skinny Dave had his bass out, tuning it, sitting with his legs crossed on a stool. There was something weird about that guy. He always seemed like he was scared, like a rabbit or something.

Frankie sauntered in wearing a velvet smoking jacket. His shoes were black and shiny with pointed toes and he was very nonchalantly smoking a cigarette. Surly grimaced at him.

"Right," said Surly. "We have three days booked in here before we go on tour. Three days to finish the album."

Frankie made a show of drawing in a long inhale on his cigarette. He squinted at Surly and let out a stream of blue smoke. It curled in the air like storm clouds.

"Damn," said Chester. "How we gonna get through that many songs?"

Surly turned on him. "We have to. Your man there, Blackmore, is getting impatient, and the last thing we need is for him to lose interest."

"Who's Blackmore?" I asked, but Surly was already gone, clomping up the stairs to the control room above us.

"Sir Charles Blackmore," Frankie said. "The head of Labyrinth Records. Don't you know anything?" He glared at me, then turned and tipped his head at Miguel, and together they walked over to the keyboard stack. I watched him pass a small packet to Miguel, folded up like a little envelope. Miguel tucked it into his jacket and they spoke in hushed tones for a few minutes.

Then Frankie came back at me. "Listen, pal," he said. I'm not sure he even knew my name. "Miguel's gonna run you through the chord changes for the new stuff. He's got the charts."

"It's okay," I said. "I don't need charts."

Frankie grinned and swung around to the rest of the band. "Our boy here doesn't need charts. He's got golden ears."

Skinny Dave seemed to get smaller.

"Frankie," said Chester. "Lay off the kid. He's doing his best."

Frankie whirled on me again. "Let's get something crystal clear, pal. You're only here because we don't have time to get anyone better. You got that?" He sneered, daring me to say something back, but I stayed quiet. I knew what was good for me. After an uncomfortable minute, Frankie called over to Miguel. "Show him '29 Streetlights.' Get him on the acoustic." Then he loped off after Surly, up to the control room.

Chester watched him go and shook his head sadly. "That boy's a mess," he said.

Miguel nodded in agreement.

"Probably," Chester continued, "she'll be good for him."

Way up above us in the control booth, we saw Frankie at the console, and there beside him was Ariadne, the girl with the camera. He leaned into her and whispered something and her face lit up. Then Surly saw us gawking up at them and rapped on the glass. I could see his mouth moving, swearing at us, but none of the mics were on yet.

"Are those two together now?" I asked.

"Something like that," said Chester. My face must have showed disappointment because he cocked an eyebrow at me. "You best keep your distance, Boss. You don't want to be messing with that."

I nodded unhappily. Like I said, I knew what was good for me.

♫

We worked on three songs that day, the two that were half finished and the new one, "29 Streetlights." I laid down a guitar solo on one called "Between Life and Fantasy" and we listened to Pete's last song, "Sometimes Magic." That one was the very last thing he ever sang on, so it was bittersweet to hear it. We decided not to add anything to it. We just decided that it was finished.

By my count, that made a total of five songs. Not nearly enough for an album. Frankie still had to do some overdubs too. The lead vocals usually went on last, and Frankie would have to do them by himself, cocooned off in a sound booth. And who knows when that was ever going to happen.

To make it even weirder, I still didn't know if I was officially in the band or not. Nobody had said a thing, one way or the other.

It must have been about midnight when we spilled out onto the street. Surly had a couple of limos waiting to take us back to the Dorchester, but there, under a lamppost, stood Rudy, looking forlorn.

"Aw, shit," I said.

"What's up, Boss?" said Chester. "You know that guy?"

Surly had climbed into the first limo with Frankie. Ariadne had long since left and Skinny Dave had skipped out the minute we finished the bed tracks. The remaining limo was still parked against the curb, with the chauffeur holding the door open for me and Chester and Miguel.

Chester pursed his lips. He squinted over at Rudy.

"I know him from back home," I said.

"You sure he's all right?"

"Rudy," I called to him. "What the hell are you doing?"

"Nothing."

I glanced over to make sure Surly's limo had pulled off down the street. "C'mon, then, get over here."

Rudy tucked his head down and crossed the street toward us. He was wearing the same clothes I'd last seen him in, his clunky hiking boots and the Dr Pepper T-shirt, and when he arrived at our sidewalk, Chester appraised him.

"You need a ride, Boss? We can drop you off somewhere."

Rudy was wide-eyed. "You're Chester Merriweather. Holy. And Miguel Rosario."

Miguel nodded, then rolled two fingers across his mustache, like he was straightening it.

"C'mon, man," I said. "Be cool."

"Holy," said Rudy again.

"This is Rudy," I said to the others. "I used to play in a band with him."

"You a musician?" asked Chester.

"Well, jeez, not like you guys."

"All right, my man," said Chester, clapping a big hand on Rudy's back. "Where you headed?"

Rudy glanced at me to see if it was all right. I nodded and we all clambered into the back of the limo. It was pretty roomy inside, with a black leather bench seat facing forward and two more individual seats facing back. Rudy squeezed in between Chester and Miguel on the bench seat and I sat in one of the others facing them. We'd barely pulled away from the curb when Miguel slipped the little packet out of his jacket pocket. I'd already guessed what it was, but Rudy's mouth formed a little O at the sight of the coke. Miguel didn't even bother to lay down lines; it would have been too bumpy in the limo anyway. With practiced fingers he rolled up a five-pound note and snorted a little right out of the packet.

He passed it to me and for a moment I didn't know what to do. I took the packet and the rolled-up bill and, what the hell, took a good snort of it too. The sensation in my nose was like carbonation, fizzing and bubbling all through my sinuses. It tasted slightly sweet too, and I felt a rush of energy and, I don't know, confidence, I guess.

I passed it along to Chester. "Nah, man. I don't touch that stuff." He shuffled it over to Rudy and I nodded at him to give it a try. Rudy came up with his right nostril coated in white powder, his pupils dilated, and the hugest grin on his face.

"I play bass," he said, out of the blue. "And a little guitar."

"Is that right?" said Chester. He turned to me for confirmation.

"Rudy—" I began. I looked over at Miguel, but he was looking out the window, lost in his own thoughts.

"You got a gig here, man?" Chester asked.

"I didn't bring my bass," said Rudy.

"I mean, you got work? You got a job?"

"Not really."

Chester turned to me. "They're looking for road crew, you know. You should talk to Bobby."

"Me?" I said.

"You wanna help out your friend here?" Chester held my gaze for a moment until I kind of sighed. It's not that I didn't want to help Rudy. It's just that he didn't really belong here. This wasn't his world at all.

Rudy reached up to a little switch on the roof above him. He flicked it and the sunroof began to shunt open. "Look at that," he yipped. "That's some good electronics right there."

"Rudy," I said, trying to sound stern. "You probably shouldn't stay here. You should probably go home to Evelyn."

Chester stared at me across the expanse of leather and carpet. "Who's Evelyn?"

"My mom," said Rudy. Above us, through the sunroof, I could see a star hovering high in the night sky, almost like it was trying to tell us something.

♫

The thing is, Rudy had helped me a lot. The day I turned eighteen, I walked out of my last group home. *Fuck that*, I thought. It was late September and I'd just had my birthday and I didn't think anyone in the world really cared about me. I'd quit school and I had about twenty bucks in my pocket. I also had the Martin guitar, though, and my little black duffel bag, and I thought that was all I really needed.

I headed straight for the bus station. It was nighttime, snowing a little. I didn't even know where I was going, but I didn't care. For the first time in my life I was in control of myself. No one else could tell me what to do.

The bus terminal was cold. I was sitting, the only guy in a row of plastic blue chairs. My guitar case was at my feet and I was studying the board trying to decide which bus I should take. I only had enough money for a one-way ticket and maybe a little something to eat.

I was just sitting there, trying to decide—thinking I should maybe just sleep in the bus terminal—when Rudy burst in, all flustered, his hair a haystack. This was only a few weeks after his dad had died. Cancer, like I said. Anyway, Rudy looked around the waiting room and zeroed in on me.

"Levi," he began. "Holy jeez, what are you doing?"

"I'm leaving. I've had enough of this shithole."

Rudy eyed my guitar case. "No. You can't go. Not yet."

We'd had the band going for about a year already, so I thought that's what he meant. Really, it was only him and me at that point, so I don't know why it mattered. I was going to say something snotty, but I couldn't think of anything. I had a big lump in my throat, if you really want to know. I looked over Rudy's shoulder. There was a bus for Vancouver leaving pretty soon. *Maybe that one*, I thought. *Maybe I should just take that one.*

Rudy moved in front of me. His coat was wet from the snow.

"I need to go. There's nothing for me here."

"No. You can't go yet."

"Please," I managed. "I have to be a musician. I'm going to be famous."

"You can live in my mom's basement. She said so."

"Evelyn said that?"

He considered me. His lower lip was trembling just a bit.

"I'm going to be famous," I said again, like that counted for anything.

"I know," he said. "But not yet."

"C'mon, Rudy. Don't do this to me."

The bus for Vancouver was leaving in ten minutes. They'd just made the announcement.

"Look," he said, taking a seat beside me. "There's some stuff I need to tell you."

The bus station was buzzing with fluorescent lights. The floor was a jigsaw of dirty boot prints. Everything smelled like cleaning product and Rudy was shaking a bit, like he was cold, only he wasn't. He was trying really hard not to cry. It was weird.

"It's Evelyn," he began. "There's stuff you don't know about her. When she went to Juilliard."

"Juilliard," I said derisively. "Like I haven't heard that about a million times."

Rudy looked straight ahead. "No, it's more than that. She got kicked out."

That shut me down. Surprised me, in fact. I always thought she was really good.

"Some stuff happened there, okay? I'm not supposed to say."

"What stuff?

"I'm not supposed to say."

"Rudy, c'mon. I'm going to miss my bus."

"They kicked her out and she lost her chance."

"Why are you telling me this?"

"Because now, she wants for you to, I don't know—"

"What?"

"I don't know. She wants to make sure you don't screw up too."

Another announcement came over the PA. It was a bus for Saskatoon. It was just pulling in. "I'm not going to screw up."

"Yeah you are. You're screwing up right now. What do you think is going to happen if you get on a bus right now? Listen, there are people who care about you, Levi, who want to help you, but you have to let them." He held my gaze for a moment and then he sighed, deeply, like he was giving up on something. Giving up on me, I guess. "All right," he said. "Do what you want. I don't care."

"Aw, jeez, Rudy." Like I said, I had twenty bucks in my pocket, and Rudy was looking down at me with this great mop of hair and his big sad eyes and I thought, shit, he was probably right. I was screwing up. I took in a gulp of air and blew it out slowly.

"The basement?" I said.

"Yeah, she's got it all ready for you." He stood up, the beginning of a grin on his face.

So I stood up too. I was trying really hard not to cry. I picked up that old guitar and followed him out of the terminal, back out into the snow.

♫

The next morning, at the Dorchester, I was staring at myself in the bathroom mirror when I heard Surly come barging into our hotel suite. I was still sharing the room with Chester. In the mirror I could see that my hair had grown, and I'd been giving it a bit of a toss to see how it looked from different angles.

It was already midmorning and I thought we were supposed to be going back to the studio for another go at the songs, but Surly had other plans.

"Get yourselves dressed," he announced. "We're going to a happening."

I came out of the bathroom.

"A what?" said Chester. He was lazing on his bed.

"A happening," insisted Surly. "You two got to get yourself dressed."

Chester heaved himself up into a sitting position. “Boss, what about the recording sessions?”

“We’ve still got two days there. Christ, do I have to explain everything?”

“I guess you do,” Chester said.

“Look,” Surly said. “We’ve got more important things to do today.”

“More important than recording?”

“It’s a happening. At the Indica Gallery. The place is legendary. It’s where John Lennon met Yoko Ono.”

I stood at the door to the bathroom. “Yoko Ono’s going to be there?”

“Jesus, no. I’m just saying we got to make connections. It’s part of the plan. So get yourselves together. We’re going.”

“Aw, Boss,” said Chester.

“It’s for Ariadne.”

I came forward a few steps.

“She’s got a photography exhibit down there,” said Surly.

Chester sank back down onto the bed. “A photography exhibit? Can’t say I’m really interested.”

“Um,” I said.

Chester shot me a warning look. Surly swung his gaze on me.

“I’ll go,” I said.

When I slid into the back of the taxicab, Frankie was taking a good belt from a mickey. I don’t know what it was but I could smell it, like a bad perfume.

“What?” Frankie snapped. “What are you looking at?”

Surly whirled around in the front seat. “Frankie, put that away. You need to be presentable today.”

“You don’t need to worry about me,” he said. “I’m good.”

He was wearing a really nice suit, except instead of a tie, he had a long silk scarf wrapped around his collar. His hair shone with some kind of pomade and I could see the comb marks at the sides, raking backward, sculpted almost, and I had to admit he had the look. He had the look of someone famous.

There were quite a few people on the sidewalk outside the gallery, and a guy was at the door checking people as they went in. The main floor was a bookshop, but books aren't really my thing, so I was happy to follow Surly and Frankie through and down the stairs to the gallery in the basement.

It was buzzing down there. Wineglasses were coming around on silver trays and there were loads of people, all dressed up and probably wondering who the hell I was. I was still wearing my old jean jacket and my Adidas running shoes, so I tried to blend into the walls. I just tried to make myself invisible.

Ariadne made her entrance in a dark blue dress with her hair swept up like Audrey Hepburn's in *Breakfast at Tiffany's*. She looked really glamorous, that was for sure. Everyone was hovering around her, clinking glasses, and she was smiling, though she kept glancing past them all like she was looking for someone. Someone who wasn't there.

The room was white and all along the ceiling were rows of tiny lights that were angled down, each of them illuminating a single photograph in a frame. The photographs weren't large—maybe twelve inches tall by ten inches wide. I wandered over to look at the first one and it was this old village up on a rocky hillside. You could see the winding pathways going off between the houses, and everything was whitewashed so that the houses looked like a haphazard stack of sugar cubes.

The next photo was of a sunset over a dark sea. It looked like the same place, except that on a little rise in the foreground were some ruins, something really ancient, like maybe the remains of a temple or something.

Surly appeared beside me. "Where'd Frankie bugger off to?"

"I don't know. I thought he was with you."

My guess was that Frankie was off in the can, slugging down more alcohol. He seemed to be having a real hard time getting over Pete's death, and no wonder. As far as I knew they'd been childhood pals.

"Christ," Surly muttered, and he plunged off to look for him.

I moved to the next photograph and an older woman pushed in beside me. She leaned right in and I could hear her jewelry rattle. "She does not have her father's eye, that much is certain."

"Her father?"

"Imagine," she hissed. "Having the nerve to try and sell these ghastly photographs."

"They're for sale?"

The woman considered me. Her face was as long as a horse's. "You'll notice he's not even here today."

"I'm sorry," I said. "Who's her father?"

She stepped back and took in my jean jacket and running shoes. "Dmitry Christos," she said, like any idiot should know who that was. "The film director?"

"Okay," I said.

"Her father is a genius. He's won twice at Cannes. And all this," she waved her arm around at the walls. "Well, just imagine."

The woman harrumphed and walked off, and I went back to the photo of the sunset and the ruins. The pictures were pretty good, if you ask me. I would have bought one if I'd had any money. All of them had little captions underneath, two lines usually, like bits of a poem, but the photo of the sunset only had four words.

At that moment Ariadne stood nearby, and I wondered if she'd heard anything the older lady had said. I thought not. She was by herself now and was twirling the stem of her wineglass, looking wistful.

"Um," I said, and her eyes hovered over to me. They were green like jade and for a moment I froze. "This one is pretty good."

Her eyes narrowed a little. "That's the Portara," she said. She had an accent, British of course, but with a hint of something else under it, something more exotic. "It's a door, or the remains of one. The door to the temple of Apollo."

I leaned down and pretended to read the caption.

"I call it *The Wine-Dark Sea*," she said.

"That's beautiful. Is that Shakespeare or something?"

"No, it's Homer." She glanced around the room like maybe there was someone else she should be talking to.

"Homer," I repeated. "Nice." I knew I was sounding kind of stupid but I just plowed on. I couldn't help myself. "And where is this exactly?"

"It's Naxos, in Greece."

"You're from Greece?"

"I was born there, yes. And, of course, my father is from Naxos." She waited a beat. "Which is all anyone here seems to care about."

"He's a film director?"

Ariadne's face blanched. "He's not here," she said. "He couldn't make it." Her lips tightened like I'd said something wrong.

"I'm sorry," I said. "Was he supposed to be here?"

She shook her head. "He's never here."

She looked at me then, like she was seeing me for the first time. "Am I supposed to know you?"

"I'm in Downtown Exit. Frankie's band."

"Ah," she said. "Frankie."

Frankie had in fact just reappeared and Surly was pulling him toward us. Frankie looked a bit ruffled, but he straightened up when he saw us. He swooped in at us and gave Ariadne a peck on both cheeks, just like the Europeans do.

"How are you holding up?" she asked, laying a hand on his arm.

Surly threw me a *Get lost* look and I took a step back, out of their little circle of attraction. A hush had come down over the room. Frankie's eyes welled up and he looked down. Ariadne squeezed his arm and leaned in closer to him. *"Heard melodies are sweet,"* she said. Her voice was soft, almost a whisper. *"But those unheard are sweeter: therefore"*—Frankie's eyes rose to meet hers—*"ye soft pipes, play on."*

Holy, I thought, *that was really good.* Maybe it was that Homer guy again. Frankie took in a shuddering breath and Ariadne pressed into him and they held each other.

"Let's just leave them be, shall we?" Surly announced. He smiled an ingratiating smile at Ariadne and yanked me away, but he didn't have to try very hard. Ariadne had already forgotten me anyway, and Frankie, well, I could see that he was the object of all her attention.

♫

We were at Abbey Road the next day by noon. Chester and his drums were surrounded by sound baffles, like he was in an office cubicle or something, and I could only see him when he stood up. Skinny Dave sat on a stool on the other side. Miguel was in a corner with his keyboards, trying out different patches, most of which were these otherworldly bleeps and toots.

Frankie was nowhere to be found and everyone was feeling a bit tense. We all hoped he was writing and would burst in any second with a new song. In the meantime, we fiddled around on our instruments, just waiting, while Surly paced back and forth in the control booth.

I'd brought my old Martin acoustic and I opened up the case, really just to tune it, to make sure it was okay. There were loads of other guitars, of course—Pete's guitars—but I still liked mine the best. It wasn't in the greatest condition, but I'd been playing it for so long, it felt like an old friend. I lifted it out of its case and strummed an E chord.

Surly rapped on the glass and leaned down into the console mic. "What was that you were playing when we auditioned you?"

"My song?"

"I don't care who wrote it. Just play me something."

So I played the opening arpeggio of notes that starts "Hello Juliet." I'd written it a couple years before. It was probably the first decent thing I'd done.

"That's real sweet," said Chester, peeking over the sound baffles.

Miguel nodded and Dave looked up for once.

Surly Bob came through the headphones again. "You got some lyrics for that?"

"Sure," I said. I'd been wanting to change a few things, but it was mostly finished. It was sort of based on the play *Romeo and Juliet*, or the movie, anyway. I'd seen it a bunch of times at school because I never could get the hang of the book. I had all the bits and pieces, though, Verona and the star-crossed lovers, and it was all set to a pretty good little melody.

I sang the first line, and just as I did, way up above us, Frankie came waltzing into the control booth. Ariadne was with him and they were tucked into each other, sharing some private conversation. As soon as he entered, he realized I was singing something that was not his, and he sort of jerked upright. I didn't like the look on his face so I stopped singing.

"What's going on?" I heard him say. He was pretty far from the console mic but the tone in his voice was unmistakable.

Surly waved him away. "Keep playing," he said to me.

"What is the key?" asked Miguel. His hands were hovering over his Vox organ.

"It's in G. Pretty straightforward."

I played the opening lick again and Miguel laid down some ambient chords over it. He understood the structure right away. Chester didn't play any drums at the beginning, but he tapped on his hi-hat to keep time. Skinny Dave started in with a low pulse on the bass guitar and it all clicked into place. That was just the verse but it sounded pretty good.

When I glanced up again at the control booth, Frankie was standing over the console glaring at me. He'd muscled in beside Surly and left Ariadne behind. She was watching me too, though. She was listening to my song.

Surly was working at the sliders on the mixer, adjusting the sound. Frankie said something, but Surly kind of brushed him off and leaned down into the console mic. "Right. Why don't you take a few minutes, show the boys the rest of the song."

It didn't take much to put it all together. We ran through the whole song a couple of times and then we recorded it, simple as that. We'd still have to overdub some instrumentation later, and of course I'd have to record the lead vocals, but I could tell it was shaping up nicely. By the third take we pretty much had it.

"Right, then," Surly said. "Let's have everyone up here and we'll listen back on the speakers."

We trundled up the stairs. The control booth was small. There was a couch at the back but most of the space was taken up by the mixing board. It was huge and complicated, with faders and rows of buttons and little red lights all lit up, and beside that was the tape machine, a real workhorse, with two-inch tape looped through its reels.

Ariadne had sat down on the couch. She was trying to stay out of the way, but I caught her eye and she smiled up at me, a sort of half smile like she wanted to encourage me but didn't want Frankie to notice. She had her dark hair tied back in a ponytail and she wore a white turtleneck sweater. Around her neck hung a thin gold chain, and she raised her fingers to the medallion at the end of it. It was gold and smaller than a penny and it was embossed with a tiny figure I couldn't quite make out.

"I'm not fucking singing on that fairy music," Frankie snapped.

Surly Bob seemed unconcerned. "Levi, you can do the lead vocal, right?"

"Sure." I could feel Ariadne's eyes on me.

"Now wait just a goddamn minute," said Frankie. "I'm not letting this clown—"

"Levi will sing it, Frankie," said Surly.

"I'm not singing backup vocals neither."

"Quit your whinging. No one's asking you to do anything."

Surly Bob sat down in the padded chair at the mixer and pressed play, then he leaned back, his hands behind his head, and listened. We all did. Chester tapped his foot and Miguel nodded in time. The monitor speakers sounded great. My old acoustic guitar chimed. Skinny Dave's bassline thumped like a heartbeat and the keyboards were celestial. And there in the control room, right from the beginning, we knew we had something special.

"Right," said Surly Bob. "I don't hate it."

♫

After our session, back at the Dorchester, I knocked on Surly's door.

"What is it?" he called out.

"It's me. It's Levi."

"Jesus. Just come in."

I opened the door. The first thing I saw was a giant oak desk. Surly must have gotten the staff to turn his room into a kind of office. He sat behind the desk with a cigarette between his thumb and forefinger. He stabbed it at me, gesturing for me to sit in a chair and wait for him to finish whatever it was he was doing.

He had an open ledger in front of him. He was doing all the accounting for the band. I knew that was part of his job and I could see the columns of numbers in his cramped handwriting. He had little piles of cash to his left on the desk, and once he made a note in his book, he moved the money into a metal box. It was just a little bigger than a shoebox, but it looked solid, that's for sure.

I sat down on the chair but he didn't look up. "I've got a friend," I ventured.

"Bloody brilliant, that is."

"He's here, in London."

Surly raised his eyes to meet mine. "And what do you expect me to do about it?"

"Well, I thought when we go back on tour, we could get him some work on the road crew."

"Who?"

"My friend. Rudy. He knows a lot about band equipment. I used to—"

"Can your man tune a guitar?"

"Sure."

"Can he drive a truck? Does he have his license?"

"Yeah, I think so."

"Right. A couple of our roadies have fucked off back to the States to tour with Sabbath. Just your luck."

"So—"

"Thirty bob a week," he said. "But your man there, he has to pay for his own meals."

"Okay."

"And he'll need to sleep on the bus."

"There's a bus?"

"And if he buggers anything up, if he breaks something, it comes out of your paycheck."

"About that," I began. "My paycheck—"

Surly closed the cashbox and latched it. "The money's coming," he snapped. "You don't need to worry about that." He tucked the box down beneath the desk, and for a moment, all I could see was the top of his head. He was getting pretty bald up there, a bit of a comb-over going on.

"Let me explain something to you," he said when he popped back up. "We don't have any money. Not right now. The record company pays for the studio. They pay for our gear and our lighting, the tour trucks, all of it. And we have to pay that back. And how, you may ask, do we do that?"

"I don't know, Bobby."

"Touring," he said. "The money from the shows is ours." He studied me for a moment to see if I was understanding. "The rest of it is just a gradually expanding mountain of bills and debts." He pinched his cigarette between his thumb and finger and studied me. "What is it you really want, Levi?"

"I don't know. I guess I want to know if I'm officially in the band or not."

"You understand I'm doing you a bloody great favor here, right?"

"Yeah, I know."

"No," he said, "you don't. You don't have a bloody clue." Surly stuck the cigarette back in his mouth. "Let's just get this second album finished and then we can worry about whether or not you're going back to that piano lady of yours."

"What?"

"Never mind." He waved his cigarette abstractly. "Forget it. No one understands a damn thing I do around here. And now I've got you to worry about."

"I didn't—"

"I said to forget it."

"Okay," I said. He went back to studying the ledger, and after a moment, without looking up, he asked, "Are you still here?"

"I'm going." No one had to tell me when I wasn't wanted. I knew that feeling well enough.

29 Streetlights

A gold record hung on the wall. It wasn't pure gold, I can tell you that much, but it was set on a background of black velvet in a polished wooden frame. It was for the first Downtown Exit album and of course that was nothing to do with me. I didn't play a damn note on that thing. Gold records were for selling one hundred thousand copies and I was sure hoping the second album would be as good. There was writing on the little gold plaque at the bottom and I put my finger on the *X* in Downtown Exit. Like I said, it was my favorite letter. I always thought the shape of it was pretty cool.

Chester laid a meaty hand on my shoulder. "Boss, you gonna stand there all day gaping at that thing?"

"Maybe," I said.

We were standing in the hallway outside the offices of Labyrinth Records. The walls were strewn with gold records, lots of them, including the reggae band that made Labyrinth its first million.

Chester considered me and sighed. "And you're wearing that to the press conference?"

"What's wrong with this?" I tugged at my jean jacket.

"Boss, you got to start looking the part."

"Aw, jeez, Chester."

"And you got to work on your moves."

"What moves?"

"See, you don't even know. You're like a wooden puppet onstage, all jerky." He went into an unkind pantomime.

"C'mon, man. I don't look like that."

"You got to be smooth. Like Jimmy Page. You got to play to the audience. You watch Frankie. He knows how to do it."

"Easy for a drummer to say. You get to sit through the whole show."

"Shee-it," he said. "Your skinny white ass wouldn't last an hour behind the drums."

Somewhere down the hallway we heard Surly Bob calling for us. He didn't sound too happy.

"Drum sitter," I said.

He grinned. "And you a damn marionette. Now c'mon. They're waiting for us."

I stepped along after him. The carpet shushed under our feet, and when we turned the corner at the end of the hall, Surly Bob was there standing at an open door. He had his arms crossed over his chest. His pinstripe suit was definitely too small for him—it was all bunched up around his shoulders. We slunk past him into the room.

It looked like a boardroom that had been converted for the press conference. There were a bunch of reporters standing along the back wall, and a long table was set up at the front on a raised dais. Miguel and Skinny Dave were already there. There was a bit of a shuffle when we came in, and a camera flash went off, but the guy immediately lowered his camera. He must have thought one of us might be Frankie, who, as usual, was the last to arrive. The reporters returned to their notepads and Chester and I sat down at the table next to Miguel.

The windows overlooked the London rooftops. Labyrinth Records was in the financial district, and we were up on the third or fourth floor, so the view was all chimneys and slate-gray roofs, like something out of *Mary Poppins*.

I guess I was a little lost in my thoughts, because Chester nudged me in the ribs.

"Quit it," I hissed.

"You got to sit up a bit. Look like you know what you're doing."

The table in front of us had a cheese plate. All kinds of it set on a platter with a little flat knife for slicing off pieces, and beside that sat a big crystal decanter with bubbly water and slices of lemon floating in it.

I was about to say something back to Chester when Surly came around in front of us, blocking our table from the line of reporters. "Right," he said. "You remember what I told you?"

"Frankie does all the talking," Chester said, parroting back what Surly had already told us about a hundred times.

"That's right. You're to just sit here and shut it."

"So, where is Frankie?" I asked.

"He's coming. You just let him and me do all the talking."

"Fine by me," said Chester, reaching for a piece of cheese.

Frankie swept in a few moments later, in a white T-shirt and jeans with the cuffs rolled up like he was some kind of movie star from the 1950s. He was wearing aviator sunglasses even though there was nothing but fluorescent lights above us. At his side was an older man, maybe forty or fifty, with a goatee and a precisely trimmed mustache like one of those Russian czars, the last one, the one who got shot. His hair was close cropped and flecked with gray, and he wore a nice suit, no tie. Just an open-collared white shirt. His face was tanned like he'd just come from playing tennis. Surly sprang forward to greet the older man, grinning deferentially. The cameras were starting to go off now, clicking and flashing.

"Who's that?" I whispered.

"That's Sir Charles Blackmore," said Chester. "He owns the record company."

Blackmore checked his watch, a chunky gold thing, then said something to Surly that made his countenance darken. I don't know what it was but it sure took Surly down a few notches. He tried to be professional, though. He put a hand on Frankie's back and steered him over to the little stage we were on. Frankie took his seat, still with his shades on, and looked out at the reporters like he was the King of England, and Surly stepped back out front and raised his hands to get things going.

"All right, all right," Surly called, and a quiet fell over the room. "Downtown Exit is here today to announce the release of their second record."

There was a scratch of pens on paper, then a guy near the front stood up. He had a little notepad flipped open, and a pen ready to catch whatever was said. "Mick Scott," the man said. "*New Music Express*."

Surly nodded at him to go ahead.

"Downtown Exit," he said, mostly to Frankie. "Congratulations on your first album. It's been quite a success."

Frankie made a show of lighting a cigarette, leaning in slowly, taking in a long inhale. He tipped his head in acknowledgment but didn't say anything.

The reporter went on. "My condolences on the loss of your bandmate Pete Gunnerson. I understand he was one of the original members of the band."

"That's right," said Surly, stepping forward again. "But we ask that you respect the band's privacy as they grieve the loss of their friend." Even I could tell that Surly had rehearsed that line. "This press conference," he went on, though he took a quick look over at Blackmore, "is all about the new album."

The *New Music* guy frowned. "Well, will you be replacing him with"—he checked his notepad—"Levi Johnson?"

"It's Jaxon," I said. "With an *x*."

Surly threw me a withering look.

"I want to say a few things about Pete," Frankie said, and all the reporters went still. He took off his sunglasses, almost wearily, and laid them with a clack on the table. Then he tapped his cigarette out, slowly, making sure he had everyone's attention. His eyes, I noticed, were bloodshot. "About Pete," he began, "I loved that guy. He was my best friend."

"Frankie," Surly began.

"No, no, I want to say this. I—" Frankie paused, collecting his thoughts. "Right until the end, we were working on new songs together."

Surly spoke up. "Tell them about '29 Streetlights,' Frankie."

"We were recording, you know. We'd written this new song and we both thought it would be one of our best."

" '29 Streetlights,' " Surly said, nodding at the reporters who dutifully wrote the name down.

"That Pete, he was good with words," said Frankie. "It tells a story, like a movie." Frankie turned to Chester. "Chester, my man, you know what I'm talking about, don't you?"

Chester nodded but didn't say anything.

"We all grew up together," said Frankie. He laughed but it sounded rehearsed. "Me and Pete, and Chester was just down the road, right? The next town over. Small towns. That's where we're from. We're just small-town boys."

"So when shall we expect to hear this new song of yours?" another reporter chimed in. "Caroline Coon, from *Melody Maker*," she said as an afterthought.

"The album's not finished," said Frankie.

Surly glanced at Blackmore, who didn't look surprised by Frankie's admission.

"Is it fair to say that Pete's death has set things back a bit?" the woman asked.

"No," said Surly. "It's almost ready. Nearly there. Meanwhile, the band is going on a short tour—next week—starting in Amsterdam."

At that, Blackmore cleared his throat and tried to catch Surly's eye. I could tell there was something going on. Something really was bubbling in the air, some thread of tension. Did Blackmore not know about the tour or was he just pissed because the album wasn't finished?

Surly continued. "And we have hired Ariadne Christos to photograph the band on tour."

I think I gave a little start at that. I was hoping nobody noticed.

There was a flurry of paper flipping, and another reporter piped up. "Mr. Novak, can you address the rumors that you're seeing Dmitry Christos's daughter?"

Frankie opened his mouth to reply, but the *New Music* guy cut in. "I'm sorry, I have to ask what really happened out there on the balcony." He lowered his pen and notepad as if to say that things were now off the record.

"What do you mean 'happened'?" said Frankie.

"Well, Pete Gunnerson tumbled off it, didn't he? Am I to understand that—?"

Frankie reared back as if he'd been hit. "Pete couldn't control his cravings."

"We all miss Pete," said Surly, "but the police have labeled his death an accident."

The reporter was undaunted. "How are you going to be able to sustain the momentum of your first album without him?"

"Listen, pal," said Frankie, rising from his seat. "I'll sustain your momentum."

"I beg your pardon?"

Frankie came off the dais and Surly moved forward to intercept him. Surly was shorter than Frankie, but he planted his feet, like a sumo wrestler. Frankie tried to get around him, poking his head around Surly, stabbing his finger at the reporter.

"You don't talk about Pete," he spat. "You don't know a goddamn thing about this."

"Easy there, champ," Surly warned.

"Fuck you."

"Frankie."

"All of you can just fuck the hell off." Frankie wriggled out of Surly's grip and pushed past Blackmore out the door.

Surly turned on the reporter. "You are not to print any of that." He stared him down for a moment and then plunged out the door after Frankie.

Blackmore sighed as if he'd seen all this before. "I imagine we're done here," he said. "Thank you for your time, everyone."

The *New Music* guy flipped his notepad closed and shook his head. A rustle went through the crowd and they all started packing away their cameras and notebooks. Blackmore checked his watch once more and then trailed out the door. And that was the end of that.

♫

A few minutes later, Surly reappeared at the door. There were a couple reporters lingering at the back. Me and Chester and the guys were sitting at the table helping ourselves to the cheese platter. I didn't want to say anything, but I was starting to wonder about Pete's death now. If he really did just fall.

"Levi!" Surly barked. He was red in the face with a little vein sticking out on his forehead. "Get out here. Now."

I got up and followed him out.

"I thought I told you to keep your mouth shut," he said.

"I didn't say anything."

"You did. Now, come with me." Surly charged down the hallway and I scurried to keep up with him. We went around a corner and in through a sort of anteroom, stopping abruptly at the open door to Blackmore's private offices, and holy crap, it was like Buckingham Palace in there. Blackmore himself sat at a huge desk, all glass and dark polished wood. Behind him, an antique globe sat on a wrought iron stand.

Blackmore waved us in. He'd taken off his suit jacket and rolled up the sleeves of his white shirt, and his elbows were resting on a manila folder on the enormous desk.

"Please take a seat," he said, and gestured to one of the upholstered chairs.

"Go on," said Surly, and he sort of pushed me forward. "We need your signature on a few things."

I sat down. Surly remained standing. I could feel him behind me, watching.

"So you're the new one?" Blackmore said.

"I guess so."

"I understand you've really come through for the Exits." Blackmore threw me a smile, but it looked kind of fake, if you want to know the truth. His voice was very posh, very British, and his eyes were hooked on me, like he was psychoanalyzing me or something.

He opened the manila folder and pushed a sheaf of papers and a pen across the desk toward me.

"Just a little business to take care of," he said, clasping his hands together and setting them down on the desk. His watch clacked a bit on the polished wood.

"What is it?" I asked.

"Levi," said Surly. He stepped forward, hovering over my shoulder. "This is your contract."

Blackmore pierced Surly with a look like he didn't really want him there. "You'll need to sign in several places, Mr. Jaxon. It's all laid out quite clearly."

"Okay," I said. I'd had a piece of cheese from the tray and my fingers were sticky. I wiped them on my pants and picked up the pen, hovering it over the top sheet of the contract. There were a lot of big words so I looked up at Blackmore. "Would it maybe be okay if I got my friend Rudy to look these over? He's really good at—"

"For Christ's sake, Levi," said Surly from behind me. "We don't have time for that."

"Does this mean I'll get paid? Can you tell me that much?"

Blackmore put up his hand. "I can assure you that you will be paid. I'm sure Mr. Malone has explained everything to you."

I looked back at Surly. "But what exactly does it say? Does it mean I'm officially in the band?"

"Bloody hell," hissed Surly. He grabbed the pen out of my hand and leaned down over me. He flipped a couple pages over and studied the contract for a moment. "Look," he said. He crossed out a couple of lines and then began to write underneath them. " 'Levi Jaxon,' " he read out loud, " 'is a full member of Downtown Exit.' Are you happy?"

Blackmore scowled. "Mr. Malone, please. That's a legal document."

"Are you satisfied, Levi? You just need to initial it and you are officially in the band."

"I'll need to initial that now too," Blackmore said. He looked pretty pissed off.

Surly pushed the paper and pen back at Blackmore and he scrawled a *C* and a *B* beside the new entry, then kind of floated it back to me.

I took the pen back and initialed it underneath Blackmore's. I could feel Surly's breath on my ear. He swiped the pages back to the beginning and went through the whole thing again, pointing at a few other places where I needed to initial. At the bottom of the last sheet, I signed my whole name. I wrote a great big *L* for *Levi*, then squiggled out my last name. My handwriting was pretty messy but I guess you could read it.

When I was done, Blackmore reached forward and swept the papers back toward himself. He signed the bottom sheet as well, then shuffled the papers back into order and slipped them into the manila folder.

"Jesus," said Surly. "Was that so hard?" He kind of grunted and turned to Blackmore. "I'll need a copy of that."

"Me too," I said.

"Of course." Blackmore clasped his hands together on the desk, his watch clacking on the desktop again. He smiled once more. "Welcome to our little stable of artists, Mr. Jaxon. Welcome to Labyrinth Records."

♫

We did a couple more days at Abbey Road, but really it was just to finish off the songs we already had, including mine, "Hello Juliet." And after that, we were just waiting around for the tour to begin. Rudy got hired on as a roadie. I hadn't seen him, but I'd talked to him on the phone and he seemed pretty pleased with himself. I was kind of glad he was coming too. Maybe I did need the support. Evelyn was going to be furious at us but we'd have to deal with that later. Right now, there were a whole lot of other things going on.

The day before we were to leave, Chester came into the hotel room. "Boss," he said, and he had this big dumb smile on his face.

I was sitting on the bed watching *Benny Hill*. I didn't really get it most of the time. It wasn't that funny. I kind of missed *Gilligan's Island*, to tell you the truth. I snapped off the TV and turned to him. "What?" I said. "What are you grinning about?"

"I got a surprise for you." He fished in his pocket and brought out an envelope. It was stuffed with large British bills, the purple ones, the twenties.

"What's that for?"

"It's from Surly. It's your pay."

"Yeah?" I said, and put out my hand to take it.

Chester whipped it away. "Not so fast. First, I'm supposed to get you all decked out."

"Decked out?"

"Down at Stirling Cooper."

"What's Stirling Cooper?"

"Well, Boss, you heard of Jimi Hendrix?"

"C'mon, man."

"You heard of Mick Jagger?"

"Yes, Chester, I've heard of Mick Jagger."

"Well those guys all used to get their clothes down at Stirling Cooper"—he flapped the envelope at me—"and that's where we're going. First we'll get your threads and then we'll work on your marionette moves."

Stirling Cooper, as it turns out, was on Oxford Street not far from the Marquee Club. Or actually, it was just down a side lane tucked off the main street. I followed Chester through a little alley to a door with a dragon painted on it, which was pretty cool if you ask me. A bell rang when we opened the door, but other than that, it was quiet inside. No sign of Mick Jagger at all.

Chester went straight for a wooden hat rack and reached for a fedora. He put it on, angling it a bit on his head. "What do you think? Does it make me look jaunty?"

"Jaunty?"

Chester laughed and it boomed through the room. He put the hat back on the rack and charged off deeper into the store. There were shelves of pants on one side and racks of shirts on the other. Mostly he was considering the shirts, and halfway down he stopped and flashed an iridescent blue one at me.

"I already have a good shirt," I said.

"Not like this one, you don't. Come here, my man, feel this. That's pure silk."

I touched it and it was cool and smooth as cream.

"That one's good for the stage," he said. "That shit will breathe."

He stepped across the floorboards, picking at shirts and pants, flinging them over at me until I had a stack in my arms as high as my shoulders. Chester hardly noticed. He pulled out a pair of white bell-bottoms with red stars sewn around the bottom.

"Oh, come on," I said.

"Nope, you got to start looking the part. What size are you?"

"Twenty-eight, maybe."

Chester tossed them on top of my pile. "Those'll work. We got to get you some shoes too. Platform shoes. Tall ones."

"Aw, jeez. I don't know."

"You got to stand out, Levi. I'm telling you."

"Yeah, but—"

"You're not in Kansas anymore."

"I'm from Canada, Chester. You know that. Stop treating me like a baby."

He stopped and eyed me. "Why you going all serious on me?"

"Because . . . you shouldn't make fun."

"All right."

"I had a hard time growing up, okay? I was in foster care. My whole life."

"Shee-it." Chester glanced away, and when he spoke again, his voice was softer. "Lots of fathers run off on their kids, Levi. That ain't nothing new."

"Yeah, but my mother ditched me too. She wanted nothing to do with me."

"Whatever happened, I'm sure they regret it." He paused. "Look." He dug his wallet out of his back pocket and flipped it open. In a little plastic cover was a photograph of two kids. They looked young, maybe six and eight or so.

"Those yours?"

"That's Annabelle and Harley," he said proudly.

"Cute kids," I said. "How come you never talk about them?"

"Because," he said, and he snapped the wallet closed, "I haven't seen them in more than ten years. They'd be almost grown up by now." He shook his head. "I screwed up, Levi. Things got a little out of hand."

"I'm sorry," I said. "I didn't know."

"It's hard being a father and a musician at the same time. Damn near impossible."

"I figure my dad was a musician."

"You got some God-given talent, I'll give you that. That song of yours, it's good, you know. It could be a hit for anyone else."

"What do you mean 'anyone else'?"

"Never mind," he said, "I just mean it's real good." He started walking off. "Now, c'mon along. You gotta keep up. There's a whole lot more interesting stuff at the back."

I followed him to the back of the store where there were some really outrageous things. On a faceless mannequin head sat a purple buccaneer hat, triangular, like something from *The Three Musketeers*. It had gold piping along the edges and a long shiny feather coming out the back.

Chester lifted it off the mannequin head and turned the hat around wistfully. "Pete would have liked this."

"He liked that pirate thing, didn't he?"

Chester held it out for me.

"I don't think so."

"Nope. I don't think so either. Not your look." He placed it gently back down onto the mannequin head.

"Chester," I said. "Can I ask you a question?"

His eyes stayed on the hat.

"What do you think really happened to Pete?"

"They screwed him over is what happened. He should never have let that happen."

"Yeah, but did he really fall off that balcony? He wasn't, like, I don't know, pushed?"

Chester stiffened. "Shee-it. Frankie's bad but he's not that bad. Nah, Pete fell. He was off his head on those pink blotters."

"Okay."

Chester heaved out a big sigh. "Hell, Levi," he said. "You look at the album. You look at 'The Blues Don't Live Here No More.' Who's got the songwriting credits on that?"

"Frankie," I said. "Frankie writes the songs."

"Wrong," said Chester. "The credits say Novak and Gunnerson, but that song was one hundred percent Pete."

"Pete wrote that?"

"Of course Pete wrote that. Pete wrote all the songs. And now—"

"But they both get credit?"

"That's the way the contract is written. All the songs are Novak and Gunnerson." He lowered his voice to a whisper. "Look, Frankie is a great singer. No doubt about it. And he can write a verse or two, but I'm telling you, Pete was the true talent. Pete wrote most of everything."

"For real?"

Chester looked both ways, to see if anyone was listening. "Pete should've got all the royalties. He should never have split his publishing rights with Frankie. That's all I'm saying. It's a lot of money."

"Yeah?"

"Yeah," he said. "Publishing is where the real money is. Don't you know nothing?"

"Surly said we get our money from touring."

"*We* do," said Chester. "The boys in the band. But as far as recording goes, it's the songwriters who rake in the cash. It's the guys who write the songs."

"Okay."

"Listen, Levi. Just don't sign anything. Especially when you're high. That's how they get you."

"Oh."

"Aw, hell," said Chester. "They already got you, didn't they?"

"I had to sign it," I said. "Otherwise I wasn't going to get paid."

"Boy wasn't going to get paid," said Chester to the mannequin head. He squelched his lips together. "Look," he said. "Did you at least read through it?"

"I didn't have time." Chester was staring at me and I had to look away.

"You didn't even read it?"

"I don't know, Chester. No, I didn't read it, okay?"

Chester sighed deeply. "All right, all right. I hope you didn't just do something real stupid."

I nodded a little but I didn't look at him again—mostly because I knew he was right.

♫

We were to check out of the Dorchester the next morning. I was going to miss that place. It was the first really fancy hotel I'd ever stayed in, even if I had to share a room with Chester. I hauled my stuff downstairs while Chester was still packing up, and the elevator pinged open to an empty lobby.

Everything had a sort of golden hue and the floors were so polished they reflected the pot lights in the ceiling. There were windows all along the front, and I'd barely made it five steps before I saw Ariadne sitting by herself on a green couch behind a little coffee table. I imagined she was waiting for Frankie, but she saw me and nodded a hello. And then I didn't have any choice except to go over and drop into the antique-looking chair opposite her.

"Uh . . . hi," I said. I put down my old duffel bag on the floor. It looked out of place among all the expensive stuff. Ariadne had a little round suitcase, like a hatbox almost, and beside it, a bigger aluminum case. "Is that your camera?"

"Yes," she said. "And the lenses, of course."

She'd been drinking tea and she set the teacup down on the table. It was fine porcelain. Even the saucer was beautiful.

"I really liked your photos," I said. "At the gallery."

"Thank you. In the end, they all sold. I was quite pleased with that."

"That's great."

"Yes," she said and she smiled, a sort of sad, sweet smile. "It's Levi, isn't it?"

"Yeah."

"You're American?"

"Canadian, actually."

"Ah," she said, as if that explained something. She lifted her teacup again.

"Um," I started again. "Can I ask you something? That thing you said to Frankie—about 'melodies unheard'?"

"It's Keats," she said. She looked at me over the rim of her teacup and her eyes were studying me now. "I do love that one," she went on. *"Beauty is truth, truth beauty—that is all ye know on earth, and all ye need to know."*

"Nice," I said.

"Are you interested in poetry?"

"It's okay."

"Well, you seem to know your Shakespeare." She put down her cup. "I liked your song. What was it called?"

"You mean 'Hello Juliet'?"

"Yes. It was really quite lovely."

"Thanks," I said. Her gaze was fixed on me, like she was trying to figure me out, and I would have said more but Chester appeared just then, lugging his suitcase toward us. It was the size of a steamer trunk. I don't know what the hell he had in there.

He plopped down beside Ariadne, and I guess they already knew each other a little, because she turned to him and they began chatting. She glanced over at me once or twice but I didn't feel like I was in the conversation anymore. They were talking about places they'd been, places I'd never even heard of, so I just sat quietly and smiled at her whenever she looked over.

And then, a few minutes later, a rumbling noise came from out front of the hotel. We all turned at the sound, and a bus pulled up to the entrance. It had a two-tone paint job, silver along the top and black along the bottom, with two sets of tires at the back and massive side-view mirrors that stuck out like wings. The door on the bus opened and out stepped Surly.

"That for us?" Chester asked.

"I guess so," I said.

Surly barged in through the hotel doors, a doorman at his heels, telling him that he couldn't park the bus there.

"Bobby," Chester called out. "You got us a tour bus?"

"Of course I did. We're going on tour, aren't we?" He stomped toward us. The doorman had given up. He was standing, looking a little lost, by a giant potted plant just inside the door.

Behind us, the elevator dinged open and Davey and Miguel appeared. Miguel had an old suitcase, a cracked and battered thing, and in his other hand he carried his accordion case, which was in even worse shape. Davey had a duffel bag kind of like mine.

"Bobby got us a bus," Chester said, smiling.

Surly took everyone in. "Where's Frankie?" he started.

"I imagine he's still in his room," Ariadne said.

That vein popped out on Surly's forehead. "Christ on a kite, the ferry leaves in three hours."

"Shall I go up and hurry him along?" She rose and brushed at her dress.

"If you wouldn't mind."

Ariadne turned to me. "Could you watch my camera?"

"Of course," I said. "I'd be honored, I—"

Chester gave me a little punch on the arm so I'd stop rattling on like a fool, but she was already striding across the lobby toward the elevators. No one had told her the room number, so she must have already known it, and I wasn't sure I liked that too much.

Surly remained standing. A few more minutes went by and I could see the doorman speaking with the manager at the front desk. They were looking over at us and I was pretty sure the manager was about to tell Surly to move the damn bus.

"Listen, lads," said Surly, and he checked his watch. "Why don't you start loading up your things?"

"What about Ariadne?" I asked. "I'm supposed to watch her camera."

"Bloody hell, I'll watch it. Chester, why don't you go on up and see what's taking them so long? Jesus. We've got a two-hour drive to Dover."

"I'll go," I said, jumping to my feet.

"Both of you go. Davey and Miguel can start loading our things." He turned back to us. "Just get them down here. On the double. It's room 302."

Frankie being late was nothing new, but I could see that Chester looked concerned. I trailed after him and we bypassed the elevator and headed for the stairs. "Chester," I said. "Is something wrong?"

He didn't answer. He clumped on ahead of me, up the stairs, hauling himself up by the banister, taking two steps at a time. When we reached the third floor, he barreled down the hallway to Frankie's room and I just tried to keep up.

Chester rapped on the door. "Frankie, Ariadne, you in there?"

There was no answer.

Chester tried again. Three short knocks. "Frankie?"

He put his ear to the door. Nothing.

The elevator opened at the far end of the hall and a man came scurrying down the hallway toward us. He was wearing a white lab coat and holding a small leather briefcase. "Hotel doctor," he said. "Are you the ones who rang?"

I turned to Chester, but he wasn't looking at me. He stepped away from the door, and the man checked the room number. It was right there in big brass numerals. He knocked. "Hotel doctor," he called.

"We already tried that," Chester said.

The man rattled at the doorknob, and as he did, it swung open. Ariadne stood there and her face was ashen. "Hurry" was all she managed.

The room was dark, but behind Ariadne I could see Frankie sitting on the bed, his head slumped down. He still had his pajamas on. The doctor scuttled over to him and seemed to catch him right before he toppled sideways.

"What's going on?" I said.

Ariadne didn't answer. She just stood at the open door, all of us peering in. Frankie's head seemed to bobble a bit and he looked over at us vacantly. The doctor was pulling a blood pressure cuff out of his little satchel and hiking up Frankie's sleeve. Frankie's eyes wavered down to it, like he didn't know what it was.

"Frankie," said Chester. "You all right in there?"

Frankie didn't answer but his eyelids were fluttering.

"Should we do something?" I asked.

Ariadne met my eyes and shook her head. "He's taken something. I don't know what."

Chester blew out a breath.

Ariadne turned to him. "Maybe you should go on ahead. Just go on without us."

"But what about your camera?" I said. "Your things?"

"Could you have the bellhop bring them up here?"

"Yeah, sure, but—"

She looked back at Frankie and seemed to make a decision. "I'm going to call Mr. Blackmore," she said. "You go on ahead. We'll try to catch up." She strode back into the room and picked up the phone on the side table by the bed. Frankie's eyes were still open but they were vacant, and the doctor was already tapping at a syringe he'd pulled out of his bag. I think the phone was already ringing on the other end but Ariadne looked over at us and cupped her hand over the mouthpiece. "Please," she said. "Just go."

The doctor plunged the syringe into Frankie's arm. His eyelids fluttered again and he slumped forward.

"Jesus," I said.

Chester grabbed my arm. "You heard the lady."

"Yeah, but we can't just—"

"Levi. She's the best one to take care of him right now. She knows the whole story."

"What story?"

"Levi, I'm trying to tell you. There's more going on than you know." He took another quick glance at Frankie and shook his head. "We best just leave. You hear me? We got a ferry to catch."

Between Life and Fantasy

At the docks near Dover, we drove up onto a ferry the size of an ocean liner. The truck with our gear went up the ramp ahead of us and then we pulled the bus in behind it. Surly levered the bus door open and it unfolded with a whoosh. Chester hopped out first, down the corrugated aluminum steps, out into the dark and cavernous car deck. It smelled of diesel fuel, and the ferry's engines were already thumping though we hadn't started moving yet. We all single-filed out between the rows of cars to a metal door and then up a clanging stairwell to the passenger deck above us.

The passenger deck was actually pretty nice, with seats like in a movie theater. Up front they had a couple televisions mounted on the walls. There were windows all along the sides, though they were spattered with sea spray, and there was nothing to see beyond them anyway but the gray horizon stretching out into the distance.

I didn't bother to sit down. I'd never actually been out on the sea before so I opened a hatch at the rear of the passenger deck. It led out to the promenade deck. A cold wind was coming off the English Channel, and down below us the dockworkers were scrambling with ropes as thick as their arms, getting everything ready for our departure.

Just as the ferry sounded its horn, a silver-gray car came racing down the road toward the pier. It had a fancy front grill and big shiny fenders, and when it pulled to a stop below us, a uniformed chauffeur hopped out to pull open the back door.

And it was Frankie, of course. And Ariadne, who stepped out with him, her hair blowing in the wind. She put a gloved hand over it to keep it in place. Then, to my surprise, Rudy emerged from the depths of the car and kind of stumbled out into the fresh air. I thought he was supposed to be with the gear truck.

Behind me on the promenade deck, Surly Bob came banging out through the hatchway, his pants flapping in the wind. "Is that them?" He pushed past me to the railing. "Frankie!" he bellowed.

"I don't think they can hear you," I said.

"Bugger it all, that's a Rolls-Royce. Who's paying for that?"

Rudy and the chauffeur were hauling luggage out of the trunk while Ariadne had already tucked her arm into Frankie's. He leaned into her and they ambled toward the ramp up onto the ferry. He looked better, maybe a bit shaky, but better.

Another great blast came from the ferry stacks, and the ropes were coiling in through a hole in the hull. Frankie and Ariadne disappeared up the ramp beneath us. Rudy lumbered after them. He'd humped his backpack up onto his shoulders and picked up Frankie's suitcase with one hand. He had Ariadne's hatbox suitcase in the other hand, with her aluminum camera case stacked on top of it, holding it in with his elbow. He was really struggling with it all, stopping every few steps to hoist things up and carry on.

"Leg it, man," yelled Surly, though of course Rudy couldn't hear us either. Then, only a few seconds after he'd made it into the hold, the ramp began to lift in a clank of chains and a squeal of metal.

Surly stomped off back inside but I stayed out. I kind of wanted to be alone, and besides, the white cliffs of Dover were out there, just to the north. They rose up out of the sea mist, stark and white, hovering there like they weren't even real.

The ferry lurched once and began to pull away from the pier. Seagulls swooped and screeched. I pulled up the collar on my old jean jacket, and I was just turning to go back inside when the hatch opened again and Ariadne appeared. She was wearing a big sheepskin coat and she had delicate white gloves on her hands. She waved when she saw me, like she'd been looking for me.

"Hey," I said. "I'm glad you made it. How's Frankie?"

"Frankie is Frankie," she said. "He's going through a rough patch."

"I'll say."

"Peter's death was hard for all of us, but for him—"

"They were best friends."

She glanced at me and her brow furrowed a bit, then her gaze went to the coastline dropping away behind us. She stood for a moment, silent, watching the distant cliffs, her gloved hands on the railing.

"The cliffs of England stand," she said, and her voice was soft. *"Glimmering and vast, out in the tranquil bay."*

"Beautiful," I said. "Is that Keats again?"

"No, that one is called 'Dover Beach.' It's Matthew Arnold."

"I like it."

She smiled and went on, *"Ah, love, let us be true to one another! For the world, which seems to lie before us like a land of dreams."*

I struggled for a moment to hold the line in my mind, to memorize it before it drifted away. "How come you know so many poems?"

"I studied poetry. At Oxford."

That figured. Obviously she was well educated. Completely out of my league.

"I did the early Victorians," she said. "Tennyson, of course, but also the Romantics: Keats, Byron, Shelley. But—" She didn't finish. She stood still for a moment and then shook her head. "It's silly, isn't it?"

"Silly, no. Why would—?"

"Because no one really cares about them. They're just old poems."

"But they're beautiful."

"Yes, they are." She clasped her gloved hands a little more tightly around the railing.

The engines had relaxed into a steady thrum and we were pulling away from the land surprisingly quickly, a long white wake churning behind us. The English Channel was slate gray and Ariadne reached up toward her collar and drew out the thin gold chain around her neck. She pinched her fingers around the tiny medallion.

"What is that?"

"This? It's a Saint Christopher, the patron saint of travelers. I suppose it's meant to help you if you're lost."

"Are you lost?" I said. I meant it as a joke, but her eyes had gone a bit misty.

"It was my mother's. I never really knew her. She died when I was still quite young."

"Oh, I'm sorry."

"It was a long time ago."

"I never knew my mother either," I offered.

She turned to me, her green eyes hanging on me. "Then you know how it feels."

I nodded.

"Honestly, Levi, I am a little lost here. I left Oxford because it just seemed so pointless."

"It's not pointless."

"It is, Levi." She let out a stilted little laugh. "So, here I am. Taking photographs for a rock band. And Peter is gone and—"

She stopped, and I was wondering why she was calling him Peter all the time. That seemed weird.

"So," I ventured. "Did you know Pete pretty well?"

She sighed and gazed out over the waves. She wouldn't meet my eyes again. "Perhaps," she said, "perhaps we should go in now."

"Okay," I said. It was getting cold anyway. England was sinking into the sea, and the sky had lowered over us, gray and heavy.

♫

A few heads bobbed up when we came in through the hatchway. The air inside was warm and the engine noise was more subdued. Chester and the other guys looked like they were having a meeting, all clustered there in the middle seats. They'd gathered around Surly, who was standing, explaining something.

Surly spotted me and stopped talking. "Levi! Get over here. This is important."

"I'll talk with you later," said Ariadne. She smiled at me and then wandered toward the seats at the front. I went over to the guys.

"Okay," I said. "I'm here." I slid in next to Chester.

Surly glared down at me. "I was just saying that Labyrinth has decided to release a single."

" '29 Streetlights,' " said Frankie. He was looking better, a bit more like himself, but he didn't seem too happy with Surly.

"Okay," I said. "But that's great. Isn't it?"

"No," said Surly. "It's only a trial balloon. They want to see if the album is even worth finishing."

"Oh."

"And," he went on, and he stared pointedly at Frankie, "they're saying '29 Streetlights' is too long."

"It's not," said Frankie. "Every word of it is important. You can't cut it down."

"It's almost six minutes. No radio station is going to play a song that long."

Miguel spoke up. "I am thinking we could take out the second chorus and go right into the guitar solo."

"But keep the guitar solo?" I asked.

"No," said Frankie, and we both shut up. "I'm not cutting it down."

"We'll do what we have to do," said Surly. "The full version can still go on the album."

"Fuck that," said Frankie.

"Hey," said Chester. "Tell him about the B side, Bobby."

I looked up at Surly. "Is it 'Between Life and Fantasy'?"

"Nope," Chester said. "Guess again."

"Well, I don't know."

"They want it to be 'Hello Juliet,' " said Chester.

"You're fucking kidding me."

Surly nodded. "It's true. Blackmore's decided on 'Hello Juliet.' "

"Wow," I said. I sucked in a breath and sank back into my chair. My song was going to be on a record, just the B side of a 45, but holy shit, that was amazing. I blinked a couple of times and let it sink in. "Wow," I said again.

"It's not a done deal," Surly cautioned. "They want the single out as soon as possible. As soon as Frankie agrees to shorten it."

Frankie rose from his chair. He was still a little wobbly. "Fuck you," he said. "Fuck all of you. I won't do it." And with that, he stumbled off down the aisle to go sit with Ariadne.

♫

After that, the band kind of dispersed. I found myself a seat near the back. There were rows and rows of empty seats. The ferry could have held a couple hundred people but today there were maybe thirty or forty passengers in total. Out through the windows, a thin drizzle was coming down and the ocean was a steely gray.

Chester had gone to sit up near the televisions. They were playing some old black-and-white movie, and he watched it for a while and then fell asleep, his big head lolling back on the headrest.

I heard a metallic clunk and turned to see Rudy at the hatch that led back down to the car deck. I waved at him and he made his way over to me, a little unsteady in the shunt and shift of the ferry. He was carrying my guitar case. He'd hauled it up from the gear truck and he sort of hefted it up to show me, grinning like an idiot. He laid it on an empty seat and then shuffled over it to come and sit beside me.

"The guitar is supposed to stay on the truck, Rudy."

"Yeah, but it's yours, Levi. The rest of the stuff is theirs, but this guitar is yours. You should keep it with you."

"You're going to get yourself in trouble."

"No," he said. "It's your guitar. I brought up your guitar."

"Well, thanks, I guess."

Across the rows, Frankie was eyeballing us. Ariadne had maybe fallen asleep.

"What's up with him?" I whispered.

"I don't know."

"What were you doing with him anyway? In the car there?"

"I'm just doing what they tell me to do, Levi. They needed some help is all."

"All right," I said. "Forget about it. Listen, I've got something to tell you."

"Something that will get me off this damn ferry?" The ferry was rolling a little now, the floor heaving just slightly beneath us. I didn't mind but Rudy looked a little green.

"Labyrinth is putting out a single."

"Whoop-de-doo."

"No, Rudy, listen. They want to put my song on the B side."

"They what?"

"'Hello Juliet.' They're going to put it on the B side."

"Why would they do that?"

"Jesus, Rudy. Because I'm in the band now. I signed a contract and everything."

"What?" His face puckered up a little. "Tell me you're joking."

"No, no. I know what you're thinking but it's all good. I'm officially in the band now."

"Did you have someone go through it first?"

"You weren't around," I said. "What was I supposed to do?"

"So you don't even know what's in it?"

"No, Rudy, I don't know exactly what's in it. But—"

"Levi." Rudy was dead serious now. I knew that look. It was the exact same one Evelyn would give me.

"It's okay," I tried.

"No it's not," he said. "You don't know how to read."

"Rudy." I looked around the ferry. The last thing I needed was for Surly or Frankie or Ariadne to overhear that. Especially Ariadne.

"Do I have to remind you of that?" he went on. "You don't know how to read and—"

"Jesus, Rudy. Keep it down, will you? Nobody knows about that."

"Why do you think I'm even here?"

"I know. I know."

"Crap," said Rudy. "Evelyn is going to kill me."

"It's not your problem."

"It is, Levi. You signed a fucking contract."

"C'mon, man." I was getting irritated now. "I'm not dumb."

"I know, Levi. But . . . jeez."

I wanted to say more, to tell him everything was going to be fine, but Frankie had stood up. He'd been eyeing us across the rows and now he was tottering toward us.

"Oh, shit," said Rudy.

Frankie stopped at the end of the aisle, towering over us, a real ugly look on his face.

"Hey," I said.

But Frankie wasn't looking at me. He had Rudy in his sights.

"Did you do what I asked you?" he said to Rudy.

"No, not yet. I—"

"Then get the fuck back down there."

"Sorry." Rudy stood up and kind of inched himself along the seats.

"Wait," I said. "Rudy. Where are you going?"

He didn't answer. He scrambled out into the far aisle and through the door that led down to the car deck.

"What's going on?" I said to Frankie. "Rudy's not—"

"Not what?"

"C'mon, man. He's a friend of mine."

"Doesn't mean he's not a pansy."

"A what? Jeez, Frankie, he doesn't work just for you."

"Listen, pal, you don't tell me what to do, okay?" He glared at me. "You think you're some kind of fucking Jim Morrison or something?"

"Jim Morrison? Who said anything about Jim Morrison?"

"You're not that good looking and you don't tell me what to do." He started to walk away but he stopped. "And another thing—stay the fuck away from Ariadne. Don't think I didn't notice."

♫

I sat for a long time, by myself, thinking about what Rudy had said. There were teachers who tried to help me with my reading problem, at least in the early grades, but then, just when I would start to get the hang of it, well, I'd get shuffled off to another school and I'd be right back at square one. I knew the alphabet. I could recognize all the letters, but I had to sound out each syllable like a little kid, and it was embarrassing, if you want to know the truth. I mean, I could pick out letters and make out simple words, but yeah, I couldn't really read.

Over the years I learned to hide it pretty well. Maybe because of music, I got really good at memorizing things. The teacher would say something and I'd just hold it in my head until I needed it again. I didn't get great marks but usually it was enough to scrape by, until high school, anyway. That's when it really went all to shit. I never finished, even though Evelyn was always telling me I should go back. I guess I thought, who needs books if you're going to be a musician?

I looked over at my old battered guitar case and a funny thing began to happen. A little tune started in my head. That's the way it goes sometimes. A melody appears out of nowhere. This one was in 3/4 time, with a sort of sea shanty feel to it, which I guess made sense under the circumstances.

Now, those little scraps of music come and go, almost like dreams, and it's best to catch them while you can. What I had was probably sixteen bars long, and my guitar was there right beside me, just asking to be played. I hoisted it up and headed out to the promenade deck. I needed to find a place where I could test out the little melody and see if it amounted to anything.

Outside, it had stopped raining. England had disappeared and there was nothing but dark ocean all around. I walked past the wooden benches—they were for nicer days than this—and around to a narrow passage that ran up alongside the ferry. I could see the lifeboats there, hanging from chains. There was a bit of an overhang along the passageway and I found a sort of niche in the wall with another bench set into it. It was windy, but about as protected a place as I was likely to find, so I plunked myself down and hauled out my old Martin.

I paused for a moment to remember the music that had been floating through my head. I strummed a G chord and tried to hum a bit of it but it seemed too low in pitch. I had a capo in the little felt compartment inside the case along with some picks and the blue ribbon that Rudy had brought me. The problem was, when I flipped the compartment open, the ribbon kind of fluttered and got caught by a gust of wind. I watched as it lifted out, and it was so slight, so inconsequential, that it danced up and over the open lid of the case, even as I rose to grab for it.

"Damn it," I said out loud.

For just a second it looked like the ribbon might settle back down onto the wet deck, but instead it lifted higher and twisted and went soaring over the railing, out over the steely dark waves below. I watched it float on the currents away from the ferry until it was lost from view.

And that killed me. It was like a bit of my childhood was gone, like a bit of me was gone. I set my guitar back down into the case and slammed the lid closed.

I stood and walked farther along the narrow passageway past the lifeboats, to where another hatch appeared. I tried the handle on it, thinking it would take me back into the passenger deck, but instead I entered a metal stairwell. I closed the door and it was suddenly quite dark and very echoey.

I sang a note to test the reverb and my voice ricocheted off the metal walls in a really nice way. The fragment of song was still repeating itself insistently, so I went down a half a flight of stairs and fished out my guitar again, trying not to think too much about my old blue ribbon.

I took out my capo and tightened it down onto the third fret. I had a pretty good idea of what key the song should be in. B-flat was always one that worked well with my voice. The chords rang around that metal staircase and I hummed through the melody a few times, and a sort of chorus came to me too, a real lilting thing, pretty but kind of melancholy. And just for something to stick in there, I sang the words "wine-dark sea" over it and it fit perfectly. I'd been thinking that that would be a good name for a song anyway. In fact, I'd thought that when Ariadne first mentioned it, way back at the Indica Gallery.

That seemed like a long time ago. And Calgary, well, that was like a whole different lifetime. Evelyn and Rudy had helped me, that was for sure, but now I was making it on my own. There was Frankie to deal with, and Surly, but one of my songs was going to be on a record and that was something. That was something I'd only dreamed about back in Evelyn's basement.

But dreams come with a price, I guess. Things with this band were already pretty crazy and we'd barely begun the tour. I tried to push all that out of my mind and focus on the music. On my music.

I tinkled away on the chord pattern, B-flat to E-flat to G minor and back again. It wasn't anything the Exits would ever do. It wasn't their style, but I liked it. There was something genuine about it. Something true.

Something that was really me.

Painted Ladies

A couple hours later, we reached Ostend, halfway up the coast of Belgium. Even before the ferry docked, we trailed Surly back down to the car deck, all of us excited to actually be on the European continent. Surly climbed in behind the wheel of the bus. He didn't look comfortable driving but he nestled into the seat and began to jiggle the massive gearshift. It was topped by an orb the size of an eight ball and he had his cashbox set down on the floor beside it. I think he liked to keep the money nearby at all times.

The rest of us filed into the seats. Our stuff had gone into the holds below and there was tons of room. Surly said we'd pick up more people as we went along on the tour, promoters and reporters and groupies, but right now it was just us, scattered across the twelve rows of seats. They were cushy with armrests, and the windows had curtains. There were even overhead compartments like in an airplane. At the far back was a closet-sized toilet—though you didn't want to sit across from it, that was for sure.

Surly took a few more practice tugs on the gearshift, and when it was clear for us to go, he edged us forward, down the ramp and off the ferry. It didn't take long to get onto the motorway, heading north, up to the Netherlands. The Belgians and the Dutch had apparently gone nuts for "Painted Ladies." It was a top-ten song in both countries, so we were starting the tour in Amsterdam and working our way back down. Our first show was at the Oude RAI, and according to Surly, we'd sold out the place, all ten thousand seats.

Pretty soon we were passing farmlands lined with low stone fences and beech trees. It was flat as hell but at least the sun had come out. I was sitting midway back. Ariadne was sitting with Frankie near the front. His head was slumped against her shoulder, asleep I think, but she stared out the window. I could see her face reflected in the glass, watching the countryside flicker by.

When we finally got to Amsterdam, we barely had time to stop at our "hotel," which was actually a line of canal boats moored along the Amstel River. Surly had booked five of these long thin tugboats and I was once again sharing with Chester. We had the middle boat and he wasn't too thrilled about it at all. These boats weren't meant for big guys and he bumped his head pretty good when we first went in. They were beautiful inside, though, all decked out with polished teak and brass railings.

We only had a few minutes to drop off our stuff and clean up a bit, and then it was back on the bus and off to the venue for the sound check. The RAI looked like an old barn, but it was actually a pretty important venue. Led Zeppelin played there before us on their *Houses of the Holy* tour. Imagine that. Jimmy Page ripping out his incendiary solos, strutting across the very same floorboards as us.

By now, we had a fancy rider for our shows, meaning that the promoters had tables set up in the dressing room with fruit bowls and cheese platters and, at this show, ice buckets of Heineken. They always had a twenty-six of Chivas Regal for Frankie too, though everyone knew that wasn't such a great idea.

Our stage clothes arrived on racks, including the new threads I'd bought with Chester. I was just scooping through the hangers when Frankie came strutting in. He usually had his own room before the shows, so this was a first. Surly was hovering in the back, studying the rider table, mentally checking off the bananas or something.

I held up a pearl-buttoned silk shirt in front of one of those dressing room mirrors with the light bulbs all around it. My face stared back at me. My hair was definitely longer now, almost down to my shoulders, and maybe I did look a little like Jim Morrison. I didn't quite have his square chin or brooding eyes, but I thought, yeah, that's not bad. That's not bad at all.

In the mirror, I saw Frankie smile at me, and that caught me by surprise. "Levi," he called over. "Need a beer? Chester, what are you drinking?"

Chester was sitting on a couch. He cocked an eyebrow at Frankie. "Already got myself a Tab," he said, holding up the can.

"I'm okay too," I said. I had a half-finished beer sitting on the vanity. "Cheers, though."

Frankie came over with a cold Heineken in his hand. "C'mon, live it up a bit. Take advantage, yeah? This is the big time."

"Okay," I said. "Thanks, man."

I thought it was a breakthrough, Frankie being nice to me. Maybe Ariadne had talked to him. Or maybe he'd decided to go with the record company on the single. I don't know but it felt like maybe he was finally easing up.

I drank the beer and got into my clothes. I'd gone with the white bell-bottoms, the ones with the stars along the bottom. I felt a bit ridiculous in that getup but, like Chester said, I had to start looking the part.

Twenty minutes later, we were strutting out onto the stage. The place had already gone dark, and I could hear the crowd begin to cheer and stomp. For me, though, something was already not feeling quite right. My hands felt thick, and like, I don't know, like they weren't my hands anymore.

When I got to my place onstage, it got worse. The neck of my guitar seemed like it was bending, like it was made out of rubber. I clamped down harder on it to keep it straight. My feet seemed to be stuck to the floorboards too. They felt so heavy I couldn't lift them, though I could move the rest of my body just fine.

Out front, Frankie greeted the crowd and then Chester counted us in, and I just focused on playing the chords, trying not to get distracted by the weirdness. I made it through the first couple of songs, but I felt myself losing it. And I was pretty sure I knew what had happened.

We were going to do "Hello Juliet" in the set tonight for the first time, but just before we got to it, Frankie bounded across the stage toward me. It was the lull between songs. The crowd was roaring and the lights had dimmed down to a single blue spotlight. That was supposed to be my cue for the intro, but Frankie's face leered in at me like a Halloween mask.

"You ready for your song?"

"No," I mumbled. There was no way I could sing a lead vocal.

"Having a little trouble there?"

"No."

He smirked at me and pranced back to center stage and began the introduction to "29 Streetlights" instead. And I knew what he'd done. He'd dropped something in my beer.

Rudy was watching from the sidelines and he knew something was up. Ariadne was there too, her eyes peeking above the viewfinder on her camera. I tried to nod at her, but she disappeared around the back and I didn't see her again.

I went through the whole show, trying to maintain control over the neck of my guitar. I knew when a solo was coming and I tried not to mess it up. I sang the backup vocals, but my voice seemed dislocated from my skull. It was like someone else was saying the words and each phrase didn't really make sense with the one before it. They were just memorized, meaningless sequences of sound.

And then I had a moment where I felt like I was Pete, like I was falling and there was nothing I could do about it. I blinked and that went away, but it scared me, that's for sure. Whatever Frankie had dropped in my beer—because that's what he'd done—well, it wasn't going to stop me. I wasn't going to be like Pete. When we came to "Painted Ladies," I leaned into the solo, letting the neck of my guitar bend as it wanted, and I just went with it. I dipped one knee forward and did a sort of lunge like something Jimi Hendrix might do. It felt good but I thought I probably shouldn't risk another. The whole of gravity seemed to shift with that move, the stage tilting like the deck of a ship.

There were tiny reflections on everything. Little sparks of light came off Chester's cymbal stands and the microphone, even off the tuning pegs of my guitar. The little lights were flashing and glinting, dancing out into the air and floating around like fireflies.

When we finished the last song, I was so high that Rudy ran out onto the stage to help me off. Chester climbed down from his drum riser to take my other arm. "Easy, Boss," he said, walking me along like you'd walk a toddler.

Ariadne's face appeared in front of me too. "He's high," she said.

I tried to straighten up, to protest that I was fine, but my eyes must have been like saucers.

"You're going to be okay," Chester said. "Here, just step forward, one foot in front of the other. That's right."

"Unh," I said.

Miguel and Dave had gone off the other side of the stage, but Frankie was still on the stage, bowing, bathing in the roar of the crowd. "Thank you," he shouted into the microphone. "Thank you, Amsterdam."

Rudy and Chester got me back to the dressing room, Ariadne trailing behind them. They laid me down on the couch faceup. On the ceiling above me, a water pipe ran in a straight line, then bent ninety degrees and went out through the wall. I thought I could see the water bulging, a lump running through it like in a Bugs Bunny cartoon.

Rudy sat with me for a while. Ariadne went to get me a glass of water. Chester paced up and down. At one point, he leaned over me, his big brown eyes on mine. "Listen," he said, "you got to be more careful."

"Uh-huh."

Rudy frowned at Chester. "You think Frankie spiked his drink?"

"Frankie's the star. You understand what I'm saying? His world fell out from under him and now he's doing everything he can to stay on top." He paused. "But it ain't gonna work. Something's got to give."

♫

When I woke up the next morning, it took a while for me to remember where I was. I felt the gentle sway of the water beneath me and it all came flooding back: the ferry, Amsterdam, tripping out at the RAI, and Ariadne's concerned face hovering over me. And now I was back on the canal boat on the Amstel River and I must have slept all night.

Outside I heard the tinkling of a bell. Slowly, I got up and opened the door to a cold blue sky. It was June already, but I guess we were pretty far north, because the morning air was pretty chilly. I was still in my underwear and my head felt like it was stuffed with cotton batting.

Up on the pier, Chester sat on a little blue bicycle with a flower basket, jubilantly ringing the bell.

"Jeez," I said. "You want to maybe lay off on that?"

Chester hunched over the bike. He was way too big for it, that much was obvious. He rang his bell again. "We rented bikes," he said.

"I can see that."

"Boss, everyone's going into town. There's the Red Light District, the hash bars. It's Amsterdam. You don't want to miss this."

"What time is it?"

"It's nearing noon," said Chester. "C'mon, join us."

Behind him a row of buildings rose up, brightly colored, each one three or four stories tall, all of them as skinny as the spine of a book. I didn't quite know what to make of it.

"Where's Frankie?" I asked.

"You don't want to bother with that."

"I'm just asking."

Chester heaved a great sigh, then stepped off his bicycle. He leaned it against a piling and came down the ladder onto the deck of our canal boat. I backed into the door hatch to let him in.

"Boss," he said, "I'm only going to say this once."

"What?"

"We need this tour, all right? I need this tour."

"Yeah, but you saw what he did. That fucker dropped a hit of acid into my beer."

"I know. It's not right, but we just gotta get through this tour. We gotta get back on our feet."

"How am I supposed to do that on acid?"

"It ain't for everyone, that's for sure. You know why Pete did it so much?"

"I don't care about Pete."

"He said he took it to make himself more creative."

"That's bullshit."

"Of course it's bullshit. I'm just saying he was under pressure, to keep writing music, to always have the next best idea."

"You saying I should be taking acid?"

"Damn, no. I'm saying you're our last great hope."

"Me?"

"You think Frankie doesn't know that?"

"Fuck Frankie."

Chester studied me. "I'm agreeing with you. He can be difficult."

"I'm done with him. Next time he—"

"You don't get it, Levi," Chester pressed his lips together. He eyed me up and down. "Am I going to have to lay it out for you? Frankie is the face of this band whether you like it or not. You're both going to have to work together if we have any chance of finishing this album."

"Then why has Surly even got us on this stupid tour when we should be recording?"

"Because we need the money."

"I don't trust him, Chester. He never tells us what's going on. It's like he doesn't even care."

"Hey, hey," Chester said. "Bobby is about the only guy really looking out for us."

"Doesn't seem like it."

"What do you think he keeps that cashbox for? That's our money. That's our money from the shows. Don't you know nothin'?"

I shrugged.

"The record company can't touch that. Surly is on our side. That man is planning all the time, trying to keep one step ahead of the game. So, my advice?"

"What?"

"Forget about what happened." Chester took a step back. "Look, man, we're in Amsterdam. When you ever gonna be back here again? Just put some damn pants on and come join us for some fun."

I shook my head.

"Suit yourself." He held my eyes for a moment, then turned and climbed back up onto the pier and reached for his bike.

"Drum sitter," I called out.

"And you a damn marionette," he said. He climbed onto his bike; he towered over the metal frame. He rang his little bell one last time, then set off down the boardwalk, a big bear of a man on a tiny blue bicycle.

♫

When I finally got myself together, I figured maybe I should try and catch up with Chester. I needed some fresh air, that was for sure. I clambered up the little ladder onto the boardwalk. A street ran alongside it, with those tall, skinny houses on the far side, and just down from that was our tour bus, parked against the curb.

I walked over and rapped on the door of the bus. Rudy's face appeared in one of the windows. He'd been sleeping on the bus—it was his job to guard it—and when he winched open the door, he didn't look so great. There was a crease mark across his forehead and his Dr Pepper T-shirt had a big orange stain down the front.

"Hey," I said, and I climbed up into the bus. It was pretty dingy in there. It smelled like stale beer and cigarettes. Rudy had a screwdriver and he went back to the underside of the overhead compartments.

"What are you doing there?" I said.

He grunted and bent down, trying to get a better look. "Trying to make this dump more habitable. There's speakers under here, but they're not hooked up. I thought maybe if I could—"

"Rudy?"

"What?" he said, and he rose up again.

"Chester's gone to the Red Light District."

"So?"

"Jeez, Rudy. It's Amsterdam. There's hash bars and girls and, c'mon man, maybe we could—"

"I'm supposed to stay with the bus."

"Says who?"

"You want me to get fired?" He pointed the screwdriver at me. "You can go and get high if you want to. You're the big rock star now."

"C'mon, Rudy. I didn't mean it like that."

"Someone has to look after things. Someone has to be responsible."

"What's with you?"

Rudy sank down into one of the seats. "Nothing," he said.

"Rudy, what is it?"

"Frankie," he said. "He's such a dink."

"Tell me about it."

"I had to hide his drugs."

"What?"

"He has, like, a shaving kit, filled with stuff. He made me hide it." He dangled the screwdriver at me. "I opened up a panel, just behind the third seat there. The panels screw right off."

"Aw, jeez, Rudy." I looked up the aisle. "It's in there?"

"What was I supposed to do? I can't exactly tell him no."

"What about Surly? Does Surly know?"

"Frankie said he'd kill me if I told anyone. And we're crossing international borders. Use your head, Levi. The whole tour is over if Frankie gets busted with dope."

"Yeah, but that's not your job." I would have said more, but someone was outside, pushing at the door. It whooshed open, and Surly came charging up the steps with the cashbox tucked under his arm.

"I've been looking for you," he said, fixing me with a glare. "What the bloody hell was that all about last night? You're taking acid now?"

"Jeez, Surly. Frankie spiked my drink. It wasn't—"

"What did you call me?"

"Bobby," I tried again. "That wasn't my doing. He—"

"Don't call me Surly. And don't let me catch you doing acid. I'm not going through that again."

"I won't. Jeez."

"Bloody hell, do I have to babysit all of you?"

"No, of course not."

"Well, it sure seems that way. C'mon, you're coming with me."

"But we were going to—"

Surly glanced at Rudy. "You too. Get a move on."

Rudy put down the screwdriver. "Where are we going?" he asked.

"American Express. I need to change some money. Every country is a goddamn different currency. Now, let's go."

I exchanged a look with Rudy. We trailed off the bus after Surly. He locked it up and then stomped off down the boardwalk. We skittered after him, the fairy-tale houses rising up on our left, the slow river flowing by on our right.

"You want me to carry the cashbox for you?" I offered.

"Bugger off. You don't touch the cashbox."

"I'm just asking."

"Well, don't."

"Then why do you even need our help?"

Surly stopped suddenly. "Listen," he said, "there's a hell of a lot of money in here. Something happens and I'm going to be wanting a couple of extra guys with me. You know what I mean?"

"Like bodyguards?" asked Rudy.

"Jesus Christ. You just keep your eyes on the cashbox. Make sure nothing happens."

We plodded up a side street away from the river, and down a couple more blocks to a modern-looking building with plate-glass windows and a big American Express logo over the door. Inside, there was a big board with the exchange rates above a counter, and all along one wall were little booths with telephones for long-distance phone calls.

"Why don't you boys call home?" suggested Surly. "I'm sure your mothers want to hear from you." He was already surveying the exchange rates on the board and he walked off toward the front counter. A woman stood behind the desk there, like a bank teller or something.

"We *should* phone Evelyn," I said.

"Why would we want to do that?"

"Shit, Rudy, she's your mom. When's the last time you talked to her?"

"I don't know. She's probably mad at me."

"Yeah, probably. But she'll be worried. We should call."

He muttered something else I didn't quite hear, but I went into one of the little booths anyway. Rudy stood in the doorway behind me. I knew the phone number, of course, but I didn't know the long-distance codes. I glanced out through the window toward the woman at the counter. She had glasses, big thick black ones with horn rims, and she was watching us. I picked up the phone but there was nothing, no dial tone or anything. The woman signaled for me to wait. She pressed at a button on her side of the counter and then something clicked and a dial tone buzzed.

My finger was hovering over the rotary dial. "Rudy," I said. "How do I work this thing?"

He leaned in and read a card beside the phone and called out the international codes for me. I dialed the numbers slowly, waiting for the rotary dial to click back all the way around before I stuck my finger in for the next number. Then the phone began to ring, far, far away, in Evelyn's living room.

"Evelyn," I said when she answered. "It's Levi."

"Levi." She sounded tired. "Where are you?"

"Amsterdam," I told her. "We played a show here last night." The phone line hummed but she didn't say anything. "The band is really good. The lead singer is a piece of work but other than that it's great."

Rudy shuffled in behind me. He let out a sigh.

"Is that Rudy?" said Evelyn. "Is Rudy there with you?"

"Yes," I said. I held up the receiver to him, but he waved his hand like he didn't want to talk to her.

"Evelyn, he's kind of busy right now. He said he'll phone you later."

Rudy shook his head.

"Is he brushing his teeth?" Evelyn asked. "Make sure he brushes his teeth."

Rudy grabbed the phone from me. "Mom," he said, "jeez, can you cut it out already?"

Over by the counter, Surly was talking to the woman with the glasses. He was getting pretty animated, waving his hands up at the exchange-rate board while the woman was trying to explain something to him. The cashbox was open and he'd scooped up a wad of bills. He was pushing them at the woman, but she backed away a step like she didn't want to touch the money. I think he was trying to get a better rate and she wasn't going for it.

On the phone, Evelyn was doing most of the talking. I could hear the drone of her voice punctuated by Rudy saying, "Yes, Mom," and "I know, Mom," and "Yes, of course I will."

After a while he handed the receiver back to me. "She wants to talk to you."

"Hi, Evelyn?"

"Levi, are you in trouble?"

"What? No. Why would I be in trouble?"

"No need to get snippy with me."

"I'm not—"

"An airmail package arrived for you. It's from Labyrinth Records."

"Oh, that's my contract. I'm in the band. Officially."

Rudy gave me a sympathetic look, and I knew what was coming, so I headed her off. "It's good," I said. "They really want me in the band."

"Levi," she said slowly, and I knew that tone. "Send Rudy out. I need to talk to you alone."

"What?" I said.

"Just send Rudy away from the phone, please."

I put my hand over the receiver. "Rudy," I said, "go and see what Surly is doing. He's getting pretty worked up out there."

"Why me? Why do I always have to—?"

"Rudy, just give me a little privacy, will you?"

"Okay, okay." He went out and I held my hand over the receiver for a moment more, waiting for the door to close. I watched him lope across the office to the counter.

"All right, Evelyn. What is it? What's the problem?"

"You know perfectly well what the problem is, Levi. Did you have Rudy go over that contract with you?"

"No. Rudy wasn't there."

"So you signed it? In your condition?"

"My condition? C'mon, Evelyn. It's not a condition."

Outside at the counter, I could actually hear Surly yelling now. He gestured vaguely at me and that vein thing was sticking out on his forehead. Rudy was standing nearby, but not too close, and the woman at the counter had backed away another step. She was being calm about it. She pushed her glasses farther up her nose and tried to explain something.

"Evelyn," I said, "you'd really like it here. There's a lot of culture."

There was a long, empty pause. I could hear her breathing.

"Evelyn?"

"Levi," she began, and her voice sounded different. "I need to tell you something. Something about the audition."

"My audition?"

"Now, don't be angry."

"Angry? Why would I be angry?"

"Well, it's like this. I set it up."

"You what?"

"I made some phone calls, all right? Did you really think your little cassette tape was going to get you anywhere?"

"Hold on." I held the receiver away from my ear for a second, trying to clear my head. Surly was shouting now. Something was going on out there.

"What do you mean you set up the audition?"

"Well, certainly, I had no idea things would turn out like this."

"But you set it up? How is that even possible?"

"Levi. I'm trying to tell you something important here."

"But you can't just—"

"Levi Jaxon, would you just hush up for a second and listen?"

I sucked in a breath. "Okay, what? What exactly did you do?"

There was a pause on the other end like she was thinking, and when she started up again, her voice was softer. "I wanted you to succeed. I wanted for you to do better than I had done."

"Okay, but—"

"No, you listen to me, young man. Things have moved along very quickly, and I don't think you fully realize."

"Evelyn," I said. "I'm in a famous band. Things are going well."

"I just want you to be careful, Levi. That's all I'm trying to say. You are in way over your head."

"I'm not."

"You are. You're a talented young man but you have no idea how dangerous these people can be."

"Nobody's dangerous, Evelyn."

"I'm just asking that you be careful. That you and Rudy—"

Outside, Rudy was signaling to me. "Just a second, Evelyn."

Surly was acting funny. He'd suddenly gone rigid. I could see him standing in front of Rudy. He was still at the counter, but something was clearly wrong with him. He stumbled backward and Rudy put out a hand to catch him. Surly whirled around and his face had turned a sickly gray. His eyelids were sort of fluttering.

"Aw, crap. I have to go." She was still speaking as I hung up the phone.

I jumped up out of the little booth and came around and reached Surly just as his knees buckled. He'd grabbed for the cashbox, only managing to sweep it off the counter with his arm. Then he crumpled to the floor and the cashbox crashed down beside him, exploding money across the floor.

The woman behind the counter leaned forward and peered down at him over her horn-rimmed glasses. Her expression didn't change.

"Holy shit," I said. "What's happening?"

Surly was motionless, sprawled out on the floor in his cheap pinstripe suit. It looked like he was dead or something. I knelt down over him. He was breathing, but it was in short gasps and his lips were turning blue.

Rudy bent down beside me. "We've got to give him a chest massage."

"A what?"

"You know, that thing—" Rudy made a fist and slammed it down on Surly's chest, and as he did, Surly Bob's eyes popped open.

"Jesus," he grunted. "Get off me."

"Bobby," I said, "are you okay?"

He blinked but his face was still pretty gray. His eyes darted from us to the lady's face high above us at the counter. She was still staring down at the three of us.

"Christ on a kite," he said. He struggled to get himself up, and I put a hand under his arm and helped him into a sitting position. His legs were splayed out in front of him like a child's. He shook his head to clear it and fumbled in his jacket pocket, drawing out a vial of pills. He snapped the lid off and popped a little white pill into his mouth.

"Christ," he said. It was more of a sigh than anything else.

"Are you okay?" I asked again.

Rudy was already scampering around collecting the money. I righted the cashbox and shuffled it across the linoleum to Surly. He reached for it and scooped it in closer to himself.

He grunted and wriggled around up onto his knees.

Rudy was darting back and forth, picking up money. It was in a lot of different currencies and he was gathering handfuls and coming back and dropping them into the cashbox. It was a mess.

After a couple of minutes, I helped Surly to his feet. He was unsteady, but he grimaced and tried to regain himself. I picked up the cashbox and handed it to him. He tucked it close to his chest.

"Did you get it all?" he asked Rudy.

"I think so."

Surly glanced back at the woman behind the counter. "Thanks for fucking nothing," he said. "We're off to Belgium tomorrow and your guilders are useless there."

She muttered something under her breath and went back to work.

"Jesus," Surly said. I got around one side of him and Rudy was on the other. We helped him out the door. "What the hell am I supposed to do with Dutch guilders?"

♫

Halfway back to the canal boats Surly passed out again, so me and Rudy pretty much lugged him the rest of the way, heaving him between us like a sack of potatoes. Rudy was carrying the cashbox with his free hand and I looked over at him.

"Why didn't you tell me?" I asked.

"Tell you what?"

"That Evelyn set up the audition."

Surly's eyes furled a bit at that but he was pretty out of it.

"Aw, jeez," Rudy said. "She told you?"

"So you knew and you didn't tell me? You showed up with that dumb ribbon and some speech about how I was so talented, when the whole time it was all just a setup?"

He looked away. "It's no big whoop, okay? She only told me after you left."

"So what did she do? Are you telling me she just phoned Labyrinth Records and said, *Hey, I've got this guy, he's pretty good, you should put him in Downtown Exit*?"

"I don't know what she said. She told me after you left. I was just as surprised as you."

"But—"

"Shit, Levi. I don't know, okay?"

Sir Charles Blackmore's uppity face flashed before me. How would she have known him? How could she have known anyone at Labyrinth Records?

"Rudy," I said. "It's me. You can tell me. I need to know."

"Look," he said, "can we just stop for a second? I need to get a better hold on him."

Surly grunted a bit but his eyes were still closed. His head was flopping between us and he was heavy as hell.

Rudy kind of juggled the cashbox up higher under his arm and leaned in to get a better grip on Surly.

"There's lots you don't know," Rudy went on. "Lots of stuff happened when she was in New York."

"Like when she got kicked out of Juilliard?" I kind of hiked up Surly too on my end and we started walking again.

"Yeah, like that."

"So why did she get kicked out? You've never told me."

Rudy shook his head. "First, you have to promise you won't say anything."

"I won't. Jeez."

"Evelyn was going to be a concert pianist and there was this competition. The Leventritt."

"I never heard of it."

"Yeah, well, you never heard of a lot of things. The Leventritt is this big competition in New York and Evelyn was in it. It's a ten-thousand-dollar prize, Levi. That was a lot of money in those days."

"So?"

"If you win you get to play with the New York Philharmonic."

"Okay."

"So there's my mom, and she's young and glamorous, and she's really good. She steps out onto the stage, probably in that glittery dress. You know the one?"

"Yeah, I know it."

"Well, they didn't let her play. She was disqualified. They didn't let her get anywhere near that piano."

"Okay, but why?"

Rudy wouldn't meet my eyes.

"Rudy. You can tell me."

Surly groaned between us and he lifted his head. "Christ," he said, and his eyes opened. "Where are we going?"

"We're almost at your boat, Bobby," I said. I looked over at Rudy, but he wasn't talking anymore. Up ahead the canal boats bobbed in the water and there was music coming from one of them. It was Led Zeppelin, their second album, side one, track one, and when we got a few steps closer I could see that the hatch on Surly's boat was open and that the music was coming from there.

"Shit," I said. "Who's in there?"

"Just get me to my bunk," Surly muttered.

I left Rudy holding Surly and I stepped carefully down onto the deck. I peered in through the hatch and there was Frankie. He was sitting on a couch with a girl on either side of him. Pretty girls. Blondes. They looked like they could be twins.

Behind me, Rudy helped Surly down onto the deck. I reached back and together the three of us hobbled into the cabin.

Frankie sat up when we entered. "What's his problem?" he said.

"Bugger off," said Surly. "Just get me to my bunk."

We helped Surly in. Those canal boats were pretty nice, really. The main room was as comfortable as a little living room. Frankie was nuzzled into the girls on a black leather couch. The girls really did look a lot alike, blue eyes, high Scandinavian cheekbones. One of them was wearing a toque.

Surly glared at them as we helped him by. The ceiling was low, and we had to duck through to the back where there were small bedrooms on either side, each one with just enough space for a bunk and a little shelf. Me and Rudy laid Surly down in the left-hand one.

His color had come back but he was unsteady. His eyes were unfocused, and he closed them as soon we got him down. Rudy set the cashbox at the end of the bed between his feet, and I pulled off his shoes, clunky rubber-soled things.

"Should we just leave him?" asked Rudy.

"I thought we were supposed to watch the cashbox."

"I can stay and watch it, at least until Bobby wakes up again."

"All right," I said. "You gonna be okay with—?" I tipped my head back toward the front room.

"I don't know. I'll just stay out of his way, I guess."

"Okay," I said. I was a bit relieved. I just wanted to get out of there. I was still trying to get over the fact that Evelyn had set up my audition. I mean, how was that even possible? And what did it say about me? Maybe that I didn't really deserve to be in Downtown Exit. Maybe all of this was just one big lie.

I had to go out past Frankie, and I thought maybe I wouldn't say anything. I would just keep my head down and breeze past him. The Led Zeppelin was still playing, that weird part in the middle of "Whole Lotta Love," but as I drifted past, Frankie stuck out his leg to stop me.

"C'mon, Frankie, let me by."

"Have you met my new friends?" he asked. "The Sisters of Mercy. I don't even know their real names."

One of them fluttered her eyelashes at me. I could see a powdery circle of cocaine around one of her nostrils. I stepped over his leg and headed for the door, then stopped and turned.

"Hey, Frankie," I said. And I glared at him. "Where's Ariadne?"

"She's not here. Obviously." He put his hand on the leg of the girl to his right and leered back at me.

"Listen, it's one thing to fuck me over, but you shouldn't hurt Ariadne."

"You don't know what you're talking about," he said. "And if you want to get wasted onstage, that's your business."

"I know it was you, Frankie. Maybe Pete liked that shit, but I don't want it."

Frankie rose. I could smell alcohol on his breath, and I could see that his hands had balled into fists.

"You ain't Pete. No matter how hard you try. You ain't no Pete."

"At least I can write a song," I snapped.

Frankie's eyes narrowed. I was pretty sure he could beat the crap out of me. He was from New Jersey, after all. The Sisters of Mercy sat behind him, blinking and giggling. Over at the door to Surly's bunk, Rudy peered out at us.

"We all have our secrets, though, don't we?" he said, leaning into me, pushing at my chest.

"Fuck you."

"You're such a fucking freak. You can't even read."

I glanced over at Rudy, who was standing there still as a statue. Shit, Frankie must have heard us on the ferry.

"Maybe," he said, "Ariadne would like to know about this little problem of yours."

"Fuck off."

"You fuck off. You think I can't do this without Pete?" One of the girls, the one with the toque, reached out for him, but he pushed her hand away. "You don't get it. You don't get it at all. Me and Pete, we came from nothing. Dirtbag little towns. Our families had nothing. You think I'm just going to forget about that? You think I'm going to forget about Pete?"

"For fuck's sake. I never said that. When did I ever say that?"

"'29 Streetlights,' that one's mine," he said. "I wrote the verses. Pete just wrote the chorus and most of the lyrics."

"Okay," I said.

"It's a good song. You know it's good."

"It's too long."

"It's five minutes and forty-three seconds. 'Hey Jude' was, like, eight minutes."

"We're not the Beatles, Frankie."

"That's exactly what Bobby said."

"We could make it shorter. Just for the single."

"You don't get it, do you? Each verse tells a story. That's the town we grew up in. Me and Pete. It's not just another pop song."

"Then let Bobby talk to them again. I'm sure—"

"Fat lot of good he's doing us." We both glanced over at Surly's bunk. We could just see his feet. They were in woolen socks and cocked at an angle, the cashbox set between them. Rudy was still standing at the door, not moving. "I'm thinking we should fire him," said Frankie.

Frankie slid an arm around the girl with the toque and settled back into her. "What do you think? Should we just fire the fucker?"

"Surly's taking care of our money."

Frankie eyed me. "You know he was in jail, don't you? That guy is an ex-con."

"He was?"

"They say he killed a man once."

"Surly?"

"Some manager," said Frankie. "Collecting our nickels and dimes. I say we could do better."

"I don't know."

"Aw, fuck it. I don't care anyway." The second girl leaned in and kissed him on the cheek, and he sort of grinned lopsidedly.

"I'm going," I said. "I'm going to catch up with Chester."

" 'Painted Ladies,' " said Frankie.

"What?"

"The song, dumbass. You go on down to the Red Light District and you'll see. It's just like the song."

♫

I *was* thinking about that song, if you really want to know. It's about a guy being lost. About being far from home and all you can find to comfort yourself are those painted ladies. That and a bottle of wine. It's crazy how close that was to how I was feeling.

I found a bicycle for rent not much farther along the pier. I got one a lot like the one Chester had, blue, with a little basket up front. I didn't really know where I was going, but I pedaled off in the direction Chester had gone even though there was zero chance of catching him. It didn't matter. I just had to get out of there.

I rode along the river for a while until I came to an old wooden drawbridge. It was like something out of a Van Gogh painting and, past that, I saw my first real canal. It kind of veered off from the real river, and it had a pathway alongside it, so I turned to go down it. There were more of those skinny houses, all pressed tightly together, each one a different color, candy colors, bright reds and blues, and I don't know, something about them reminded me of gingerbread houses.

The canal began to get busier. There were groups of tourists taking pictures of a statue and past that I saw a woman walking. She was wearing a sheepskin coat and she had a camera strapped over her shoulder, and I knew right away, even at a distance, that it was Ariadne.

I sped up a bit, standing up off my seat to get a better purchase on the pedals. "Ariadne," I called.

She stopped and turned, and when she saw me, her face lit up.

I swung in alongside her and hopped off the bike. "Get some good shots?"

"Yes," she said. She had a little spiral notepad in her hand and she tucked it down into the pocket of her coat. I imagine she kept track of her shots in there. "It's lovely here. I've always liked Amsterdam."

"You've been here before?"

"I have, yes, many times." She studied my face. "Are you feeling better? What exactly happened to you last night?"

"Oh," I said. "Well, I—"

"Never mind. It's not my business."

"No, it's just that, well, Frankie is—"

"Frankie is what?"

"Maybe you better not go back to the boats right now."

"Is there a problem?"

"No, it's just—well, you might not want to go back there yet. Frankie's kind of . . . busy."

Ariadne clamped her lips together. "Oh, I don't care," she said. She hoisted up her camera and pretended to adjust something on it.

"That's a nice camera."

"It's a Hasselblad. A 1600F."

"Okay."

"Don't you want to ask if it's my father's?"

"No," I said. I knew better than that. We began walking along the canal. I clanked my bike alongside me.

"Well, the Hasselblad is mine now. Father presented it to me when I left Oxford. So I could make something of myself. Or at least that's what he said."

"Yeah?" I said.

"He was never really happy with my schooling anyway," she said. She stopped and fixed her green eyes on me. They were especially translucent in the crisp afternoon air. "And I'd come to realize that what I was learning wasn't . . . Oh, I don't know."

"Wasn't what?"

"Wasn't real, I imagine." We began walking again. It was really kind of beautiful along the canal. "I was especially interested in the Romantics," she went on, "in their interpretations of Greece. Because they were interpretations and not the real thing. Do you know what I mean?"

"Kind of."

"Tennyson and Keats and Byron, they wrote about Greece as if it were some sort of heaven on earth."

"It's not?"

"No," she said. "It's not. In fact, things are very bad there just now."

"I'm sorry."

"There was a military coup. Many people had to flee."

"Like your father?"

"Yes, like my father."

"We could maybe go for a coffee," I said. "Until things . . . settle down, I mean, back at the boats . . . with Frankie."

"Yes," she said. "Thanks."

We strode along in silence until we came to a little place.

"Here?" she said.

"Sure." This one, it turned out, was an actual *koffiehuis*—where they only sold coffee and pastries. I left my bicycle propped up against the wall outside, and we ducked in and ordered at the counter, then sat at a little round table near the front. Joni Mitchell was playing through the speakers, that song about skating away on a river. Ariadne rested her chin on her hand and stared out the window.

"You okay?" I asked.

"I'll be fine."

"I'm sorry," I said. "Frankie can be so—"

"I'm not sure I can do this much longer," she said.

I could tell she was hurting, and I knew I needed to say something. "It's not right," I started. "How he treats you."

Ariadne turned her big green eyes on me. "I'm not really Frankie's girlfriend, you know."

"You're not?" My heart clamped up a little.

"Frankie is still sorting things out. He needs my help. He needs all of our help."

"Oh, I don't think he needs any help from me."

She threw me a look like a teacher might give a slow student. "No, Levi. He does. It's terribly hard on him. All this hiding."

"Frankie?"

Ariadne kind of cocked her head at me. "Oh," she said, as if she'd suddenly realized something. "You don't know, do you?"

"Know what? About him hiding?" I was kind of confused now.

She looked down at the table. "I'm sorry. I shouldn't have said anything."

"Ariadne, what's going on?"

"Well," she began, hesitantly.

"Ariadne, please. I don't know what you're talking about."

"Levi, Frankie is gay."

"What? No. I just saw him. He was with those two girls. He—"

"It's all a big show. He's trapped. He's supposed to be this massive rock star that all the girls swoon over, but—"

"So you're not together?"

"Honestly," she said. "Maybe I better tell you something. Just to be clear."

I didn't like the sound of that.

"I was with Peter before—"

"You and Pete?"

"We'd only been together for a few weeks before . . . before he fell."

"Oh, man," I said. Ariadne was looking down at the table. Her face had fallen. It had sorrow written all over it.

"It's been very difficult," she said. "For everyone. Peter was a lovely man. Brilliant, really."

"Wait, wait." I really wasn't sure I was getting this. "Are you saying Frankie was in love with Pete?"

"It's complicated. Things are not always so easy to put into pigeonholes."

"Wow."

"But, no, Levi. It's not what you imagine. Frankie was mostly in love with Peter's talent. They grew up together. Really, they were more like brothers. Closer than brothers. And when the band came together, Peter was the songwriter and Frankie, well, Frankie became the face of the band. And that's a certain pigeonhole too."

"Frankie is handsome. I'll give him that."

"Yes, but that's not who he really is. Can you imagine what it must be like for him?"

I kind of clamped my lips shut. I knew when to shut up.

"Peter was the one person in the world who understood him. He was the one person Frankie could confide in. And now I've gone and ruined everything."

"Oh, man," I said again.

"Frankie couldn't even go to the funeral. They had to ship Peter's body home, and of course, Frankie was dragged off on this tour." She stopped again and hung her jade-green eyes on me. "It's been very difficult for everyone."

"I didn't know. I didn't know any of this."

She sighed. "I'm sorry. I've blathered out everything."

"It's okay."

"No," she said. "It's not. It's not my place to say anything. Really, I should never have—"

"Ariadne." I reached over and put my hand on hers. "I saw how you handled things in the hotel room. You were great. It's like you stepped in when Pete couldn't be there."

"I don't know," she said. "I don't know what I'm doing anymore."

The Joni Mitchell was still playing and a long silence fell over us. After a minute or two it was almost unbearable and I thought I needed to say something. Anything at all to change the subject.

"I love this album," I said. "*Blue*. Do you know it?"

Ariadne nodded. "I met her once."

"Who? Joni Mitchell?"

"Well, my father and I did—" She waved her hand, as if it were nothing. "He used to take me sailing in the Greek islands. My father has a sailboat. It's called *The Northern Star*." She paused, looking off in the distance, and a tiny smile swept across her lips. "Really, he's a very good sailor. It's the only place we can be together . . . where he can relax. Where he doesn't have to be the famous movie director."

"Holy. You met Joni Mitchell?"

"It's really quite lovely out there on the sea." Her hand went up to the St. Christopher medal around her neck. "Of course, now, we can't go back to Greece."

"It's really bad?"

"It's complicated. Politics."

A guy with a ponytail brought our orders and Ariadne stopped talking. She had an espresso in a tiny cup with a tiny saucer. I had a normal-sized coffee and a pastry. I gulped down a mouthful of coffee and realized it was exactly what I needed.

"So," I said. "Joni Mitchell."

"Once," she said, "we were sailing off the southern coast of Crete and we docked at a port called Matala. And there, on the beach, there's a place called the Mermaid Café."

"Wait a second, I know that song."

"It's not there anymore," she said. "But it was then. I must have been, I don't know, sixteen maybe, and there she was: Joni Mitchell. My father didn't know who she was, but I was thrilled. I told him about her and he dragged me over to meet her. I told her that her song 'The Circle Game' changed my life."

"What did she do?"

"She smoked her cigarette and she studied me with those deep eyes of hers and she just gave me a little nod of thanks, that's all. She never said a word. I went back to the beach, but my father sat with her for a while. The funny thing is she knew who he was. They talked about films. You know, my father had done that documentary on the Rolling Stones."

I almost choked on my pastry. "That was your father?"

"Yes, and Joni was an aficionada of European films anyway, so it was natural that—"

"Wow."

Ariadne stared out the window, her fingers still on the St. Christopher. "I thought she was a genius. I still do. And they were both famous, Joni Mitchell and my father. They were famous, and that hadn't brought the slightest bit of happiness to either of them."

Someday, Sunday

We left the next day, midmorning, earlier than usual. It was only about a three-hour drive to Brussels but there was always lots to do before a show. Surly had got himself a tweed driving cap and he certainly seemed in better health than yesterday. The rest of the guys weren't so great. Everyone had made a big deal about partying in Amsterdam and now they were sleeping, their heads bobbing with each bump in the road. The Sisters of Mercy were riding up front, sitting with Skinny Dave. Skinny Dave, of all people. Rudy was at the back, on the seat beside the toilet, kind of avoiding everybody.

Frankie had more or less pulled an all-nighter. He'd disappeared, God knows where, and he looked pretty worse for the wear. He was sleeping now, by himself, curled up in the fetal position in row three. He stunk a bit and it looked like maybe he'd thrown up. He was a real mess, if you want to know the truth.

I went back to sit with Ariadne. She had her camera out, the aluminum case tucked into the compartment above us. She was watching out the window, and every once in a while she'd raise her camera, then think differently of it and lower it again, leaving it dangling from the strap around her neck. It looked pretty heavy, if you really want to know. She had a little spiral notebook resting on her lap, like a flip pad, and she brought it up.

"You keeping track of your shots in there?" I asked.

She flipped the little notebook shut. "Just writing down my thoughts," she said, and she tucked it down beside her on the seat.

We drove on in silence and eventually we passed a row of wooden windmills, somewhere outside Utrecht, ancient brick towers with their crossbeams revolving in the breeze like tiny white sails. Ariadne raised her camera and fired off a shot.

"That should be a good one," I said, and she turned to me, almost like she'd forgotten I was sitting there.

"I'm trying," she said. "It's a little challenging to get the aperture just right. Especially when you're moving." She held the camera up. It was a boxy old thing but obviously well made. I'd already seen that a part of the top popped up into a viewfinder and along the side was the little crank for advancing the film.

"Well, I thought your photographs at the gallery were beautiful. You're very good at it."

She nodded. "Thanks. The trick is to capture the real thing, the real person, and not just the image, you know what I mean?"

"Ah," I said. *"Beauty is truth and truth beauty."*

"Exactly," she said, and smiled at me. She lifted her camera again and swiveled around to face me.

"Oh, no, Ariadne."

"Let me take your photo. The light is wonderful just now."

I was still wearing my old jean jacket and I hadn't combed my hair. "But I look awful."

"No," she said. "You just look like Levi."

♫

Surly edged the bus off the E19 down into the center of Antwerp. Antwerp was more than halfway between Amsterdam and Brussels and I think he was ready for a break. More of those gingerbread houses appeared and Surly drove us down into a large square. He pulled the bus over by a sort of park. A fantastic fairy-tale building rose up at the end of the square.

"Right," said Surly. He turned off the engine and stood. He hiked up his pants and grimaced down the aisle at all the sleeping heads. He clapped his hands once, a sharp report. "All right, you lazy sods. If you got the stomach for it, it's lunchtime."

There was a bit of movement in the bus. But not much. Surly reached down and hauled up his cashbox. He set it down on the driver's seat and opened it. Then I saw his expression change. His face went white, then red, and I thought he might be having another one of his seizures. I took a quick glance back at Rudy, but Rudy had dropped his eyes like he was trying to avoid me. People were stirring and you could tell that something was happening. Some thread of tension went wafting through the bus.

Surly scooped up a wad of bills. "Where's the rest of the money?" he barked.

Ariadne blanched a bit. Frankie jerked awake.

Chester was sitting up near the front, quite close to Surly. "Boss," he said. "What's going on?"

Surly leaned down to dig around in the cashbox again. "Someone's nicked five thousand quid from the cashbox."

"Bobby," Chester said. "I really don't think—"

Surly rose up and came down the aisle. He was glaring at me. "Levi. You put the box on the bed when I was . . . when I was . . . Where's my fucking money?"

"I don't know," I said. Ariadne had sunk down a little beside me.

"Don't be cute," he said. "Where is it?"

"Bobby, I don't know what you're talking about."

"Well, it didn't just go traipsing off on its own."

Rudy uttered a low groan at the back, and everyone turned at the sound.

Surly eyed him. "You know something about this?"

Rudy looked around helplessly. "No."

"All right," bawled Surly. "Everybody off the bus. Bring your things with you."

"Oh, Boss," said Chester.

"Everyone out, now."

Frankie sat up. He looked pretty rough. His famous hair was uncombed, and he was unshaven. But still, he looked handsome, like a rugged detective on one of those television shows.

Surly levered open the door and stomped down the steps. He stood waiting just outside the door.

"Bring all your things," growled Surly. "We're going to do a search."

Crap, I thought. *This is going to be bad.*

Frankie lurched up out of his seat. He was shaky, that's for sure. People were milling about, reaching up into the overhead bins, bringing down bags and purses and little packs. Surly stood out there on the grass. The Sisters of Mercy were clutching each other, whispering desperately in Dutch.

Rudy lumbered up the aisle. He sidled into me as I was helping Ariadne get her camera case down. He just stood there looking guilty.

"Rudy," I hissed. "What do you know about all this?"

"Nothing." His backpack was down below in the hold. He just had that stupid fanny pack in his hand.

"Rudy?"

"It was Frankie," he said. "Don't say anything."

"Aw, jeez, Rudy."

We all marched out and stood on the grass in front of Surly, our things arranged in front of us. "That's right," Surly was saying. "Open everything up. Empty your pockets."

"C'mon, Boss. Is this really necessary?" said Chester.

"That was our money, Chester."

"It's not all of it, is it?" I said.

"It's a bloody good chunk of it." Surly had marched over to the Sisters of Mercy. He was having an especially good inspection of their things but nothing was coming up. "Right," he finally said. "You two, fuck off out of here."

The two girls scampered away, off across the park toward the big building at the end of the square. I think it was a train station.

Frankie had lit a cigarette. He had a smirk on his face like he was daring Surly to say something. Surly edged up in front of him. "What do you know about this, champ? You steal my money?"

Frankie took in a long, slow drag. "It's our money."

"It's all of our money," said Surly. "And we need it. Hotel rooms, meals, your fancy fucking clothes. You think this stuff is free?"

Chester was looking at Frankie too. "You take that cash, Frankie?"

"Fuck Surly if he can't keep track of things."

"Christ," said Surly.

"Someone's got to take charge here," said Frankie. "Our manager here seems to have forgotten what's important."

"What's that supposed to mean?" said Surly.

"Someone's got to stand up for us. Someone's got to tell Labyrinth to back the hell off on '29 Streetlights.' "

"What are you talking about?" said Chester. Miguel and even Skinny Dave had kind of formed a huddle around him. "What did you do, Frankie?"

"I'm looking out for us. Someone's got to."

Surly's fists were balled up. I thought he might take a swipe at Frankie. Everyone else just stood still, not making a move, waiting to see what might happen.

Surly checked his watch. "Bloody hell. We've got to go. We can't lose this show. We're going to need every penny now." He shook his head and glared at Frankie. "I'm not done with you. This is not the end of it."

Ariadne had grabbed on to my arm. She stood beside me, shivering.

"All right," said Surly. "Everyone back on the bus. It's another hour to Brussels. We'll figure it out there."

♫

We arrived outside of Brussels at about five o'clock and drove straight to the venue. I'm telling you, these arenas are weird places before shows. Voorst Nationaal was huge, a big sea of cement with maybe five thousand plastic seats rising up in tiers, up into the darkness. It was like a junior hockey arena but bigger, and more of a circle than an oval. I stood out on the floor where they'd be setting up the sound- and light boards. The gear truck had arrived well before us and the guys had already got the scaffolding and PA set up beside the stage. It was kind of strange seeing it all from out front. A whole bunch of guys were swarming around, taping down cables, hauling in our amplifiers, setting up the microphones.

Chester and the guys were in the changing rooms beneath the stands, but I'd already put on my clothes for the show, a kind of frilly shirt and some black velvet bell-bottoms. I was still wearing my Adidas, though. I'd change my shoes later. You can't be walking around in platform shoes all day. It's hard on the ankles.

They were clattering out rows of chairs on the main floor, hauling them out by the dozen on these big pushcarts. It was quite an operation. Other than that, the place was empty of people. It was almost ominous, this vast cement palace and all these empty seats. We had a little while to go before sound check, so I thought I'd have a look around.

Rudy was standing over by one of the exits. I'm not sure why he wasn't up on the stage helping set things up.

"Hey," I called out, and he sort of froze. It looked for a second like he might try and make a run for it, but he didn't. I strode across to him, but he was already looking past me, over my shoulder. And when I turned to see what he was looking at, there was Surly trudging across the floor toward us.

"Stop right there," Surly called.

"Aw, shit," I said.

Surly marched toward us, his pinstripe suit bunching around his shoulders, that vein thing sticking out on his forehead. "All right, you two," he said. "Out. No one else needs to hear this." He followed us out into the corridor that ran around the periphery of the concert venue. There were stalls out there where they sold beer and chips and things, but they were all shuttered. It was still a couple hours before showtime.

"Right," said Surly. "So what do you know about the missing money?"

"Rudy?" I said.

"Crap," said Rudy, and Surly whirled on him. "What? What do you know?"

"It's in the wheel well," Rudy said, his voice shaking. "Behind the right front fender."

"The money?" said Surly.

"Not exactly," Rudy said, and he looked at me for help.

"Then what? What's in the wheel well?"

"About two kilograms of pure cocaine."

"Bloody hell."

"It was Frankie," bleated Rudy. "He bought, like, a ton of cocaine, more than he could ever use, and then he told me to hide it."

"And it's in the wheel well?"

"Jeez," said Rudy. "What was I supposed to do?"

"For fuck's sake, Rudy," I said.

"I know, I know."

"Are you stupid? You gave the cashbox to Frankie?" said Surly.

"No," said Rudy. "You were out of it. We laid you down on your bunk and you were out of it."

Surly snarled. "And you just let him have it?"

"No, I'm not saying that." He backed away a step. "He asked to see it and what was I supposed to say? He took it, just for a moment. I don't know what he did. He turned his back. He was with those girls and they were laughing and—" Rudy looked at me again for help.

Surly advanced a step toward Rudy. He was pretty red in the face. "You're supposed to watch the cashbox."

"Okay, okay," I said. "I'm sure there's an explanation."

"Bloody hell, you think I don't know what's going on here?" said Surly. He glared at me.

"There's nothing going on," I said.

"What's Frankie doing with that coke? Tell me."

"I don't know any more than you, Bob."

Rudy stood behind him. "Am I fired?" he squeaked.

"Christ," said Surly, "don't be such a wanker." He stomped off down the corridor and I knew where he was heading. He was off to find Frankie, in the dressing rooms. And that wasn't going to be good.

♫

Rudy took off the other way. He skittered down the corridor and I watched him disappear up a stairwell.

"Rudy," I called out. "C'mon, man."

I went after him. I was a little angry, if you want to know the truth. I hit the stairwell and it looked like it led up to the seats at the back. I could hear Rudy's footsteps echoing on the stairs ahead of me. I knew he heard me behind him. I kept going until I finally came out on this mezzanine level, high above the arena, at the top of the first level of seats. Rudy stood there at a railing. He was waiting for me.

"What the fuck are you doing?" I said. "I told you, right from the beginning, don't wreck things for me." I was a bit out of breath, and I stopped and bent over a bit.

"I didn't," he said. "Holy hell, Levi. You're supposed to be on my side. You're supposed to watch out for guys like Frankie."

"How am I supposed to watch out for him? He's the main guy in the band."

"And all you want to do is hang around Ariadne, because you're the big rock star now and she's so—"

"Rudy, why did you even come here if you can't do the job?"

Rudy was really rattled. He looked scared as hell. And even though we were a million miles from anybody, he leaned into me and whispered. "Cripes, Levi. I'm here because I'm supposed to look after you. And you're supposed to look after me. Don't you know anything?"

"Why the hell does everyone keep saying that to me?"

"Because you don't know anything. There's tons you don't know."

"There's things you don't know too," I said, but he wasn't listening.

Way down below us on the stage, the PA system hissed to life. You could hear the electricity. Then, with almost a thump, the house lights went off above us. The stage lit up in a pool of purple spotlights and the rest of the arena dropped into darkness.

Far down below us, a figure stepped out onto the stage. It was Frankie, you could tell, even from this distance. "What's he doing?" I said. "We're not going on for another two hours."

"He's probably looking for me," said Rudy.

Way down on the stage, Frankie was marching back and forth. The rest of the roadies had cleared out, sensing trouble. It was just Frankie, all alone, prowling around on that big empty stage.

"Don't you get it?" said Rudy, and I have to admit, I didn't really. He was staring at me, maybe expecting an answer. "He's the guy that's wrecking things. Not me. This was your big chance, Levi. I'm trying to help you here. I'm trying to make you see that—"

"It's okay. You need to relax."

He shook his head and took a deep breath. "Oh, man, Mom's going to be furious."

"Rudy," I said. "I don't think Evelyn has anything to do with this."

"Shows you what you know," he said, and then something inside him kind of cracked. "Fuck, fuck, fuck, fuck."

"Rudy?"

"Okay." He sucked in a breath and tried to calm himself. "Here's the thing."

"What?"

"Shit. I'm not supposed to tell you."

"Tell me what?"

"Evelyn," he said. "It's about Evelyn."

Down on the stage, Frankie was looking off into the arena. He'd shaded his eyes with his hand, like he was scanning the empty seats for us. Rudy kind of yanked me down a little.

"Evelyn," hissed Rudy. "At that competition. This guy came out of the wings and they wouldn't let her play."

"I know that," I said. "But why?"

He risked a look over the railing. The stage lights were still on, but Frankie had gone. Rudy stood up. "Because she was showing, okay? She was, like, seven months pregnant and it was 1953 and you're not allowed to—"

"She was pregnant?"

"It was all this huge scandal. She got pregnant and she wasn't married, and they kicked her out of Juilliard. She lost her chance."

"Aw, shit, Rudy. I'm sorry."

"You're sorry?"

It was suddenly cold up there. The rows and rows of seats lay below us, empty, quiet as ghosts. "It's not your fault, Rudy. I know that ended her career, but—"

"Shit, you think it's my fault? Holy jeez, you're dumb."

"I'm not dumb, Rudy. I just can't read."

Rudy turned away from me. He put his hands on the railing and watched the roadies come back onto the stage. "Cripes," he said. "Do you get it now?" He turned back to me. "Do you see how shitty this is for me?"

"I get it, Rudy. That's super shitty."

"No," he said. "You don't." He shook his head slowly. "You don't get it at all." He just stood there, waiting for me to catch on.

And maybe it was starting to dawn on me. He'd said 1953.

"But—" I began.

"She was seven months pregnant," Rudy pressed on. "And they wouldn't let her play."

"Yeah," I said. "But—"

"And that baby was you," said Rudy. "That baby was you."

♫

Well, holy shit. That was news. Evelyn was my mother. I mean, it made sense. Why the hell else would she be helping me out all the time? And I remember, clear as day, when that junior high band teacher arranged for us to meet. Well, she didn't know. She didn't know who would be turning up. But she took one look at me and even though she hadn't seen me for twelve years, well, she must have known. She probably knew right away who I was.

I should have known too by the look on her face. Only, of course, she didn't say a word. She couldn't. At least not as long as Rudy's dad was alive. But what I didn't get was, why didn't she tell me after he died? What was the big deal about that? Why didn't she just sit me down and tell me? I didn't understand. I really didn't.

Jesus. I did not feel like doing this show, that's for sure. It was nearly time for us to do our sound check. I could see one of the roadies adjusting the lights, and another was already tapping at the mics.

Rudy had disappeared again, making himself scarce, but I didn't have that luxury. I trudged down to the dressing room and stopped at the door before I went in. I took a deep breath and pushed it open. It was a pretty gloomy changing room. Just a cement floor and some benches and lockers and a row of fluorescent lights on the ceiling. Everyone was grouped around Frankie, who sat on one of the benches looking dejected. Surly was hovering over him and a stony silence met me when I entered. Ariadne sat in the corner. She tipped her eyes up at me and nodded, just slightly.

Chester was there, and Miguel and Skinny Dave, all of them clustered around Frankie with Surly just in front. Frankie looked up at me. "Guys," he said. "I did it for you. I'm trying to tell you, we can sell this stuff in Paris for way more than—"

Surly was glaring at him, not saying anything.

"Frankie," said Chester, and he stepped in front. "You took our money. How are we supposed to get paid now?"

Frankie looked up at him. "Chester, my man," he said. "You know I'm good for it."

"No," said Chester. "I'm not sure you are. And what about Miguel here, and Dave and"—he pointed over at me—"you gonna get that money back for them?"

Everyone was grim. It was all super uncomfortable and I glanced over at Ariadne again. She shook her head like I shouldn't say anything.

I stepped forward anyway. "What about Ariadne? Do we have enough money to pay her, at least?"

Frankie pinched up his lips like he hadn't thought of that. "Ariadne," he said. "I'm sorry. If everything wasn't such a disaster, I wouldn't have to—"

"It's all right," she said.

"No, everything is fucked. And nobody is listening to me."

"How much cocaine is it, Frankie?" asked Surly.

"It'd be worth double the price in Paris, Bobby. I'm telling you."

"That's not how we do things, Frankie. We'll have to get rid of it."

"No, that's my . . . That's our money. Why isn't anybody listening?"

"Because you're an idiot," said Surly. "We have to find a way to fix this."

"How are we gonna do that?" said Chester.

Frankie suddenly stood up. He was white as a ghost. He burst past me and fled the dressing room. I think maybe he was crying.

Surly watched him go. It looked like Ariadne was going to go after him but Surly put a hand up to stop her. "Just hold on," he said. "Maybe I've got an idea of what we can do."

"What?" said Chester.

"There's maybe a way to save '29 Streetlights.' "

"What are you thinking, Boss?"

"In Paris," he said. "We'll have a party. A big party, with loads of important people, and we'll just give it all away."

♫

We could hear the crowd coming in. They were opening the gates. We could hear them surging in, filling the venue. It was like a low rumble of thunder. We didn't do a sound check after all. We'd just run out of time. I managed to gulp down a beer, just to calm myself, and then, in no time at all, we were strutting out onto the stage with the lights blazing down and the crowd out front roaring.

All those people thumping up and down, yelling and clapping, and they didn't have the slightest idea how we were feeling up there. I was on autopilot. I hardly moved from my spot to the left of Chester. He kept looking off to the side of the stage, maybe because we weren't sure Frankie would even show.

But he did. He came bouncing out onto the stage like he always did, though he was clutching a bottle of Chivas Regal in his hand. He didn't bother to put it down. He took a big slug from it and went right to his microphone.

And the crowd went nuts. Chester clicked us in, and we started playing. We'd already done this a million times and it wasn't hard. And Frankie, I've got to say, was on fire. That guy lived for the stage. The crowd was going crazy and he egged them on, holding up that stupid bottle, then snatching the microphone out of its stand and strutting across the floorboards like he was a goddamn jungle cat. Jesus, what a showman.

I don't remember much. I remember we played "Someday, Sunday." That one's a slow one, and the stage lights went blue and the crowd settled down. I have to play that one on my acoustic and usually Rudy'd be the one to come out and help me switch guitars. This time there was no one there. I had to dip back into the shadows behind the amps and find the damn thing myself, and when I strode back out, Frankie was sitting at the edge of the stage, like he was on a dock or something. It was strangely intimate.

I plucked out the beginning chords and just let the song drift over me. It's sort of a sad one but bittersweet, you know. Like there is hope. It's one of those songs that's just about ordinary everyday things. But about how they're important too. It's about enjoying the little moments I guess and, I don't know, the crowd just listened and I think they got it.

And that's the thing about music. It goes deeper than other stuff. I looked over at Frankie, and goddamn the fucker, I just felt bad for him. He was trying his best to put on a good show because that's all he knew how to do. That's what he was really good at, and fuck all the rest.

♫

After the show, we filed back onto the bus. It was all a bit of a blur. There'd be no hotel tonight and we'd be driving through the wee hours all the way to Paris. We'd picked up quite a lot of people now, a concert promoter and his crew, a few more groupies, and a couple of overeager roadies. Everyone was drinking and smoking for the first hundred miles or so, talking about the show. There were beer bottles rolling around in the aisles and the skunky smell of joints being lit up, and everyone was happy for a while.

I sat with Rudy. He'd slunk onto the bus when no one was looking. Frankie was so drunk by now that he wouldn't have known if the Queen of England had stepped on board. Ariadne was off by herself too, up near the front, lost in her own thoughts.

Rudy and me didn't say a whole lot to each other. I think he was regretting telling me about Evelyn. He kept glancing over at me, but I ignored him. Really, I was just trying not to freak out. There wasn't much comfort in finding out who my true mom was, not under the circumstances. I mean, obviously I was a mistake, and even more than that, I'd generally fucked up her life. I was the reason her dreams never came true. That was my fault and I wasn't feeling too good about it, that was for sure.

Gradually the partying died down. People started to drift off to sleep, but I was still wide awake and so was Rudy. It must have been about three in the morning. Rudy hadn't got the speakers rigged up yet, but Miguel had a little cassette tape player propped up on the seat beside him. He was sitting a couple seats ahead of us and he was listening to Elton John, the *Goodbye Yellow Brick Road* album. It was about halfway through the first side. The song "Candle in the Wind" was playing. It was sad and beautiful and gentle all at the same time, and that kind of matched my mood. Outside, it was raining, rivulets sliding down the windows, and God knows where we were. Someone said Normandy but all I knew was that we'd crossed over the border and we were somewhere in France.

Frankie was keeled over, up in his usual seat. He'd drunk a whole twenty-six at the show and now he was halfway through a second bottle. He held it tucked into his chest, like a baby, but I couldn't tell if he was asleep or not. It was quiet on the bus now, just the rumble of the engine, the hush of conversations, and the delicate chords of Elton John.

Then Frankie broke the calm. He staggered up out of his seat, and everyone who was still awake turned at the movement, aware that he wanted their attention. Rudy nudged me in the ribs and I saw what he was looking at. Frankie, for whatever reason, was holding up the screwdriver, the same one Rudy had been using. The thing is, he was holding it like it was a knife or something. Like he was going to stab someone. I saw Surly, driving, glance into the rearview mirror, trying to see what was going on behind him.

Frankie growled something and everyone froze. Miguel flicked off the music and Frankie stumbled down the aisle toward us, stabbing at the air with that stupid screwdriver. It was like something out of a slasher film. He stopped at our row and leered down at me and Rudy. Rudy was beside me in the window seat. Frankie was rearing up over me.

"You," Frankie spat, and I couldn't tell if he meant me or Rudy. He was wobbling pretty good and he leveled the screwdriver at Rudy. I don't know how sharp the thing was, probably not at all, but still, I imagine you could do some pretty good damage with it.

"What'd you say to Bobby?" Frankie growled.

Rudy kept his mouth shut. I thought maybe Frankie might still settle down, turn it into a joke maybe. But he glared down at us and then hefted up the screwdriver like he was going to plunge it into something.

"Huh?" Frankie pressed. "What'd you tell him?"

"Nothing," said Rudy.

"You the one who ratted me out?"

"No, Frankie. I didn't think—"

I started to stand up and Frankie jabbed the screwdriver at me. He missed by a mile. In fact, it kind of stuck into the back of my seat, right up near the top, by the pillow part. He yanked it back out and a bit of cotton fluff came wafting out of the hole it made. "Sit the fuck back down," he shouted.

Surly had been watching in the rearview mirror. He slowed and turned the big steering wheel, hand over hand, banking us over to the shoulder of the roadway. He shut off the engine and everything went quiet. We'd pulled up alongside an ancient stone wall and, behind that, an old church, half in ruins, almost lost in the rain.

"Get off the fucking bus," Frankie said. He was holding the screwdriver like a switchblade now.

"Frankie," I tried. "He's with me. I need him."

"Either he gets off the bus or you get off the bus, how about that?"

At the front of the bus, Surly hoisted himself out of the driver's seat. He marched down the aisle toward Frankie. "Jesus Christ, Frankie."

Frankie didn't move, though he'd heard him well enough.

"Why don't you just take it easy here," Surly said.

Frankie still didn't turn back. The screwdriver bobbled in his hand, but I could tell he was listening.

"It's over," said Surly. "The money's gone. We're just going to have to deal with it." Surly caught eyes with me, signaling for me to do something.

"Maybe put the screwdriver down, Frankie," I said. I rose slowly and this time he didn't stop me. "We can figure this out."

"Fuck that," said Frankie. "This fat fucker squealed on me."

"I already knew," said Surly, from behind him. "You think I didn't know who took the money?"

"I want him off the bus."

I tried again. "He'll leave. Right, Rudy? As long as you give me the screwdriver."

"Now," said Frankie. He made another mock swipe at Rudy. "Get off the fucking bus. You're done here."

Rudy stood.

"Just put the screwdriver down," I said.

"You fucking put the screwdriver down."

"I don't have a screwdriver, Frankie. Look, just give it to me, okay?" I was standing in front of him. I wasn't trying to be a hero. I just knew he wouldn't stab me, though he probably did want to plunge it into Rudy. I could see the gauze of drunkenness in his eyes. So I just reached out, as quick as I could, and snatched it out of his hand.

"Hey," he said, and he looked down at his now-empty hand.

Rudy edged past us, his face contorted with confusion. He squeezed by Surly and trundled up the aisle to the front. Frankie watched him go.

"Don't fucking tell lies about me," Frankie snarled after him.

"It's okay, Frankie," I said. "Everything is cool. He's getting off the bus."

I nodded at Surly and he plodded back up to the front, behind Rudy. He swung the lever that opened the folding door. Outside the rain was splattering down. We could hear it pinging on the roof of the bus.

I moved forward too, past Frankie.

"Hey," Frankie said again. His words were slurred. "Where you going?"

"I'm just going to give him some pocket change, Frankie. He needs to go home."

"Fucking right he needs to go home."

Rudy stood all alone at the open door and I walked up the aisle toward him. It was completely silent on the bus. Surly sat down in the driver's seat with a grunt. He just stared out through the windshield, eager to get going again.

I stepped out into the rain with Rudy. We opened the hold and I pulled out his backpack. At least he had that. I gave him some money too. It was, like, twenty British pounds, but it would have to do. He slumped, the shoulders of his T-shirt already darkening with the rain. "The truck is behind us," I told him. "The gear truck. Just wave them down when you see them."

Surly grimaced down at me from the driver's seat. "You coming?"

"Yeah, just a second." It was really raining hard, and I was thinking, this is the shittiest summer ever. "Rudy," I said, and he turned his big brown eyes on me, weary but resigned. "Just watch for the gear truck. It's coming. We'll talk about this later." He shrugged and wrestled up his old backpack. He didn't say anything. He just lumbered off into the rain, hunching under the weight of that stupid backpack.

I climbed back on the bus and Surly closed the door behind me. I smiled awkwardly at Surly. Frankie had slumped back to his seat, his eyes vacant, his fist wrapped around the bottle again. We pulled out and I peered back, but Rudy was almost lost in the darkness. He was walking back along the road, beside the stone wall.

I sat up front for a while with Surly Bob, watching the miles crawl beneath us. We passed through a small village. Everything was stone walls and hedgerows. "Listen," said Surly. He glanced over at me. The bus had quieted. "Maybe we don't give sharp things to Frankie anymore."

"Yeah," I said.

"We just got to keep going, you know. And hope it works out."

"I know," I said. But I really didn't.

Sing, Sing My Song

We came to the outer arrondissements of Paris just after dawn. I thought I might see the Eiffel Tower but there was nothing but train tracks and parking lots and warehouses. Then gradually it changed. The sun was coming up and Surly steered us down a long, wide boulevard with cream-colored apartment blocks on either side. They all had wrought iron balconies and high casement windows and chimney stacks that looked like pipe organs.

I didn't sit with Ariadne. I was still grappling with the fact that Evelyn was my mother, and I didn't think I'd be able to tell Ariadne, or anyone, without bawling like a baby. And then there was Rudy. Shit, just watching him walk off in the rain like that. He was my brother—well, half brother, I guess—and I was hoping he'd got a ride with the gear truck. I was hoping I'd see him at the gig.

We dropped everyone who wasn't in the band at a street corner. There was a big hotel there, and they'd have to fend for themselves. Ariadne stayed with us, of course. And Surly said he had something extra special planned. A bit farther on, he turned the bus down a narrow side road and pulled up in front of a big marble entranceway with ornate ironwork lettering above a glass door.

"L'Hotel," Surly read out loud, and he turned to grin at us like we should all know what it was. The hotel looked nice enough, but I couldn't see anything special about it. "It's L'Hotel," he said again, and he dropped his smile. "This is where all the famous people stay. Oscar Wilde?" he said. "Maybe you heard of Oscar Wilde?"

"Who?" asked Chester.

"Bloody hell," said Surly. He shook his head at us and stomped off the bus.

A doorman stood inside the marbled vestibule and, as we tumbled out of the bus in the early-morning light, his lips pursed in distaste. Ariadne said something to him in French and he tipped his head at her, almost in resignation.

Inside, the lobby was circular—a rotunda, I guess you'd call it—with marble pillars and a high domed ceiling like something from another century. It was pure luxury and Surly had arranged that we'd all be getting our own rooms. I don't know how. I thought we were short of money.

In the lobby Ariadne caught me by the arm. "What was that all about?" she said. "With you and Rudy?" She'd seen everything on the bus, of course: Frankie and the screwdriver and Rudy being marched off in the rain.

"I don't know."

"Levi?"

"I'm sorry," I said, and fluttered a hand at her like I couldn't talk about it right now.

Surly was at the counter and he turned and dangled the first key at her. He was at least gentlemanly enough to let her have the first room. She stared at the key for a moment, then swiped it out of his hand. She looked exhausted, like maybe she'd had enough of us. She cast another glance at me, her whole face a question. Then she hoisted up her things and walked off to the spiral staircase that wound up from the rotunda.

Frankie was being propped up by Chester. He was out of it. I wasn't sure he'd even remember what happened on the bus. We got him booked in next, and Chester more or less carried him across the lobby and into the Oscar Wilde Suite. I'd heard of Oscar Wilde, though I wasn't quite sure who he was. It turned out that he'd actually lived in this hotel for a couple of years, right on the main floor here. Someone said later that Oscar Wilde had died in that suite, but we weren't supposed to tell Frankie that.

The rooms at L'Hotel were not that big but they were elegant. Each one was unique. And when I finally got up to mine, it had walnut paneling along the bottom half of the wall and red embossed wallpaper on the top half. The curtains were a thick velvet with a gold brocade along the edges, and the lamps on either side of the bed looked like antique lanterns.

I headed straight for bed. I didn't even bother to change out of my clothes. I just flopped down onto the covers and was out like a light. I really needed to catch up on some sleep. In just a few hours, we'd be climbing onstage again, trying to pretend we were having the time of our lives.

♫

When I woke up, it was midafternoon. I had a shower, then caught a cab down to the venue. Surly told us these Paris shows were to be the highlight of the tour. We were playing three sold-out nights at Olympia Hall, which was almost a hundred years old. In the dressing rooms there were old black-and-white photographs of cancan girls from the 1930s, and Nazis sitting at tables in the 1940s. They had pictures of Ray Charles and Billie Holliday and even Miles Davis up there on the walls.

The stage was still bare, but Chester was already out there setting up his drum kit. He liked to do that himself. He was down on all fours, adjusting the kick drum pedal. Miguel was sitting on a wooden chair nearer to the front of the stage, playing his old accordion to the empty hall. Beyond him were rows and rows of red velvet seats, and above that, a balcony with more seats disappearing off into darkness.

"Does he always do this?" I asked Chester.

"Most times, yeah, he does."

It was beautiful, what he was playing. Some traditional folk song or something.

When Miguel wheezed out the last note, I nodded appreciatively. "That was pretty," I said. "Did you always play accordion?"

"Yes," he said, and patted at the top of the old accordion. "I call her Gypsy. She belonged to my *abuelo*."

"Ah," I said, though I didn't know what *abuelo* meant.

"My grandfather," Miguel explained. "It would be impossible for him to play in a place such as this. He was a poor man."

"Yeah?"

"But I will play for him, no?" Miguel glanced up at the ceiling, like he was looking to heaven. "Maybe he will see all this and be happy."

That gave me a little lump in the throat. Evelyn would have loved Paris, that's for sure. She would have loved this old concert hall. It was everything she dreamed of, everything she worked for, and I still felt pretty shitty about ruining that for her. I felt pretty shitty about a lot of things. I could see now that that's all Evelyn really wanted for me, just for me to do well, for me to be happy. Her chance was gone but she'd given me mine. And maybe that's all Rudy was doing too. Just trying to help me out. The thing is, I still hadn't seen him. I was starting to think he was lost.

Miguel took off the accordion, sliding the big straps off his shoulders, and he laid it gently into its beat-up case. He nodded at me, then picked up the case and walked off the stage. I watched Miguel go and Chester eyed me from the drum kit. "No sign of your friend yet?"

"Nah. The gear truck came in midmorning, but they said they didn't see him."

"He'll turn up."

"Shit," I said. "Evelyn is going to freak out."

Chester frowned. "Who's Evelyn again?"

"She's my mom," I said, and Chester kind of cocked his head like I'd said something he didn't quite understand.

♫

Things didn't get any better when, an hour or two later, Surly came barging into the dressing room. "Right, you lot," he said. "Gather around. I've got some bad news."

Frankie wasn't there but everyone else was. I had one foot in the leg of my white bell-bottoms, and I had to do a little jig to get the other one in.

Surly considered me. "You gotta look sharp tonight."

"Boss," said Chester. "We always look sharp."

"Extra-special sharp," said Surly. "Your man there, Sir Charles Blackmore, he's come over from London to see the band."

Davey looked up at that. Miguel stroked at his mustache.

"Yeah?" I said.

"It's not good," said Surly. "They're deciding tonight."

"Deciding?" said Chester.

"All right," said Surly, "it's like this. We're late on delivering the album and now they're thinking they might drop us from the label."

"Shit," said Chester. "What about the single?"

"Bloody hell. They're not budging on the length of '29 Streetlights.' They're going to cancel the single too. So you got to be on your toes tonight. We've got to win them back."

And sure enough, Blackmore was standing there when we came out of the dressing room. He was backstage in a shiny silk suit. He ignored us, though, making a show of checking his big clunky watch like he didn't really want to be there. He and Surly were studiously avoiding each other, and it was only when Frankie came along that Blackmore broke into his big fake-tan smile. Frankie nodded back at him and then just walked right out onto the stage. He wasn't supposed to go out yet, and of course the crowd roared when he appeared. Frankie started waving his hands above him, and me and Chester had to scurry out there to catch up with him.

It was all a bit awkward. Frankie stood waiting for us at the front of the stage, already sort of draped over his microphone. I hurried to strap on my guitar, and when Chester saw I was ready, he clicked us in and the whole place detonated.

We were good live, there's no doubt about that. Anything you hear on the records is nothing compared to how we sounded live. We started with "Between Life and Fantasy" and Chester was right away walloping at his drums. Miguel hunched over his keyboards like a mad scientist, and on the far side of the stage Skinny Dave was dancing a bit, shuffling from one foot to the other, which was about the most I'd ever seen him move. Frankie, of course, stalked back and forth across the stage like he owned it, a purple spotlight trailing him around, glistening on his slicked-back hair.

Blackmore was standing off in the wings, watching us. He stood just behind the curtains, an impenetrable look on his face. I knew he was taking it all in, and he couldn't help but nod a little in time with the music. Like I said, we were pretty good live.

Ariadne was offstage too, on the other side, taking photographs. She caught my eye a couple of times and smiled.

When I stepped forward for "Hello Juliet," Frankie swept his hand out in a caricature of invitation. "Time," he said into his microphone, "for someone to do their little song."

I went up and leaned into the microphone at the front. Fuck Frankie, I thought, and fuck Blackmore. This was my moment. I took in a breath and made sure to properly introduce the song.

"A long time ago, I wrote a song about love." My voice boomed through the PA system. It was my voice and yet not my voice. The crowd cheered at the word *love*.

"This was before I even knew what love was. But now I know. Now I know for sure."

The crowd kind of went crazy at that and I made a point of looking over at Ariadne. She blinked up at me, hovering over the viewfinder on her camera, and I'm pretty sure she smiled again.

"Off our next single," I went on pointedly. "This is 'Hello Juliet.'"

Frankie was glaring at me the whole time, but I stepped back and began the little arpeggio, that tinkly little thing that begins the song. The crowd quieted, and this time, I made sure to sing the hell out of it, my voice cracking a couple times, but just where it should, just where it would have the most emotional impact. Miguel's keyboards washed over the melody. And I felt for a moment like I was just floating with the sound, riding the beautiful noise of it. Chester kicked in with the drum fill and the whole thing swelled through the old hall.

It was a moment of pure magic.

I saw a couple of girls in front start to tear up, holding on to each other, swaying to the sound, but best of all was that the lights were dimmed for the song. It was mostly a slow song, and all around the auditorium, the crowd held up their Bic lighters, hundreds of them, thousands of them, and by the time we got to the organ solo, it was like a sea of bootleg stars out there, flickering and twinkling, and at the end, when I sang that last line—the band having died away, just me and my old Martin guitar—well, there was a split second of complete silence like I had stopped time for a moment.

Then the crowd began to roar, a huge thundering ovation, and I stepped back from the microphone and bathed in the light of all those stars.

♫

The next morning, I slept in a bit. I could have lain there all day, except that Rudy was still missing and I really needed to find him. So, I got up, put on my old jeans and a T-shirt, and wandered down the stairs.

Near the front desk, Ariadne was sitting in a high-backed chair. Surly sat across from her and they were talking, discussing something. Her back was to me, so Surly saw me first, his eyes rising over her, clamping onto me. "Levi," he called, and I could see Ariadne kind of freeze.

"Levi," Surly said again. "How's the room?"

"Nice," I said, and went over. "Have you seen Rudy?"

Surly ignored that. He was glaring at me. "You want to tell Ariadne here that she should stay on?"

"What?" I came alongside them, and Ariadne's eyes hooked onto me, wide and imploring. She was wearing a raincoat, a beige one, and out through the front windows, it did look kind of gray.

"She wants to leave the tour."

"But we just got here."

"Christ," said Surly. "That's what I'm trying to tell her. We've got two more nights in Paris and then—" He stopped midsentence. "Listen, the party is planned for tonight."

"What party?"

"The one I told you about," said Surly. "Jesus, Levi. We're in a bit of a spot here. Labyrinth is not happy. And we've got to dump the you-know-what."

Ariadne's mouth went tight.

"Lots of important people coming tonight, so it's all set. And, Ariadne," he turned to her. "We need you there."

"No," said Ariadne. She put her hands up and rubbed at her eyes as if she'd already said this a bunch of times to him. "I'm sorry. I really have to go."

"Bloody hell," said Surly, and all of a sudden he turned nasty. "What? You're going to go running off to your daddy as soon as times get tough?"

She stood abruptly.

"You can't leave," said Surly. "This is exactly what we talked about . . . for your future."

Ariadne didn't look at him. "Things have changed," she said.

"Ariadne," I said, "what's going on?"

"My father. I've spoken with him." She shook her head. "There's been some news from Greece."

"Let me talk to him," said Surly.

"No. You are not to speak to my father." Over by the front desk, the hotel clerk was watching us. Our voices had risen unpleasantly. Surly stood up too. He staggered a bit and sank back down into his chair. He was sweating and his breathing was ragged.

"Bobby," I said, "you okay?"

"Bugger off," he said, and he waved a hand at us. "I'm fine. Just . . . Ariadne, don't leave. Not yet. Really. It's all set for tonight. You have to trust me."

Ariadne considered him. He reached into his suit pocket and brought out those little white pills again. He popped one in his mouth and blinked up at us and tried to smile. "Just think about it, will you?" I could tell it was taking every bit of strength he had to sound conciliatory.

"I don't think so," she said. She looped up the belt on her raincoat, and pivoted, and walked off toward the front doors.

"Levi," Surly croaked. "Go after her."

"Me?"

"Bloody hell, man. Go after her."

♫

I pushed out through the glass doors and turned left. Ariadne was already almost at the corner where the little street turned onto a wider boulevard. The sky was rolling with dark clouds, but I didn't care. I trotted after her and caught up to her on the boulevard. She stopped when she heard me and whirled around. She didn't look happy. "What?" she said. "What do you want?"

"You're leaving?" I started.

"I need to be alone now."

"Ariadne," I said, as gently as I could. "Please don't go."

She heaved a sigh. "Why, why do men always have to make things so complicated?"

"I don't know."

She shook her head slowly. "Listen. It's not about you. It's not even about Bobby."

"Then what? Why are you leaving?"

"All right," she said. She paused and brushed a strand of hair from her eyes. "In Greece. The coup is collapsing. My father wants me to come right away."

A woman walked past us, elegantly dressed. She had a tiny dog on a leash, skittering ahead of her on the sidewalk.

"Things are changing," she said.

"Okay."

"My father is in Cannes. At the villa. But he wants to return to Greece." She sighed. "And he wants me to come with him."

"But is it safe?"

"Look," she said. "Let's just walk. I'll tell you as we go."

Paris, I could see, was a place of very small cars. And the people, men and women both, wore scarves around their necks even in the middle of summer. We passed by a shop with a striped awning. Fruits and vegetables were set out front in tilted wooden bins. I had to walk quickly to keep up with her.

"Ariadne, slow down. I need to tell you something."

She stopped all of a sudden. "Honestly," she said. "What is going on with you?"

"Something's happened," I said, and her eyes wavered on me. "Rudy," I began. "He's my brother. Well, my half brother, technically."

"Rudy?" she said. "What do you mean?"

"I just found out. Evelyn is my real mother." I paused and shook my head. "I didn't even know. My whole life I didn't know . . . though now I guess it's kind of obvious."

"Oh, Levi." She put a hand on my forearm.

"I'm sorry," I went on. "I know you lost your mother, so I shouldn't even—"

"That was a long time ago," she said, and her eyes didn't leave mine. "Are you quite all right?"

"No. Not really."

"Levi, knowing the truth about something should be a good thing."

"Yeah, but she gave me up, right? She never wanted me."

Ariadne's eyes were locked on me. "Are you certain about that?"

"Well, no. But she could have tried."

"I imagine it was incredibly hard for her."

"Probably," I said. "But—"

"And now," said Ariadne, "you know a little more of who you truly are, isn't that right?"

"I guess so."

"And that should be a good thing." She held my gaze for a moment longer and then she said, "Listen, I want to show you something."

"Okay."

She smiled and tugged at my arm, almost playfully, and I followed her across an intersection, down the boulevard. The apartment blocks rose above us on either side, centuries old, stately facades of cream-colored stone. Then after a couple of blocks, the boulevard opened up, quite suddenly, onto the River Seine.

"Holy," I said.

The river was wider than I'd imagined. It cut right through the most ancient parts of Paris, flowing slowly, a kind of greenish blue. Across from us, on the far side, was a massive stone building, ornate, like a palace or something. The banks themselves were walled and all down the river were bridges with arches and statues and iron lampposts. And for the first time I could see the very top of the Eiffel Tower in the distance, hovering there like a dream. All I could think was how much Evelyn would love this, how, if it weren't for me, she might have seen this for herself.

"Down there," she said. "Do you see? It's the *bouquinistes*."

On the sidewalk above the walled banks of the river were green metal stalls, their lids propped open like tiny shops.

"The what?" It sounded like books.

"I'll show you."

And as we got closer, I could see that there were books, all right, tons of them. I felt a little heave in my chest, but she started off toward them and I just had to follow.

Some of the *bouquinistes* had racks of postcards, draping down to the pavement, and there were newspapers hung over wooden dowels like laundry. There were etchings of Paris in another stall, and calendars, but most of all there were books, piles of them, hundreds and thousands of books.

"This is one of my favorite places in the world," said Ariadne. She was beaming, flushed with excitement.

"Yeah?" I said. I was trying to look interested, but this was dangerous territory for me. I couldn't read any of the titles. I imagined most of them were in French, so I thought I could play it that way. If it came to it.

She slowed at one of the stalls, scanning the books. Most of them were little paperbacks, dog-eared, and some of them looked pretty tattered. She nodded at the aproned shopkeeper, who sat beside his stall on a stool. Then she reached for a small book and held it out to me.

"What's this?" I said, and tried to stay calm, to act normal.

"This one," she said, "has some of my favorites."

"Okay," I said, and I took the book from her. I flipped through it quickly. I was pretty sure it was poems.

"Do you have a favorite?" I asked.

"I love them all."

"Sure, but if you had to pick."

" 'Ulysses,' " she said, "by Alfred, Lord Tennyson. That one is a masterpiece." She closed her eyes. *"That which we are, we are; one equal temper of heroic hearts, made weak by time and fate, but strong in will."*

"Oh, that's good," I said, and meant it. I was already trying to memorize it. To hold on to the words in my head.

"I had the most tremendous fight with my father over that one. I wrote my thesis on it, quite convinced it was the greatest poem ever written."

"It's not?" I said.

"Honestly, Levi, I can picture my father now, jabbing his finger in the air, his dark eyes blazing. 'We Greeks invented poetry,' he'd say."

"Yeah?"

She laughed and shook her head. "It was always Homer this and Sappho that."

"But I thought you liked Homer. The wine-dark sea and all that."

"Oh, I do. But I just see things differently from my father. Levi, how can I say this? My father, he sees in pictures. He visualizes everything."

"Well, yeah. He's a film director. He filmed the Rolling Stones."

"That's not what he usually does. Have you even seen any of his films?"

"No, I—"

"He makes things so real. So visceral. If there's a chase, you can feel it, right there in your heart. And he does it all with pictures."

"That's cool."

"And you, you're different. You think in music, right? I imagine you have whole symphonies crashing around in your head."

I nodded. "Something like that."

"I don't think that way. I live for words, Levi. I live for poetry." Her fingers reached for the St. Christopher medal.

"Maybe you should be a writer," I said.

"Maybe I should. Here." She broke away. "I'm buying this book for you. You must have it."

"Oh, I don't know."

But she was already paying the man, and he leaned forward to take a bill from her, digging into his apron for change. She held up her hand to say she didn't need it and he nodded his acknowledgment.

So I was stuck with the book and I didn't know quite what I was supposed to do with it. We began to walk again, along the Seine, and I just held it low, down at my side, hoping she wouldn't mention it again.

We stopped at one of the bridges. "I do like talking with you, Levi. It seems like we understand each other."

"So," I said. "Does that mean you'll stay?"

She laughed gently. "Let me speak with my father again. Maybe I can stay on for the other Paris shows, but then I really must go."

♫

Our second show went even better than the first, and Surly had the party planned for after, back at the hotel. He'd been talking about it like it was a pretty big deal. I thought I heard him say that one of the Rolling Stones might show up.

We were pretty wound up after the concert anyway, so Chester and I went up onto the roof to smoke a jay before the festivities. I'd brought my old guitar up to the roof. I don't know why. I just did. I put the case down and we sat by the iron railing near the edge of the roof, staring off over the rooftops of Paris. In the distance, we could just see the two towers of Notre-Dame.

"Look at that," said Chester. He held the joint out to me. "That place is damn near a thousand years old."

"Cool," I said. And it was. Nothing was that old where I came from. I took a giant inhale on the joint and handed it back.

"No sign of Rudy yet?" Chester asked.

"No. Evelyn is going to freak out."

Chester frowned. "Who's Evelyn again?"

"She's my mom," I said. "And Rudy's mom too."

"Wait. You two are brothers? I thought you said you were in foster care?"

"I don't want to talk about it. At least not now."

Chester eyed me. "Suit yourself." He took another long philosophical toke, then offered the joint to me again.

"Listen," he said. "You ever wonder about why things happen? About how you were born and when you're going to die?"

I blew out. "I think you're stoned, Chester."

"I am, yes. That's why I ask."

"I'm not thinking about death right now, that's for sure. This is about as alive as I've ever been." I gave him back the joint.

He nodded as if he considered that a good answer. He took what was left of the joint and pinched it to his lips. At this point, it was nothing more than a small squeeze of brown-stained paper, though it still had a flickering spark at the end.

"Hey, why don't you play us a little something?" Chester said, then he took a last little hoot on the joint.

I was already lifting my guitar out of its case. I was thinking I could show him that little tune I'd composed back on the ferry. See what he thought of it. And just as I dug out my capo from my case, the door to the roof opened and Miguel stood there in the light, his accordion in one hand, an open bottle of wine in the other. It was like we all had the same idea at the same time.

"Hey there," said Chester, waving him over. "Levi's about to play us something."

Miguel tottered over. I could see he was a little drunk. Chester held what remained of the joint up to him, but he waved it off. Chester shrugged and tossed the roach over the iron railing. It flared for a moment and flittered off into the darkness, six floors down.

I started in on the song, just sort of humming the melody. Miguel grinned and set down his wine bottle. He patted the top of Gypsy, his accordion. It really was a beautiful old thing, shiny blue, with pearl keys on one side and buttons like tiny white marbles on the other. He was watching my hands, working out the chords, and almost right away he started in on it. He closed his eyes and pulled at the bellows of the accordion. A breathy fat chord wheezed out of it and it went along perfectly with what I was doing.

"Nice," said Chester.

Miguel and I played through the chord changes a bit, and I hummed what I thought would be the melody. Then I had an idea. I'd stuffed the book Ariadne had given me down into the little compartment of my guitar case, where the blue ribbon had been. The lid was still open, and I could see it in there.

"Hey, Chester," I said, "pull out that little book there, will you?"

"This?" he said. He reached over and lifted it up, holding it out at arm's length, eyeing it suspiciously.

"Yeah, can you find the poem by Tennyson? 'Ulysses'?"

" 'Ulysses'?" He cocked an eyebrow at me, but he opened the book and scanned the table of contents. "This one by Alfred, Lord Tennyson?"

"Yeah. Yeah. Read us a bit of that."

Chester cleared his throat. "Let's see," he said. *"We are not now that strength which in old days moved earth and heaven."*

"Keep going. What's the part about heroic hearts?"

Chester pinched his lips and studied the book. *"Come my friends,"* he read. *" 'Tis not too late to seek a newer world . . . for my purpose holds to sail beyond the sunset.* Starting from there?"

"Yeah, yeah." I was thinking maybe I could match some of the lines to the music. Maybe we could make it fit. Maybe too I was just stoned, but I thought it was worth a try.

We worked through the lines and I tried them out in the melody, and some of them were really good. Miguel caught on right away and the accordion came alive in his hands, haunting and sorrowful. Chester held up the book, chanting out the lines, and we pieced it together, bit by bit, seeing what would fit and what wouldn't. Seeing if it made any sense at all.

And right there up on that Paris rooftop, we wrote the first full draft of the song. I already knew what I was going to call it: "Wine-Dark Sea." It was perfect and it all just came together in less than an hour.

"That's pretty good," Chester said.

Miguel had been standing the whole time, swaying with his accordion. "Yes," he said. "I am liking it very much."

"You got a particular fascination with this Tennyson fellow?" Chester asked.

"It's Ariadne's favorite."

"So this song is for her?"

"Maybe," I admitted.

"Boy's got moves," said Chester appreciatively. He laid the book back down in the case.

"It's not for the Exits," I said. "It's not their style."

"It is true," said Miguel, and he patted his accordion again.

"We're good," I went on. "Maybe we don't even need Frankie. Maybe we should form our own band."

Chester scrunched his lips together. "I've been meaning to talk to you about that, Boss."

"What?"

"The contract you signed, it says—"

"I had to sign it. I didn't have a choice."

Chester considered me. "No need to get defensive. I'm just saying you should have read it first."

My face must have blanched.

"The thing is, they got us locked up pretty tight."

"And what's that supposed to mean?"

"It means we can't do diddly-squat without Blackmore's permission. We can't really be writing our own songs."

"Aw, fuck that."

Chester shook his great head. "You can say whatever you like, Levi, but I'm telling you, they got us locked up tight." Far down below us, taxicabs were pulling up to the front door of the hotel, one after another, and scatters of people were going inside. "Hey," he said. "Who exactly is supposed to be coming to this little soiree tonight?"

"I don't know. Mick Jagger maybe. Or Keith Richards."

"Well, shee-it. Maybe we best go down and meet our competition."

"I will leave now," Miguel said. He picked up the bottle of wine from where he'd left it.

"You're not coming to the party?" said Chester.

"It is not for me," he said, and he turned and headed for the rooftop door.

"How about you?" asked Chester.

"Fuck yeah, I'm in." I took one last glimpse at the Paris rooftops and packed away my guitar.

♫

A staircase wound down through all the floors, all the way down to the lobby. It had curving iron banisters and a bloodred carpet runner, and on each of the landings there were massive mirrors in ornate frames. I glanced in one as we passed by. My hair was much longer now, a sort of dirty blond. And I thought, *Yeah, I do look like a rock star. I look like a fucking rock star and I don't care what anyone thinks.*

When we got down to the lobby, Surly stood outside the Oscar Wilde Suite. We could hear music inside. It was a David Bowie album, the *Ziggy Stardust* one.

"Evening, gents," he said. "You're a bit late."

"Boss," said Chester, "we're musicians. We're always late."

"We got all the radio guys in there, disc jockeys, music programmers. So no drama, all right?" He kept looking past us, at the front door, like he was waiting for someone.

Chester frowned. "You really think the Rolling Stones are coming?"

Surly glared up at him. "You just wait," he said. "You'll see."

In fact, a car had just pulled up outside. Surly made a little noise in his throat. It was a long black limousine and the doorman was already hopping out, across the sidewalk, to open the door.

I turned to see Sir Charles Blackmore climbing out of the back.

"Aw, hell," said Surly.

Chester didn't move. "That's not the Stones."

"Jesus, no," said Surly, and he pushed at Chester. "Get inside. Quick. I'll head him off."

Surly reached for the door and opened it. The music swelled and we entered one of the most dazzling rooms I've ever seen. It was a pretty big suite, but it was packed, wall to wall, with people. Frankie was sitting cross-legged on the king-sized bed in the middle of it all. Above him, on the wall, was a mural. It had a green background, like felt, and was embossed with dancing golden peacocks. I'm not kidding. Their tails curled out across the green background like fine lines of filigreed gold. Jeez, it was like being in a sultan's tent or something. And on the opposite side of the room, there was a door that led out onto a sort of garden terrace. Ariadne was out there, taking pictures.

I started to make my way through the crowd toward her, but there was quite the party going on. There were guys in suits and others in jeans, some girl in a fur coat and another in almost nothing. Some of the people were sitting on the carpet at the side of the bed. A few more stood by the walls. One guy in a suit was doing lines off the top of an antique reading desk. There were bottles of booze on almost every surface.

Frankie spotted us and beckoned us forward like it was a royal audience. "Hey," he called over the music. It was still the David Bowie playing. I edged through the crowd with Chester, and Frankie plucked up a little envelope from the bed and offered it to us.

"Nah, man," Chester said. "You know I don't do coke."

"It's a party," said Frankie. "Live it up a little. Levi, how about you?"

"No thanks, Frankie."

"C'mon, take it." He thrust it at me. "A little token of my appreciation."

"I don't want it, Frankie." I was thinking he had some nerve. He'd stolen our money and spent it all on coke and now he was doling it out like candy. I looked around the room and almost everyone had one of these little packages. It was obvious what he was doing. Most of these guys were radio people, or at least that's what Surly had said.

"Last chance," Frankie went on. He held my gaze for a moment longer before laying the envelope back down on the bed. "Then fuck it. I don't need you anyway."

"What's that supposed to mean?"

"That I can do just fine on my own."

Outside, on the terrace, I saw the flash of Ariadne's camera going off. She looked in at me and waved, and I was about to say something when I heard the door open behind me. The room suddenly went quiet. Someone turned off the music and Blackmore stood just inside the entrance. A few people got up from the floor, dusting themselves off. The guy at the reading desk stood up and wiped at his nose.

Blackmore marched into the room, and the crowd parted for him. He wore a light gray suit with a burgundy scarf. He looked like somebody's rich dad. He stood at the foot of the bed, staring down at Frankie. No one was saying a word.

Surly stood in the open doorway behind him.

"Frankie Novak," he said, and obviously he saw all the little packets of cocaine. "What is going on here?"

Frankie swung his feet over the edge of the bed. He rose up, a little unsteadily. " '29 Streetlights,' " he said. "I'm making everyone promise that they'll listen to it."

Blackmore grimaced and cast a glance back at Surly, who stood unmoving in the doorway. "This is highly unethical."

"I'm just giving everyone a little incentive," said Frankie. He was smirking at Blackmore. "Maybe they'll play a longer song after all."

"It's illegal," Blackmore said. "It's payola."

"C'mon," said Frankie. He was pretty stoned. "It's a party."

The room had gone awfully still. The guy at the reading desk had already surreptitiously dropped his little envelope into his suit pocket, and almost everyone was waiting, deferentially, to see what Blackmore might do.

Another flash went off. Ariadne was at the door to the terrace. I don't think she realized exactly what was happening.

"I will have to ask your young lady there to stop taking photos." Ariadne had just stepped into the room. She'd just raised her camera to take another photo of Blackmore. She stopped when she saw his expression.

"Do you not understand?" said Blackmore, turning back to Frankie. "People go to jail for payola schemes. I could go to jail."

"No," said Frankie. "It's just—"

Blackmore signaled for Surly to come forward. "Perhaps we can clear the room," he said.

"C'mon," pressed Frankie, " '29 Streetlights' is me and Pete's last song together." He was really stoned, and he was struggling to understand what was being said. He looked a little crestfallen, really, and I almost felt sorry for the guy. Almost.

"We don't come from rich families, not like you," Frankie went on. "This song could make bundles of money. For you and for me, and for Pete . . . Well, Pete's family, I guess. They're nice people." Frankie looked around the room, like he was looking for someone to back him up. Ariadne managed a smile for him. "They're good people. And Pete's share will—"

"Mr. Malone," said Blackmore. You didn't often hear Surly called by his real name. "Would you like to explain something to our little friend here?"

Surly had come in to stand by me and I could almost feel him sweating.

"Explain what?" asked Frankie.

"Well," Surly began, "the thing is, Pete's royalties, they—"

"They what?"

"They won't be going to his family."

"It's all very clearly laid out in the contract," said Blackmore.

" 'In the event of death,' " Surly quoted, " 'the songwriter's royalties revert wholly to the publisher.' "

"What?" Frankie's voice sounded very small.

"We will be collecting his half of the royalties," replied Blackmore, and he jutted out his chin, like he knew what he was saying was unpleasant but he was going to say it anyway.

"Nothing goes to his family?" said Frankie.

"A contract is a contract, Mr. Novak. You will continue to receive your share of the songwriting royalties, of course, but the other half automatically transfers to our publishing arm. I'm sure you understand."

Frankie's face had really fallen now, and Blackmore tried a conciliatory smile. "But, please, everybody," he said. "We at Labyrinth are proud of Downtown Exit, with or without Peter Gunnerson, and I'm sure—"

"Fuck you," Frankie said. All eyes swiveled back to Frankie. His face was a broken mess. With everyone watching him, he jumped from the bed and charged past us and out of the room.

And then I did feel bad for him. Frankie sure as hell wasn't an easy person to like, but he obviously had a bit of a conscience, at least when it came to Pete. It made me think of Rudy again, who was supposed to be taking care of me. Or was I supposed to be taking care of him? I didn't know anymore. I just knew that he was lost, somewhere in the north of France.

Ariadne was standing just inside the door to the terrace, her camera in her hand. She looked terrified. She glanced at me and then she bustled out of the room after Frankie.

"Ariadne," I said, but she was already gone.

♫

The party picked up again once Blackmore had left, but it didn't seem so celebratory anymore. The Stones never showed up, that's for sure, and everything gradually died out. It was maybe three or four in the morning when everyone was finally gone, and it was just down to me and Chester.

I was sitting on the edge of the bed and he'd gone over to pick through the bottles on the reading desk. I'd already drunk most of a bottle of tequila by myself and was pretty out of it.

"You think they got any Tab in here?" Chester said.

"I doubt it."

He clinked around and drew up a bottle of Jamaican rum. He turned around to show it to me.

"I'm kinda done," I said.

He looked down at the bottle. "But there's no Tab," he said, and his face twisted up.

"Chester?"

He put the bottle down, but slowly, like it was really hard. “I used to drink a lot,” he said. “I told you about my kids, Levi, but the truth is, I left them. I ran away with this pretty young thing. Took me a long, long time to recover from that little dalliance.”

“Was she pretty?”

“Shee-it, Levi. That girl damn near killed me. That and the drinking.”

“And you don’t see your kids anymore?”

“They wouldn’t know me from a hole in the wall. I should never have run away.”

“People shouldn’t run away,” I said. “You got to stick it out for the ones you love.”

“You know, Boss, you’re smarter than people give you credit for.”

“Thanks.” I set my tequila bottle down on the floor. “Maybe,” I said. “Maybe we ought to smoke another of your famous doobies instead.”

“Yeah, you’re probably right.”

Chester drew out a little baggie from his pants pocket. There wasn’t much left, just twigs and seeds and a bit of green dusty powder at the bottom. He dumped it out onto a rolling paper and rolled up a pinner, licking the edge of the paper to seal it.

He came over to where I was sitting and stopped for a moment to consider the peacock mural above the bed. “You really think Oscar Wilde died in this room?” He lit the thin joint and took a big draw on it, still squinting up at the mural.

“Probably.”

Chester nodded. He held the smoke in for a moment, then slowly exhaled. “Surly said he drank himself to death.”

“Oscar Wilde?”

“Yeah.” Chester sat down on the bed beside me. He handed me the joint. “So listen,” he said. “The reason I was asking before, about birth and death and stuff.”

“Jeez, Chester. You’re kind of wigging me out here.”

“It’s Frankie. He’s troubled. I’m worried about him.”

I took a hoot on the joint. I didn’t really want to hear this.

“He’s got himself so tangled up I don’t think he even knows who he is anymore.”

"He's a mess, all right," I said.

"Levi," Chester said. "I don't think you get it. If something happens to him, we're in trouble. You know what I mean?"

"Chester, can't we just enjoy ourselves for a change?"

"I'm just saying," he said. "If Frankie goes down, we all go down."

And right on cue, the door cracked open and Frankie came sweeping in.

"Hey!" he said, spreading his arms wide. He was exhilarant, all coked up, and he careened into the room. Ariadne appeared in the doorway behind him. She held on to the doorframe to steady herself. Her camera still dangled from a strap across her shoulder. She looked a bit pale and I was surprised she was still up.

"You okay?" I said to her. I rose up onto my feet.

"I am extraordinarily drunk," she said, and grinned. "And I think I must go to bed."

"No, no," said Frankie. He reached back and tugged her into the room.

"Frankie," she protested. "It's almost morning."

"Here," he said, and he steered her over to the upholstered chair in the corner. She sat down with a sigh.

"Where have you been?" I said.

She wobbled her eyes up to mine. "We went for a drink," she said, and she giggled a bit and held a finger up to her lips.

Frankie laughed, a bellow that was overblown and unnecessary. "We've had the most wonderful chat," he said.

"A chat?" I said.

"Honestly," said Ariadne. "I think things are going to be okay now. Frankie has promised to stop drinking and—"

"Not until later, my dear. This is our last hurrah. It's finally just us. It's finally time."

Chester swung his big numb face toward him.

"We're going to have a séance," Frankie announced.

"Aw, c'mon, Frankie," I said.

"No," he said. "I've been waiting all night for this." He skipped across to the reading desk beside Ariadne and plucked up a delicate silver candleholder, like a little Aladdin lamp. It even had a long thin candle tapering up out of it.

Frankie lifted it. "Look," he said. "It's perfect."

"I don't think—" I began.

"We'll talk to the dead. And who should be first?" He glanced up at the mural. "Oscar Wilde?" He was really very high, exuberantly so. He clapped his hands like he'd suddenly had a thought. "Or, no, no, we should bring back Jim Morrison. You like that, Levi? Jim Morrison? He's buried in Paris, you know. I know exactly where."

Chester's eyes hovered up to mine. "See?" he said. "Our boy's not right in the head."

Ariadne was falling asleep in the chair, her eyelids half shut. Her camera was tucked under her arm, but her head was drooping to one side.

"Or maybe I should talk to Pete," said Frankie, and his face drained of its glow. He suddenly became very serious. He set the candle down on the bed beside Chester. Chester struggled to get up. After a couple of attempts, he managed to hoist himself onto his feet. The little silver lamp swayed a bit on the bed when his weight left it, but the candle stayed upright. Frankie worked a book of matches out of his shirt pocket. He lit a match and cupped it and set it to the candle. We all stood there for a few moments, watching the candle flickering on the bedspread, and it was kind of beautiful, if you want to know the truth, just this little wisp of flame, kind of blue right at the wick.

"Are we supposed to say some words?" I said. Ariadne's eyes had closed completely. I think she was asleep. Frankie was frozen, mesmerized by the candle. He didn't say anything. It was Chester who made it fall. He sat down again on the edge of the bed and it was enough to make the candle wobble. A little gloop of wax went rolling down the side of the candle, and then all at once it toppled over.

We all saw it, but nobody moved to right it. The flame flickered for a moment, then caught on the bedspread, just a little circle at first, and still we just stared at it, dumbstruck, too drunk or stoned to do anything about it. There must have been something flammable in the bedspread, because it started to spread pretty quickly.

"Frankie," I managed. "The candle."

"That's Pete," he said. "I think he's angry." His pupils were the size of dimes.

"The bed's on fire," I said.

"Shit," said Chester, and he stood up. He shook his head at the flames and lurched out of the room. I could hear him stomping out into the rotunda, back toward the stairs.

"Ariadne," I called. Her eyelids fluttered and opened. I bumbled across the room and put a hand under her forearm. "We have to go."

The room was already starting to fill with smoke. She rose unsteadily to her feet, blinked a couple of times, and wrinkled her nose at the smell. "What's going on?" she said.

"We have to go," I said. "We have to go now."

Falling Up

I woke up the next morning in the bathtub, naked, with very little memory of how I got there. A frantic knocking was coming from the door.

"Hold on," I said, and I sat up. My head was throbbing.

"Levi," I heard through the door. It was Ariadne. I stood up and grabbed one of the big fluffy hotel towels, wrapping it around my waist.

"Levi, open up."

"Just a second." I checked myself in the mirror and a sorry mess of a face looked back, wan and unshaven, with squinty bloodshot eyes. I opened the door anyway and Ariadne barged in. She was fully dressed, and she was tying the belt around her beige raincoat, ready to go out.

"Frankie is missing," she said, "and my camera is gone."

"What?"

"Frankie's gone and so's my camera."

She shot past me into the room. I cinched the towel a little tighter around me. And she turned, seeing me for the first time. "Did you happen to pick it up last night?"

"I don't think so," I managed. The events of last night started to come to me then. The after-party, the séance, the fire. Shit. The alarms going off and everyone out on the street in their pajamas. Only after the fireman had put out the blaze did we trundle back to our rooms. Then I think I drank some more. So stupid.

She paused long enough to consider me. "You look frightful," she said.

"I don't feel so hot."

"Where is everyone? I knocked on some of the other rooms. They're all empty."

I stood before her, acutely aware of the fluffy towel around my midsection. "Maybe I better get dressed." I pulled a T-shirt and some jeans out of my little duffel bag. It wasn't easy with one hand clinging to the towel, trying to hold it around me. As I went past her, back to the bathroom to change, the phone began to ring, a bristling insistent jangle.

"Would you like me to answer that?"

"Yes, please. Make it stop."

I closed the bathroom door, but heard her answer and then her side of a very short conversation. By the time I'd changed and come out, she'd already hung up.

"Who was it?"

"The front desk. There's a message for you."

"The front desk?"

"Levi," she said. "Can you please focus? My camera is gone. I must have left it in Frankie's room. And Frankie is missing."

"Okay, okay," I said.

I was starting to remember more now, and oh, shit, I knew we were in a whole bunch of trouble.

♫

It must have been about ten by the time Ariadne and I stumbled down the stairs. Sir Charles Blackmore stood there in the lobby. He was dressed in his flashy suit and he did not look at all happy.

"Mr. Jaxon," he said. "Do you have any idea where Frankie might be?"

Across the lobby, the door to Frankie's suite was open. It looked pretty bad in there. I saw a policeman rummaging around, maybe taking fingerprints or something. And on the other side of the lobby, Chester and Miguel and Skinny Dave all sat together, pressed into a couch. Chester shrugged at me.

"He's vanished," Blackmore said. Ariadne came up behind me and Blackmore considered her, his mouth creasing into a grimace. A lingering stench of smoke hung in the lobby.

"Right," I said. "Give me a second. I have a message at the—" I pointed to the front desk. The guy there was scowling at me, waiting, and when I went over he lifted a piece of paper.

"You are Levi Jaxon?"

"Yes, that's me."

"You have a phone call from Evelyn Wheeler."

"Okay," I said. She'd probably heard about Rudy. *Shit, shit, shit.*

The guy eyed me. He was being a bit snotty, if you ask me. "You are to phone her back. Immediately."

"I will. As soon as I'm not hungover anymore."

"Mr. Jaxon," Blackmore called from behind me. He was shaking his head, impatiently. "We have more important matters to deal with."

"What?" Really, I was getting pissed off at the guy.

"As you can see," said Blackmore, "there has been considerable damage to Frankie's room."

Ariadne was hovering at his side. "Please, Mr. Blackmore," she said. "My camera is missing. I think we may have left it in there."

Blackmore turned to scowl at her. "Let me remind you, young lady, that you do not have permission to take photographs, especially incriminating ones."

"Pardon me?" she said.

He shook his head. "I must insist that you—"

He didn't finish. Surly came barreling out of the suite. He headed straight toward us. "Where the bloody hell is Frankie?" he bawled.

"How am I supposed to know?" I said. Jesus, my head was really throbbing.

Surly glared at me. "What exactly happened in there?"

"Nothing, I—"

Blackmore harrumphed. "Mr. Malone," he said. "The fact is, you are all being asked to leave the hotel. The damage is considerable and if you are very lucky they will not press charges."

"My camera," insisted Ariadne. "It's a Hasselblad. Please. If I could just check in the room."

"It's not in there," Surly said. He studied us a moment longer, then plunged off up the stairs.

"Do you think Frankie might have it?" Ariadne said.

"Frankie Novak is missing," Blackmore said. "And there has been a fire in his room. In the Oscar Wilde Suite, of all places. The situation is quite intolerable."

Ariadne threw me a look like I should step in here. I hooked my hand under her elbow and faced Blackmore. "Can we go now?" I said.

Blackmore raised an eyebrow. "You will need to clear the things out of your room," he said. He was going to say something more, but a commotion was building outside the front doors and the doorman was looking over at us. The man at the front desk too had bent forward over the counter, trying to see what was happening outside.

Out through the glass doors, past the vestibule, a crowd had gathered on the sidewalk. Paparazzi, it looked like. I could hear them calling for Frankie, and they were bunching forward with their cameras, almost to the doors.

Blackmore strode over to the glass doors, brushing past the doorman. Blackmore looked imposing, that's for sure. He pushed through the door, and the sound of the reporters poured in through the open doorway. They were yelling out questions. Some in French, some in English. "Gentlemen," I could hear Blackmore say. He raised his hands to quiet them.

I leaned into Ariadne. "I think I know where Frankie is," I whispered. The doorman was watching us. He was still holding the door open behind Blackmore as if he was expecting us to go out behind him.

"Where?" asked Ariadne. I walked her to the door, but Blackmore was blocking the way. He had his back to us, and he was pumping his hands, trying to quiet the ruckus. A flashbulb went off and I was momentarily blinded by its light.

"We have no comments at this time," Blackmore announced. "But I can assure you—"

One of the paparazzi said something in French. "Why are the police here?" another called out. He wore a fedora like a private eye in an old Hollywood movie. "Is Frankie Novak dead?"

"Of course not," Blackmore said. "Downtown Exit has a new album coming out. He can't be dead."

We tried to slide by Blackmore, but he wasn't budging. The reporter in the fedora saw us.

"Who are they?" he asked, and a jumble of voices came in behind him.

"Nobody important," said Blackmore. He pursed his lips at us just as we sidestepped him. Another flashbulb went off. "Hold on a moment," he said. He made a grab for my arm but we were off. We sank into the swarm of reporters and pushed through them and out the other side. We just kept moving at a quick trot, without looking back. When we got to the end of the street, Ariadne stopped, her eyes wide. "Where are we going?"

"The cemetery," I said.

She stopped cold. "Pardon me?"

"Frankie. He's gone to the cemetery."

"Of course," she said. "Père Lachaise."

And then we both said it together. "Jim Morrison's grave."

♫

We hurried along, left, up the boulevard. "Do you think they'll follow us?" she said.

I risked a glance back. "I think we're in the clear. Crap. Did you see Frankie's room?"

"Are you quite certain my camera's not in there?"

"They said it wasn't. Maybe Frankie took it."

"I can't afford to lose it. I can't." She shook her head and wouldn't meet my eyes.

At the end of the block were some steps leading down under the street. Above the entrance, wrought iron lettering spelled out a name in a kind of art nouveau design. I guess I was staring at it. It was in French, obviously, but still, Ariadne glanced at me sideways. "*Métropolitain*," she read. "It's the Métro station."

"I know," I said. "But is it the right station?"

I could feel the rush of air coming up the steps. "We can start from any station," she said, and looked at me oddly. "But we may have to change lines a few times."

"Okay."

"Are you quite all right?"

"I'm fine. Let's just go."

She studied me for a moment more and then we bustled down into the darkness. By the time we got to the platform, I was surprised to find she was holding my hand. She didn't let go either. Not until the train pulled into the station.

♫

The train shunted through the tunnel, the fluorescent lights buzzing and flickering overhead in the car. The inside walls of the train were spray-painted with graffiti, some even on the seats, mostly unintelligible black squiggles. Ariadne's fingers went to her St. Christopher medal as she studied the Métro map above the doors. It was a maze of colored lines and numbers and station names in French.

We went around a curve and the brakes squealed. The lights kept flickering above us. We rumbled into the next station, and Ariadne put a hand on my knee to tell me that this was not our stop. Honestly, I still felt pretty crappy, and I don't think she felt very chipper herself.

I tried to smile. "We'll get your camera back. I'm sure of it. Maybe Frankie has it. Probably he does."

"I'm worried, Levi. Frankie is out of control."

"I thought he promised he was going to quit."

"Yes, after one last binge."

"You figure he's still on it?"

"He has a whole satchel full of drugs. Enough to kill him." She paused. "And where do you suppose he might choose to—?"

"Wait. What are you saying?"

"You know what I'm saying."

"Oh, shit."

"So, we have to hurry."

Our train ground into the next station. Ariadne eyed the map above the doors just before they swished open. "We change here," she said.

A few stops down the next line, we got off the train. We tramped up the steps from the Métro, blinking in the daylight, getting our bearings, and just down the street, the marble gates of Père Lachaise Cemetery rose up. The sky hung low, gray, and sullen, and we didn't talk.

We were walking quickly now, and we passed in through the gates, and holy shit, it was spooky in there. The path was lined on either side with creepy-looking trees. And tucked between them were tombs, tons of them, like little stone temples.

Ariadne led the way. She seemed to know where she was going, and at one intersection in the path she stopped and sniffed at the air. She wrapped her raincoat more tightly around her. "This way," she said.

I caught the whiff of marijuana too. We went up a little incline and the pathway was lined with more old tombs, marble things with iron gates and peaked roofs. Ariadne slipped off between two of them, stepping onto the grass. I followed and we came out in front of a small square grave squeezed between a couple of bigger ones. The headstone was simple, just a roughly chiseled block of stone. On top of it were a couple of half-burned candles and an empty bottle of wine.

Embossed on a copper plate set in the tombstone was the name. "'James Douglas Morrison,'" Ariadne read. "'1943 to 1971.' And look," she said, "the inscription under his name. It's in Greek."

"Can you read it?"

"Of course I can. I'm Greek."

"Well, what does it say?"

She studied it for a moment. *"According,"* she translated, *"to his own demons."*

"Whoa."

"No, but the meaning is not—" She shook her head. "It's not the same in English. It means something more like *True to his own spirit.*"

"Do you think Frankie was here?" I asked.

"If he was, where is he now?" Ariadne's brow furrowed and she looked around.

"Do you hear that?"

Someone was coming. I could hear a guitar being played and a jumble of footsteps coming through the tombs from the other way. The music drew closer, and Frankie sauntered in, strolling along like the Pied Piper of Hamelin with a small crowd, maybe a dozen people, all marching in behind him. He was strumming on a slightly out of tune acoustic guitar.

I didn't even know he could play.

"Ariadne," Frankie called out. It was clear he hadn't been to bed yet. He looked awful, his face drained of color, his eyes bloodshot and puffy. I guess he'd just kept going all this time, wired to the gills. He held up the guitar triumphantly. "And my old pal Levi."

The fans crowded in behind him. "Play another one," someone said.

Frankie plunked down hard on the edge of Jim Morrison's tombstone. "I know a song," he said, and he flashed a smile at Ariadne.

"No," she said. "Don't play that one."

"Which one?" I said.

"We wrote a song together," said Frankie. "Didn't she tell you?"

Ariadne looked sheepishly at me.

"You what?"

"I only helped him with the lyrics."

"Show him your notebook, Ariadne." His vacant eyes drifted back to me. "She keeps her poems in there."

Crap. I was an idiot. I was the one who told her she should be a writer, when she already was. And of course she'd be writing lyrics. I just didn't know she'd be writing lyrics for Frankie. I hadn't thought of that at all.

Frankie began a song in E minor, a bluesy thing, deep and sorrowful. The crowd hushed. I have to say it was beautiful. And Frankie was not half bad on guitar. He closed his eyes and sang, gruff at first, like a sideman in a smoky bar, then his voice gathered strength and he rang into a chorus that shook my spine.

"Without love, the lost don't ride. I've seen heaven from the other side."

"Jesus," I said. Ariadne clutched my arm. Someone started to cry.

Frankie played on, this amazing song, and at one point, a girl came forward tentatively. She'd brought a bouquet of flowers and she laid them at Frankie's feet. There wasn't a lot of room. Really, Jim Morrison's grave was kind of small and crammed in between a bunch of bigger ones. Everything was gray and bleak.

No one clapped when Frankie finished the song. There was a solemn hush and a raindrop fell from the sky. It plopped on the tomb beside us. Then another one came down. An umbrella popped open. Ariadne pulled up the collar of her raincoat. She held out her hand to test the drops. "Frankie," she said, and he struggled to focus on her.

He stood gingerly. He passed the guitar to a frail young man with very long hair. It must have been his. Frankie had gone a strange color, as if he might be sick.

"Can you walk?" I asked.

His head bobbed up. "No, but I can sure as fuck sing."

"I know you can, Frankie."

He smirked at me, and Ariadne took his arm to support him. I swung around to the other side and hooked my arm through his.

Frankie's eyes wobbled across to me. "Come to rescue me, have you? The great white knight coming to save the day?"

"C'mon Frankie," I began.

He turned to Ariadne. "Did he tell you his little secret yet?"

"Jesus, not now, Frankie." We were on the pathway now. I could see the gates in the distance.

"What's he on about?" Ariadne said.

"Ha," said Frankie. "You don't have the balls to tell her."

Goddamn it. I wanted to hit him, just to shut him up.

"He can't read. The dumb shit never learned how."

I stopped in my tracks. I felt almost sick to my stomach.

Ariadne's eyes had gone wide. "Is that true?"

"Can we maybe just talk about this another time?"

"Levi?"

"Yes, yes, it's true, all right? Can we talk about it later?"

"Okay," she said.

We continued on in silence. I looked over at her a couple of times, but she didn't look back. *Goddamn it.* The other people had mostly scattered in the rain. A few followed us out through the marble gates. They ambled off toward the Métro with awkward goodbyes. One of the girls lingered, but not the one who'd brought the bouquet. She said, "I love you, Frankie," and he tipped his head in agreement. She looked sad and turned to follow the others across the street to the station.

Ariadne put up her hand to hail a taxi, and almost immediately, a cab swung up to the curb in front of us. We clambered into the back, the three of us, Frankie trembling and barely able to sit up.

Ariadne sighed and said the name of our hotel to the cabdriver. Frankie's head drooped down. "Frankie," Ariadne said. She nudged into his shoulder and said his name again a little more sharply, and he blinked and gaped at her, bleary-eyed.

"Do you know," she enunciated, "where I might find my camera?"

"Camera?" he slurred.

"Bobby said it's not in your room."

"That Bobby." Frankie began to chuckle. "What a clown."

"Frankie," I said. "This isn't funny."

"Bobby has it. I saw him carrying it up to his room after . . . everything happened."

"You're sure?" Ariadne asked.

"They were fighting over it," he said. "Blackmore was trying to get the back open, to rip out the film. I don't think he liked your photos."

"But Bobby has my camera?" pressed Ariadne.

"And why wouldn't he tell us?" I said.

"I don't know," said Frankie. "I'm just telling you what I saw. Blackmore sure didn't like those pictures."

♫

At L'Hotel, the doorman came at us. *"Non,"* he said, putting up his hands. *"Non, non, non."*

Ariadne spoke to him in French. And, no big surprise, we weren't allowed in. The Exits were banned from the hotel, forever. Ariadne translated, saying that they'd moved our luggage up the street to another place. At least the rain had stopped.

"Frankie," I said. We were propping him up between the two of us. "We still have a show tonight. You have to get your shit together."

"Fuck that," he managed.

I glared over at Ariadne. "This is the guy you gave your lyrics to?"

"No. I said I helped him with the lyrics. He needs help, if you must know."

"No kidding."

Frankie thumped between us. He let out something like a laugh.

"Levi," she said. "I don't care anymore. I just want the camera back."

We'd gone down a block or two. "Do we even know where we're going?" I said. But before she could answer, I heard someone calling out my name. It was Chester, standing there at the end of the boulevard, waving, his shape unmistakable. He must have been watching for us. He came loping toward us, which was good because Frankie was almost completely deadweight now, his shiny shoes dragging on the pavement, his head bobbing like a partially deflated balloon.

Chester swung in and took over from Ariadne. "What's up, my man?" Chester gave a little heave and took over most of Frankie's weight.

"He's out of it. Shit, Chester. We've got a show in, like, four hours."

"And my camera is missing," said Ariadne. She threw me a look.

"And her camera is missing," I repeated. "We think Surly has it."

"You don't want to be talking to Surly right now. He's on the warpath."

"What's his problem?" I said.

"Him and that record company guy, Blackmore. They're at each other's throats."

We hoisted Frankie into the lobby of the new hotel, and it was maybe a mark of how scuzzy it was that nobody even batted an eye when we carried him in. "Where's Surly?" I asked.

"Room beside us," said Chester. "317, I think. But I'm telling you, he's in a mood."

"Okay," I said to Ariadne. "I'm going to get your camera for you."

"Thanks. We'll talk later?"

"Yeah." Not that I knew what I was going to say. She'd finally found out the truth about me. The girl who was going to be a writer . . . and me, the guy who can't even read.

♫

I knocked on Surly's door and he opened it in his pinstripe suit, a cigarette dangling from his lips. "You find Frankie?" he began.

"Yeah, we've got him downstairs. He's out of it."

"Christ almighty." He checked his watch. "Right. I've got something that will fix him up." He started to close the door, but I just stood there. I wasn't leaving. "Something else you want?" he said.

"Yeah, what about Ariadne's camera?"

"Jesus," he said. "I've got it, okay? I grabbed it before those cheese-eating monkeys could get at it. I got the rest of the coke too. There were still packets everywhere."

"Cheese-eating monkeys?"

"The French police, Levi. Jesus. You should have seen the place. There was enough evidence in there to put us all in jail for the rest of our lives."

"But you have the camera?"

"Blackmore's furious about it. It's illegal to pay radio stations to play songs. Especially to pay them with drugs."

"I just want the camera back."

"What? You and Ariadne a thing now?"

"Surly, just give me the camera."

"What did you call me?"

"I mean Bob. Bobby. C'mon. Let me have the camera. Ariadne's pretty upset."

"Don't bloody well call me Surly. I don't like it."

"Then stop being so fucking . . . surly."

"Point taken." He grunted and ducked back into the room. I heard him puttering around and a moment later he came back with the camera.

I took it from him, but I held his eyes. I really didn't know if I could trust him.

"What? What the bloody hell do you want, Levi?"

"I want to know what's going on. What's going to happen to us after Paris?"

"Blackmore's a right bastard, Levi. With his contracts and contingencies and options. He's got us coming and going."

"Are we still on for the album?"

"Of course we are. Don't you worry. I've got a plan."

"C'mon, Bob. How are we supposed to finish it now?"

Surly grinned at me. "Ariadne's father," he said. "The famous movie director. I've just spoken with him."

♫

We had about three hours to go until the sound check and I felt like crap. The second hotel was a dump: moldy carpet and paint peeling off the walls. I know I was supposed to phone Evelyn, but I sure as hell wasn't going to do that, not now. Not while Rudy was still missing. Jesus, I'd almost forgotten about him in all the craziness, but now it was starting to weigh on me. Everything had gone off the rails and I needed to start fixing things. I needed to start making things better.

Ariadne had a room on the fourth floor. I knocked on her door and it swung open before I could even finish the second rap. She stood there expectantly, and I raised the camera.

"Oh," she said, taking it from me. "Thank goodness."

She cradled the camera in her hands, examining it. She popped open the film compartment. "It's empty."

"Did you have a lot of photos on it?"

"Just the last Paris show and the party. But it doesn't matter. I have more film. The most important thing is that I have the camera back."

"It really is a good one, huh?"

"It is." Her aluminum camera case lay on the bed open, an empty Styrofoam indentation where the camera should have been. She closed the back of the camera and laid it in the case.

She wasn't really looking at me. "It's not really mine."

"What?"

"It's not really my camera." She turned to me. "My father only lent it to me with the expectation that I would follow in his footsteps. It's what everybody wants. It's what everybody expects." Her lower lip was trembling. "But I didn't want this. I didn't want any of this."

"It's okay, Ariadne."

"It took years, Levi. Years to convince him that I wanted to be a poet. That I wanted to study poetry. He was not happy. He—"

"Really, it's okay."

"No," she said. "You don't understand. I went to Oxford to learn. To learn everything I could about writing and poetry. And I did learn. But it still wasn't me. It was just two-hundred-year-old dead men telling me what I should think about Greece, about my homeland. It was exactly like he said it would be."

"So maybe you need to write your own poems."

"I know that. Do you think I don't know that?"

"And not just lyrics for Frankie."

She frowned. "What's that supposed to mean?"

"No, I just—"

"Honestly, Levi. That's exactly what I'm talking about. I'm tired of doing what other people expect me to do. I just want to be my own person. Is that so hard to understand?"

"I'm sorry," I said. "I don't want you to leave. That's all."

She tightened her lips even further. "I have to, Levi. Once again, I don't have a choice."

She just stood there by the bed, looking off into the distance.

"Ariadne?"

"The military coup in Greece. I told you. It's finally collapsing."

"But that's good, isn't it?"

"No. My father wants to go back. And he wants me to go with him. We have a house there, on Naxos."

"Maybe it'll be okay."

"I don't know," she said. "It's all very uncertain. But he wants to return. To show people that—" She stopped and shook her head. "It's always about appearances with him."

"Well, I guess it's important that—"

"And you," she said. "Why didn't you just tell me that you couldn't read?"

That stopped me. "I don't know, Ariadne. What was I supposed to say? It's not something I want people to know. And here you're an Oxford scholar and everything."

"I'm not."

"But you're an expert on poetry and I can't even—" I stopped again. I really didn't know how to go on.

Her jade-green eyes hung on me, but I don't think she really knew what to say either.

"Ah, love," I began. *"Let us be true to one another! For the world, which seems to lie before us like a land of dreams."*

"Oh, Levi," she said. "You remembered."

"See, that's the thing. I do remember. I remember everything."

♫

I made my way down the dark staircase back to the room I shared with Chester. He was snoring on the bed. The carpet smelled like stale cigarette smoke and a fly was buzzing around on the window. The window had a view of a brick wall across from us and that was it. I climbed into the shower, and even though it was lukewarm, it was the most refreshing thing I'd felt all day. It made me feel like maybe I could get through the show tonight.

I tried to think. I tried to imagine a way in which this could all turn out for the best. I stood there, the water running in rivulets down my back, swirling into the rusty drain. And then it came to me.

It came to me what I should do.

I got dressed and tiptoed out of the room. Chester was still sleeping, but I had a couple hours and I didn't have to go far. I walked back to

L'Hotel. It was just a couple of blocks away. I thought he might still be there. And I was right.

Blackmore stood in the lobby. He was talking to a man in a trench coat, a detective maybe. The door to the Oscar Wilde Suite was closed but a faint stench of smoke still hung in the air.

He glanced up at me when I pushed through the door. There wasn't a doorman to stop me, and the detective drifted away over to the front desk, maybe to interview someone else, I don't know.

"Mr. Jaxon," said Blackmore. He looked very tired.

"I need to talk to you."

"I have nothing to say to you. The lawyers will handle things from here on out."

"No," I said. "We're not done. Maybe you think '29 Streetlights' is too long."

"I am not speaking about Frankie. I will not—"

"Just listen," I said, and I was a bit surprised at myself. Maybe he was too, because he shut right up.

"You need to release 'Hello Juliet.' It should be the A side. It's a good song."

"That has been considered," Blackmore said.

"Then do it. You've seen how people react to it at the concerts. It's good. It could be a hit."

Blackmore narrowed his eyes on me. "The problem," he began, "is in marketing. It's not Frankie singing on it, so—"

"Fuck Frankie," I said, and watched Blackmore's reaction. I could tell he was thinking.

"Be that as it may," he finally said, "it's 1974. Albums sell. Singles are no longer—"

"It's a start," I said. "And if it does well, it buys us time. Downtown Exit is a good band, Mr. Blackmore. You need to put 'Hello Juliet' out as a single."

Blackmore held my gaze. "Your band has sorely tested my patience."

"I know."

"The fire, that's a very serious matter."

"I'm just trying to tell you we can do better. We can make up for all of this."

"Well, I shall have to think about it."

"That's all I wanted to hear." I tipped my head in acknowledgment and turned to go. "Show's in two hours," I said.

"That's right," he said. "Your last show."

I pushed out through the doors of L'Hotel and didn't look back.

♫

The limousines came for us about an hour later. Surly climbed into the first one with Frankie and me. I didn't say anything about my little talk with Blackmore.

Frankie was still pretty wiped out. He slumped down in the leather seat, barely holding his head up.

"Right," Surly said. He dug in his coat pocket, pulled out a pill bottle, and spilled one out into his hand. These pills were also white, but they didn't quite look the same as his other ones. And they definitely weren't medicine. He put his hand under Frankie's chin. "Open up," he said, and he popped the pill into Frankie's mouth. Frankie's eyes fluttered for a moment, and we waited while he swallowed it.

"Levi?" said Surly. He held the open bottle toward me. "A little pick-me-up for you?" He rattled the bottle at me and the chauffeur at the front glanced in his rearview mirror. His eyes quickly darted back to the road.

"Bennies," Surly said. "They'll get you hopping again."

"No thanks. I'll make it through on my own."

He grunted and tucked the little bottle back into his suit jacket. "You fall apart up there, don't blame me."

When we pulled up to the Olympia, a crowd was lined up along the sidewalk. Someone started screaming when we stepped out. And the cameras were out, that's for sure. Frankie was slow, but he managed to raise his hand and wave, and a whole lot of flashbulbs went off. We pushed through a cordon, young girls thrusting pieces of paper at us asking for autographs, reporters yelling out questions. Surly led the way, elbowing and shouldering his way through, and we made it in through the front doors.

I know we could have driven around to the back, to the stage doors. That's what we'd done the previous two nights, but I guess Surly wanted to make a statement. He wanted to squeeze out every drop of publicity he could. And who was I to say otherwise?

In the dressing room, I had some salty chips, and I chugged a whole bottle of Perrier water and began to feel a little bit better. Ariadne appeared. She'd come separately but she had her camera. She raised it to show that she'd still be taking photos tonight, and maybe to thank me again for getting it back.

This was it. Her last night with us, the last night of our disastrous tour. I wanted to see her after the show, and I started toward her to ask if she could stick around, but just before I reached her, someone wheeled in our racks of clothes and I stopped, and when I looked up again, she was gone.

For our final concert, I picked out a black velvet dinner jacket. I thought it might look cool. Frankie put on a white shirt with suspenders, and for the first time, they put a bit of eye makeup on him. Under the current conditions it made him look a bit creepy. It made him look like the guy in *A Clockwork Orange*.

We went out in a blaze of lights, kicking into "Painted Ladies," and Frankie came momentarily to life. He waved a silk scarf around and yanked the microphone out of its clip. For a while I thought the night might go okay. Chester and I exchanged glances, nodding to each other, knowing we just had to get through the set.

The crowd was riotous. They knew all the songs. They held up their hands and clapped over their heads. They roared, they screamed, they surged back and forth like currents in the ocean. But by about the third song, Frankie was done. I could tell. He stopped moving around the stage and mostly just leaned on the mic stand. Then he began to forget lyrics.

So I made a show of it. I stepped up to his mic and sang along with him, as if we'd rehearsed it that way, both of us pushing into the same microphone, and that close, I could see that his eyes were unfocused. There was nothing going on behind them.

The crowd didn't seem to notice, or else they must have thought it was part of the show, but as we neared the end of "29 Streetlights," Frankie was singing only fragments of the proper lyrics, staggering a bit at the effort of staying near the mic. So I stepped right in front of him and took over the lead vocals.

That brought him to life again. He was having none of that. He tried to muscle around in front of me, but I wouldn't let him.

"Frankie," I hissed. "Just get off the stage. We'll finish the set."

"Fuck you," he slurred.

"Frankie," I tried again. "Please, just get off the stage."

He was going to ruin everything.

Miguel was already doing the piano entry to "Falling Up" when Frankie shoved weakly at me. The crowd kind of went quiet. There were people gawking at us in the front row, their expressions confused and concerned. I couldn't really see much farther back than that.

I wiggled in front of the mic to sing the first line and Frankie grabbed at me. I tried to shuffle him off, but he swung at me and his fist connected with my jaw. It fucking hurt. He hit me pretty hard, if you want to know the truth. I almost went down, but I recovered and dodged away before he could hit me again. Miguel stopped playing but Chester kept thumping on. Then Skinny Dave stopped too, and Chester realized something was happening. He gave one last big crash on the cymbals and he reared up over his kit, his big face gaping down at us from between the tom-toms.

I grabbed ahold of Frankie, both of us tugging at each other like in a hockey fight, swinging each other around by our shirttails. I was a lot more sober than he was, so I finally just let him go, and he crashed backward and landed hard on his ass.

That's when Surly came bellowing out onto the stage. Frankie was on his back on the floorboards, struggling a little, trying to get up. And over at the side of the stage, I spotted Ariadne. She'd just lowered her camera, her face pale. She'd caught the whole thing on film, the moment my dreams went down the toilet.

There was really nothing more I could do at that point, so I stepped back up to the microphone. "Goodnight, Paris," I called out, and then all the lights went out.

10 That's the Sound

The photo was on the front page of *Le Monde* the next day, a pixelated black-and-white image of Frankie punching me, my chin snapping back, a shower of sweat leaping from my face, and him with his fist still swinging through the air, a slightly glazed expression on his face. The caption was in French, of course, but it was credited to Ariadne Christos. I was pretty sure that was Surly's handiwork, though, because Ariadne was gone. Probably to her father's place. She hadn't said goodbye and I had a terrible feeling I was never going to see her again.

A bunch of reporters had already tracked us down to the new hotel, so we couldn't really go out. In fact, we were hiding at the back, where they had some tables set up for their free breakfast. Plates were stacked on a counter there, but the breakfast was long over. Too bad. I would have killed for a coffee and some toast. I'd lain awake for a good part of the night, wondering if my time in the Exits was now officially over.

Surly was passing around the paper, looking pleased with himself. Chester took one look at it and let out a booming laugh. Miguel pinched the end of his mustache and shook his head sadly. Frankie wasn't there at all. He'd been whisked off the stage after the fight and I didn't know where they'd taken him. Davey was gone too.

"All right, lads," Surly announced. "I've been on the phone all morning. *Rolling Stone* wants to run the photo. *Der Spiegel*'s doing a spread this Saturday, and I haven't seen it yet, but it's in *The Guardian* too." He turned to me, looking almost appreciative. "And you, you're a regular Rocky Marciano." He put up his fists in a mock boxing stance and poked one playfully at me.

I wasn't much in the mood for joking. My jaw was sore, and a blue-black bruise was forming on my cheek. We could hear the reporters outside shouting for us to come out. A policeman even showed up to stand guard at the hotel doors. It was all a bit of a shitshow and it got a lot worse when Blackmore came bristling in through the front doors. We all saw him stomp over to the front desk to ask where we were.

"Oh, bugger," Surly said.

Blackmore came raging across the lobby toward us, his hands swooping like he was shooing geese. "Up, up," he said. "You can't stay here." And we bobbed up, one by one. "This way," he said, and we marched back to the front desk, where an old man sat smoking a cigarette. Blackmore had a word with him in French, and the man pointed us to a door at the side of the lobby. Blackmore thanked him and then strode to the door and held it open, tapping his foot, waiting for us to follow.

"Down," he said.

We trooped past him down a set of wooden steps and into what looked like an old wine cellar. It was all bricks, with arches and niches, like something out of the Middle Ages.

Blackmore came down after us and we sort of staggered to a stop, standing like schoolchildren waiting to be picked for a sports team. Surly tucked in behind me. I could feel his breath on my neck.

"Now then," Blackmore began. "I want to make something perfectly clear here."

I stiffened. I thought this was it. I thought this was where they fired me.

"I've had quite enough." He glared at us one by one, reserving a particularly penetrating gaze for Surly. "Your manager has apparently not fully apprised you of the situation. Isn't that correct, Mr. Malone?"

We spread apart so that Surly was fully exposed.

"I was going to tell them," he muttered, but Blackmore held up a hand to stop him.

"Two months overdue, Mr. Malone."

"We have six songs finished," said Chester. "And '29 Streetlights,' it's long, so that should count for two."

"Which is still not enough for an album, Mr. Merriweather," said Blackmore. "Go on. Tell them, Mr. Malone."

Surly was sweating now. "We owe them some money."

"And how much would that be, Mr. Malone?"

"One hundred and eighty thousand dollars."

I heard Miguel gasp at that, and holy shit, that was a lot of money.

Chester raised his hand to ask a question. Blackmore ignored him. "Rental of the recording studios," he said. "Trucks, lighting, marketing, and now damage to the room at L'Hotel. It's a considerable amount of money." Blackmore turned to me. "Not to mention the damage to the label's reputation. And that's just the beginning."

"Can I ask a question?" said Chester.

"No, you may not. Those monies are due immediately."

Surly lifted his chin. "If you would just let us finish the album, we can more than make up for that."

"Nothing would give us greater pleasure," said Blackmore. "And so we have decided to issue a *final* deadline. My lawyers are drawing up the papers. You will have five days, and not an hour more, to have the master tapes handed over. For a full album, Mr. Malone. At least ten songs."

"Jesus," said Surly.

Chester raised his hand again. "Is that one hundred and eighty thousand divided by five?"

"Mr. Merriweather, that is the least of your worries. If the master tapes are not received within the allotted time, we will be initiating further legal action."

"Bloody hell," said Surly.

"It is a breach of your contract, as I have warned you over and over."

"What's that supposed to mean?" I asked.

"It means that we will sue you for lost profits, for the money we expected to make from the album."

I gulped. "And how much might that be?"

"Five million dollars," said Blackmore. "Possibly more."

"Ay Dios mío," Miguel whispered.

Chester blinked and I felt my empty stomach buck. A bit of bile came up my throat, but I swallowed it back down.

Blackmore let that little piece of information hang in the air for a moment. "And now," he went on, "before we are completely finished here, I have one more disturbing piece of news. As of this morning, David Barrons is no longer in the band."

"Say what?" said Chester.

"He's on a plane back to the States as we speak. He has made private arrangements to settle with us. But that, frankly, is none of your business."

With that, he whirled on his shiny shoes and clipped back up the steps.

"Bugger," said Surly, and we all turned on him.

"What the hell happened with Davey?" I said.

We surrounded Surly and he put up his hands to appease us. "Boys, don't listen to him. That's rubbish. If we can make a good album, they're not going to turn it down. They stand to make a lot of money. You heard him—they'll make five million at least."

"And if we don't?" asked Chester.

"He's frightened," Surly said. "He doesn't want to lose Frankie. He knows Frankie can sell records."

"Speaking of," Chester said. "Where is Frankie?"

"Don't worry. It's all part of the plan."

"But," I said, "do we really owe them one hundred and eighty thousand dollars?"

"It's a drop in the bucket, Levi. A drop in the bucket."

Chester's lips compressed glumly. "Shee-it."

"Chins up, lads. I've got it all worked out." He glanced up at the door at the top of the stairs. Blackmore was gone, but still, he lowered his voice. "I have spoken to Mr. Christos."

"Ariadne's father?" Chester asked.

"And we've worked out an arrangement. He expects us shortly."

"To do what?" Chester said. "Star in one of his damn movies?"

"Better than that, Chester. You'll see. We're heading to the South of France. Everything is going to work out just fine."

♫

We were down to three guys—well, four counting Surly—and there was nothing to do but pack up, get on the bus again, and keep going. We had to make that deadline. I left a message for Rudy at the front desk—the old man was kind enough to scribble a note—just in case he came looking for me. And where the hell was he anyway? I really didn't know.

Surly was already in the driver's seat when we lugged in our suitcases. The bus was looking a lot worse for wear, I've got to say. Somewhere it had got a big scrape along the side and one of the side-view mirrors had been sheared off completely. The front fender panel was loose, like someone had taken it on and off too many times, which of course they had. And the bus was emptier than it had ever been. I took a seat across from Surly, and Miguel slipped into the one behind me.

"What exactly is this plan of yours, Bobby?" said Chester. He was still standing, bent down, looking out through the windshield.

"First, we have to get to the gear truck. We don't need the lighting racks anymore, but we do need our instruments."

"Are we stealing them?" said Chester.

"Technically?"

Chester waited.

"Well, technically, yes. But we have an album to finish."

Surly closed the door and ground the bus into gear, working the big stick shift on the floor. He pulled away from the curb and Chester lurched and sat down hard on the seat behind Surly.

The apartment blocks of Paris reared up on either side of us with their ornate facades. They were all starting to look the same, to tell you the truth.

"Where exactly are we going?" I asked.

"I told you. We're off to the Côte d'Azur." Surly looked up into the rearview mirror to see our reaction.

Nothing.

"The French Riviera?" he prompted. "Cannes?"

"To Ariadne's father's place," I said.

"Look," said Surly. "I already told you, I spoke to Christos. It's all been arranged."

"Do you think Ariadne will be there?"

"Save the rumpy-pumpy for later, sport. We're going to record there, at his villa."

"But how are we supposed to record at some guy's villa?" Chester asked.

"You'll see," said Surly. "All in good time. First, we have to get our instruments back."

♫

The gear truck sat in a compound on the outskirts of the city. The sky was already darkening into sunset but there was still enough light to see. The place was surrounded by a chain-link fence and a gate where two sections of the fence swung in. The truck, I guess, was being kept in there, all loaded up with equipment, ready to go back on the ferry to England.

"You got a key to that?" asked Chester, pointing to the padlock and the heavy iron chain around the gate poles.

Surly ignored him. He drove the bus forward, inching it up to the gates until the bumper was right up against the padlock and chain. He kept edging the bus forward in little lurches until the metal at the front started squealing and scraping. The gates slowly spread apart, wrenching at the chain that held them until, with a crack, the chain snapped and the gates swung open. Something flew up and hit the windshield and a long crack spiderwebbed across the glass.

"Nice plan," said Chester.

Surly didn't answer. The gear truck was in sight and he drove in behind it. "Five minutes," he said. "Grab what you can."

We rolled up the back of the gear truck and scampered inside. I hauled out a small MESA/Boogie amp and a couple of guitar cases. I couldn't exactly tell which guitar was which, but for sure I got the

Les Paul and another bigger, squarer case that I thought might be a Stratocaster. I couldn't see my own guitar case, though. I dug around behind the speaker cabinets, but I couldn't see it anywhere. And there wasn't time. Surly was yelling at us to step on it.

I ferried the guitars to the bus and loaded them on board. There wasn't even time to shove things into the hold below, so we just dragged everything onto the bus.

I headed back to the truck for a second time and Chester passed me with his kick drum. "Forget something?" he said.

"I can't find my guitar. The Martin."

Surly was lumbering by with a handful of cables. "Jesus Christ, it's in there somewhere. Just look harder."

I hopped back up into the truck, desperately pulling at crates and amplifiers, but I just couldn't see it. Darkness was falling faster now and everyone else was already back on the bus. Surly honked the horn at me to hurry.

"Shit," I said. And then I found it. My guitar. The old case was tucked in behind one of the big keyboard cases and I just about burst into tears when I saw it. I had to clamber over a few things, but I managed to yank it out.

Surly had the bus in gear as I stepped through the door. "You got it?"

"Yeah, thank god," I said, plopping down into my seat.

"Right, then we're off."

He hit the gas and it was like a bad getaway scene. He spun the tires and threw up a bit of gravel and we careened out through the broken gates without even bothering to close them. It only seemed like a few minutes before we were back on the highway.

I sat with my hand protectively on the old battered guitar case. I'd had this thing for a long time, and maybe it was just an old guitar, but it was a Martin, and it was mine. It was the one thing in this world that was truly mine.

We drove south, our headlights pushing ahead of us on the asphalt. We passed under a blue autoroute sign saying we were on the A6, but none of us were speaking. We bumped along silently, our equipment heaped along the aisle of the bus, until, maybe twenty or thirty miles outside Paris, something under the bus started making noise, a metallic clanking, like something had broken.

Surly tried to ignore it but Chester pressed him. "You check the oil, Boss?"

Surly kept his eyes on the road.

"Maybe a wheel coming off?" Chester went on. "The front of the bus is pretty smashed up."

"Bloody hell," muttered Surly.

The noise was getting worse, insistent. It sounded like it was coming from under the bus. We pulled over at a rest area. Surly turned the bus off and a silence spread around us, then the clanking began again.

"What the hell?" I said. "It's coming from the hold."

We trailed off the bus, and Surly unlocked the hold and swung the door up. A sullen face peered out at us from the dark.

"Rudy," I said. "What are you doing in there?"

Rudy unfolded himself. His T-shirt was filthy. His chin was stubbled with the beginnings of a beard, blondish red, and his hair haloed out around his head. In the shadows, I could see his backpack laid down and his foamy too, rolled out where he'd been sleeping. There was nothing else in the hold but a stench like he'd been living in there for a couple of days.

"Christ on a kite," said Surly.

"Shit, Rudy. How long you been in there?"

"I don't know. I slept in a park for a couple nights. Then I found the bus and crawled into the hold. Only I didn't know I'd locked myself in." A crescent moon was rising above the treetops and Rudy looked around. "Where are we? Are we going back to England?"

"Nope," I said.

Jeez, he really was a mess. We helped him onto the bus and he walked stiffly down the aisle to the back. Chester got his backpack and we gave him a bottle of water and, when we headed off again, I went and sat with him.

He scrunched over and I tucked in beside him. "You okay, man?"

"Not really," he said.

"Shit. There's lots to tell you. Things have gotten pretty crazy."

"I don't want to hear about it."

"There was a fire and then we got kicked out. And Frankie punched me and—"

"Well, you probably deserved it."

"Rudy, c'mon, man. You're supposed to be on my side."

"You were supposed to be on my side." He wasn't looking at me.

"And the contract," I said. "Shit. That Blackmore guy, he says we owe them money. Like, a lot of money."

Rudy sighed and turned to me. "I told you, you shouldn't have signed that contract."

"Well I did. Okay? It's done. And besides"—I paused significantly—"I fixed it. I talked to Blackmore. They're maybe going to release 'Hello Juliet' as the single."

Rudy's eyes narrowed. "Your song?"

"Yeah, and that would pay some of it back. Especially if it does well."

He shook his head. "Maybe."

"Rudy. C'mon, man. I'm trying."

"You'd better be."

"What's that supposed to mean?"

He sighed again. "All right. It's like this. Mom might be selling the house."

"What? Why?"

"Because," he said, "because of exactly what you said." He waved his hand abstractly. "Because you owe, like, a gazillion dollars to the record company."

"No," I said. "It's not my fault. I didn't know."

"Levi, I just want to go home. Okay? I've got no reason to be here anymore. I just want to go home."

"No. We can still fix this. I wrecked Evelyn's chance once. I'm not going to wreck mine." I paused and looked long and hard at him. He was my brother—well, my half brother. "And I need you here, Rudy. I need you to help me with this."

♫

Sometime before dawn, Surly pulled over to get gas. There were stars in the sky and almost no traffic. All the world seemed silent and dark and strange. The fuel pumps looked almost alien under the fluorescent lights.

The other guys were asleep, spread out across the seats, but I watched as Surly filled up the truck, then made a call from the phone booth outside the station.

"Who you calling at this time of night?" I asked when he climbed back on board.

"Change of plans," said Surly. In the dark, I could see a rare grin on his face. "We're going to Switzerland."

"Switzerland? Why? What about Cannes?"

"Don't worry, we just need to make a pit stop in Geneva. It's just over the border."

"Okay, but why?"

Surly grinned even wider. "Now you're going to see what I've been talking about. Now you're going to see."

Geneva *was* right over the border. A couple of hours later we arrived, and the border guards there barely glanced at our papers before lifting up the boom gate. We drove pretty much straight into the old city and then stopped for breakfast as the sun was coming up.

We loaded up on buttered bread and marmalade and coffee. Goddamn, that marmalade tasted good. We paid in French francs because we didn't have any Swiss money, but they accepted it and we drove on. The early-morning light was silver on Lake Geneva and the low mountains on the other side were a hazy blue.

"That is some crazy beautiful," said Chester.

We wound up into the rolling hills, and the view of the shimmering lake and meadows of green was even more spectacular. In front of us, a little Swiss village appeared with a white church and a tall wooden spire, looking like a toy model for a train set. Cows crossed the road, great bells clanging around their necks, and in the distance, the purple mountains rose up into the clouds.

Then, out of nowhere, two motorcycles roared up behind us. One got in front of us and the other stayed in back, boxing us in. They were Harleys—big bikes, loud as hell—and the guys riding them wore black leather jackets with skulls stenciled on the back. One guy had a helmet that I was pretty sure was a Nazi thing from World War II. Surly didn't seem too troubled by them. He nodded at the guy in front of us, who waved for us to follow him.

"What's going on, Bobby?" I asked.

"You'll see. Just be cool."

We drove up onto a smaller road that ended at a massive iron gate. The first biker put up his hand and we pulled to a stop behind him. The other motorcycle pulled up alongside us, sort of fencing us in. I watched the guy on the first motorcycle pull something from his jacket. It was a gun.

Rudy rose from his seat near the back. He trundled up to the front.

"Shit, Rudy," I hissed. "What are you doing?"

"I'm not scared." He had that damn screwdriver in his hand. I don't know why everyone thought that was some kind of weapon. Because it wasn't.

Surly levered open the door. He said something to the first biker, who was still straddling his Harley. Surly stood blocking the door of the bus. The guy got off his bike and ambled up to the gates. He had that gun out, a big one, and he kept looking back at us, ready for any sudden movement. He leaned into a callbox beside the gate, his eyes still on us, and said something into it.

Rudy inched up behind Surly. "You need help?"

Surly glanced back at him and saw the screwdriver in Rudy's hand. He began to laugh, a sort of coughing chortle, and he swiped at Rudy, like he was telling him to quit the joke. But then the biker came toward us and was eyeing Surly coldly. He'd been holding his gun loosely but now he raised it a bit.

"Jesus," said Surly. "Let's all settle down, here. We're just here for the truck." He stepped down off the bus. "Just tell him Bobby Malone is here"—he glanced back up at Rudy—"with his bodyguard."

The guy nodded, and after a moment the iron gates creaked open.

"Right," called Surly. "You lot stay here. And Rudy, grab the cash-box. You're coming with me."

We waited outside the bus, just getting some air, but we were pretty wary of the biker that remained. Maybe twenty minutes later, we heard a rumble coming down the lane behind the gates, then a big truck appeared. It could have been a furniture delivery truck for all we knew, except that somebody had painted it in camouflage. Rudy was behind the wheel and Surly was in the passenger seat.

"What's that supposed to be?" said Chester.

"Hell if I know," I said.

Miguel was beside us. His eyes had gone wide. He was staring at it like a kid who'd just seen Santa Claus.

"Shit, Miguel," said Chester. "What is it?"

"That," he said, "is the Rolling Stones Mobile Studio."

"That thing?" said Chester. "It looks like a beat-up old moving van."

"The Stones have recorded 'Brown Sugar' and 'Wild Horses' on it, and all of *Exile on Main St.*"

We took in the old truck. It still didn't look like much.

"Led Zeppelin," Miguel went on, "recorded their third album and their fourth."

"*Led Zeppelin IV*?" I said. "It was recorded on this?"

"It is the greatest album ever made," said Miguel, and he crossed himself like he was in the presence of something holy.

Chester considered the truck again and blew out a long, low whistle of appreciation.

Rudy pulled the truck to a stop beside us. Surly climbed down from the passenger side, beaming and swinging his cashbox. Rudy was carrying two cardboard boxes, like fat pizza boxes, but he looked a bit pale, if you want to know the truth. Miguel and Chester followed Surly around to the back of the truck.

"What you got there?" I asked Rudy.

"Tapes. Two-inch recording tapes." He looked like he was in kind of a daze.

"What happened up there?"

"I saw Keith Richards," he said.

"Keith Richards?"

"He was there. He was standing right in front of me."

"Did you talk to him?"

Rudy's eyes were saucers. "He was standing right in front of me."

"Holy shit."

Surly opened the back doors of the truck, revealing a shallow space and a couple of sliding doors with the famous Rolling Stones logo painted across them—those crazy lips with the tongue hanging out, blowing a great big fat raspberry at the world.

Surly lowered a small metal stepladder and clambered up into the sort of anteroom at the back, then he slid the inside doors open. In the main cavity of the truck the walls were just sheets of plywood, but at the far back there was a state-of-the-art mixing board and a couple of giant speakers. On the right-hand side sat a floor-mounted reel-to-reel tape recorder.

We all climbed up, gawking at the equipment.

"You hear that?" said Surly.

I listened for a second. There was nothing.

"That's the sound of fame. Of legends being born."

"Damn," said Chester.

"Look," said Miguel, and he pointed at a black patch on the ceiling. "It is burned. You can see."

" 'Smoke on the Water,' " Rudy said. "It's from 'Smoke on the Water.' "

I couldn't believe it. It was like looking at rock and roll history.

Everybody knew the story. Deep Purple had been recording a live album, right here in Switzerland with this very Rolling Stones Mobile Studio, when the casino they were playing went up in flames. The Mobile Studio was parked outside, but it was close enough that it almost burned down too. No one was killed, but Deep Purple wrote "Smoke on the Water" about it. You listen to the lyrics. They talk about this recording truck right there in the song, and here we were looking at that very same truck.

"Okay, okay," said Surly. "You all want to get down now? We still got some driving to do."

"We're going to be recording on this?" I said, hopping down.

"Soon as we get to the villa."

Behind us, the gates were closing, the metal creaking. The biker was gone now, and Chester and Miguel clanked down the ladder steps. Surly closed the back doors and we stood together in a sort of huddle.

"Right," Surly said. "Who's going to drive the bus and who's going to drive the truck?"

"He said I could drive the truck," Rudy said.

"Who?" I asked.

"Keith Richards."

"Yeah," said Rudy. "He asked if I could work a stick."

"Can you?" said Chester.

"Sure. I said I drove the delivery truck sometimes, at Kmart. And he said, 'Cheers,' and gave me the keys."

"Right," said Surly. "Everybody back on board. We got an album to finish."

♫

Surly pulled out ahead of us in the bus. I'd volunteered to go with Rudy in the Rolling Stones Mobile. We drove along in silence for a while, Rudy with his hands at ten and two on the wheel, me staring out the windshield trying to get a grip on what had just happened. Below us, Lake Geneva appeared again, sparkling in the sun.

Rudy glanced over at me. "There's a little problem," he said. "We're supposed to be transporting this truck back to England. For Led Zeppelin."

"No shit?" I said. "Zeppelin?"

Rudy frowned, his hands still on the steering wheel.

"Wait a second. But we're taking it to the French Riviera."

"Yup."

"So you're telling me we've stolen our musical instruments and now we've stolen a recording studio from Keith Richards?"

"That's what it looks like."

"Aw, shit. This is getting really fucked-up."

Rudy squelched up his lips a bit, but he kept his eyes on the road.

"Shit," I said. "Evelyn is going to murder us."

Rudy wouldn't look at me.

"Rudy?"

He kept staring pointedly ahead but his lips had plumped up a bit more.

"Is she really selling the house?"

"I don't know why she thinks you're so special. It's not fair."

"Rudy," I said. "Jeez."

"She's my mom too, you know."

"Of course I know. Rudy, what are you even trying to—?"

"In New York," he went on. His eyes were fixed firmly on the road. "She must have had a boyfriend. Did you ever think of that?"

That was exactly what I was trying not to think about. Whoever was there with her in New York, well, that'd be my father.

"Who the hell was he?" said Rudy. "And what did he do to my mom?"

"I don't know."

He glanced over at me. "You don't know much, do you?"

I swallowed, hard.

Rudy stepped on the accelerator. We were falling behind, and we couldn't let the bus get too far ahead because we didn't really know the way to the villa. The highway here wound through a thick forest. It was a good highway, smooth and all, but the truck was a real elephant. We kind of lumbered along, even when Rudy crunched it into another gear. It took us a little while to catch up to the bus again.

And when we did, something was clearly wrong. The tour bus was swerving, almost drunkenly, weaving over the white center lines and then back again. Rudy honked the horn, but just as he did, the bus careened over to the far side of the road. They were lucky no other cars were coming. Then the bus corrected, but it swung back way too far on our side and went off the shoulder and right off the road. It hit the dirt and threw up a shower of rocks before grinding to a halt in a cloud of dust.

"Holy shit," I said, and Rudy went pale. We pulled in behind the bus and scrambled out to see if everyone was okay. Surly was unconscious in the driver's seat. Chester and Miguel were hovering over him, trying to wake him up. Surly was breathing, but it was shallow, with a gurgle of phlegm coming up from deep in his lungs.

"His medicine," I said. "He's got pills in his coat pocket."

Chester fumbled into Surly's coat pocket, then pulled out two little plastic pill containers. Both of them had little white pills, round like aspirin. They looked pretty much the same.

"Which ones?" I said.

Chester held up the vials. "These ones are amphetamines . . . bennies," he said, shaking the pill bottle.

Miguel was holding Surly's head up and his eyelids fluttered, so at least we knew he wasn't dead. "The other ones?" Miguel said. "What can be the other ones?"

Chester held up the other bottle to read the label. "Methadone hydrochloride."

"Methadone?" I said. "Isn't that what they give you to get you off heroin?"

All of us stared at Surly.

"Shit," said Chester. "Do we give him more, or is he ODing on these things?"

Surly grunted. He raised a hand weakly. "Water," he croaked. "Just get me some bloody water."

I rummaged through the overhead bins. The bus sat at a weird angle, so I had to brace myself to stay upright. Finally, I found the water and passed a bottle to Miguel, who held it up to Surly's mouth. Surly slurped at it and seemed to improve a bit. He struggled to sit upright, and the color started coming back to his face.

"Bobby," I said. "What's going on? Are you on heroin?"

"I was. Not bloody anymore."

"And now you're on methadone?"

Surly kind of grunted. "Lesser of two evils," he managed.

"But how long have you been doing this? How long is—?"

"The trouble is," began Surly, "methadone is just as addictive as the smack. All except you don't get any pleasure from it. So then you end up taking more, and well, fuck off, you don't want to hear about it."

"Maybe we should get you to a doctor," I said.

"No. Doctors only cause more problems. Just let me drive."

"I don't think that's a good idea, Bobby," Chester said.

A few cars had gone by, slowing down to look at the bus in the ditch.

"We should get going," said Rudy.

"Okay," I said, "I'll drive the bus. Rudy, you go on back to the truck."

"No. Bugger off. I can drive."

Chester and Miguel exchanged a look.

"Look, Boss," Chester said. "How about we let Levi have a turn? Just for the next little while."

"Goddamn it," said Surly. "Fine. Just follow this route until you hit the A8."

Chester got an arm under him and helped maneuver him to the back. He really didn't look very good.

I lowered myself into the driver's seat and had a good look around, seeing where the stick shift was, where the headlights were, all that stuff. At least the bus had stayed upright. I started the ignition and waited while Rudy walked back to the truck behind us, then I gunned it. The bus lurched forward and I clawed onto the road and managed to get the beast up onto the highway. Rudy was behind me and we started out again.

♫

We drove on for a while. The sun was climbing in the sky. Chester had been watching Surly, asleep in the seat opposite. He looked up at me. "Hey," he said, and I glanced back at him. He'd risen out of his seat and took a step toward me.

"What?" I said.

"I'm thinking we should check on the money. It's ours, right?" He took another look at Surly. "Maybe we should see where we're at, you know, just in case something happens to Bobby."

Miguel looked up at that. He was in the seat behind where Chester had been sitting. I checked Surly in the mirror. He was completely out of it.

"Now's our chance," said Chester.

"I'm not sure—" I began.

"What if he's on heroin again? Don't you want to know how much we have left?"

"Yeah, but—"

We all kind of looked at one another and then Chester leaned down and opened up the cashbox. Surly didn't stir. If anything would have brought him to, it would be someone touching his damn cashbox.

I took a quick peek down at it. At the top was a sheaf of papers. "What's that?"

Chester drew it out and held it up.

"Oh, shit," I said. "I think that's my contract."

"What's it doing in there?" said Chester.

"I don't know."

Chester put it on the seat and kept digging in the cashbox. I risked another quick glance and saw, for sure, that there was still a lot of money left.

"Hey, look at this." Chester lifted a wad of bills from the cashbox. It wasn't like any kind of money I'd seen before. It was a sort of faded brown and the top one had an ancient-looking figure with a beard printed on it. The writing didn't look like English. "What do you think that is?"

"Greek," Miguel said. "They are Greek drachmas."

Surly groaned and his eyes flickered open. He was coming to.

"Close it up," I hissed.

Chester put everything back—including my contract—and pushed the cashbox back into place by the stick shift. Surly stirred some more and blinked and then started to haul himself up. Chester moved to help him into a sitting position. For another minute or two, Surly just bounced along in the seat looking vacant.

"Bloody hell," he finally managed. "Where are we?"

"Maybe a hundred miles north of Cannes."

"Let me drive."

"Bobby," said Chester. "You need to take it easy."

"Bugger off," he said, and he tried to get up.

"Boss, you gotta be straight with us. How bad is it, you know, with the methadone?"

"Jesus, Chester, I'm doing what I have to do, all right?"

I glanced up into the rearview mirror. Surly's color had come back. "Is that why you were in jail?" I said.

"Who said I was in jail?"

"Frankie."

Surly made a sound deep in his throat, kind of a growl, but it didn't have much power in it. He was still pretty weak.

"Boss?"

"I told you, that's none of your bloody business. Frankie shouldn't have opened his big mouth."

"But did you really kill somebody?"

"Frankie said that?"

"Yeah."

"Levi," he said. "Just forget about it. You don't want to know." Surly craked his neck this way and that, like he was loosening it up. He took in a deep breath and looked directly at me in the mirror. "You of all people don't want to know."

Something was starting to niggle at me. "Bobby," I said. "When did all this happen?"

"Before you were born. So you don't need to worry about it."

I shifted my eyes back onto the road, but there was something in Surly's voice. Something he wasn't telling me.

That man was hiding something. I just didn't know what.

Funny, How That Goes

The villa sat on a rocky promontory halfway between Cannes and Nice. I could see it up there through the windshield, as big as a castle. The bus choked and burped up the hill and Rudy followed behind us in the Rolling Stones Mobile Studio truck. It was steep, this road, and I kept ducking my head to gawk up at the villa. Holy crap, it was glorious.

The road leveled out and we came to the entrance, two square brick pillars with a gate already swung open between them. We drove through, then down a short laneway and out into a wide graveled drive. There was a fountain in the middle, burbling and sparkling, with a little patch of rosebushes around it. The villa rose above us like a fortress, its stone walls covered in ivy, vines as thick as hockey sticks.

I turned off the ignition and Rudy pulled the truck in behind us. I heaved on the crank to open the door and Surly climbed out first with the cashbox in hand. He seemed to have recovered pretty well. "Mr. Christos?" he called out.

The front door was set into a little alcove between two fluted columns, and a balcony jutted out above it with a marble railing and thick curved balustrades. The louvered doors behind the balcony were open and I could see curtains up there fluttering in the breeze.

Surly called out again and a figure emerged on the balcony. I was still sitting in the driver's seat, but my heart clamped shut for a second because it was Ariadne. She came out wearing a sundress, barefoot, like Botticelli's Venus stepping out onto the seashell. I was still wearing my white bell-bottoms and a blue silk shirt, and suddenly I felt a little ridiculous.

"Go away," she called down at us.

Surly stepped across the gravel toward the villa. He shielded his eyes from the sun and gazed up at the balcony. "Ariadne," he said, "we're here."

"No. Go away."

I came down off the bus. It was bright out there, well into the afternoon, and it was warm, almost muggy.

"It's horrid, that photograph," Ariadne called down. "How could you give it to the press?"

Surly's shoulders were hunched, like he knew he was in for another fight. "You were hired to take photographs, Ariadne. That was the deal."

"Not photos like that. I am not your paparazzi."

"It was good publicity." He cast a glance back at me. "And look, Levi is fine. A little bruise there on his cheekbone, but he's fine."

She looked down at me and her lips tightened.

"I'm okay," I said. "Really. Everything's okay."

"Ariadne, where's your father?" Surly said. "We have an arrangement."

"He's not here."

"What do you mean, he's not here? I spoke with him on the phone just two days ago. We have the recording truck. We're all ready to go."

"He's gone. He left without me."

"Ariadne, we had a deal."

Ariadne sighed and shook her head in resignation. Surly took another step toward the front door. "And where's our boy, Frankie?"

"He doesn't want to talk to you either."

"Is he all right?" I asked.

"Why don't you ask him yourself?" she said, looking beyond us.

We all turned and there was Frankie, coming out of a garage-type building at the far end of the drive, pushing a wheelbarrow. He looked nothing like his usual self. He wore a plaid work shirt and jeans streaked with mud, and he came toward us in rubber boots that slapped almost up to his knees.

What the hell? I thought. I looked up again, but Ariadne had disappeared back into the villa.

Frankie pushed the wheelbarrow toward us, crunching through the gravel. There was an outboard motor sitting in it, its propeller circling slowly at each lurch of the wheelbarrow. He glanced at the Rolling Stones truck as he trundled by it, and Rudy had to quickly duck down below the steering wheel.

"Is that what I think it is?" Frankie said. He set down the wheelbarrow.

Surly grinned. "That's it, all right."

Frankie grimaced. "You're too late. We won't be needing it anymore."

"Frankie, my boy. We have an album to finish."

"Nah," said Frankie. "I'm out." He rubbed his hands together and hefted up the wheelbarrow again. "I'm not giving them any more of Pete's money."

"You are contractually obligated," began Surly. He sort of rattled the cashbox at him like that had anything to do with it.

"Fuck that. I'm done. You guys can carry on if you like, but I'm done with Downtown Exit."

The front door flung open and Ariadne came out onto the little porch. She was still barefoot. Frankie looked up at her. "You want I should let them into the ballroom?" he said.

"The ballroom?" said Surly.

"It's around the back," said Frankie, and he started pushing the wheelbarrow forward. "You gotta follow me."

Ariadne kind of sighed again. She stood there, looking beautiful, and I tried to catch her eyes. "You're to sleep in the pool house. And record in the ballroom. You can't come in any farther. I'm still putting things away." She turned and went back into the house. She didn't exactly slam the door behind her but it sure closed with a solid thunk.

"She's pretty pissed at you," Frankie called back.

"Why?" I said. "I thought—"

"Because her father has already left. She took too long getting here and now her father is gone. Without her."

"Aw, shit."

Frankie clomped off through the gravel. Chester and Miguel were still on the bus, pressing their faces to the windows like a couple of kids. Surly glared up at them. "Christ," he called to them. "Don't just sit there like a couple of wankers. Start hauling in the stuff already."

Rudy was peeking up just above the driver's-side window. He signaled to me that I shouldn't say anything. Frankie was oblivious anyway. He humped the wheelbarrow off around the side of the villa and Surly and me tottered after him. There was a little red cinder path around the side, and the villa towered above us. The walls were stone, old as the hills, and there were windows set high above us that looked almost medieval.

The outboard motor in the wheelbarrow was clanking, and the path sloped down a little so that Frankie had to plant his rubber boots with each step, holding the wheelbarrow so it didn't get away from him. I came up almost alongside him. "You need some help?"

"Look, pal. I don't want to fight anymore, okay? That was humiliating."

"You swung at me first."

"I was drunk," he said. "What did you expect?"

"Boys," said Surly, and he bustled up between us. "Let's all try and get along here."

"Fuck that," said Frankie. "And fuck Blackmore. I'm doing my own thing from now on. I could go solo. I could—"

"No, Frankie. Listen to me," said Surly. "We have to finish this album first. We have to."

"I'll do what I like, Bobby."

"No, actually you won't."

"You threatening me?"

"Frankie." The cashbox was still wedged up under Surly's arm. "There's a clause. 16b. It's part of your contract."

Frankie stopped. "What does that have to do with anything?"

I stood there, looking from one to the other.

"16b," Surly repeated. *"This contract supersedes any other contract and remains in effect for any member who chooses to resign and/or chooses to embark on a solo career."*

Frankie's face dropped.

"Even if you went solo," said Surly, "your music would still fall under this contract. Do you understand?"

"I can't even quit?"

"No. You can't. Labyrinth owns you." He paused to let that sink in. "Look, Frankie, we just have to finish this bloody album. If it does well, then maybe we can renegotiate."

"So we just let Blackmore win?" Frankie shook his head. "Then how about I do nothing? How about I never sing another note in my life? They can—"

"We still owe them the money, Frankie. A lot of it. We have no choice. Now, you want to quit your whinging and show us where this so-called ballroom is?"

Frankie pushed at the wheelbarrow again and lurched off around to the back of the villa. He didn't stop and we trailed after him. "Ballroom's in there," he said, and tipped his head back at the villa. "I'm not singing anymore."

He kept on going, humping that stupid wheelbarrow out across the lawn. Surly threw me a look and stomped after him. "Frankie," he called. "C'mon. It's not as bad as it sounds. Can we at least talk about this?"

♫

There was a swimming pool at the back, edged with flagstones, and beside it was a kind of gazebo thing that I think was the pool house. A manicured lawn ran out past that, a long swath of green, and at the end of that was a semicircular terrace and a low stone wall where the property seemed to drop off into nothing. Beyond that, stretching out into the distance, was the Mediterranean, greenish blue, sparkling in the afternoon sun.

"Wow," I said.

Along the back of the villa were windows. Some of them were

French doors, and the doors nearest me were opened just a crack, so I thought I'd take a quick peek inside. I slipped through, and it was a ballroom all right, a vast expanse with chandeliers and a polished wooden floor inlaid in a herringbone pattern. The furniture was covered in drop sheets, all except for a grand piano at the far end of the long room. It sat under the windows, its lid propped open, its ivory keys yellowed with age.

"Hello?" I called out, and I could hear the acoustics of the room bounce back at me, a crisp natural reverb.

It was perfect. I went back out around to the front and Chester and Miguel were hauling things off the bus. The Rolling Stones Mobile Studio was still sitting there, but now the back doors were open and the ladder was down.

"Rudy," I called, and heard a muffled answer from inside the truck. I went to the back and stepped up the ladder. The little vestibule at the back had shelves and cables, miles of them, rolled up on big wheels like garden hoses. Behind that were the sliding doors, the ones with the famous lips painted across them. They were closed. "Rudy? You in there?"

I slid the doors open and a cloud of smoke billowed out. Rudy sat on a stool at the mixing board with a massive joint in his hand. He was hunched over the board with a manual of some kind propped up on the sliders and sound meters.

"Rudy. What are you doing?"

"Someone's gonna have to work this thing." He flipped a page of the manual. "It's a Helios console," he said, and took a toke from the joint. "There are lines in for forty-four microphones. We route them onto twenty-four channels, you see, and then, and then—"

He stopped as if seeing me for the first time.

"What the hell are you smoking?" I asked.

"There was a bag of weed stashed in here. Look." He flipped open a panel under the mixing console. "It's like a secret compartment."

"Cool." I moved in closer. Rudy had turned on the mixing board, and there were rows and rows of sliders and buttons and little lit-up windows with gauges like miniature speedometers.

"Listen, Rudy," I said. "Did you notice something weird about Surly?"

"Like he keeps passing out all the time?"

"No, that's . . . Well, I'll tell you later. No, there's something else. He said something about when I was born."

Rudy squinted up at me. He was pretty stoned, but even so, his brow furrowed in confusion. "What are you trying to say?"

"I don't know. He was being all mysterious. He said there were things I didn't want to know about."

I stopped suddenly. Chester appeared outside. He had his bass drum hauled up in front of him like he was in a marching band or something. He raised his nose and sniffed at the air and then set the bass drum down into the gravel.

"Rudy," I said. "We'll talk about this later."

Chester hauled himself up into the truck. "Well shee-it," he said appreciatively. "What have we got here?"

"There was, like, a huge bag of dope," said Rudy, "in the hidden drawer here. See?" Rudy flipped the lid of the secret compartment up and down a couple of times. It squeaked a bit and I offered up the joint to Chester.

Chester took it and held it up, appraising it. "You suppose this is Keith Richards's private stash?"

"This is nothing," said Rudy. "I bet he's got mountains of the stuff."

"Damn," said Chester. He took a big draw on the joint, held it for a moment, and then blew out a stream of smoke. His eyes traveled over to the tape machine. Rudy had already got one of the two-inch tapes wound onto it.

"My man, you know how to work this thing?"

"I think so."

"Rudy," I said, "nice work."

"You just got to figure things out," he said. "It's not that hard."

He looked up at me like he was talking about more than just the recording equipment. He held my gaze for a moment until I got it. And I did. Rudy was my brother. We'd been through shit before and we always managed to figure it out, together.

"You're right," I said, and I gave him a little nod to show I understood. "We can make this work."

After that, we got pretty high before we realized we'd have to drive the truck around to the back. The little cinder path was not really meant for vehicles, let alone trucks, but for sure the only way to record would be to get the truck as close as possible to the ballroom.

Rudy started it up and Chester and me just went on ahead of him, walking backward, guiding him along. We took it real slow. Rudy took out a bush at the edge of the cinder path, but we got it back there. Then we still had to back it in between the villa and the pool.

I thought the whole damn thing might topple into the pool, but Rudy just backed in real slow, and when I put a hand up to stop him, he sort of slithered out the driver's-side door. There wasn't much room between him and the villa, that was for sure.

Chester was staring at the pool.

"Hey, man," I said. "Everything cool?"

He looked up at me and his mouth was tight. "It ain't nothing," he said, and shook his head. "The pool. It just reminds me of my kids."

"You got kids?" Rudy said.

"I messed up," Chester said, and shook his head again. "They must be damn near grown up by now."

"You don't talk to them?"

"I took off on them."

"Why would you do that?"

"Damn, Rudy. So I could bathe in the wonder of your sweet smile."

"Okay, okay," I said. "Why don't you guys lay off the smoke for a while. We got to start setting up."

The truth is, Chester's little speech reminded me that I was supposed to call Evelyn. I had some questions for her, that's for sure. But I stood there, just for a moment longer, staring at the pool. The sunlight was sparkling on it like little stars.

♫

I set myself up near Chester's drum kit. I had my old acoustic guitar, of course, and a Les Paul, but the third guitar case I'd grabbed from the gear truck turned out to be one of Davey's bass guitars. Chester gave a great guffaw when he saw me lift it out of its case. It was a big thick Fender Precision Bass, and the strings were fatter than anything I was used to.

Chester grinned over at me. "You think you can play that thing?"

"It's got strings, doesn't it?"

"Not the same thing at all," said Chester. "But you try it out. You just keep the beat with me. *Boom, boom, boom.* You understand? That's how we get it done."

"Chester," I said. "Why are you always making fun of me?"

"Because I like you, Boss."

Rudy was stringing cables in through the French doors and Miguel was over by the grand piano. He had his little cassette player and he'd set it up on top of the piano. The thing had an AM/FM radio band on it and he'd tuned it to a station. I don't know where it was beaming from, but they were playing some pretty good stuff. First some Moody Blues and then a little bit of Steely Dan. I liked it.

After the end chords of "Rikki Don't Lose That Number," the announcer came on and said something in French, and Miguel perked up. The next song started playing and it took me a second to realize what it was. Rudy noticed it first and then Chester looked over at the radio. There was a moment of almost stunned silence.

"That's 'Hello Juliet,'" said Chester. I had already risen up, listening, and out of that little radio speaker came the sound of my guitar. And then it was me singing, on the radio. "Holy shit," I said, and bounded over to the piano. "Turn it up."

We all gathered around. Rudy's mouth was open. Chester was bobbing his head and smiling. And me, well, I couldn't believe it. They say there's nothing like hearing your own song on the radio for the first time. And that was true, for sure. My heart was thumping and my hands were trembling. I wanted to shout. I wanted to tell the whole world, *That's my fucking song. Hey, everybody, that's my song on the radio.*

Out through the windows, Surly was trudging back across the lawn carrying his stupid cashbox like he wasn't ever going to let another human touch it. Chester waved at him frantically, and Surly furrowed his brow and picked up his pace. He marched in through the French doors.

"Bloody hell," he said. "What is it now?"

"Quiet," Chester said. "Just listen."

The second verse was starting. That bit about Romeo. And Surly froze.

"I'm on the radio," I said. I was grinning from ear to ear.

"Christ on a floating kite."

"Quiet," said Chester again, and we all listened right to the end of the song, the five of us gathered around that little radio player. It's probably the happiest I've ever been in my life.

And when it was over, Miguel gawked up at me with a strange expression.

"What?" I said.

"It is nothing. A mistake perhaps. The man, in French." He nodded at the radio. "He has said something about Pete."

"Pete's gone," I said. "This is the new Downtown Exit."

"Play us a little something there, Miguel," said Chester, and Miguel started up on the piano, a bouncy little tune, and Rudy started clapping out time. Chester took me by the arm and swung me out onto the dance floor, twirling me around like we were square dancing or something.

And then Ariadne appeared. She stood at the doors leading into the ballroom and we all stopped pretty quick. "Honestly," she said. "You are such children."

"Ariadne," I said. I must have been grinning like an idiot.

She looked a little alarmed at first, but then stepped toward me.

"My song," I sputtered. "My song was on the radio."

Her eyes widened. "Your song?"

"They were playing 'Hello Juliet' on the radio."

"Oh, Levi," she said, and to my surprise, she lurched forward and wrapped her arms around me. "That's wonderful. That's just what you wanted."

I could see Chester over her shoulder. He threw me a wink.

Surly was standing there too, his pinstripe suit bunching up around his shoulders, the cashbox cradled in his arms. He still seemed a little surprised by it all. "That is good news," he said. "I don't know why they didn't tell me."

Ariadne pulled away from me.

"I need to use your phone," Surly said.

Ariadne scrunched up her lips.

"Please, Ariadne. I need to use your phone. I have to know what they're up to."

She sighed. "It's down the hall, in the front entrance." She stepped aside and Surly went out. She turned to follow, and I went after them.

Surly was already stomping down the long hallway. There were closed doors on either side and all along the walls were framed photographs. I stopped at the first one, and just ahead of me, Ariadne stopped too.

"Hey," I said. "These are your photos."

The one beside me was that one from the gallery, that print of ancient ruins up on a little hill. The sun was setting on the old marble blocks and the ocean swept off into the distance behind it.

Ariadne stood there, watching me.

"But what are they doing here?" I asked.

"It was my father. He bought them all, anonymously. Isn't that just like him?"

"This one," I said, and pointed at the photo. "I really like this one. I'm kind of glad he got it."

"That's the Portara," she said. "The door to the temple of Apollo."

"And who was he again?"

"Apollo was the god of music, Levi."

"Right."

"And also the god of poetry."

"Well, that's kind of appropriate, isn't it?"

"It doesn't matter anymore." She looked up at me. Her lower lip was starting to tremble.

"My father's gone. He's probably in Athens by now."

"He really left?"

"And now I'm expected to close up the villa for him. To take care of everything. And I don't know how I'm supposed to—"

"I'm sorry, Ariadne. I know we held you up in Paris."

"It's all right. My father is not the kind of person to wait. I just thought he wanted me to go with him. I should have known better."

"I'm sorry."

"All the staff have been dismissed. The kitchens are empty. And I don't know what I'm supposed to do here. Maybe I can join him later in Greece, but I don't have—"

"There's money," I said.

"Pardon me?"

"Greek drachmas. In Surly's cashbox. There's tons of them. They must have been for your father, for renting this place."

"No, I'm sure—"

"So, it's yours now. There's tons of them."

She stared at me. "Are you quite certain?"

"If you need to go, go. He's your father."

Down the hall we could hear Surly on the phone. He was already yelling about something.

Ariadne brightened a little. "Then I'll have to start making arrangements. I'll need to—" She looked past me, back toward the ballroom. "Where's Frankie?"

"He took that boat engine somewhere, I think."

"The sailboat," she said. "It'll need to be dry-docked in Nice. And then I'll—"

"And then you'll need to leave," I finished for her. She nodded and turned to face me.

"Levi," she said, and I waited. "I'm sorry it has to be like this."

"I'm sorry too, Ariadne. Really I am."

She nodded again and gave me a weak smile.

"But I have a song on the radio," I said, trying to lighten the mood. "Maybe everything's going to work out after all."

She didn't answer and I held her gaze for a moment longer. Then she turned and stepped off down the hallway. I could hear Surly somewhere down at the front entrance. He was still on the phone, yelling. And I wondered what that was all about.

♫

The pool house was made from the same rough stones as the villa. It was octagonal, with tall windows around all its sides. The floor was bare cement, but somebody had set up a row of cots for us, like a military camp hospital or something. Along the far wall, there were a bunch of plastic pool chairs stacked up against the windows, and beside them a set of shelves that held towels and some floaty things for the pool. It kind of smelled of chlorine, if you really want to know the truth.

I thumped my black bag down onto one of the cots. I'd brought in my guitar too. I'd taken it out of its case and was strumming on it, just sitting on my cot. Chester was stretched out on the cot beside mine, his hands behind his head, his feet crossed. Rudy was setting up microphones in the ballroom and we thought it'd be faster if we just got out of his way.

We hadn't been there long when Surly came crashing in, his face a bit red, that vein sticking out on his forehead. Chester rose a little from his cot and I stopped playing my guitar. Surly marched over to the last bunk and sat down hard. "Bloody hell."

"What's up, Boss?"

"Jesus," said Surly, and he tapped out a cigarette. "It's one step forward and two back with those people."

"What'd they say?" I said.

Surly lit his cigarette and took a long hard pull on it. Then he let the smoke drift out slowly. "First," he said, "they did release 'Hello Juliet.' But only in France."

"Okay." Why did I get the feeling this wasn't good news?

"It's already hit the charts." He wasn't making eye contact with me. In fact, he was deliberately avoiding my gaze. "It's number seven."

"Well, that's great, isn't it?"

"They sent it up like a trial balloon," he said. "Because of our Paris shows and maybe because of our little party too. The French programmers, Levi. Maybe they liked our little stunt with the coke. Blackmore's not too happy about that."

"But it's number seven?" I said.

"I told Blackmore we were finishing up the album at Dmitry Christos's villa and that shut him up." Surly shook his head and looked down.

"Is there something more?"

"Don't worry. I'm going to fix this. I've got a plan."

"What's that supposed to mean? Fix what?" I got up and laid my old guitar down on the cot. Surly was staring at it like he was thinking. There was something going on for sure.

"What is it, Bobby? What's going on?"

"You got a broken tuning peg there, huh?" I thought that was a weird thing to say, like he was deliberately trying to change the subject. It's true, five of the tuning pegs were the original silver pegs, but the sixth was a plastic replacement part. Surly took another puff on his cigarette. He eyed me through the smoke. "You know, I used to play a little."

"Yeah?"

"I was never very good. Lots of guys better than me."

Chester sat up. "Bobby," he said. "Why didn't you ever tell us you played guitar?"

"Because it didn't go well. Can we just forget about that for a second? We got more important problems to deal with here."

"But you played guitar?"

"Levi. There's a problem, all right? If you would just stop to think for a second, you'd know there's a problem."

"What problem?"

"Bloody hell. Do I have to explain everything? It's Frankie."

"What about him?"

"Someone's gonna have to tell him that it's not '29 Streetlights.' "

"Oh, shit," I said, and Surly glared at me.

"You're the one who changed things, so you're the one that has to tell him."

"Me?"

"I'll give you ten minutes. Then I'll come down to make sure he hasn't hit you again."

♫

The lawn swept out behind the pool house all the way to the cliffs, and I trudged across the grass, swearing a bit under my breath. At the end of the lawn, a couple of steps led down to the semicircular terrace. It was skirted by a low stone wall. And beyond that and far below was the sea, spreading all the way out to the horizon. I could see a big sailboat moored out there in the little bay. It was white and sleek and anchored to a floating red ball maybe a hundred yards from the shore. I was pretty sure it was *The Northern Star*.

A dirt trail wound down the cliff, zigging and zagging all the way to the beach below. I could see a small shed there, a sort of boathouse, and a wooden dock sticking out into the water. Frankie and Ariadne were out on the dock, looking at something in the water.

I stood for a moment on the stone terrace high above them. The crystal waters of the Mediterranean spread in front of me, flat as a mirage, sparkling in the slanting sun. For a moment, I thought to call down to them, but they looked so peaceful down there, like a couple of kids on the last day of summer.

I was still wearing the clothes I'd arrived in, my white bell-bottoms and my stupid platform shoes. That's all I'd managed to salvage of my concert wardrobe. It was really hot out now, but I plunged down the dusty path anyway. I wobbled once or twice on those high heels. *Really stupid shoes*, I thought, but I kept going, and finally I came out into the little bay. From here you couldn't see the villa above us. There was nothing but the lapping of the waves on the pebbled beach.

I came out onto the beach and I saw what Frankie and Ariadne were doing. There was a little skiff, a rowboat really, tied alongside the dock. I imagine they used it to ferry things to the larger sailboat, out in the bay. Frankie had just set the outboard motor onto a cleat at the back of it. He was bent over it, adjusting something with a wrench. Ariadne stood over him. She was wearing a chiffon wrap over a bathing suit and was telling him something.

I clunked out onto the slats of the dock and Ariadne and Frankie both turned at the sound. Frankie stood up when he saw me. His hands were covered in grease. "Well, shit," he said. "If it ain't our little Levi."

Frankie looked good, muscular and quite sober, and I was all the more aware of how pale I was, and how skinny.

"Frankie," I began, "they're setting up the stuff in the ballroom. You have to come up." I said all this but really I was looking at Ariadne.

"Nah," Frankie said. "I don't think so."

"But we have to finish the album."

Frankie shrugged.

"C'mon, man," I said. "We can record that song you did in Paris, you know, at Jim Morrison's grave." Ariadne was watching me, and she nodded at me to continue. To keep encouraging him.

"It's a good song. We should record it."

He shrugged again but it was a "maybe" kind of shrug.

"And about that—" I went on.

He waited, staring at me. Ariadne gave me another little nod.

"It's just that, well, we heard the single has come out."

He picked up a rag and started trying to clean off his hands. "They fucking edited it?" he said.

"No," I started, "not exactly."

" '29 Streetlights?' " For a moment, he brightened. "They kept the whole thing?"

"No, Frankie, that's not—"

He just stared at me. "Then what? What, exactly?"

Ariadne murmured something and I looked at her. She was staring past me, up the path that led back up the embankment. When I took a glance behind me, I saw Surly huffing down it, waving at us.

"Oh, crap," I said.

"Right," said Ariadne. "I'm off, then." She stepped down into the skiff and I could tell she was used to being on the water. The boat only rocked a bit and she sat down on a slat near the back. "I'll leave you boys to it."

Frankie stood back. He was kind of grinning and he gave a circular motion with his hand for her to start up the engine. It was just a pull cord, like on a lawn mower, and she tugged on it and it started up right away, a sort of chugging sound.

"There you go," said Frankie. "Works like a charm." He bent down and unfastened the rope that tied the skiff to the dock.

Ariadne waved at us, then turned to face the open water. She opened up the throttle, which was on a long hockey stick kind of thing sticking out of the engine. She turned it and the whole thing swiveled, and the little skiff puttered out into the bay.

Surly thumped up onto the dock behind us, a bit out of breath.

"What's with her?" he said.

"She has to get the sailboat ready," I said.

"For what?"

"For leaving. She's leaving, Bobby, and you have to give her her money."

Surly eyed me. "You been digging around in the cashbox?"

"It's hers, Bobby. You were supposed to pay her father."

Surly shrugged.

Frankie was looking at both of us. He'd stuck the wrench in his back pocket and was back to wiping his hands on the little rag.

"Did you tell Frankie the news?"

Frankie met my eyes. He looked healthy. Really, he did. The muscles in his jaw flexed. "What exactly are you trying to say?" he asked.

"The single," I said. "It's 'Hello Juliet.' They put my song on the A side."

A sort of bemused expression lit across Frankie's face. And that wasn't what I expected.

"What?" I asked.

"It's not your song," said Frankie.

"No," I said, "it's 'Hello Juliet.' They put it on the A side. That's what I'm trying to tell you."

"You poor dumb fuck," said Frankie. "They've screwed you too. Didn't you tell him, Bobby?"

Surly took out his pack of cigarettes. He was sweating, dark stains coming right through the armpits of his pinstripe suit. His face was flushed, and I wondered if he might not have another attack.

Way out in the bay, Ariadne had arrived at the sailboat. A little ladder hung over the back, and she tied off the skiff and stepped gingerly up into the back of the boat.

Surly snapped open his lighter and took in a deep draw on his cigarette.

"Wait, no," I said. "It's my song. I wrote it."

"Actually, it's not," said Surly. "Downtown Exit songs are Novak and Gunnerson songs. That's the way the publishing works."

"But—"

"It's a good song," said Surly. He jabbed his cigarette at me. "I'll give you that."

"Of course it's good. I wrote it."

"Settle down. I'm just explaining how the contract is written."

Frankie squinted at me. "They put my name and Pete's name on all the songs. I thought you knew that."

"So you get the royalties?"

"Half," said Surly. "Labyrinth gets the other half."

"Shit," I said. "So I get nothing?"

"It's not technically your song, Levi." Surly shook his head as if there were nothing he could do. He took another drag on his cigarette.

"No. That can't be." I felt almost sick to my stomach.

"There's more," said Surly, and he looked over at Frankie.

"What?" said Frankie.

"Now, listen. The both of you. Don't take this the wrong way."

Frankie stared him down. "What now, Bobby?"

"It's Pete," he said. "They've had a little brainstorm over at Labyrinth and they're saying that 'Hello Juliet' should be Pete's last song."

I looked over at Frankie and his face had gone tight. I felt like I was going to puke.

"All right," said Surly. "It's like this. The only way they can market 'Hello Juliet' is by saying it's Pete Gunnerson's swan song. They're going to say that he wrote it and that he sang on it and that it's the last damn thing he did before he died. It's a great angle, actually."

"But that's my song. That's me." I was struggling to even talk now. I couldn't believe it. "That's me singing and playing the guitar."

"Yeah," said Frankie. "That ain't right."

Surly held up a placating hand. "Now, listen, boys. I can still fix this. You don't have to—"

"No," I sputtered.

"Just hear me out. I've got a plan."

"No," I said. "You should just shut up now. And you"—I whirled on Frankie—"you need to fuck off." I paused. "In fact, both of you can just fuck off and die."

I spun around and ran off the end of the dock. I didn't bother to kick off my shoes or anything. I just dove into the water. It came up faster than I thought and suddenly I was under. The world disappeared for a moment in a gurgle of bubbles, but I kicked my legs and surfaced and began to swim toward the sailboat.

♫

When I popped up again, the boat seemed pretty far away. Ariadne was at the back of it, watching to see if I could swim okay. I was actually a pretty decent swimmer. Evelyn used to take me and Rudy to the pool when we were teenagers. I always liked it.

My platform shoes were definitely an impediment, though, so I stopped, took a deep breath, and reached down and yanked them off one by one, letting them drift to the bottom. My shirt was plastered to me, but my bell-bottoms were a light cotton and not too bad. I kicked forward and swam toward the boat, but the next time I looked up I didn't seem to have gained on it at all.

It was pretty far. I had to stop a couple times to correct my direction. When I got closer, I tucked my head down and swam hard, pulling through the water with my hands, kicking with my stupid socks slowly pulling off my feet. I didn't stop again until I was almost there, around the back at the ladder. The name of the boat was painted across the back in curlicue lettering but of course I couldn't read it. I knew what it was called anyway.

The waves were nudging at me, bumping me into the hull, so I got a grip on the ladder and tried to get my foot up onto the lowest rung. I was kind of twisted up like a kid on the monkey bars. Ariadne stood above me.

"What are you doing, Levi?"

"What are *you* doing?" I said back.

"Here," she said. "You have to wait for the waves to lift you. Use the water." I let go and paddled around, my head up, like a dog. The sea was rising and falling, but gently, and I reached up to the highest rung and just waited, and sure enough, the next wave lifted me, and I got my foot on the lowest rung, and then it was easy to step up. Near the top, Ariadne reached down to take my hand, and she pulled me over the gunwale, and I slopped down into the boat like a fish being reeled in.

"They've stolen my song," I said.

"Who?"

"Frankie, Surly, everybody. They say I signed away the rights." I hauled myself up and looked back at the shore. "Now they're saying it's Pete's song." Frankie and Surly were already walking back up the path to the villa. Surly had his hand on Frankie's shoulder. They were tucked into each other like they were having some kind of secret conversation. "Bastards," I said.

I began to peel off my shirt and Ariadne sat down on the bench that ran around the deck at the back. A massive steering wheel stuck up in front of us and beyond that was a sort of hatch that led into the cabin. Above us was the boom, poking out horizontally from the mast, the sail folded down over it and wrapped in a tarp.

Ariadne was staring up at me. "What are you going to do?"

"I don't know."

I put a hand on the boom to steady myself and pulled off my one remaining sock, kind of hopping on one foot to get it off. I flung it overboard. She watched it flop into the water.

"Maybe," I said. "Maybe we should just sail away. Go to Greece. Like, right now."

"Greece is about two thousand miles away, Levi. It would take us weeks to get there."

"But I don't want to be here anymore."

"Levi," she said again. And she patted the bench for me to come and sit beside her. "I'll have to dock the boat in Nice. That's where we keep it for the winter."

I sat down beside her. My pants were sodden, and a little pool formed beneath me.

"Have you ever been on a sailboat before?"

"Not really."

She shook her head in resignation. "Well, then . . ." She didn't need to finish that sentence. Up on the embankment, Surly and Frankie were still climbing, almost at the top now, almost at the stone terrace.

"Ah," she said. "Just look at us. We're two lost souls."

"Yeah. Funny, how that goes."

She stopped and looked at me with those big jade-green eyes. "That's actually quite a nice imperfect rhyme."

"It is?"

"I need to write that down. Here." She stood up. "Come inside. Let me show you around."

I got up and followed her, edging around the big steering wheel. The top section of the hatch came off like the lid of a box and then the doors below just slid open to either side. A wooden ladder, maybe three steps or so, led down into the cabin.

Inside, it was mostly polished wood. There was a little kitchen to the left, and another nook to the right with a desk and a two-way radio and some charts laid out showing the tides or currents or something. Ariadne sat down there, still in her chiffon wrap. She picked up a pen.

"You're writing down those lines?"

She looked up at me and smiled. "Yes." She held up a little scrap of paper and read it out loud:

> *"I met my love in paradise.*
> *We had coffee on the Spanish Steps.*
> *She said, 'Ah, look at us, we're two lost souls.'*
> *And he said, 'Funny . . . how that goes.' "*

"You just came up with that right now, like, out of the blue?"

"It's a start. Maybe it needs some work, but—"

"No, no, it's good." I looked at the paper. I could make out a couple of the words. "But what are the Spanish Steps?"

"That's where Keats died."

"Jeez," I said. "Is it really so easy for you to write like that?"

She handed the paper to me. "Tell me, Levi, what do you hear with this?"

"You want me to write a song to it?"

She just sat there expectantly, and I held up the paper. And she was right. A melody was already forming in my head. Her words were already turning into music. I hummed a bit of it, then tried it out with the words.

She stood up, standing very close to me, reading the words over my shoulder. Then she leaned forward and kissed me on the cheek. The touch of her lips was soft and warm.

She shuffled around closer to me, and I put down the paper and wrapped my arms around her. Her skin was still warm. Outside, the sky was getting dark, purpling into evening.

Then she took my hand and led me to the berths near the front. They were a little like the ones on the canal boats in Amsterdam. Kind of odd-shaped, a bit triangular, just big enough for a little bed and some shelves.

And we made love there with the sea shushing at the hull. And through the porthole above, I could see a star hovering in the evening sky, twinkling and glittering down on us like a land of dreams.

The Other Side

The music was slow and haunting, just a simple piano line, just a pulse of chords. It must have been around midnight when we got back. Light was spilling out from the ballroom windows, out across the pool to the lawn beyond. The Rolling Stones Mobile Studio was no more than a dark lump parked up against the wall, and we stopped, me and Ariadne, to listen to Miguel playing the grand piano.

"Wait," said Ariadne. "You can't go in there like that." I was barefoot. My pants were still a little damp and I had no shirt. I think I was shivering. "Just a second," she said, and disappeared into the pool house. When she came out she had a couple of big fluffy bathrobes. They were folded up. They must have been on the shelves.

I took one and unfolded it and slipped it on. She got into the other.

"I'm off to bed. You should go on in."

Rudy appeared at the back of the truck. "Shit, Levi. Where have you been?"

Ariadne smiled up at him. "Goodnight, boys," she said, and walked off around the pool. There was a staircase on the far side of the villa. She headed toward it and gave us a sort of backward wave as she left.

Rudy grinned at me. He came down the ladder and stood beside me. "She's cool," he said. "Did you two just—?"

"Rudy, it's none of your business." I turned again to listen to the music. "Shit, did they tell you about 'Hello Juliet'?" I said. "Those fuckers screwed me over. They—"

"Yeah. I heard. Surly's trying to fix it."

The back doors of the Rolling Stones truck were open. The ladder was down, and spools of cables ran out of it and down along the ground and into the ballroom.

"How's he supposed to fix it?"

"Look," said Rudy. "I don't know. Surly's working on it, okay? Frankie feels real bad about it too."

"You talked to Frankie?"

"Yeah, he knows I'm here. I don't think he gives a shit."

"This is all really fucked-up, Rudy." I looked up into the back of the truck. "I don't know how they expect me to record anymore. I mean, why would I want to when—?"

"Levi, things are all set up."

"And who's supposed to be recording us? We don't have time to get a proper engineer."

"No," said Rudy. "So—"

"Wait," I said. "It's you? You're doing it?"

"Jeez, Levi. Yes, me. Okay? Just go in and put on your headphones. Everything's set up. It's all ready to go."

The French doors opened just then, and the piano music poured out. Chester stuck his big head through the door. "Levi, there you are."

I stood there in my stupid bathrobe, barefoot, a bit pissed off at the world.

"You got to come in. We're going to record."

"Jesus, Chester. I don't want to. And what about Frankie, he—?"

"Listen. I think we got it figured out. Maybe we got a way out. Just come on in."

"Aw, fuck, Chester. They stole my song."

"Naw, listen to me. I think we got a way out."

"How?"

"Well," he said. "Labyrinth pays for the recording studio, they own the songs, right?"

"Yeah, but—"

"This time, they're not paying for the studio. We got the Rolling Stones Mobile Studio. They're not paying for that, so they don't own any of the recordings."

"Are you sure about that?"

"Frankie figured it out. He says—"

I threw up my hands in frustration. "But what about me? What about 'Hello Juliet'?"

"Boss," he began. "I'm real sorry about that."

"What did I ever do to deserve this?"

"Well, we burned down a hotel room," Chester said.

"And the tour bus is pretty banged up," said Rudy.

"And we stole a bunch of equipment," Chester went on.

"And," said Rudy, "we kind of stole the Rolling Stones truck."

"Yeah," I said. "But besides that, we've been pretty good."

"Look, Boss," said Chester. "I'm only a drummer." He eyed me, making sure I was listening. "I'm only the drummer but I love what I do, you know what I mean? And I especially love to drum in a band as good as this one."

"I know."

"No, you don't," he said. "It's like I'm the heartbeat. When I'm sitting behind the kit, I get to be the heartbeat of the whole band. I get to be the heartbeat of the whole damn world. You couldn't pay me enough to stop." He paused and grinned. "Be nice to get paid a little, though."

That made me smile.

"This is not about Labyrinth. It's not about Blackmore or Surly or any of that stuff. It's about the music, Levi. It's what we do. It's who we are."

"Aw, shit, Chester," I said.

"So, you coming in or what?"

♫

Surly came at me right away. "Bloody hell, where have you been?" The ballroom had been completely transformed. Cables lay across the parquet floor like spaghetti. Microphones were everywhere. Miguel sat at the grand piano under one of those big chandeliers. Frankie was in jeans and a plain white T-shirt. He was standing in front of a microphone just beside the piano. There were still drop cloths over most of the rest of the furniture, but it had all been pushed off to the sides now so that it was just us and our circle of equipment, buzzing and humming and all ready to go.

Surly pulled me toward my little station of guitars. "Is it true?" I asked him, and I kind of shuffled off his arm. "Are we really going to own everything this time?"

Surly glanced over at Frankie. "Well," he said, "we're checking into it."

"But Chester just said—"

"It's not quite that simple, Levi. But trust me. I'm working on it."

I went over and sat down on my squat little amplifier. My pants were still a bit damp and a little itchy and I had the big fluffy bathrobe wrapped around my shoulders.

Frankie grinned over at me. "What the hell have you been up to?"

I tucked my bathrobe in closer, fumbling to cinch up the cloth belt around my waist. "Screw off," I said.

"Listen, Levi," he said. "You don't have to like me. You don't have to like any of this."

I didn't say anything.

"Believe me. I hate it way more than you do, the way they're using Pete."

"Listen, Frankie. I don't know what happened between you two. I don't even care."

He grimaced. "That's not—" he started. He took in a big gulp. "Listen, Levi, I can't help it. I can't help who I am."

"For fuck's sake, Frankie. I don't care if you're gay, all right? I don't care if you're a little green man from Mars." I paused. "I only care about the music."

Chester was watching me from across the room. Frankie was speechless for once.

"Shit," I went on. "You're a hell of a singer. Okay? That's the only important thing here."

Frankie was staring at me. He wasn't sneering like he usually did. In fact, he kind of shrugged. "I am pretty good," he agreed.

"All right," I said. "So, let's just get on with it."

Somebody—probably Rudy—had already set up my Les Paul. I hoisted it up and plucked at the strings one by one to make sure they were in tune. A set of headphones lay on the amplifier beside me. Everything was mic'd up and plugged in, the cords running along the floor like the tributaries of a river, joining others, all running into bundles, taped together, and heading out through the doors to the Mobile Studio. Crap, I had to give Rudy credit. It really did look like everything was working.

I tucked the headphones down over my head and the ambience of the room hissed back at me. Rudy's voice came through my headphones. "Ready when you are."

We ran through the song a couple of times, and when we had it, Rudy started rolling the tape. Miguel started off with a lilting blues run on the grand piano, and Frankie leaned into his microphone, growling out his words, as intense as I'd ever heard him. Really, the song was haunting and beautiful. It was about death, all right. Seeing heaven from the other side. It was about Pete being gone and about finally owning up to that fact. It was sad and beautiful and mysterious and absolutely perfect. And when the last chord faded away, the room went silent. We all froze until we heard a click in the headphones, and we knew that that was Rudy shutting off the tape machine.

Surly stood up. He'd been sitting on a chair by the windows, trying to be quiet. "That's it," he said. "That's pure gold right there."

♫

We all trundled out to listen back to the tape. It was quiet outside. The Rolling Stones Mobile Studio sat like a dinosaur, its guts spilling out the back, bundles of cable as thick as my leg. The swimming pool was as dark as a mirror and the pool house beyond it was silhouetted against the sky.

"Rudy," Surly called.

His face appeared at the back of the truck, his hair a frazzle, straw-colored like a scarecrow's.

"Did you get all that?" he asked.

"Yeah," he said. "Hop on up." He disappeared back through the doors. And when we all squeezed into the truck, Rudy was cuing up the tape. It was thick—black two-inch recording tape—and he'd written the name of the song on a piece of masking tape and stuck it on the reel.

The Helios console was at the back, a vast field of faders and buttons and sound meters. Rudy had laid a line of masking tape along the bottom of the faders. In felt pen he'd written what each track was: Frankie's vocal mic, my guitar, and so on down the line. There were about eight different tracks just for the drums. Surly bent over the mixing board, studying the layout.

"Good work, Rudy," he said. "Let's have a listen."

Rudy pressed the play button and the music started up.

Chester turned to Frankie. "It's good, Boss. Pete would've loved it."

Frankie bowed his head, and no one said anything for a minute. We were all just remembering Pete. Then Frankie said, "I think it needs a guitar solo."

Miguel nodded at me like he thought that was a good idea too.

"And someone needs to play bass," he said.

I looked at Rudy.

"Me?" he said.

"You play?" asked Frankie.

"Well, a little."

Surly nudged Rudy out of the way. "Right, then. I'll handle things out here. How many tapes do we have?"

"Two," Rudy replied. "The one on the machine and this one." He showed him the second box, not yet used.

"How many songs you figure we can get on each tape?" asked Surly.

"I don't know. Maybe three or four on each."

"Right, you want to show me how to do it?"

Rudy hit the rewind button, and a counter at the bottom of the machine began to whirl back through numbers. "So 'The Other Side' is on the first five minutes of the tape. Let me just set it to the beginning."

Surly was leaning over the tape recorder.

"Then you just press record?"

"Yeah. Press play and record at the same time and you're ready to go."

"Simple as that?" said Surly.

"Yeah, and then you come over to the mixing board."

"You're not as dumb as you look, are you?"

"Nope," said Rudy. "You just punch in the tracks you need. These little buttons here."

"I know how to work a mixing board."

"Right, of course."

We all went back inside and took our places again. Rudy lumbered over to the big square bass guitar case that was sitting behind my amp and lifted out the Fender Precision. He tried out a few runs on it. His big fingers were totally suited to the bass guitar, not that he was great, but he could do a simple bassline. I was pretty sure of that.

I put on my headphones and could hear them hissing. Everything was turned on. I went over to my vocal mic. "Bobby," I said, "you ready out there? You know what you're doing?"

There was no answer.

"Bobby," I said. "You there?"

His voice came through the headphones. "Just bloody go."

"Roll it from the beginning, then."

"Wait a second," he said. His voice was thin in the headphones. I could hear the click of the machine. "Right, it's rolling."

The playback came through my headphones, Miguel's piano run at the beginning and then Frankie's lead vocal coming in, haunting and tortured. Across the room, Rudy tucked his head down, listening in his own headphones, and he played his first note, just a thump, just an open E. But it sounded good. It grounded everything.

I sang a bit of a harmony on the chorus since my mic was still live, and then about three-quarters of the way through there was a little section that was instrumental, and Frankie nodded at me. I lit into a guitar solo, nothing fancy, just something melodic, and it sounded pretty good right off the bat. And when the final notes of the song faded out, we all stayed still for another few seconds until we heard the click of Surly shutting off the machine.

"You get that?" I said into the mic.

"Got it. Want me to rewind it again?"

"Nah," Frankie said. "I think that's it." He was watching me from across the room. "Nice work."

I tipped my head.

"I mean it. You're good."

I didn't say anything.

He studied me for a moment more. "Listen, Levi. We're in the same boat here. You're just another guy Blackmore is screwing." His eyes hung on me. "You know that, right? You're not any different from the rest of us."

"I know," I said. "I know."

♫

It was really late when we finally finished up. Frankie went off into the villa and the rest of us trailed out to the pool house. I couldn't sleep. I just lay there on my cot, thinking about all that had happened in the last twenty-four hours. Chester was snoring on the cot beside me. Miguel was a bit farther on, just a lump in the shadows, and Surly was there too, on the far cot. I could hear him breathing and I wasn't sure if he was still awake.

It was maybe two or three in the morning, which meant that it would still be early evening in Calgary. Quietly, I got up, slid into my jeans, and pulled on a T-shirt. When I stepped out onto the flagstones, they were still warm under my bare feet. A full moon was up, and everything was cast in silver.

I tiptoed over to the French doors and let myself in. Everything was dark and silent, and my feet slapped a bit on the parquet floor. I was really hoping I wouldn't wake Ariadne, but the place was huge and she was upstairs somewhere, so I thought I was good.

I went down the hall to the front entrance. It was like a lobby, all marble with potted plants and stuff, and a massive staircase led from there up to a mezzanine level. To the side of the staircase was a little nook and black rotary phone on a shelf. I picked it up and started dialing.

It rang three times before Evelyn finally picked up. “Hello?” She sounded very far away.

“It’s me.”

“Well, young man. It’s about time. I’ve been worried sick about—”

“Rudy told me everything,” I said, cutting her off.

There was silence on the other end.

“Why didn’t you tell me that—that you’re my mother?”

“Oh, Levi. You don’t know how hard I—”

“I’m not phoning to fight with you. I just want to know why.”

“It’s not what you think,” she began. “I tried to make things right. I really did. And then everything—”

“I’m not blaming you. I just want to understand.”

“Please tell me that Rudy is okay. At least tell me that.”

“He’s fine, Evelyn.” I couldn’t bring myself to call her Mom yet. “He’s here with us. He’s been doing good.” What I didn’t tell her was that he was sleeping in the truck. We couldn’t close the doors on account of the cables spilling out of the back, so he was guarding it at night. That and a big bag of killer weed.

“I always told him,” Evelyn went on, “that if he just applied himself, he’d do quite well.”

“Evelyn, please. This is not about Rudy.”

“All right, then.”

“First of all, tell me, was it Bobby you phoned? It was him, wasn’t it?”

I heard her sigh. “He was not to say anything to you.”

“But how do you even know him?”

“Levi, it was a long time ago.”

“Then tell me. I need to know.”

There was a pause on the other end, then Evelyn started in on it. “When I was in New York, I used to spend a lot of time at the folk clubs in Greenwich Village.”

“You?”

“It was exciting. Jack Kerouac, Allen Ginsberg. There was quite a scene going on.”

"And you played piano there?"

"No," she said. "Don't be ridiculous. I was studying classical music. You know that." She paused. "There was one club in particular that I used to go down to."

"To hear the folk singers?"

"Yes, if you must know."

"Oh, man. It was Bobby, wasn't it?"

"I knew him, yes."

A terrible thought was dawning on me. "Evelyn, do you want to tell me who my father is?"

"Levi, that's not important anymore."

"No," I said. "It is important. You have to tell me."

"I don't think it—"

"Is it Bobby?" Jesus fucking Christ. I couldn't believe it. "Is Bobby my father?"

There was silence on the other end. But just for a moment. Then Evelyn began to laugh. "Levi Jaxon," she managed. "That is the most patently ridiculous thing I've ever heard. Bobby Malone? Why, that man couldn't—"

"Well, if he's not my father, then who the hell is?"

"Language, Levi. Please."

"Well?"

"You don't have to worry about that. Your father has been gone these many years."

"Gone where?"

"Really, Levi, that's neither here nor there. It doesn't matter anymore."

I had a big lump in my throat, if you want to know the truth. I mean, sure, I was glad it wasn't Surly. That would be too much to bear. But if it wasn't him, then who? And why the hell had she called Surly to set up my audition? What was that all about?

"Evelyn—"

"He was a musician, Levi. Just like you. But now he's gone, and I don't want to talk about it anymore."

I didn't know what to say. My hands started shaking and there was a long silence on the phone. I finally just said that I had to go. I pressed down on the button to hang up, but I kept the receiver held up to my ear. I stayed there for a long time. I just listened to the dial tone. I think it was A-flat.

♫

When I went back outside, I saw a little spark glowing in the darkness, way out by the terrace, and I knew it was Surly having a smoke. I could just make out his silhouette. He was sitting on the low stone wall that looked out over the sea.

I walked across the grass toward him, and when I got there, he looked up, almost like he'd been expecting me. He was just sitting there waiting for me. He stamped out his cigarette, but he didn't stand up.

"You phoned her?"

"I couldn't sleep," I said, plopping myself down beside him. "What else was I supposed to do?"

"And she told you everything?"

"Not quite everything."

He peered at me closely. "What all did she say?"

"I got some questions for you."

"All right," he said. "Take it easy."

"Just tell me what really happened. I have a right to know."

"Aw, Christ," he said. "She was new to the city, all right? All rosy-cheeked and wide-eyed. She was in a bit over her head, if you ask me."

"Did you like her?"

"Look," said Surly. "It was a long time ago. She used to come by the club where I worked. She used to come in with friends, students from Juilliard, I guess."

"What did you do to her?"

"Nothing, Levi. I just worked at the club." He shook his head, remembering. "Christ, Levi, I was wishing I could be up on that stage. There were some really good players there. Guys way better than me."

The moon was glowing. Everything was shimmering like it wasn't quite real.

"Evelyn was a knockout. It's not like you weren't going to notice her." Surly seemed lost in his own thoughts. "Later on, she just came in by herself."

"Bobby, what happened to her?"

He wasn't really meeting my eyes.

"He was a guitar player. He was good, handsome as hell. And Evelyn was young."

"Shit," I said. "She fell in love with some guitar player?"

"Of course she was in love. That was the problem." He shook his head and looked at me. "Christ, I can see his face in yours."

I felt a hollow in my stomach. I waited for him to go on.

"Lots of girls came in. He took advantage of them. Who wouldn't? She didn't stand a chance."

"Jesus, Surly. You're talking about my mother."

"Don't call me Surly."

"Then don't be an asshole."

"Levi, I'm trying to tell you. You don't have to worry about this anymore."

"No," I said. "It's my father. I have a right to—"

Surly stared me down. "He's gone. Long gone."

"Where? Where did he go?"

"Jesus, Levi. He's dead. All right? He's dead."

"What? How do you know that?"

"Because I killed him."

♫

Surly heaved himself to his feet. He stood there a moment, then strode off down the trail to the beach. He didn't look back.

"Bobby, wait." I scrambled after him. The path was really kind of steep. The full moon shone across the cliffs and, out in the black sea, the sailboat was bobbing, ghostly and pale, its mast swaying back and forth like a slow metronome. I had my Adidas on again, so I caught up with him pretty quick. “Hey,” I said. “You have to tell me what happened.”

We were already halfway down when he suddenly stopped. He whirled on me. “It was an accident, all right? Now fuck off.”

He kept going, stomping down the path, and he didn’t stop till he got to the bottom. I didn’t stop either. He crunched off ahead of me, across the pebbled beach toward the dock, and I finally just made a grab for his elbow. That was a mistake. He swung around and slammed his fist into my gut. For a moment I couldn’t breathe. I bent over like I was going to puke.

“Ow,” I finally managed. “What was that for?”

“That’s so you fuck off with all your questions.”

I straightened up slowly. Out on the dock, the little rowboat was clattering against the boards with that stupid outboard motor attached to the back. The beach was pretty much silver in the moonlight and little waves were frothing onto the shore.

Surly stood there glaring at me. He felt for his cigarette pack and brought it out. “Listen,” he said. “Evelyn used to come down damn near every weekend.”

He popped the cigarette between his lips. He didn’t light it, but it wobbled when he spoke.

“I didn’t see her for months, then one day in the spring she showed up again.” He lit a match and held it to the end of his cigarette. It flared up and then glowed red as he took a deep inhale. He let it out and then squinted at me through the smoke. “You could see right away she was pregnant.”

“Oh, jeez,” I said.

“She’d come to tell him, and that bastard tried to steer her off. He didn’t even care.”

“So you killed him?”

“Bloody hell, I told you, it was an accident.”

“But you went to jail?”

“Yeah, I went to jail.”

Out beyond the bay, the stars were shining. The moonlight shivered across the water.

"Levi, Evelyn tried her best. She tried to make everything right for you."

"I don't know about that," I said.

"None of this should have happened." He watched me for a moment. "It was just like any other afternoon and I was doing some cleaning up before the night's show. I remember, I was mopping the floor.

"The place was empty except for this old drunk who used to sleep there in the afternoons. All the chairs were up on the tables and I was kicking the soap bucket along, just mopping the floor, and that's when he came in. He was playing that night and he'd come in with his guitar.

"We had a raised-up area at the back for a stage. And down the hallway was the dressing room. It was just a storage room really, but he nodded at me as he went past and I knew what he wanted. I propped my mop up against the wall and followed him."

"What did he want?"

Surly took in a deep inhale from his cigarette and I waited for him to let it out. "Smack. I sold him his smack."

"His what?"

"His heroin, Levi. Jesus. Do I have to explain everything?"

"Well, I don't know."

"So he was in the dressing room and he'd put his guitar case on the table. He'd opened it and taken his guitar out and leaned it up against the wall. When I came in he was digging around in the compartment for his spoon and, you know, his lighter and things."

"His spoon?"

"You have to cook it up, Levi. You mix it with water and bring it to a boil. Jesus."

"Okay."

"So I sold him a fiver. Christ, I'd barely handed the bag to him when she appeared at the door."

"Evelyn?"

"She must have been standing there for a moment already, not wanting to interrupt us. She was wearing a coat, and one of those little pillbox hats. But you could tell. You could tell right away she was pregnant.

"*What are you doing?* she said. He had the spoon in his hand. It was blackened along the bottom and he had the little baggie of brown powder in his other hand. Me and him stood there, still as statues. She was glaring at him, her eyes burning holes in him.

"*I came*, she said, *hoping against hope that you might reconsider.*

"*I already told you*, he said. *That thing's not mine.*

"*It is*, she said. *I've only been with you.*

"And that's when he called her a whore. Her face reddened. Her lips went tight and she stepped forward and slapped him, hard, across the face, and, bloody hell, he dropped the bag. Jesus, it burst all over the floor. It wasn't a lot, but it was a fiver and it exploded in a cloud of dust on the floor. There was powder everywhere.

"He looked down at what was left of the bag and I could see his expression darken. And then, Christ, he hit her, closed fist, smacked her in the jaw, and she looked startled and crumpled backward. I was already moving on him because he was readying to hit her again, and she was whimpering, down on the ground, pushing herself away from him.

"I grabbed at his arm but he kind of shook me off, and he called her a whore again, and he was towering over her, ready to belt her a second time. She skittered back out into the hallway, trying to get away from him, and I grabbed him by the back of his shirt.

"He whirled around and threw a punch at me, a roundhouse, but I ducked, and I was still holding on to his shirt, so I swung him around, using his momentum against him. And he went crashing backward. He landed against the back wall and his guitar was leaning there. He didn't land on it exactly, but I remember it falling down, twanging and cracking."

"And one of the tuning pegs snapped off?"

"Yeah."

That was my guitar, my old Martin. I should have known. I should have known where it came from.

"What about Evelyn? Was she okay?"

"I was reaching for her, wanting to help her back up onto her feet. She was out in the hallway and I was in the doorway. I turned just in time to see him coming at me, charging across the room like a runaway train.

"So I clotheslined him. I put my arm straight out and caught him right in the throat. Right in the Adam's apple. He sank to his knees and put his hands up to his neck and started choking. He slumped down, then he crumpled over sideways and his face went gray and his lips went blue. Christ. He was dying right in front of us. Evelyn was clambering onto her feet again and I stood over him. And she looked at me, and to the end of time, Levi, I will never forget that look on her face."

I didn't say anything. My heart was beating so hard I could hear it in my ears.

"I must have broken his windpipe, Levi. I didn't mean to." Surly looked me in the eyes. "He was coming at me. I didn't have a choice."

♫

Surly walked off to the end of the dock. The moon cast a long shimmering swath across the black water. The sailboat was out there, bobbing slightly, and Surly stood silently at the end of the dock.

It was getting colder now. The water sloshed up through the planks of the dock, but I stepped out to where he was standing. He didn't turn when I arrived. He finished his cigarette and flicked it down into the water. Then he sighed, a deep exhale. "That's when Evelyn helped me out, Levi. That's what she was like. Of course, you should know that better than anyone."

"What do you mean 'helped you out'?"

"There was a beat cop," he said. "He usually stood out on the corner at Fourth and Tenth. That old drunk had gone to get him. It all happened pretty quick." He let out another huff of air. "I was thinking I'd really buggered up things and she looked me right in the eye and said, *You didn't kill him.*

"*No*, I said. *I did.* Jesus Christ. He was lying right there on the floor in front of us.

"And that beat cop was already coming in through the front door. I could hear him. He knew me. He knew I was bad news and I thought that was it. This time it was all over for me. The cop came barging down the hallway, waving his nightstick, yelling for me to stop right where I was, and Evelyn stepped in front of him. She was very matter-of-fact. She told him to call for an ambulance because the man on the floor had just overdosed.

"He was lying there and there was heroin splattered across the floor and the spoon was sitting there on the table, and really . . . that's how you die of an overdose, Levi. You stop breathing. Who's gonna say anything different?"

"But you went to jail?"

"For selling heroin, Levi. Not for murder. Five to ten, instead of life."

The stars spilled across the sky. And the moon shone down on us. Surly turned back to look out over the dark sea. "I didn't hear from her for twenty years. Until, one day, the phone rang. And there she was, calling in her favor."

"What about my guitar?"

"Evelyn put it back in its case when the cop went out to call for an ambulance. She cleared the stuff out of the compartment and she just took it." He paused and looked at me. "Maybe it was always meant for you, Levi." He kind of nodded at the thought. "Maybe that guitar was always meant for you."

Wine-Dark Sea

At some point, I must have slept, because suddenly, it was morning. Music was coming from the ballroom and the sun poured in through the pool house windows. I sat up on my cot, rubbing at my eyes. Everyone else was gone. It was just me.

I got dressed and stepped out into the morning sun and just stood there by the pool, trying to wake up. It was a beautiful morning, gentle and calm, or it was until Surly thumped out through the ballroom doors. He was wearing shorts, for God's sake, and a floral shirt that was unbuttoned all down the front. His stomach was white and flaccid, and he had rubber thongs on his feet like he was on holiday.

"Nice getup," I said.

"Bugger off. Someday, I'm gonna sit by a pool, and it's going to be my pool and I can just sit there and relax."

"Maybe," I said.

"Someday," Surly said wistfully. Then he seemed to realize that he was talking out loud. He kind of grimaced at me. "But not bloody yet. We got work to do."

Without another word, he climbed into the back of the recording truck. I headed into the ballroom, where the little AM/FM radio was playing. It was that new band Supertramp. Terrible name, I thought.

Miguel was over by his keyboards, sitting cross-legged on the floor. He had the back off his Vox organ. He liked to do that. To mess with the electronics, to try and get some different sounds.

Chester was behind his drums, tightening something. “Morning,” he said, and I nodded back at him. Really, I didn’t know what we were supposed to be doing. We had one new song recorded but we’d need at least a couple more to finish the album.

Rudy was moving mic stands around. He had a couple new ones set up on the far side of the room, just to catch the ambience. Up above him, a sunbeam was angling through one of the chandeliers, sending little rainbows dancing against the wall.

I sat down on my little MESA/Boogie amp and pulled out my guitar. The old Martin. It was weird to hold it in my hands now, knowing where it came from, knowing why that one tuning peg was a different color. Knowing that it had been broken but then fixed.

I strummed a chord and it sounded pretty, and I was just about to say something when Ariadne came in. She was wearing capri pants and boating shoes, delicate little canvas things, and she was carrying a big tray with one of those coffee press things and what looked like a plate of croissants. I swung my guitar around so it hung off my back and rose to help her.

“Thanks, Levi,” she said as I took the tray out of her hands. I went over and set it on top of the piano.

“Damn,” Chester said, rising from his drum stool. “Don’t that smell good.”

“There’s not much left in the kitchens,” said Ariadne.

“Where’s Frankie boy?” Chester asked. “He already eat?”

“He’s gone out for a walk.”

Chester had a croissant halfway to his mouth. “You got our boy exercising?”

“Something you might consider,” said Ariadne, and Chester chuckled.

He bit off another chunk of croissant and wiped his hand across his mouth. “Hey,” he said, grinning at me. “How about you play Ariadne that little song of yours?”

Ariadne's eyes drifted over to me. "What song?"

Miguel stood up. He nodded and turned, heading right away for his accordion.

"Well," I said, "I've been tinkering with—" I swung my guitar back around. My capo was clamped onto the headstock, up by the tuning pegs, so I unclipped it and set it down on the third fret. Frankie's mic stand was there and I moved over closer to it. Ariadne sat down on the piano bench. Miguel was already lifting his accordion out of its case.

"It's that thing by Tennyson," said Chester.

"Wait," I said, "I'm supposed to tell her."

"Tennyson?" said Ariadne.

"Uh-huh," said Chester. He laid what was left of the croissant back down on the plate and strode over to his drums. "Levi wrote a little song for you."

Miguel strapped his accordion up over his chest. The keys glittered in the morning light. Rudy stopped adjusting microphones and I signaled that he should go pull out the bass. "Just listen to the first verse," I told him. "Get the feel of it, then maybe watch my fingers."

We took a minute or two to get settled. Ariadne's jade-green eyes were on me. "It's called 'Wine-Dark Sea.' "

I waited a beat and then launched into the opening chords. Miguel came in on his accordion and the ballroom swelled with music. I closed my eyes and just went with it. Chester tapped out the time on his hi-hat, and at the beginning of the first verse, he came in lightly, just on the snare and kick drum.

And I began to sing. The lines from Tennyson, all reworked, of course, and kind of stuffed into the melody. I could just see Ariadne out of the corner of my eye, listening, recognizing this phrase and that. And when I sang the chorus, Rudy came in on the bass and everything sort of crescendoed. It was sorrowful and filled with longing, sailing off on the ocean with Ulysses.

We played it just once, all the way through, and it was just one of those things. We couldn't have played it any better if we'd rehearsed it for weeks. Like on the Paris rooftop, it was spontaneous and perfect all at the same time. And when the last chord dropped into silence, Ariadne sprang up off the piano bench.

I still had the guitar strapped in front of me, but she came over and put a hand on the back of my neck and pulled me in close. "Thank you," she whispered in my ear, then she kissed me on the cheek.

Chester was beaming at me. "That's the way," he said. "That's the way it's done."

Rudy too was grinning that big dumb grin of his. Then Frankie appeared at the inner door. We didn't even hear him coming. "What was that?" he asked.

"Nothing," I said. "Just messing around on some stuff."

"Sounded pretty good."

"Thanks."

Frankie swept a hand through his perfect hair. "Listen. I'm thinking we should go through 'The Other Side' one more time. It needs something more."

"Like what?" I asked.

I reached for the headphones that were looped across the boom stand in front of me, and when I put one of the cups to my ear, I heard a hiss. It was live.

"Rudy," I said. "Were these mics on the whole time?"

"Jeez, I don't know." He glanced out the window. He narrowed his eyes on the truck.

Chester reached for his headphones and tapped at his drums. "The microphones are live."

I went to the doorway. Surly was just stepping down from the back of the mobile recording unit, wearing his stupid shorts and rubber thongs. "Shit."

"Is there a problem?" asked Ariadne.

"I think Surly just recorded my song."

Frankie raised an eyebrow.

"It was a song for Ariadne," I said. "It's not for Downtown Exit."

I charged out through the French doors. "Surly." I didn't even bother to call him his real name. "You recorded that?"

"Of course I bloody recorded it." He reared up in his defensive stance, but couldn't quite pull it off. Suddenly he just looked old and haggard.

"You can't just record me without saying anything. That was for Ariadne. It's not for you."

"I'm trying to make things right, here."

"How is this making things right?"

He drew out his cigarette pack and popped one into his mouth. He lit it and squinted up at me through the blue smoke. "Look," he said. "Keep your voice down, all right?" He looked back at the villa doors. "Frankie can't write on his own. He needed Pete. Ariadne got him through the last one, but he's done for. You think I don't know that?"

"Yeah, but—"

"We need a couple more songs to finish the album. Where do you think we're going to get them?"

"I'm not giving away any more of my songs. Fuck that."

He eyed me. "You don't have to."

"What's that supposed to mean?"

He lowered his voice. "First of all, it's not true, that thing about us paying for the recordings ourselves."

"But I thought if we pay for the recording sessions then we own the tapes. Labyrinth can't touch them."

"That's not exactly right."

"Well, shit, Bobby."

"I had to tell Frankie that," he said, "to get him recording again. Jesus, Levi, we could record in Timbuktu and they'd still own the master tapes."

I didn't say anything.

"Frankie doesn't know anything about contracts," said Surly.

"What? And you do?"

"As a matter of fact, I do." He looked at me hard. "We've got one last card to play, Levi . . . and that card is yours."

"What do you mean?"

He looked back at the ballroom doors, then motioned me up into the mobile unit. It was a mess in there. Cables dripping out of the back, ashtrays on top of the tape machine, and at the back, the lights were blinking on the mixing board like an airport runway.

Surly hefted up the cashbox from where it was sitting on the floor and he lifted the lid. On the top was my contract. Then he showed me. He showed me what he'd done way back in Blackmore's office and I had to admit it was pretty smart. It was right there in my contract, plain as day, and, I mean, I wasn't a lawyer or anything, but it seemed like a pretty good loophole.

"All right," I said. "That might just work."

♫

Ariadne was by the pool when we came out. She didn't look happy. Surly took one glance at her and stopped at the door of the truck, but he didn't come down.

"Ariadne," I said, and I slipped past him and stepped down the little ladder. "It's okay. Surly's got an idea."

"Did he really record your song?"

"Yes, but listen. There's a way for me to keep it."

She waited. I don't think she was too convinced. I could see the other guys, looking out at us through the ballroom windows, probably expecting me to throw a fit. I waved to them that everything was okay.

"Ariadne," said Surly. "You have to trust us on this."

She squinted up at him. The sunlight was in her eyes and she shook her head slowly.

"If you don't believe us, come on up and I'll show you."

She frowned and looked at me.

"It's true," I said. "Come and look." She gave a little nod and followed me up into the truck.

Surly was over by the mixing board, the cashbox still open. He'd brought out the Greek drachmas, all of them bundled into little packets. They made quite a nice little pile, actually. Surly pointed at them, a little sheepishly, if you really want to know. "That's for your father," he said. "If you wouldn't mind taking it to him."

Ariadne didn't say anything.

My contract lay there beside the piles of bills. I took her arm and led her over to it. I explained what he'd done, and she peered down at the contract. "Honestly," she said, and she looked up at Surly. "You did that. For Levi?"

"I did. You don't last long in this business if you don't have a few tricks up your sleeve."

"So," said Ariadne, "what happens now?"

"We need to dig up one more song. One more song and then tomorrow we can wrap all this up and get the truck back to England."

I turned back to Ariadne. "How about those lines you wrote on the sailboat? The thing about the two lost souls?"

"That's just one stanza, Levi."

"Yeah, but could you write more? I mean, if I can come up with some music for it?"

"I don't know," she said.

"Please. Could we at least give it a try?"

"Let me get my notebook."

We left Surly in the truck and went back out and into the ballroom. Rudy was plunking around on the bass guitar and he looked up at me expecting the worst. Chester was standing with Frankie, and Miguel was on the floor again, fiddling at the electronics in his Vox. I walked over to where my guitar was sitting, tipped up against the little amplifier, and Ariadne disappeared down the hallway.

Frankie spoke first. "What happened out there? Why've you got that dumb grin on your face?"

"Because, Frankie boy, everything has changed."

"Boss," said Chester. "What's got into you?"

"One more song," I said, "and we'll have enough. I'm not sure what belongs to who anymore, but I think I know how we can screw over Blackmore." I picked up my guitar and put the strap over my head, nestling it across my shoulder.

"Okay," said Frankie. "I'll bite. How are we going to screw over Blackmore?"

"One thing at a time," I said, enjoying the moment. "Can you play the piano?"

He frowned. "Simple chords, maybe."

"That'll work. Come on over to the grand. Let's see if we can pull another song together."

"You got something?"

"Maybe. Ariadne came up with an idea out on the boat. It's the start of a song, anyway."

A few moments later, Ariadne came back in. She was flipping through the pages of her notebook. She had a pen too, and I could tell she was already composing in her mind. "Let's start with the first verse," she said, coming around to the other side of the piano. She put her notebook on the stand in front of us.

I played a G chord and sang the first line. *"I met my love in paradise."* I remembered it, of course, and I already had a bit of melody to go with it. I looked over at her. "Are you good with this?"

"It's lovely, Levi."

Chester went for his drums. Miguel stood up and tucked in behind his Vox organ to fill things in. Rudy tried a low G on his bass, and we ran through the first few lines.

"All right, then. What do you think should come after *'two lost souls'*?"

We got most of the song down and Frankie came up with a nice little bridge section in C major. We recorded a first run-through of it and Frankie looked up at me when the headphones clicked off. "That's good, you know. That could be a hit."

"Funny," I said. "Funny, how that goes."

♫

I was sitting on the front steps of the villa maybe a couple hours later, just taking a break. I was pretty pleased with myself. We'd really come together, all of us, to write that one final song. Our old tour bus sat before me in the drive, looking pretty worse for the wear. The fountain was turned off, and tomorrow we would close up the Rolling Stones Mobile Studio and everyone would head back to England, all except for Ariadne.

And I was thinking about her, and her leaving, when two policemen wheeled into the drive on bicycles. They dismounted like they were getting off horses and leaned their bikes against the column beside the front door. I stood to meet them.

Both wore pillbox caps with flat little brims. Their dark blue uniforms had a star at the collar and big silver buttons down the front. One of them had a whistle around his neck on a leather strap but that was about it. No guns. Not even a nightstick.

The older one gave a little two-finger salute on the brim of his hat and came toward me, saying something in French. I held up my hands in a gesture of incomprehension and he pursed his lips, and just as he did, a car crunched into the drive behind him, throwing up gravel before pulling to a stop right in front of the steps. It was a sports car, a racing-green MGB, and I could see right away that Blackmore was behind the wheel. He stepped out and slammed the car door behind him. "Where is he?" Blackmore called. The two policemen watched him, stepping back a little to let him take over.

"Where is who?" I said.

"Where is Mr. Malone?" Blackmore came at me like a hawk. "And you," he said, stabbing a finger at me, "what do you know about this?"

"Know about what?"

"What do you know about stolen recording equipment?"

"The mobile unit?"

"He admits it," Blackmore said to the policemen, though I was pretty sure neither one could speak English. They nodded anyway in their stiff blue uniforms. "I'm catching hell from Ahmet Ertegun. Do you know who that is?"

"No."

"He's the president of Atlantic Records. And do you know what he wanted?"

"How should I know?"

"He was asking about the Rolling Stones Mobile Studio. And do you want to know why?"

"Because Led Zeppelin needs it?"

"You do know. That truck was expected at Headley Grange. Headley Grange, do you understand? Led Zeppelin is waiting. We're talking Led Zeppelin here. The biggest band in the world." His lips curled back. His teeth were sharp and white. "Did you not think to do things legally for a change?"

"Okay, so maybe we're a little late."

"This is costing them millions of dollars a day."

"No way," I said. "No way it's costing them that much."

He pushed past me up the front steps and gave the door knocker a mighty clack.

"I don't know if anyone will hear you."

He whirled on me furiously. "Where's he hiding?"

"Jesus," I said. "How am I supposed to know?"

He marched off, heading around the villa to the back. The policemen nodded at me, almost politely, then followed Blackmore. I heaved a sigh and fell in behind them.

Around the side of the villa, the tire prints from the Rolling Stones truck were still visible. There was the wrecked bush too, its leaves and petals strewn across the cinder path. You didn't have to be Sherlock Holmes to see what had happened. When we rounded the corner, the snout of the truck came into view. And then the pool, where Surly was sunning himself on a lounge chair, his legs splayed out, his white belly hanging out of his unbuttoned floral shirt. His chest was moving up and down like he might be sleeping.

Blackmore was gesturing at the truck and trying to explain to the policemen what it was and why it shouldn't be there. Finally, he just threw his hands up in frustration and marched toward Surly.

"Well, you've done it this time."

Surly's eyes popped open. "Bloody hell, what are you doing here?"

"That's it, Mr. Malone." Blackmore jabbed a finger at him. "You're finished."

Surly rose into a sitting position. He eyed the police. "Cops, Blackmore? Really?"

"This is not a joke. You have stolen the Rolling Stones Mobile Recording Studio."

Surly laughed dismissively. "It's not stolen." He stood up off the chair and casually slipped his feet, one by one, into his rubber thongs. He was playing it cool, but I could tell he was appraising the situation.

The older policeman, the one with the whistle, said something in French.

"What's he saying?" said Surly.

"He's telling you that the transportation of stolen goods across international borders is a very serious offense."

"We needed the mobile unit to finish the album, just like you wanted. And it's done now, so what's the big deal?"

"You are being placed under arrest." Blackmore tipped his head at the policemen.

The one with the whistle moved to take Surly's arm, but Surly deked left like he was going to go around him. It was a feint, a good one, and Surly dodged right and spun off between the two of them, his rubber thongs slapping across the flagstones. For a moment Blackmore and the cops stood frozen. Then the older cop called out *"Arrêtez,"* and began walking briskly after Surly.

"Where are the bus keys?" Surly hissed as he jogged past me.

"I don't have them."

"Bugger. I'm not going to jail again."

"Bobby," I called. I broke into a trot to keep up with him. Behind me, I heard a little toot on the whistle and the sound of police boots. Our front, Surly went for the cops' bicycles. He swept up the closest one and wheeled it a few running steps before he hopped on. The first policeman had come around the corner now and stuttered to a stop almost like in the comics. He raised the whistle to his lips again and blew. This time hard. A shrill blast rang out across the drive.

But Surly was already pedaling, fast. The bike wobbled a bit, but he charged off on it, around the corner and down the lane toward the front gates.

"Bobby," I yelled again.

But it was no use. He was almost at the end of the lane. He was a bit out of control on the bike, standing on the pedals, surging toward the gates at top speed. They were open but there were square pillars on either side, and he was going full tilt. His front wheel started wobbling, and I watched, helplessly, as the tire jerked violently and then suddenly turned completely sideways.

"Oh, shit."

His bike lurched to a stop, but Surly kept going, almost in slow motion, over the handlebars, crashing headfirst into the brick pillar on the left.

I broke into a gallop toward him, the policemen behind me. Surly was lying there, sprawled out in the gravel, and he wasn't moving at all.

I ran as fast as I could, and I was the first one to reach him.

It didn't look good. He lay facedown. I couldn't tell if he'd broken anything, but one of his legs started shaking, spasmodically. Worse, a trickle of blood was coming out of one of his ears. And there was more blood, pooling out beneath him.

"Bobby," I said, and turned him over. I know you're not supposed to. But I wasn't exactly thinking clearly just then. I cupped my hand under his neck and his eyes fluttered open.

"Bloody hell," he whispered.

"It's all right. Everything is okay."

Surly's eyes were glassy but he was looking at me. I bent down and he whispered in my ear. "The cashbox," he rasped. "Don't forget."

Chester appeared at my side. I don't know where he came from, but he was suddenly there kneeling beside me. "What'd he say?"

The cops were standing over us, trying to work out what they should do.

Surly tried to raise himself. "Get my pills," he managed, and then his eyes closed and he slumped back down.

I stood up. "You stay here. I'll go for his medicine."

I sprinted back to the pool house for the methadone bottle. I guess they worked as painkillers. I don't know. Blackmore was still standing beside the pool.

"Did they catch him?"

"Fuck off," I said, and I spun past him.

Surly's pinstripe jacket was hanging on a hook by his cot and I fumbled in the pocket for his pill bottle. Miguel was looking out from the ballroom. Rudy was climbing down from the back of the truck. "Levi?" he called, but I just kept going.

When I got back to the gates, Chester was still bent over Surly. The cops were with him and at least they'd loosened his collar. Ariadne was nowhere to be seen, which was good. She didn't need to see this, that's for sure.

I skidded to a stop in the gravel, twisting off the top of the bottle even as I bent down to Surly. He was very pale. His left leg was still kicking weakly and the pool of blood under him had grown thick, almost a black color. Surly opened his mouth, maybe to say something more, I don't know, but I dug into the bottle for one of his little white pills. I pinched one out and put it on his tongue.

"Can you swallow?"

His eyes rolled back and his eyelids closed, but the pill was in there. A heartbeat went by.

"Bobby?"

He began to shake violently, not just his leg but his entire torso, like he was having a seizure. Chester glanced at the bottle and then slapped it out of my hand. It bounced down into the gravel.

"What are you doing?" I said. "It's his medicine."

"That's not his medicine," he hissed. "Those are the bennies. You got the wrong bottle."

I pushed myself away from Surly's flailing body. I took a step back and raised my hands over my eyes like I didn't want to see anymore. I felt a hand on my shoulder; it was Rudy, pulling me back, leading me away.

Chester and the policemen knelt over Surly, holding him while he thrashed, but the convulsions got weaker, and finally he lay limp. The pool of blood glistened under him. Miguel and Blackmore had come round the front now, and they watched as one of the policemen began CPR, straight-armed, pumping down on Surly's chest.

I don't remember much after that. Ariadne came out on the front porch, but I couldn't speak. I couldn't do anything but stand there and shake as they ferried Surly's body to Blackmore's car and drove off. All of a sudden it was just very, very quiet, like the world had completely stopped.

♫

We all moved to the back, and we sat on the scatter of chairs around the pool. The strangest silence hung over us. Everything was strange on this gorgeous day. The birds were singing but none of it sounded right. It was like someone had put on the wrong soundtrack. No one spoke. There was nothing we could say. I sat heavily on the same lounge chair Surly had been sitting on.

Everyone had seen them carry Surly off. Everyone except Frankie. He came sauntering up the pathway from the sea, whistling, but he stopped when he saw us.

"What's going on?" he asked.

Chester turned a mournful pair of eyes up at him. "Frankie," he began. "There's been an accident."

Frankie didn't move. He surveyed our little group. "What kind of accident?"

I tried to speak but nothing came out. Ariadne was standing beside me. She put a hand on my shoulder. "They've taken Bobby to the hospital, Frankie," she said.

Ariadne went back into the villa. She didn't say anything. She just left. Rudy stood and trudged across the flagstones, around the pool, and up into the back of the truck.

"Where do you think you're going?" said Frankie.

"Gonna clean up the truck," said Rudy without turning. "I think we're finished here."

"What does he mean 'finished'?"

"Frankie," said Chester. His voice was gentle. "Bobby's hurt pretty bad. I don't think—"

"You don't think what?"

Chester shook his head and Frankie stared at him for a moment. "Fuck," he blurted, and strode off after Ariadne, into the ballroom.

Ariadne appeared again a few minutes later.

"Any word?" I said.

"You must come inside," she said.

We bunched in through the doors to stand in a little semicircle around her. Miguel went over to the piano bench. Frankie was sitting on a wooden chair. He'd found a bottle of liquor, bourbon or something. I don't know. I hadn't seen him drink in all our time at the villa, but he was back at it now. He took a deep slug of the stuff and watched us like a caged tiger.

"Ariadne?" I began.

"I'm sorry," she said. "He's gone."

"What do you mean 'gone'?"

"Bobby died."

Frankie bent forward in the chair like he was going to throw up.

"I am sorry," she said.

I killed him, I thought. *I got the wrong bottle. Just because I couldn't read the labels. So stupid.* Chester's big brown eyes were on me. He shook his head at me, almost imperceptibly, like he knew what I was thinking and that it wasn't true.

"There will be reporters," said Ariadne. "So please, you should gather your things. I imagine we'll all have to leave right away."

♫

Chester and I went out to the pool house to get our stuff. I couldn't help but focus on Surly's suit jacket hanging there on the hook above his cot.

"Levi. We have to move. Quick now."

I was in a daze. I moved over to my cot and hauled up my black duffel bag. My guitar was already in the ballroom and I was thinking that that's all I really needed.

"Listen," said Chester. He could see I was a bit frozen. "I'll get—" He bent down to look under Surly's cot, then rose again slowly. "Hey. Where's the cashbox?"

"I don't know," I began.

"It's not here," said Chester. He was staring at me.

I didn't know what to say to him.

"Well damn. How are we supposed to—?"

"I don't know," I said.

Chester went for his suitcase. It was huge. Like a steamer trunk or something. He opened it up to toss a few things in, but I've never seen him look so defeated. He shook his head sadly.

My platform shoes were long gone at the bottom of the sea. I still had the white bell-bottoms and a couple of shirts, but in the end, I just left them on the bed. I didn't want any of that shit anymore.

Chester heaved up his suitcase. "We'd best go into the villa," he said. "Lock everything up." I didn't answer but I picked up my duffel bag and trailed him out the door. When we came out Rudy was spooling up cables at the back of the mobile unit, and I shook my head at him. "Just leave it, Rudy. It doesn't matter anymore."

"I got the dope," whispered Rudy, and he pointed at the bulge in his pants pocket. "We got to hide it before the cops—"

"Rudy," I said. "It doesn't matter."

Out front, we heard a vehicle pulling into the gravel driveway. That was either the police or the first of the reporters, but either way, it wasn't good.

"What about the tapes?" Rudy said.

I looked up at that. "I'll get them. You two go on in."

"We only used one. It's already in its box," said Rudy. "I marked it."

I hauled myself up into the Rolling Stones Mobile Studio, maybe for the last time. I lifted the tape box, the one Rudy had written on, and I could feel the reel-to-reel tape in there. The other tape box was underneath. We never even had a chance to use it.

♫

I went into the villa, looking for Ariadne. I dumped my duffel bag in the front foyer, then thumped up the grand staircase. I found Ariadne in the room at the far end. She had her little round suitcase ready.

"They're here already," she said.

"Who is?"

"The paparazzi. They're out front." She gestured to the balcony doors. They were closed and the curtains were drawn, but I could hear them out there. I edged over and opened the curtains just a smidgen. Down in the gravel drive, there were reporters setting up cameras on tripods. Big cameras with long telephoto lenses. They were pointed right up at me.

I let the curtains fall but one of the reporters had already seen me. A voice called out for Frankie and then a few more voices rose as well. I didn't see any police yet, but now I was thinking we might need them.

"Levi, come away from there."

I took a step back from the doors.

Ariadne looked at me with her wide green eyes. "I don't know if this will work anymore. Without Bobby."

"It has to," I said. "It just has to."

We heard a bustling out in the hallway and she looked up. Not at me, but past me, out the door to the hall. Someone was coming down the hallway, and a second later, Frankie appeared at the door, clutching his bottle of bourbon.

"I think you're going to have to let me in on this little plan of yours," he said.

"You're not going to like it," I said.

"How about you let me be the judge of that."

Ariadne gave me a little tip of the head to say it was all right, that I should tell him about the plan, or at least what was left of it.

"Okay," I said. "It's about my contract. 16b. Do you remember what that was?"

There was a pause as the wheels turned in Frankie's head. "I think so."

"Well—" I began. "We changed a few things." And I told him the whole big idea. I didn't know how he was going to take it but at the end he just nodded.

"Maybe," he said. "Maybe you're going to need some help pulling that off."

Ariadne brightened.

"I want you to know, though, I'm not doing this for you."

I waited.

"I'm not doing it for myself either. But"—and he paused dramatically—"I'll do it for Pete."

"Okay."

"So what I figure," he went on, "is that when Blackmore comes back—because, you know he's coming back—you're going to need a distraction."

"I'm not sure I follow."

"Listen," said Frankie, and he held up the bottle. The amber liquid in it sloshed a bit, and he shook it, like he was making a point. "You can run your little scheme and I can make sure everyone's looking at me. It's like what magicians do. You know? The old sleight of hand."

"You would do that?"

Frankie looked at me, hard. "I know a little something about pretending, Levi. I've been doing it all my life."

♫

An hour or so later I was standing on the terrace, watching *The Northern Star* motor out of the bay. The sea was a translucent blue and the boat was a brilliant white and everything looked like a watercolor painting. I could see Ariadne, way down below me, standing at the wheel. She hadn't put up the mainsail. I don't know if she could do that on her own, but it didn't matter. The thing had an engine and she'd said she could cruise all the way to Nice and dock the boat there for the winter. As she passed the rocky outcropping at the end of the bay, she turned back once and waved, but she looked very small and very far away.

Chester came up behind me at the low stone wall. I could almost feel his presence before he said anything, and for a while both of us watched the sailboat putter slowly out of the bay. A long white wake trailed behind it.

"Boss?" he said. "You ought to come back inside."

"She's gone," I said.

"Damn." He studied me for a moment, and I felt kind of bad. We hadn't really let him or Miguel in on the plan. I really didn't want to give too much away, not yet, at least.

Chester laid a hand on my shoulder and stood there beside me. The sailboat was turning slowly, out into the open ocean.

"Someday," I said, "we're going to be talking about this like it was all just a crazy dream."

"Not sure about that, Boss."

"Chester, you've been a good friend, and I'm telling you, one day we're going to be old men and we're going to be laughing at all our foolishness."

"Aw, Boss," said Chester. "It ain't over yet."

The sailboat had rounded the point now. It was getting smaller and smaller.

"No," I said. "It's not."

He cocked his head back in the direction of the villa. "In the meantime," he said, and even all the way out here, we could hear the reporters clamoring out in the front drive. "I think we best go inside." He swept an arm around my shoulder. He was a big man, that's for sure, but he could be gentle. "Things are about to get real heavy."

Flying Ever Faster

It was late afternoon when the police roared in, in an unmarked windowless van. These were different guys—scary-looking guys—all in dark uniforms like a SWAT team. There were five or six of them and they wore jackboots and blue berets and had guns holstered to their hips. They set to work right away, backing up the paparazzi and forming a sort of cordon around the steps to the front door.

Blackmore arrived soon after in his MGB, and behind him came a sleek black limousine with two small American flags on the front hood and windows so dark I couldn't see inside.

"I do believe the cavalry is here," said Chester, coming up beside me.

I'd been peeking out the front windows, keeping tabs on the gathering crowd of reporters. It was mayhem out there, a crush of camera lenses, all aimed at the villa. All afternoon they had shouted for Frankie to come out. But Frankie was busy. Just now he was singing in the ballroom. Not one of our songs, something by Tom Jones, and he was really wailing on it.

Blackmore marched up the steps and hammered at the door knocker. I took in a breath, then opened it just a crack, and he pushed in. With him was an older man with gray hair cut close to his scalp. He held himself very upright, shoulders straight, like a man who'd spent time in the military. He moved toward me.

"Is this Frankie Novak?" he said.

"No," said Blackmore. "This is just Levi."

"Hi," I said.

He had a kindly smile, but he looked like he knew what he was doing. He looked like maybe he'd seen worse than this.

"Mr. Langford," explained Blackmore, "is with the American consulate. He'll be taking over your extraction."

"Extraction?"

Langford was looking past Blackmore. "Is Mr. Christos still here?" he asked.

"He's gone," I said.

He smiled diplomatically. "I'm sorry to have missed him. I'm a real big fan of his work."

I didn't say anything.

Langford peered at me. "I understand you boys got yourselves a situation."

"I guess so." I was still mulling over the word *extraction*.

"Well, we're here to help. We're gonna get you boys back home." He tipped his head like that was a sure thing. Like we could count on him. "But first, let me just say that I am sorry for your loss. We are making arrangements for Mr. Malone's relatives to be informed. And for his, ah, remains to be shipped back home."

"Where's Bobby now?" I said.

"Mr. Malone's remains are being held at the Centre Hospitalier de Cannes. We're working on the paperwork."

Blackmore stepped forward. "It's being handled," he said.

Chester was already heading to the ballroom, and we could all hear Frankie wailing away back there, singing at the top of his lungs. I swept my hand through the air in a gesture of invitation, and they followed me, Blackmore and this Langford guy.

The room was a disaster. Cables and instruments everywhere. Rudy was looping up cords and Miguel was disassembling his keyboard rack. Frankie stood at the microphone near the grand piano, his bottle of bourbon—now empty—still clutched in his hand. His eyes were closed, and he was singing quite wildly out of tune.

Langford remained at the door; his expression tightened.

"Frankie," called Blackmore. Frankie swayed a little and then opened his eyes.

Frankie dropped the bottle. It didn't break, but at the sharp smack of the bottle on the parquet floor, everyone stopped. Rudy looked up, a cable half-wound in his hands.

Blackmore glared at Frankie. "Just leave it. Leave everything." He swept in toward Frankie, putting a hand under his elbow to steady him. "We're leaving now. Everything's been arranged."

"Leaving?" Frankie slurred.

"Back to New York. The flights have been booked."

"Did you get that last take?"

Rudy looked over. "The microphones aren't on, Frankie. You're not recording anymore."

Frankie squinted in confusion, but he allowed himself to be led away from the mic stand.

"What's going to happen to all the gear?" asked Chester. "What about the truck?"

Blackmore scowled. "It'll be taken care of, Mr. Merriweather. It's no longer your concern."

"And the album?" Chester said.

"I'll need that master tape," Blackmore said. He'd already seen the tape box. I'd left it sitting there, conspicuously, on top of the piano. It looked like a big fat pizza box.

"Yeah," I said. "About that, I—"

"Give it to me, Mr. Jaxon."

I sighed and went over to get it. *Downtown Exit* was scrawled across the cardboard box.

"Now, Mr. Jaxon."

I picked it up and brought it to Blackmore, who snatched it out of my hands. "Right," he said. "Here's what's going to happen. We're going to go out there, hold up this master tape, and say that the album is finished."

"But what about Bobby?" said Chester.

Langford spoke up. "We're making arrangements for Mr. Malone's relatives to be informed. It's all being taken care of."

"Is there going to be an investigation?" I asked.

"I told you. It's being handled," Blackmore said.

"We think it best," said Langford, "that we get you back to the States as soon as possible."

Blackmore continued. "We'll announce that the recording was a great success. Then we'll express our condolences over the death of your manager. We'll call it an unfortunate drug overdose."

"That was no overdose," said Chester.

Blackmore snorted. "They don't know that. They'll print what we tell them to."

We were all gaping at him, dumbfounded.

"For God's sake," he said. "We have a crisis here. We have to distance ourselves."

Blackmore tucked the tape box under his arm and turned his wrist over to check his watch. "We are leaving in fifteen minutes. Gather your things."

♫

We got our stuff stacked up in the front foyer, a tumble of suitcases, and I didn't see how it was all going to fit into the limousine. Frankie was completely out of it, propped up between Miguel and Chester. His head was lolling back and forth, and he was pretty incoherent. I wouldn't have put it past him to suddenly throw up, except that, once, he caught my eye and gave me a sort of wink.

Mr. Langford opened the door and a storm of flashbulbs went off. I could see the paparazzi bunching in closer and the police trying to hold them back. Langford stepped out first, and Blackmore, behind him, held up the tape box like it was some kind of trophy. He tried to speak but there was too much noise. They just kept shouting for Frankie to come out.

Chester and Miguel hoisted up Frankie between them, but Miguel also had his accordion and Chester had his big suitcase, so it was all a bit awkward. When they got Frankie outside, he came temporarily alive again, raising his hand in a feeble wave. That guy liked an audience, that's for sure. A couple of the paparazzi had climbed up on top of our old tour bus, pointing their cameras down at him from the roof, and really, it was all a bit of a shitshow.

I stayed inside the front door, watching. Outside, one of the policemen came forward to take Frankie from Chester and Miguel. The trunk at the back of the limousine was open and Chester and Miguel stepped down to try and get their things in. Blackmore was heading for his own car, the tape box tucked safely under his arm.

And then I don't know exactly what happened. Frankie squirmed a bit, but the cop was a big mean-looking guy and he just held on tighter, and Frankie I guess didn't like that. He tried to step away, then he whirled and took a swing at the policeman. That was dumb. You don't swing at a cop, especially one of these SWAT team guys. It took about three seconds before he had Frankie facedown in the gravel, kneeling on his back.

"Oh, for God's sake," said Blackmore.

The paparazzi were really surging forward now, trying to get a shot of Frankie on the ground. Blackmore hoisted Frankie to his feet and steered him to the MGB. Actually, I think the big cop helped. Maybe he just wanted to get rid of Frankie. They got him into the convertible and Blackmore slammed the door behind him.

Chester and Miguel were still at the back of the limousine, trying to push Chester's massive suitcase into the trunk, but when Blackmore got into his sports car, they scrambled around and climbed into the limo.

I was still inside the front door. In fact, I started to close it. The cars were trying to muscle their way through the crowd, the trunk of the limo was flapping up and down on account of Chester's big suitcase, and the last thing I saw was the paparazzi scurrying forward, clicking their cameras. And no one was paying attention to me anymore.

♫

I shut the front door and the foyer was suddenly this massive empty room. My footsteps echoed across the marble floor. I picked up my old guitar and my little duffel bag. I went down the hall all the way to the louvered doors that led into the ballroom, and Rudy was standing there, looking confused. "Are they gone?" he said.

"Everything's cool. We have to hurry now."

The ballroom was silent. The drum kit, my amplifier, even Miguel's keyboards, were all still there, and I felt pretty bad leaving all that stuff. It felt like I was right back at square one. Just me and my guitar, and Rudy, I guess, just like how it used to be.

"Rudy, grab the bass guitar."

"But . . . that's not ours."

"Just take it, okay?"

He picked it up and then we hurried across the lawn to the terrace. I took a glance back. There were no reporters around the back, just the Rolling Stones Mobile Studio, looking kind of lonely.

My guitar case thumped against my thigh and I could hear Rudy wheezing along behind me, his backpack hiked up on his shoulders. At the terrace, he balked.

"Levi," he cried. He stopped and bent over double, trying to catch his breath. "You sure you know what you're doing?"

"I sure as hell hope so."

I skirted the terrace and headed down the path to the sea. I had my old runners on again, so I could move pretty fast. I reached the dock and stepped down into the skiff with my guitar and duffel bag. It wobbled furiously underneath me, but I stayed low in the boat to keep it from rocking. Rudy passed me the bass guitar and his backpack and then I held out my hand to help him in. He'd stopped, though. He was staring back at the little boathouse like he'd forgotten something. "I need a life jacket."

"Leave it. There's no time."

"I'm not drowning just cuz of you."

"Okay, okay. Just hurry."

He ran to the boathouse and I looked up at the cliffs. There was no one coming after us. It must have been five or six in the evening by now. After a minute, Rudy appeared again with a faded pink life jacket cinched around his midsection. He untied us from the dock and tumbled into the front of the skiff.

I'd never really driven anything like this before, but I yanked on the drawstring and the little outboard motor puttered to life. A long rudder handle stuck out from the motor, and the whole thing just turned on a swivel clamp. I throttled it up and steered us away from the dock while Rudy held on tight to the sides of the boat.

The water was a deep green now, and the sun was dazzling down into it like the light in a cathedral. A school of little fish skittered away from the hull and I pointed the boat straight out into the bay. The skiff was already thumping in the waves, and I could see out beyond the point that the ocean was even rougher, a steely-gray color, and Rudy clamped down harder on the gunwales. I thought he might barf.

We passed the rocky outcropping at the end of the bay and I turned the boat to head out parallel along the coast. The waves were crashing onto the rocks, great plumes of white water, and I tried to steer us away from them but still keep us pretty close to shore.

And as we rounded the rocks, there in the distance was *The Northern Star*, anchored, its sail down and Ariadne at the back, waiting for us.

We bounced across the whitecaps toward her. Rudy lifted off his seat a few times and there was a bit of spray coming over us, but I kept the little motor revving pretty good. I just hoped the boat wouldn't flip. Ariadne was watching us. She already had the little aluminum ladder down at the back of the sailboat.

I gave the rudder a good twist and we came in sort of sideways. "Rudy," I yelled. "Grab the ladder." Rudy reached for the ladder and held on. It tugged him almost right off the seat, but he didn't let go and I cut the engine. We were bobbing pretty good, but Ariadne tossed down a rope and I tied us up with a granny knot. We passed up our things, one by one, and finally we were able to hoist ourselves up the ladder and into the back of the sailboat, cold and wet and pretty exhausted.

Ariadne had a couple of blankets ready, and I wrapped one around me and sat on the bench at the back. Rudy's backpack lay at our feet in a puddle and the guitar cases were propped up side by side against it.

"So what now?" Rudy said. "We're sailing to Greece?"

"They'll be expecting us to sail for Nice," said Ariadne. "We'll head to San Remo instead."

"Right," I said. "And that's where?"

"Just over the border," she said. "In Italy."

"Wait." I lifted up the bass guitar case and set it on the bench. "Let me just check that everything's okay."

Rudy was watching me now. I flipped the latches and swung the lid open, and inside, in the felt outlines where the bass guitar should have been, there was our reel-to-reel recording tape. It still had that piece of masking tape stuck on it.

"Holy," said Rudy. "You switched the tapes."

♫

"So far, so good," I said. "You should have seen Frankie. He should get an Academy Award for his performance."

"I'll be sure to tell my father," said Ariadne, though I wasn't sure if she was joking or not. She was already scampering around the back deck, tugging on ropes. One of them pinged, it was so tight.

"All right." Ariadne turned to look at us. She was standing by the big steering wheel. "Is it too much to expect that either of you have any experience sailing?"

We stared at her blankly.

"Honestly," she said, and she shook her head. "Then you'll have to do exactly as I say. Is that understood?"

We nodded.

"There's only a light wind at present, so that will make things easier for us. Okay, Levi, see that halyard?" She pointed to a rope that was wound around a crank just by the steering wheel. "When I tell you, you start hauling that up."

"Okay," I said.

"And Rudy, you hold the steering wheel. Don't let it turn." She showed him the compass on the wheel housing. It looked like a snow globe with a red needle inside. "Try to keep us between ninety and a hundred and ten degrees. Point us east. And if the wind changes, then—"

"How am I supposed to know if the wind changes?" he asked.

"Check the mast," she said. "Look up at the top there."

We craned up our heads. A long triangular strip of metal at the top served as a weather vane, pointing like an arrow, quivering a little in the breeze.

Ariadne climbed up onto the thin part of the deck where the boom came poking out from the mast. She was pretty nimble, that's for sure. And when she called out for me to start cranking up the halyard, I did. She helped the sail up for the first few feet, making sure it was unfurling smoothly. The rope whined with each revolution of the crank, and the sail lurched up. It flapped and cracked, and when it was fully up, it ballooned out suddenly, catching the wind, and the whole boat listed over a bit with the tug of it.

"Beautiful," I said, and it was. The white sail billowed out against the purpling sky and we surged forward. Our little skiff was still tied up behind us, and it jerked with our acceleration, then fell in line behind us. And we headed out, away from the coast, out into the deep ocean.

♫

If you've never seen a sunset on the ocean with no land in sight, well, then you're really missing something. We all watched the sun dip down, red and impossibly large, slipping slowly below the horizon. The whole sky lit up, orange with wisps of purple shot through it. It lasted for a very long time.

And then it was dark. The wind had picked up a little and our sailboat shushed through the dark sea, the ropes and rigging clattering lightly, the water slapping at our hull. The moon was just rising in the east, casting a yellow swath across the water.

Ariadne and I sat at the back. Rudy stood at the wheel, his feet planted wide and firm. He looked like he was enjoying himself. It looked like he was adapting to this just fine.

I was trying to think things through. The first part of the plan was done. We had the tape. But I wasn't exactly sure how the next part was going to play out. I only knew that they'd probably be coming after us. I mean, shit, we're talking thousands of dollars here. Maybe millions. I could tell by Ariadne's expression that she was thinking the same thing.

"Levi," she started, but before she could say anything more, Rudy spoke up.

"I think the wind is changing."

At the top of the mast, the little weather vane was turning slowly, and the sail was rattling in protest.

Ariadne stood up. "We'll need to tack."

"Tack?" I said.

"Just do what I tell you to."

"How long till San Remo?" Rudy asked.

"We'll be there by morning if this wind doesn't change again." Ariadne looked a little worried, if you really want to know. She met my eyes. "I'm afraid it's going to be a very long night."

♫

Rudy noticed it first. I was at the wheel and he was staring at the stars. There was an especially bright one almost on the horizon directly behind us. I heard him murmur something and I twisted around to look.

"I don't think that's a star," he said. And I saw what he was looking at. I thought it might be the lights of a car or a truck or something way off on the mainland. It was right on the waterline, but Ariadne said we were too far out for it to be a car.

All three of us watched the light hovering—or lights, because they'd kind of separated now into two, a small red one on the right and a green one on the left.

"That's a ship," said Ariadne.

"Is it coming toward us?" I asked.

Ariadne pursed her lips. "Yes, I think it is."

"Oh, shit," I said.

The ship was getting closer and it definitely wasn't a sailboat. There were lights spilling out across its deck and I could hear the faint rumble of engines. I couldn't tell how far away it was, but it was coming up behind and gaining on us fast.

"They're going to catch us," said Ariadne. And, really, it was like a scene in a movie.

Rudy had come up beside me. His faded pink life jacket ballooned out around him and he bobbled when he moved. I was still steering the boat, but I kept glancing behind us. The other boat was moving quickly. I could make out the steely front of it surging toward us. You could see the spray coming off it.

"Rudy," I said. "Stay down."

And just as I spoke, a spotlight swept across the dark water and our sail lit up like a projector screen.

"Oh, crap," said Rudy. "It's the police again."

This Time Will Not Come Again

I still had my hands on the big hula hoop of a steering wheel, though I don't know what good it was doing us anymore. The police boat was close enough that I could see the man who was training the spotlight on us. He was definitely one of the policemen from the villa, one of those SWAT team guys. And, as they gained on us, I could see a gun strapped to his belt.

Rudy was shaking pretty bad and he'd ducked down below the bench at the back, huddling there in his faded pink life jacket.

I took another glance behind me, and I could see that there was an enclosed cockpit on the patrol boat and the lights from there were spilling out sideways across the dark water. The patrol boat was rigged out with antennas and a radar dish and a kind of megaphone speaker on the roof of the cockpit. The speaker crackled to life and a voice called out for us to stop. It was in English but with a French accent.

"We need to reef in the sail," Ariadne said.

"I don't know what that means," I said.

"We need to take the sail down before they ram us." She hopped up to stand by the mast. "Quickly, unhook the halyard."

The halyard was clamped into a cleat on my left. I unhooked the line and the rope started whizzing up through the pulleys. Ariadne was trying to fold the sailcloth over the boom as it crumpled, but it was coming down way too fast. I could feel the boat slowing right away, starting to drift helplessly in the waves.

The patrol boat was maybe fifty yards behind us now, coming up on our left. I could smell the diesel of its engines. I looked back again and that's when I saw him. Sir Charles Blackmore. He stood at the hatch, yelling something at the cop on the spotlight.

Our sailboat was bobbing now, just drifting, and I could feel the bow surge from the patrol boat pushing up behind us. They'd throttled down and were inching forward, coming up alongside us. And all of a sudden the spotlight snapped off and everything went much darker.

Blackmore stood at the hatch, looking down on us, the pale lights from the cockpit spilling out around him. And I could see Frankie in there too. The cockpit had windows all around and controls at the front. There was a cop at the wheel in there and Frankie sat behind him in a sort of captain's chair.

When the bow of the patrol boat was about halfway up ours, someone threw a hook over onto our boat. It caught on our railing and we were tugged in alongside them. It all happened really quickly. Then they shut off their engines and everything went still, just the two boats clunking together a little in the waves.

I still had my hands on the stupid steering wheel and Ariadne hopped down beside me. She clipped a little strap at the bottom of the steering wheel and said to let go. Our boat was drifting anyway, and we were hooked onto the patrol boat. There was still that sickly-sweet smell of diesel, and their deck rose above ours by about a foot or so, bobbing, all bluish-gray metal. The moon had come out from behind a little cloud and everything was etched in silver.

I counted the cops. There were three of them. Blackmore seemed to be in control, and behind him in the cockpit I could see Frankie, not looking at us, playing it cool.

Then Blackmore called down. "The tape, Mr. Jaxon. Hand over the tape."

The guitar cases were still out on the deck, and I was trying not to look at them, trying not to give anything away.

"Where is it, Mr. Jaxon?"

"They're my songs," I protested.

"You know that's not true."

The big cop at the front still stood at the spotlight. He had his hand on his gun, just resting there, ready for whatever might happen.

Blackmore shifted his gaze to Rudy. His big pink life jacket ballooned out around him, and he had a hand on his pocket where I knew he had the dope. Blackmore turned to Frankie. "Who is that again?"

"That's Rudy," said Frankie, and he came out to stand behind Blackmore.

"Right. You, Rudy, or whoever you are, hand over the tape."

Rudy looked scared as hell. "I don't have anything," he said.

"Do I have to inform you that you are an accessory here? You could be going to jail for a very long time."

"Levi?" Rudy squeaked. He looked over at me helplessly.

Blackmore eyed Rudy. He knew a weak spot when he saw it. "You have about one minute to tell us where that tape is. Hurry now. This time will not come again."

"Don't give it to them, Rudy," I said, but it was too late. Rudy whimpered a bit and reached down for the bass guitar case, and Blackmore's face lit up. Rudy popped the latches and opened the case, and there for all the world to see was the reel-to-reel tape.

Rudy looked over at me with a crumpled expression on his face. I turned to Blackmore. "Fuck you," I said, and I lurched forward and yanked the tape out of the case. I pivoted, heading for the front of the boat, just trying to get away. I edged around the steering wheel, and Ariadne just shook her head at me, but still, I didn't stop. I hopped up onto the deck that skirted the cabin and grabbed for the mast, pulling myself past it almost to the very front of the boat.

"You are being ridiculous," Blackmore said.

"No," I said, turning. "You can't have it."

The cop at the spotlight started to unholster his gun and I glared at him. "Stop," I said, and I dangled the tape out over the side of the boat. "Just stop or I'll fucking drop it."

The deck under me was swaying a little, but I held that tape out over the railing, out over the cold black ocean. Rudy looked terrified and suddenly he hucked something into the water. It was the bag of dope, like that wasn't obvious. The cop at the front forgot about his gun and went for the spotlight again. He clicked it on, and I was suddenly blinded in its light.

Then I heard Frankie. "For fuck's sake. Am I going to have to do this all myself?" And before anyone could move, he jumped down onto the deck of our boat. I pulled the tape back in to myself and shaded my eyes so I could see what he was doing. There was about a six-inch gap between our boat and theirs, but Frankie leapt over it easily. He was pretty agile, all right.

"It's in the cashbox," called Ariadne.

"Just hold your horses," Frankie said, and he ducked down into our cabin.

Blackmore called out something to the cops, but before they could react, Frankie came back out, waving a sheaf of papers.

The pages were a brilliant white in the glare of the searchlight.

"That's my contract," I said.

Frankie was flipping through the papers. He was totally bathed in light.

"It's 16b," I called out.

"I got it, pal," he said, and grinned over at me.

"What is all this?" said Blackmore.

"How about you shut up for a second and look at this?" He pushed the papers toward Blackmore.

"It's right there," I said. "Clause 16b."

I already knew what Blackmore was going to see. Surly had showed me. When I signed that contract, way back in London, he'd written in the line about me being in the band. That was useless, but Surly had also taken the opportunity to cross out the lines above it.

That was 16b, of course, and I'd already memorized it. "*'This contract,'*" I quoted, *"supersedes any other contract and remains in effect for any member who chooses to resign and/or chooses to embark on a solo career.'"*

"I don't see what that proves," said Blackmore.

"It's crossed out," I said. "That clause is crossed out."

"Go ahead," said Ariadne, looking up at me. "You just have to say it now." And I knew what she meant.

"I quit the band," I said. "I quit Downtown Exit."

"You can't do that," said Blackmore.

"I can and I do. I quit the band and that means I am no longer bound by this stupid contract. All the songs I wrote are mine."

Frankie beamed. "You tell them, Levi."

"Including 'Hello Juliet.' That's my song. You can't say that's Pete's. That's mine."

"It's true," said Frankie. "That's Levi's song."

The policeman at the front was looking at us. I think he understood English, and I could tell he was taking all this in, like he was already thinking about what he might say in court.

Blackmore glared down at us.

"So now," I said, "Ariadne will get the credit for her lyrics. Chester and Miguel, they helped on those songs too."

"That's all very well and good, Mr. Jaxon. You can run off and play your little games, but that does not diminish the fact that we have a contract for a Downtown Exit album. And seeing as that is no longer possible, you have forced us into initiating legal action. Breach of contract, as I have already told you."

"No," I said. I'd already thought about all this. "You can still have your album, Mr. Blackmore."

That stopped him. He looked momentarily confused. "I do not see how that's possible."

I looked over at Frankie. I really wasn't sure if he was going to like this. "What if—?" I began. "What if the album is from Levi Jaxon and Downtown Exit?"

"You can't have it both ways, Mr. Jaxon. Are you quitting the band or not?"

"Mostly," I said, "I'm just quitting your stupid contract."

"No," said Blackmore.

"It could work," Frankie said. "What about Lou Reed and the Velvet Underground?"

"Or Crosby, Stills and Nash," said Rudy. "With Neil Young."

"Or Ziggy Stardust and the Spiders from Mars," I went on.

"That's not even a real band, Mr. Jaxon."

"Well, neither are we."

He grimaced. But I knew we had him.

"It's a good album," I said. "It could make millions."

Blackmore didn't move. He knew he was done. He looked at the cop on the searchlight and the guy shrugged at him. The spotlight clicked off and everything went dark again. We rocked gently in the waves.

"Or," I said, "we could take the album to Atlantic Records." I held the reel up and jiggled it a bit. "Who did you say was there—Ahmet Ertegun? Maybe he'd be interested in buying out all of our contracts."

Blackmore's eyes narrowed. "I imagine you think you're pretty clever, Mr. Jaxon."

"No, sir. I just want my songs back."

Blackmore was furious but I knew he was already thinking. He pinched up his lips and finally said what I'd been waiting for him to say. "Right," he managed. "We can have another look at the contracts. I want to hear those songs first, though. I have to know that they're as good as you say."

"They are, Mr. Blackmore. I think you'll see that they are."

I took in a deep breath. Of course I knew I'd have to hand over the tape, and I knew things would probably be tangled up in legalities for a long, long time. But from Blackmore's expression, I knew we had him. I knew we'd won.

Ariadne looked up at me and smiled. She looked beautiful in the moonlight, that's for sure. And all of a sudden it felt like everything was over. It felt like the end of things.

Probably because it was.

EPILOGUE

St. Christopher and the Mermaids

The house sat at the top of the village with a terrace that looked down over the harbor. The walls were whitewashed, like all the other houses, all of them as square as sugar cubes, jumbling haphazardly up the hill. And, like all the others, the front door and the shutters were painted a deep, eternal blue.

I couldn't believe how beautiful it was when we first arrived on Naxos. The village rose above the harbor and everywhere there were steps and little winding lanes. There were no cars at all. Instead, there were donkeys, and sometimes I'd see them parading up the little lanes in the mornings, with harness bells jingling and great wicker baskets filled with melons and tomatoes and olives.

We were staying at Ariadne's old family home, waiting for the lawyers to settle things. I was told that could take months or even years, but I didn't mind. For once, I was enjoying being out of the spotlight.

The sun was going down, and I could see all the way over to Paros, the neighboring island, low there on the horizon. I was playing my guitar out on the terrace, sitting on a rickety wooden chair surrounded by flowerpots. On the low rock wall in front of me, a little gray cat was taking in the last of the day's heat. He seemed to like my playing and he sat there and licked his paw and ran it over his long whiskers.

I had Ariadne's notebook open in front of me and was working through a new poem of hers. She had written some really great lines about mermaids and stars, and about St. Christopher and not being lost anymore—and really, her words were easy to set to music. They had a rhythm all their own.

We'd docked *The Northern Star* in Nice but there were plans to eventually bring it back to Greece. Christos, I heard, was going to hire a crew. He was in Athens still, where he'd been hailed as a modern-day folk hero, a conquering Odysseus, returned at last.

Miguel had gone to Spain and Chester was back in New Jersey, both of them waiting to hear what was going to happen with the album. Frankie was in New York, in rehab. There were still things to work out with Pete's estate, but I was going to leave that to Frankie. I was hoping that with the new configuration of the band, all the contracts could be renegotiated. But that was for smarter people than me to figure out.

And Rudy? Well, he was looking after the villa. He was really good at figuring out stuff, and the biggest news of all was that Evelyn had come over to help him. It was the both of them now, taking care of that big empty villa. It made me smile to think of her, sitting at the grand piano in the ballroom, playing her Beethoven. I really liked that a lot.

The blue shutters behind me opened up and Ariadne peeked out. "Are you ready?" she asked. We were going out tonight, down to our favorite taverna.

I'm telling you, Naxos Town is really something. The oldest parts of the village have these tiny lanes that are more like tunnels than streets. The old buildings were gradually built up right over the paths, and sometimes you'd have to duck under the floor beams and hunch through the shadows till you came out on the other side.

Ariadne knew her way around, but I still got hopelessly lost, so I followed her, down the pathways and steps, all the way to the harbor. The food at our taverna was simple and delicious, and when we came in, the other tables were mostly occupied by old fishermen. They bent into each other, speaking Greek, nodding and gesturing, looking over at us and smiling.

A group of them sent a bottle to our table, something yellow and shimmering, and Ariadne told me it was Kitron, a specialty of Naxos. I brought it to my lips, and it tasted like lemons—well, lemons on fire—and I raised my glass at the fishermen, and they smiled toothlessly back at us.

At some lost hour, much later that same night, Ariadne took me by the hand and led me, not back to our little house at the top of the village, but down the weathered steps to the harbor.

"Where are we going?" I asked.

"It's a surprise," she said, her green eyes sparkling in the moonlight.

I was a little drunk, if you want to know the truth. Ariadne was giggling a bit herself. We walked to the end of the promenade, along the old harbor fortifications to the very end, where a rocky breakwater pushed out into the water. It led out to a small island, and on that little island sat the ancient Portara, the ruins I'd seen in Ariadne's photograph.

The pathway along the breakwater was maybe ten feet wide, with huge jagged rocks dropping away into the sea on either side. It didn't look all that safe and it was farther than I thought. The path was spattered with sea spray so that my Adidas got soaked through, but Ariadne held my hand all the way along. The Portara reared up above us in the darkness, a great doorway to the temple of Apollo, the god of music and poetry.

There was no temple, though. It was never finished. There was just a massive marble doorway standing there on the little island. Its sides were square blocks probably two stories high, and across the top was a marble lintel that must have weighed ten tons or more.

Behind us, the lights of Naxos Town were shining across the harbor, and I walked on, all the way to the ancient doorway, and put my hand on the cold marble. Ariadne let me have my moment with it, the great unfinished temple of Apollo.

"Should we go through?"

"After you," she said.

And I stepped through the door, under the weight of the lintel, and came out the other side. And there was nothing there at all. Nothing but the moon and the stars and the wine-dark sea.

Ariadne came through and wrapped her arms around me, nestling her chin on my shoulder. "What do you see?" she asked.

"Nothing," I said. "There's nothing here."

"No, Levi. Try harder, what do you see?"

There was no temple, no place of glory and fame. There never was. I looked out over the little hill to the dark sea beyond. "I see the truth," I said.

"Beauty is truth," she whispered, *"truth beauty—that is all ye know on earth, and all ye need to know."* And the stars glittered above us, precious and still, and everything, all at once, became clear to me.

Acknowledgments

This is the book I've always wanted to write. It's an homage, really, to a golden era of music—from around "Sgt. Pepper's Lonely Hearts Club Band" to "Bohemian Rhapsody"—a time when musicians were pushing at the boundaries of what could be done in the recording studio. And while my characters are entirely fictional, the story could not have come into being if it weren't for all those extraordinary recordings. I listened to them endlessly as a kid and I now know the extent to which those musicians had to stand up for themselves—to fight for their artistic visions. And the results are clear: We are still listening to them some fifty years later.

I'm really more of a failed rock star than a writer, but, miracle of miracles, I just happen to be playing in a band now that is far better than any band I've ever played with in the past. So, for fun, we've made a soundtrack for the book. All the songs mentioned in the novel—from "29 Streetlights" to "Hello Juliet"—are real, and for that I have to thank my fellow bandmates: Michael Dangelmaier (songwriter and keyboards), Jim Sarantis (songwriter and lead vocals), Richard Maruk (bass guitar and vocals), and Darren Stinson (drums). And me, of course, on guitar with a few songwriting credits of my own.

What was even cooler is that we got to record some of the tracks on the very same Rolling Stones Mobile Studio that's mentioned in the book. The old truck is legendary, and it's now housed in the National Music Centre of Canada, a miraculous place filled with all sorts of wonders. I'd like to thank Andrew Mosker for making that all happen, and specifically Jason Tawkin, who worked as our engineer on that project. And, as if that weren't enough, right before the world shut down with COVID-19, I managed to travel to Europe and visit many of the places in the book, including Jim Morrison's grave in Paris, the Greek island of Naxos, and, what was most amazing for me, Abbey Road Studios in London—the very place the Beatles recorded in—where I worked with mastering engineer Alex Wharton on another handful of songs for the soundtrack.

Music aside, this is my fourth book, and I'd like to express my thanks to my literary agent, Hilary McMahon, and everyone at Westwood Creative Artists for believing in me (especially considering that my first three books were nonfiction and the leap into writing a novel was by no means easy). Likewise I have to thank Simon & Schuster Canada—and especially my hardworking editor, Sarah St. Pierre. Really, there was a whole team behind this little book, and I have to say that all of them—from the cover designer to the copy editor to the marketing and publicity people—were (and are) a delight to work with.

Of course, nothing like this happens without a long line of people helping you along the way, and first and foremost on that list are my parents. From the very beginning it was my mother who, with her love of books, made me want to be a writer, and it was my dad, with his love of music (he could literally play any instrument), who made me want to be a musician. Thanks, Mom and Dad. I am nothing without you.

There was also the unwavering support of my true love, Desiree, who helped me with everything from the initial brainstorming and plotting to reading passages out loud and fixing all the little things that didn't sound quite right.

My last acknowledgment is a bit of a sad one. No one will ever know the hundreds, possibly thousands, of hours I put into this book. There were many drafts and many long, cold winter nights, and through almost all of it, my old cat Tigger sat at the end of the couch with me while I worked. He died, at almost twenty years old, just as I was finishing up the final drafts. In the epilogue, there's a little cat sitting on a stone wall in Naxos. That's for him, just so you know.

About the Author

Desiree Bilon

Glenn Dixon is the #1 bestselling author of the memoir *Juliet's Answer*. He has played in bands all his life, traveled through more than seventy-five countries, and written for *National Geographic*, *The New York Post*, *The Globe and Mail*, *The Walrus*, and *Psychology Today*. Before becoming a full-time writer, he taught high school English for twenty years. He lives in Calgary with his girlfriend.

GlennDixon.ca

@Glenn_Dixon